t

BLAZE IN, BLAZE OUT

JOSEPH LEWIS

Black Rose Writing | Texas

ISBN: 978-1-68433-853-5
PUBLISHED BY BLACK ROSE WRITING
www.blackrosewriting.com

Printed in the United States of America
Suggested Retail Price (SRP) $21.95

Blaze In, Blaze Out is printed in Baskerville

*As a planet-friendly publisher, Black Rose Writing does its best to eliminate unnecessary waste to reduce paper usage and energy costs, while never compromising the reading experience. As a result, the final word count vs. page count may not meet common expectations.

I am proud to have been in education full time for forty-four years. In that time, I served alongside some of the finest teachers and administrators who helped make my journey from teacher-coach, counselor, and administrator enjoyable. Together, we touched lives, molded minds, and embraced hearts. To each of you, I give my gratitude. I am humbled by each of you. Specifically, I want to acknowledge my mentors: Dr. Andre Nougaret, Dr. Randy Bridges, Bill Bertrand, and Robert Grimmer. Thank you and God Bless!

ACKNOWLEDGEMENTS

Not being a hunter or a fisherman, I had to rely on friends and colleagues who were. ***Blaze In, Blaze Out*** would not have happened without you. Thanks to Mr. Nick Roman for sharing his knowledge of hunting. I want to thank Roger Spencer for sharing his knowledge of fishing and boating. I want to thank Chief of Police Jamie Graff, Detective Mindy Warnick, and Deputy Alex Jorgenson for their help with police and crime scene information and procedures; James "Skip" Dahlke for his expertise with forensics; and Sharon King for all things medical and for her eyes on the first draft. I want to thank my former colleagues and close friends, Alexis White, Bob Freeman, Amy Ivory, and Nick Roman, for allowing me to use their names. I hope you like your characters. I want to thank Reagan Rothe and the team at Black Rose Writing for giving me a home; and to David King for a killer cover design. A special thank you to my wife and best friend, Kim, who puts up with the hours of writing and rewriting each night; and to my daughters, Hannah and Emily, for their love and support. I also want to thank the reader for joining me on this journey.

BLAZE IN, BLAZE OUT

Heroes aren't born, but they are created in times of strife and struggle. Everyone is capable of being a hero in their own way, often without even knowing it, they are a hero to those around them.
—Anonymous

CHAPTER ONE

He sat his boney ass on the unyielding wooden bench in nearly the same spot, sometimes for up to six or seven marathon hours give or take, minus a lunch break or whenever the judge decided to give the jury a break. It wasn't often, but it was enough.

He wondered for the hundredth time if the place was ever cleaned. The same long black strands of hair lay on the floor along with a spent staple, two paperclips, and fingernail clippings. None of it had moved in the three days he had sat there and probably wouldn't get moved unless someone shuffled their feet along the floor as they filed past aiming for a seat to watch the show. Dust bunnies and a tipped over empty paper coffee cup had been pushed in a corner. All remnants of human filth, dirt and debris. Fitting he thought, considering who had filed into and out of the massive stone structure.

The lone window in courtroom eleven on the fifth floor of Chicago's Cook County Criminal Court Building overlooked California Avenue. The view through its dirt-smeared heavy glass was a grimy cement five-floor parking garage with a smaller parking area in front of it. Buses dropped off and picked up various characters who took part in the shows in any number of courtrooms. A never-ending parade of miscreants and misfits.

A food truck fought for space between three news vans, all covering the proceedings taking place in Honorable Thomas P. Martin's courtroom. Though cameras weren't allowed past the lobby, there were several reporters sitting behind the heavy plexiglass windows separating the actual courtroom from the audience made up of family and associates, cops and attorneys, and one or two homeless folks who wandered in from the outside.

Detective Pat O'Connor couldn't sit in the courtroom until after he had testified. Until he had done so, he stood out in the hallway staring out the dirty window overlooking the Cook County jail. His testimony over, he sat by himself in the first row behind plexiglass affixed on top of a cheap wooden wall, etched and carved with a 'there is no hope' and a 'FUCK this' along with various gang symbols.

O'Connor's control when under cover, and long-time friend and partner, was red-haired and freckled-faced Detective Paul Eiselmann. He sat in the back, four rows behind and to the side of O'Connor by design and out of precaution. They had not interacted or conversed within two hundred yards of the courthouse. Though they both stayed at the Midway Marriott on Cicero, they had different rooms on different floors, and hadn't ridden together to or from the courthouse. Eiselmann drove his own rental, while O'Connor was shuttled to and from the courthouse by a sheriff deputy assigned to do so. The arrangement made sure no one would be able to connect the two of them.

Both O'Connor and Eiselmann had been on loan to a task force belonging to the state of Illinois, ATF, and FBI working a murder, and gun selling, buying, and distribution ring operating up and down the I-94 corridor in both Milwaukee and Chicago. O'Connor had been recommended by the FBI with whom he had worked several cases, mostly in Wisconsin. Where O'Connor went, Eiselmann went.

The state of Illinois was first at bat, which is why the proceeding took place in Chicago's Cook County Courthouse. After, and depending upon the outcome, the Feds would have a go at it, hoping to cement Andruko permanently behind bars.

O'Connor was the linchpin in the case against Dmitry Andruko, a Ukrainian gang lord. The Illinois Assistant State Prosecution team of Michael O'Reilly, Daniel Keene, and Heather Sullivan pinned their hopes on O'Connor. They felt he would be enough to put Andruko away after the day and a half of testimony and cross-examination.

It had taken two months of painstaking study and observation to infiltrate Andruko's gang. O'Connor ostensibly wanted to purchase high-end semi-automatic weapons. He approached Anton Bondar in a

Ukrainian bar that had been watched by the ATF. Equipped with a wireless microphone inserted into the collar of O'Connor's favorite *Cheap Trick* t-shirt, the transaction was recorded. The game was for O'Connor to play coy until and unless he met with Andruko, who the feds knew was in charge. He had $400,000 to spend and was not going to bargain with a peon.

Andruko took the bait. While O'Connor sat in the back-corner booth of the bar, he heard Andruko, in English, order the hit on a rival. Instead of the task force swooping in right then and there, the decision was made to wait to see if the hit would be carried out. Before the feds had the chance to intervene, the intended victim was shot in his own home, along with his wife. That was when the task force swooped in, rounding up the boss and five underlings.

The hit and the inaction of the feds complicated the case. There was a demotion for one and transfers for two others. However, the defense attorney couldn't use the *'You didn't protect Bogdan and Nastia Yevtukh!'* card because that would be an admission of complicity and guilt.

It was after the arrests when it got messy.

One of the five slit his own throat at some point after deposition and lockup. Two of the others died in lockup after their deposition. Because the three had died, their depositions couldn't be used.

That left two, Andrii Zlenko, Andruko's right hand man, who refused to answer any questions. It was Zlenko through Anton Bondar who O'Connor initially approached in the Ukrainian bar. And of course, Dmitry Andruko.

Ostensibly for Zlenko's and Bondar's safety, and for Andruko's safety, they were locked up in separate facilities. Zlenko and Bondar were somewhere downstate miles away from Chicago, while Andruko was held in Joliet, but moved unceremoniously to Cook County jail for the trial. All three were kept out of general population and placed under twenty-four-hour watch as a precaution.

Zlenko and Bondar were brought in as hostile witnesses. Their attorneys had advised them to plead the fifth. However, their depositions were read into the record, and O'Connor's testimony established that both were the initial contacts. O'Connor also stated that Zlenko introduced O'Connor to Andruko. O'Connor further established that

Zlenko was present during the negotiations with Andruko, making him an accomplice in the sale of illegal weapons without a permit. Most importantly, O'Connor testified to the hit ordered by Andruko made in the presence of Zlenko.

O'Connor glanced at his watch. Nearly ten, which was the appointed time to get this show started.

Michael O'Reilly turned around and nodded at O'Connor. He kept his eyes away from Eiselmann.

O'Reilly, a short and slightly built man, had silver hair, cut short and neat. O'Connor had never seen the prosecutor without a Windsor knot in his tie, without a dark suit, or without his shoes polished. For all of that, O'Reilly had a quick sarcastic wit. He had a love for his city, and he viewed his role as bringing peace and justice back to it.

Daniel Keene was taller and younger than O'Reilly, a bit doughy and rumpled. Personable, but more on the quiet side. O'Connor was slightly smitten with the third member of the team, Heather Sullivan, and couldn't guess her age. Attractive with long dark hair, solid and strong. She was never without a Diet Mt. Dew, often drinking from two different bottles at the same time.

Sullivan had provided a grand slam closing. She brought a smile and chuckle to O'Connor during the defendant's closing, offered by Peter Van Druesing. He was a high-priced attorney who most prosecutors felt was in the back pocket of the mob. Some stated in hush tones that Van Druesing had his head so far up Andruko's ass, he tasted the food before Andruko did.

Van Druesing argued entrapment, to which Sullivan threw her head back and slumped in her chair, as if to say, *'That's all you've got? Really?'* Then she shook her head as she took a long pull of her Dew.

Andruko was led into the courtroom through the defendant's entrance by three Cook County Sheriff Deputies, one in front, two behind. He was dressed in an ugly light-tan jail jumpsuit. Quite the difference from the navy-blue pinstriped suit and starched white shirt with a navy-blue tie he wore during the trial. He stopped midway, caught O'Connor's eye and mouthed something to him. O'Connor assumed it wasn't an invitation to dinner, and happy the courtroom had security cameras.

Andruko stood behind the defendant's table, took one more look at O'Connor and then turned around and caught the eye of a heavy-set, bullet-headed middle-aged man in an expensive suit sitting left of the aisle on the defendant's side of the gallery. O'Connor didn't bother to look right away, knowing that Eiselmann had already taken note of him. Casually, as O'Connor reached down and grabbed his bottle of water, he turned to see the man Andruko stared at.

Their eyes met briefly, before the big man returned his gaze to the courtroom.

Judge Martin entered and the court clerk announced, "All rise!"

The last to get up was Andruko, and he did so casually, disrespect intended.

"Deputy, can you bring the jury in, please."

Martin was a thin, late middle-aged man, gray at the temples, who peered over his glasses to look out over the gallery and the witness. He had been clearly annoyed with Andruko's attorney, Van Druesing, who had objected to most everything the prosecution team presented, to what O'Connor stated, and at the harsh, condescending cross of O'Connor as Van Druesing tried to poke holes in the testimony. Martin wasn't having it, his disdain if not contempt readily apparent. He was, however, careful not to cross the line that might cause a mistrial.

The jury had been out since mid-afternoon the previous day. They had deliberated late into the night, were brought in early in the morning, and it was only an hour later when they had reached a verdict.

The prosecution team and O'Connor didn't know what to think. The jury had sent three questions to the judge that he, the prosecution team, and the defense attorney had to confer on and then answer together. One, who was going to protect them in the event of a guilty verdict? Another, at what point did Andruko's culpability begin: during the offer of weapons for money or during the initial negotiations between O'Connor and Zlenko? The last, did the order for the hit make Andruko accountable for the actual murder of the man and his wife? Those three questions pointed towards a conviction, but the length of the deliberation threw them.

"Ladies and gentlemen of the jury, did you reach a verdict?" Martin asked.

The foreman, an older lady with longish dark hair streaked with gray, stood up and said, "Yes, we have, your honor."

O'Connor counted six sheriff deputies in the courtroom, and another four in the gallery. They tried to remain unobtrusive, but it wasn't possible.

One of the deputies took the folded paper from the foreman and brought it to Martin. He read it quietly and without expression, and then handed it back to the deputy to take back to the foreman.

"Would you please read the verdict?" Martin asked.

O'Connor noticed that the jury didn't look in Andruko's direction, but rather towards the judge, the floor, or the wall behind the judge. All good signs in O'Connor's mind.

"On the first count, we the jury find Dmitry Andruko guilty of the illegal sale of weapons and ammunition intended to cross state lines. On the second count of murder in the first degree, we find Dmitry Andruko guilty."

Van Druesing stood and said, "Your Honor, I request a rollcall vote."

Rather than use the names of the jurors, the clerk used the number assigned to each of the jurors as a precaution, for protection, and for anonymity. One by one, each juror was queried, and each responded with '*Guilty*' to each count

"Sentencing is scheduled for October 27th at 9:00 AM in this courtroom. Until then, Mr. Andruko will be held without bond in a maximum-security federal penitentiary."

"I object, Your Honor! Mr. Andruko is a prominent member of the community. He has a loving wife and three children. I request that he surrender his passport and driver's license and remain at home."

"Your Honor," O'Reilly said, "we've already had four deaths related to this case. I would not want anything to happen to Mr. Andruko. For his own safety, I request that Mr. Andruko be held without bond in a maximum-security penitentiary."

"I object. Surely, you aren't blaming Mr. Andruko for unrelated deaths, are you?"

Sullivan stifled a laugh with a cough.

Before O'Reilly could answer, Martin said, "Objection overruled. The defendant will be held in a maximum-security penitentiary. Members of the jury, I thank you for your diligence, your service, and your time. Deputies of the Cook County Sheriff department will escort you to your vehicles should you so desire. Have a good rest of the day and a nice weekend. This court is adjourned."

"All rise," the clerk said.

Martin left through the door behind his bench. The prosecution team shook hands, and O'Reilly, Sullivan, and Keene turned around, nodded and smiled at O'Connor.

O'Connor nodded, but didn't smile. He did what he did because that was his job. It was the right thing to do. He would return for the sentencing, and then he would take on the same role for Zlenko's and Bondar's upcoming trials, and then all three trials in Federal Court.

Andruko turned around, stared at O'Connor, and said something in his native tongue. Because of the heavy plexiglass window, only a few in the gallery heard or understood what was said. Andruko was then grabbed by the arms by two sheriff deputies, and pulled or pushed to the defendant's door leading to a van that would take him away to wherever.

The bullet-headed man with whom Andruko had spoken to before the proceeding locked eyes with O'Connor before he turned to leave. There was a message in that look, one that O'Connor knew well.

CHAPTER TWO

TGI Friday's sat in the middle of a battery of hotels and motels near Midway Airport. O'Connor and Eiselmann had wanted to get on the road as quickly as possible, but they didn't feel right saying no to an early lunch and a goodbye with the prosecution team.

The restaurant was empty except for a man and woman in power suits sitting at one of several high tables in the bar area. What looked like a mother-daughter combination sat facing each other in a booth in the main eating area. Other than that, it was a little early for the lunch crush that would surely arrive within the next hour.

Out of habit if not a precaution, the group chose a table in the back rather than a booth. Neither O'Connor nor Eiselmann liked having their back to any door. Not in their line of work. An added benefit to sitting in the back away from everyone was that they could talk about whatever came up without anyone paying attention. Besides, O'Connor and Eiselmann wanted to move quickly if need be, and a booth wouldn't allow for that. They weren't necessarily anticipating anything other than a celebratory and leisurely early lunch before the two-hour ride back to Waukesha, Wisconsin, which could be more or less depending upon traffic. But they didn't want to take chances.

O'Reilly raised his glass of iced-tea and said, "Thank you for your work on this case. We wouldn't have gotten the conviction without you."

Glasses clinked and heads nodded. O'Connor smiled.

"What's next for you?" Keene asked. "Do you have anything you're working on?"

O'Connor shook his head and said, "Nope. A soccer game tonight. Paul's son, Stephen, is the starting goalie on the North team. He's only a freshman but he's good."

He didn't add that he wanted to keep an eye on Brian Evans, the adopted son of Jeremy and Vicky Evans. Ever since they had gotten back from Arizona searching for the missing boy, Brian hadn't been doing well. According to Brian and confirmed by Jeremy, his therapist described his condition as PTSD. The intermittent nightmares and hand tremors were just two of the symptoms. He wasn't eating or sleeping well, either.

"This weekend, Jamie Graff and I are taking four of Jeremy Evans' kids fishing in Northern Wisconsin." He shrugged and said, "Unplugging and getting away."

"Sounds wonderful," Sullivan added. Then she laughed and said, "Not so much the fishing, but the Northwoods and unplugging."

They laughed along with her.

"You're not going?" Keene asked Eiselmann.

Paul shook his head and said, "I'm going to spend a quiet weekend with my wife and kids. Putz around the house. Maybe a movie or something. Nothing much."

"How are the boys?" O'Reilly asked. "It's been, what? Two years since the kids were set free from that ring?"

"Were you involved in that?" Sullivan asked.

Pat liked the look of her. Long dark hair and dark eyes matched her olive complexion. More importantly to O'Connor, she had a great smile and a great mind.

"Pat and I headed a team that freed about a dozen kids from a warehouse in Long Beach, California."

"Jesus, I can't imagine," Sullivan added. She shut her eyes and shook her head. "How can any of those kids have a normal life after what they've been through?"

O'Connor sighed and said, "It's been a journey for them. Some are further along than others."

"There was a boy . . . Brett, I think," O'Reilly said.

It occurred to O'Connor once again how sharp O'Reilly's mind was. He remembered names, faces and details others might forget.

"Brett McGovern and his brother, Bobby," Eiselmann said.

"Brett was the kid who rallied the kids in Chicago. He saved Pete Kelliher's life, but took a bullet in the shoulder and almost died," O'Reilly said as he squinted in the memory.

"Were both boys there?" Keene asked.

"No, just Brett. However, his uncle, Tony Dominico was molesting Bobby. The uncle was the guy who set Brett up to be snatched off the street, and then he used that to blackmail Bobby into sex."

"He's a piece of shit," Eiselmann muttered.

"He's in for life without parole in a maximum-security prison in Indiana," O'Connor added. "Both Brett and Bobby are doing okay. The two have developed into quite the athletes. Football, basketball and track. Bobby and one of the twins, Randy, wrote several songs that might be recorded by Tim McGraw."

"No way!" Sullivan said.

O'Connor nodded. "Both sing and play guitar. Bobby's also a helluva piano player."

"The others are doing pretty well," Eiselmann said.

O'Connor said, "Do you remember George?"

"The Navajo boy," O'Reilly said.

"About two months ago, George found out he had a half-brother. Same father, different mother, raised in different families on different parts of the reservation. Michael is living with Jeremy and Vicky now."

"He's the youngest of the boys. An eighth grader. He could be George's twin," Eiselmann said.

"But the two are different. George is quieter and more serious. Michael is outgoing and playful," O'Connor said.

"How many kids do Jeremy and Vicky have?" Keene asked.

"Seven. Brett and Bobby are Vicky's sons by a previous marriage. Randy and Billy are twins and the first of Jeremy's adoptions. Then George came during the summer of shit." O'Connor glanced at Heather Sullivan and said, "Excuse the language."

She waved it off.

"Brian was adopted last year," Eiselmann said. "His parents died. It was ugly. They had never recovered from Brian's twin brother, Brad, dying the same summer all the other crap happened."

"I think Brian suffers the most," O'Connor said. "About two months ago when we were out in Arizona, Brian almost lost his life protecting Brett, George, Michael, and George's friend, Rebecca."

"He survived, but has scars around his right eye," Paul said. "Some on his arm and shoulder, and the side of his head."

Pat added, "He wears glasses as a precaution because the cornea on his right eye was damaged. But, he's managing as best he can."

"He's a neat kid," Paul said. "My stepson hangs with him sometimes. He's the captain of the soccer team, and he's only a sophomore. He also kicks for the football team."

O'Connor smiled and said, "From the left hashmark, Brian kicks with his right foot. From the right hashmark, he kicks with his left. I don't know of any other kicker anywhere who does that."

O'Reilly said, "Usually kickers use one leg, their dominant leg, right?"

Eiselmann laughed and said, "Usually. The way Brian explains it, he says that in soccer, you have to use both feet and both legs or you become one dimensional."

"What are their ages?" Sullivan asked

"The twins, Brett, George and Brian are sophomores in high school. They're sixteen. The twins turn sixteen in October. Bobby is a freshman and Michael is an eighth grader. A house full of boys."

"Wow! I can't imagine that," Sullivan said with a laugh.

"It's a special family," O'Connor said. "Jeremy and Vicky do a great job with them. And there are some of us who help out where and when we can."

"Like the fishing trip this weekend," Keene said with a smile.

"Something like that," O'Connor said. He felt himself blush.

"You forgot to mention the four dogs and the horses," Eiselmann said.

"You're not serious," Sullivan said.

"Part wolf, part dog. Smart as hell," Eiselmann said.

"The horses are kept at Jeff Limbach's stable," O'Connor said.

"Limbach? Not the writer?" Keene said.

"The same. He, Jeremy, and Jamie Graff worked at Waukesha North High School back in the day. Jeremy taught social studies and was the head basketball coach before he became a counselor. Jeff was an English teacher before he became a full-time writer, and Jamie was the School

Resource Officer before he became Chief of Detectives for the city. They were known as the three J's."

"Do you work with Graff?" Keene asked.

Eiselmann shook his head and said, "Sometimes. We're with the sheriff department. He's with the city police."

A few hungry patrons, looking like businessmen of some sort to O'Connor, entered and sat in a booth in the main area. A couple of younger women entered and chose to sit at a high table in the bar area. O'Connor didn't know how to categorize them.

The conversation switched to sports, to cases, and anything light and casual. It was enjoyable and relaxing for O'Connor, who being single, seldom socialized outside of work. He was able to push away the thought of the long drive to Wisconsin in grinding traffic.

That changed when three men strolled in. Big and bulky. Dark five o'clock shadows on two of them. Dark, slicked-back hair. Sport coats with a tell-tale bulge under the arm indicating a shoulder holster.

They stood in the doorway, looked over the various patrons, studied the back table of cops and prosecutors. They took seats in a booth near the door about as far away from O'Connor, Eiselmann and the prosecution team as they could get. Casually, they'd glance in their direction. If O'Reilly, Sullivan and Keene noticed or were alarmed, they didn't let on. It would have been hard for them anyway, since their backs were mostly turned towards them.

O'Connor and Eiselmann had a clear line of sight to the front door, the hallway that led to the restrooms, and the kitchen where there was sure to be a backdoor.

O'Connor picked at his salad, and out of the corner of his eye, kept watch. Eiselmann, who could eat anything at any time, hungrily ate his grilled chicken sandwich and munched on his fries while watching the three men out of the corner of his eye.

"Gentlemen, excuse me a minute," Sullivan said as she dabbed at her mouth with her napkin. She pushed back her chair and headed off for the restroom carrying her purse.

O'Connor glanced at the three men who huddled briefly. One of the men, a tall youngish man with a short-cropped beard eased himself out of their booth and followed Sullivan towards the hallway leading to the restrooms.

"Hoss?" Eiselmann muttered quietly.

O'Connor stood and said, "Excuse me a minute."

O'Reilly was in mid-sentence when Eiselmann quietly said, "Guys, I want you to keep your eyes on me. We have company. It doesn't feel right."

That got their attention.

"Michael, casually take out your phone and call 9-1-1. Tell them who you are, where you are, and request backup, but without lights or sirens. Have them get here in a hurry."

Stunned, O'Reilly didn't move at first. Then he recovered, nodded, and did as Eiselmann had asked. Keene's hand shook as he reached for his glass of water.

"We'll be fine. I've got this, but we're going to be smart. If I tell you to hit the floor, you do it without hesitation. Understood?"

O'Reilly nodded and smiled as if a pleasantry was exchanged and said, "Crystal."

Eiselmann smiled back and pushed away from the table just a foot or so to give himself room to maneuver.

CHAPTER THREE

O'Connor had a decision to make.

Sullivan was behind the women's restroom door, while the guy who followed her was presumably in the men's room. He could either wait in the hallway or go into the men's room to see what might happen. Before he could make the decision, the man came out and the two men faced each other.

O'Connor judged that he was an inch or two taller, but the guy had at least fifty pounds on him, mostly hard-packed muscle.

The hallway wasn't wide. Still, they had at least two feet between them. O'Connor shifted so that his back was to the women's restroom.

"Can I help you with something?" O'Connor asked.

The guy cocked his head, smirked, and took a step back. His hands were open and his arms hung at his side.

Sullivan stepped out of the restroom, bumped into O'Connor and said, "Oh, excuse me."

"Stay behind me," O'Connor said without taking his eyes off of the guy.

The youngish man nodded at both O'Connor and Sullivan, raised his hands slowly in surrender, turned around and walked back into the main dining area.

O'Connor waited until the man was ten steps ahead of him. He started to move forward, but Sullivan held him back.

"Who is he?" she asked.

"Not sure. Do you carry a weapon? A handgun or something?"

"Pepper spray."

O'Connor shook his head and said, "I'd consider picking up a weapon. In your line of work, you can't be too careful. Doesn't have to be big. A .38 maybe. Or a .22."

With his eyes on the man ahead of him, O'Connor led Sullivan back to their table. The three men in the booth openly stared at him.

"They don't seem very friendly," Eiselmann cracked.

O'Reilly turned around to see who they were and said, "I don't recognize them." He turned to Keene and Sullivan and asked, "Do either of you recognize them?"

"No," Sullivan said.

Keene shook his head.

O'Connor wondered who the three men came for. One, two, or all of the prosecutors? For him? All of them? He didn't know and that troubled him. He liked to know who he was facing and why. He also recognized that the precautions he and Eiselmann had taken to hide their relationship were for naught.

Staring at the table of cops and prosecutors, the three men stood up. The bigger, older of the three took out his wallet and tossed money on the table even though they hadn't ordered. As his two partners left the restaurant, he stood in the doorway, locked eyes on one of them-O'Connor wasn't sure who- and walked out.

"What was that all about?" Sullivan asked.

"Not sure. I think we need to stay here until the cops arrive," Eiselmann said.

"Too exposed," O'Connor said as he searched for an area that was away from windows.

"Restroom. Let's get up slowly and move down that hallway," Eiselmann said. "Ready? Let's move."

Keene was the first down the hallway with Sullivan following and O'Reilly trailing. Eiselmann brought up the rear like a sheep dog herding them along. O'Connor stood at the hallway entrance until they disappeared behind doors. Eiselmann came back to join him.

"I'm guessing they were sent," he said.

"No doubt. But how did they know we were here?" O'Connor asked. "We also don't know who they came for."

"Could have followed O'Reilly and the others. They drove together in O'Reilly's car."

"Possibly," O'Connor answered without taking his eyes off the doorway.

CHAPTER FOUR

He had left New York and arrived in Chicago one day previous. Late in the afternoon on the same day O'Connor and Eiselmann had eaten their lunch at *TGI Friday's*, he drove to the Richard Daley Branch of the Chicago Library system, where he picked up a thick legal-sized envelope from a woman sitting at a computer station behind one of the stacks. He had been told to look for a redhead in a blue windbreaker.

He had shuffled around the library twice at a leisurely pace, and then doubling back once to see if he had a tail. No one had paid any attention to him.

Why would they? Thick black-framed glasses, a prosthetic nose, a rubber fat pad around his middle. He looked like a dumpy man on the backside of life. He wasn't. He was a muscled and well-maintained man in his thirties.

He sat down at a table in a corner and scanned the contents. He placed everything back into the envelope and shuffled back outside just the way he had strolled in- slowly and hunched over.

He stood at a bus stop, and then caught a bus traveling east for three blocks and got off. He headed into a small diner for a cup of hot tea. He sat at a window seat and looked for anyone watching him. After, he stood at the same bus stop and waited for a different bus that would take him north four blocks. He back-tracked two blocks to a four-story parking garage and rode the elevator to the third floor. He shuffled to his dented late-model green Ford Fusion, got in, and drove off.

North of Chicago in Skokie, he drove to a storage facility, punched in a keycode, and drove to his garage. He punched in his personal code, rolled up the steel door, and drove the Fusion inside. He shut the door, stripped off his prosthetics and changed his clothes to black leather pants with a matching black leather jacket. He pulled on a black helmet with a darkly-tinted visor, and backed his bright blue Yamaha YZF-R3 out of the garage.

He took I-94 north to highway 41 to Lake Forest, and then drove east towards Lake Michigan. At a fashionable condo, one of his residences, he pulled up in the driveway letting the beast idle under him. He pressed the garage remote and the door opened. He drove in quietly, his bike purring, and he shut the door behind him.

He swung himself off the bike, took off his helmet, and set it on the saddle ready for the next ride, which wouldn't take place until the job was over.

The first thing he did was inspect the trips he had placed on or near his door to see if any had been disturbed. They hadn't, so if anyone had entered his condo, it would have been either through the front door or slider in the living room.

He reached under the workbench at the front of the garage and slipped the SIG Sauer P365 Pistol from the Velcro straps holding it in place. Then he unlocked the door and entered the kitchen. He stood and listened, waiting and watching.

None of the trips he had in place in the kitchen had been disturbed.

He moved to the front door and none of those trips had been moved. Finally, he inspected the slider and found those trips in place. Last and not the least of importance, he walked through the condo and cleared each room. This was his usual pattern of behavior. It had kept him alive several times.

Satisfied, he relaxed.

He poured himself two fingers of scotch, unzipped his jacket, and took out the envelope that contained his newest assignment. He sat in a soft brown leather chair and read over it twice before setting it aside.

He shut his eyes and ran through several options, settling on the easiest. Take the cop while he was on his trip up in the Northwoods where people were scarce. There could be collateral damage because he wouldn't be alone. But that didn't bother him. Better to be rid of any witnesses than not, no matter the ages.

He wouldn't be the only one on this assignment. While he, himself, operated alone, there would be two others who operated as a team. They were good, but not as good as he was. His assignment was to support and take care of anyone who might have gotten away from the team of two. He had worked with them in the past and knew that they didn't leave anything to chance. He wouldn't either.

He read over the folder once more, committing it to memory, before he destroyed it.

CHAPTER FIVE

He dressed for the part. Contacts that made his blue eyes hazel. An expensive and form fitting wig that turned his blond hair brown. He could have been anyone's father or uncle. From his vantage point in the stands, he could watch a good game of soccer, but more importantly, keep an eye on the tall, long-haired, skinny cop.

The cop sat with a group of adults who he assumed were parents of some of the boys on the field. From what he had overheard, O'Connor and one other guy, another cop named Graff, were leading a carload of four boys to Northern Wisconsin at four in the morning. He would be ready. He would follow the four kids, since they would be less likely to spot a tail.

The team of two had arrived at the game before he did, and had separated. One sat above and to his left just below the press box. The other sat in the visitor's section on the other side of the stands. Neither spent much time watching the game, instead focusing on their pigeon.

They made no effort to hide who they were watching. Dangerous because if the cop was as good as he was made out to be, he would notice.

CHAPTER SIX

South was their arch rival and the only other team in the conference that was undefeated. There had been bad blood between the two in several sports, and Brian had been the recipient of it, especially in basketball the previous winter.

It was as if the shot was expected. Brian didn't know it, but the crowd in the stands stood up almost as one as he dribbled past the South stopper. The crowd leaned forward, but again, Brian didn't know it. He was intent on what was happening on the field. Specifically, what the defenders from Waukesha South were doing.

Two quick whistles from Mario, letting Brian know to send the ball his way. He followed the whistles with a shout, "Here!"

Anticipating a pass from Brian to Mario, the center-defender drifted over to Mario's side to join the defender who was already in Mario's pocket. He had been there all night frustrating the North offensive game plan. Mario led the team in goals, and that was evidently not lost on the South team. Brian was second to Mario in goals by two. A viable threat with the ball.

The left defender stuck with TJ, the taller of the two who was underrated as a striker, great with his left or right foot, and an equally adept passer. That left Brian one on one with the goalie.

Two options flashed through Brian's mind at warp speed. He could dribble in for a better shot, but that would risk the center-defender and perhaps TJ's defender fading back into the center. That would take away any shot Brian might have. The other option was to let it fly. He was twenty almost twenty-five yards out. He'd have to drill it, hooking it into the right upper ninety.

He chose the latter option.

The ball was already on his left foot. Brian was deadly with either. The goalie was on the short side, not lanky with long arms like Brian's teammate, Stephen, in their own goal.

Brian didn't hesitate. He aimed just right of the left post, knowing it would hook.

The goalie reacted too slowly and couldn't counter in time. The ball ripped into the upper ninety on the far right over the outstretched hands of the leaping goalie.

Brian charged looking for a ricochet or rebound, but at the same time looked over at the side-judge hoping no one was offside. Nothing from the side-judge. The center official blew his whistle and signaled the goal.

One to zero with just under a minute and a half left in the second half.

Brian was mobbed and found himself at the bottom of the scrum. The first to him was Mario, who tackled him, and then TJ, who piled on.

"BRIIIIIIAN!"

Brian recognized Billy's shout. He heard the other yells, cheers and applause along with the foot stomping on the metal bleachers from the North crowd, but by far, Billy's was the loudest.

Mikey helped him to his feet and gave him a hug and then rested his forehead on Brian's. The two were sweaty and a little ripe, but neither cared.

"Helluva shot, Bri."

Brian beamed as he received pats on the back and fist bumps from the rest of the team. He pointed at Billy and grinned. Billy pointed back and gave high fives to his brothers and friends standing on either side and behind him.

Brian called the team together at the fifty.

"We have a minute and a half to play. No one lets up. Mikey, direct traffic back there. Sean and G-Man, no one gets past you. Will, you and I control the middle. TJ, drift back and cover their striker man to man. Mario, they'll move Ruiz to striker. Stick to him like he stuck to you. No fouls. No cheap shots. Expect it from them. We can't fall for that. Hands in."

Everyone put their hands together on Brian's and he said, "On three, one team, one win. One, Two, Three, ONE TEAM, ONE WIN!" the teammates yelled at their captain's command.

They broke to their positions for the kick off. Brian and Will lined up not quite side by side, ready for the South kick. Brian knew that Will would hang back, allowing Brian to charge. As Brian predicted, Ruiz lined up at a striker position opposite Mario.

Ruiz would tug, pull, kick, and cleat whenever he thought he could get away with it. He already had one yellow card from a hard tackle, but that wouldn't stop him if he thought something would give him an advantage.

"Mario, keep your head," Brian said.

Mario was one of the best players in the state. He was only a freshman like several other starters on the field, but that didn't matter. He was already being scouted by division one schools.

Mario gave Brian a head nod, but then he focused back on Ruiz.

South kicked it back to their holding-mid, who sent the volley towards the North goal. Both South strikers took off, but TJ and Mario stuck on them.

Brian didn't see what had happened, but Mario fell to his knees holding his stomach. He struggled getting to his feet.

No call.

"Will, take the middle!" Brian yelled.

He shifted over to Ruiz stride for stride. He ignored Ruiz's elbows. He ignored Ruiz's cleat raking his left ankle.

G-Man cleared it, sending it back to the South end of the field stalling for time.

"Mario, take the middle and attack. I have him," Brian yelled.

Mario took off. The ball was sent from a South defender towards Ruiz. Brian stepped to intercept it, but Ruiz tripped him.

The side-judge caught it and the referee called it. No yellow card, but a free kick just the same.

"Will, take it," Brian yelled.

Will usually put the ball in play. More often than not, his kicks ended up just where he intended.

TJ lined up on the left, Mario in the middle, and Brian on the right ready for Will's kick.

He gave a little nod, called out, "Two," and kicked it over the three South defenders who had formed a wall. Mario took off. TJ and Brian hung back just a hair.

Two was a nothing call, but South didn't know it. They hesitated and Mario found space and Will's ball. He one-touched the ball towards the net that the goalie barely got a hand on, deflecting it backwards and out the back. That gave North a corner kick and more time off the clock.

"Will, take it," Brian said.

The clock ticked away. Less than twenty seconds, and Will knew it, so he took his time.

Instead of Sean moving up into the play, coach Bennett kept him back with Mikey and G-Man. He didn't want a breakaway, which sometimes happened off a corner.

"Will, you'll have to get back," Bennett yelled. "Brian, TJ, and Mario, keep your heads!" He knew that sometimes a corner kick ended up in a free for all in front of the net.

Will caught Brian's eye and gave him a slight nod. He lifted his hand signaling he was ready. He played it short to Brian. Brian dribbled twice to the center, but then kicked it back to Will. Will circled towards the middle and let fly a soft volley.

TJ was ready. He leaped into the air, but his header sailed over the cross bar. No matter, time ticked away.

Less than seven seconds.

By the time the goalie punted, the horn sounded, and the referee called the game.

North was in sole possession of first with the only undefeated record.

After the teams shook hands and shook hands with the officials, they gathered on their own sides. One team more joyous than the other.

Coach Bennett recapped the positives which were many, along with a couple of things to work on. When he was finished, Brian said, "Coach, can I say something?"

"Yup," he said with a smile.

By this time, most of the parents and fans had gathered at the fence waiting to congratulate the team.

"Guys, the box score is going to read a one to zip victory. It will probably give me the credit for the win, which isn't the case."

The team and fans reacted doubtfully.

"Mario called for the ball and two defenders went with him. TJ had the respect of the other defender who stayed with him. That's the only reason why I had an open shot on goal."

"It was a helluva shot," Mario said. "No one could have done it better."

"I've seen you and TJ and Will score like that all season. But my shot was created because of you and TJ. You two had as much to do with it as I did."

Mario smiled at him, while TJ blushed.

"Each of us has a part to play. Our defensive line of G-Man, Mikey and Sean played lights out. Stephen, you handled the few shots South sent your way without any trouble. I wasn't worried one time. Cem and Kaiden, you stopped their strikers before they ever got going. No matter how the paper prints it, it was a team win. Each of us played a part. Each of us did our job. We relied on each other and each of us came through. Don't forget that. Enjoy tonight, but it's just one win. We have another game on Tuesday. We can't let down and we can't relax."

Heads nodded and Bennett smiled, proud his team had chosen Brian as one of the captains.

"Coach, you have anything else?" Brian asked.

"Nope."

"Sean, anything?" Brian asked his long-time childhood friend and co-captain.

"Nah, you said it better than I could have," Sean said with a smile.

"Okay, hands in. On three, one team, one win. One, two, three, ONE TEAM, ONE WIN!"

CHAPTER SEVEN

Jeremy reacted to Brian's shot like everyone on the North side of the bleachers. He whooped and hollered and stomped his feet along with them. When he saw Brian's reaction, the smile and the finger pointing at Billy, his feelings sunk.

It had been weeks since he had seen Brian smile and laugh like that. It had been weeks since he saw Brian hug and high five anyone. It had been weeks since he showed any reaction like he had with Billy.

He sat back down and held Vicky's hand. Puzzled, she looked at him and said, "What?"

He shook his head.

Mark and Jennifer Erickson, Mikey's parents sat down with him. Mark had been next to him the entire game.

He said, "What's up?"

In quiet tones that he didn't want anyone else to hear, Jeremy told them what he had been thinking and then said, "The only time I notice a difference is when he's with Mikey, but even then, he's cautious and apprehensive. What is Brian like when he's at your house?"

The two boys had been constant companions on weekends since the beginning of August. Brian would spend one night at Mikey's house, and the next night, Mikey would spend the night at Brian's house with Jeremy and his family.

Mark looked at Jennifer, then back at Jeremy and Vicky and said, "Just about what you saw on the field. He's happy and smiling and teases the hell out of me. Constantly teases me."

He and Jennifer laughed, and Jennifer added, "He's relaxed and genuine. It's like he's a part of our family. After a meal, he picks up the kitchen even though I try to shoo him away. He makes Mikey help him, which is the only time Mikey picks up the kitchen."

"He's had one nightmare that we're aware of," Mark said quietly. "He's had the shakes once and that was during dinner about a month ago. He was embarrassed, but we didn't make anything out of it. Mikey held his hand until the episode ended, and we finished the meal like it was no big deal."

Jennifer smiled. "Mikey and Brian are cute together. Mikey hasn't had a friend like that since Spring. Stephen and Mikey and Bobby are close, but it is a different kind of friendship with Brian. Nothing is forced. The word that keeps popping back into my mind is genuine."

Nothing they said comforted Jeremy. He couldn't tell what Vicky was thinking. He knew she still felt tremendous guilt about what had happened in Arizona. He knew that while Brian and Brett and Billy were as close as brothers sometimes are, Brian had become more cautious and guarded around George. Even Two was closer to Brian than he was to George.

Two was the nickname the boys had given George's step-brother, Michael Two Feathers. He was now part of the Evans' clan and soon to be adopted by Jeremy and Vicky.

Brian spent much of his time by himself up in his room reading or writing or napping. He still worked in the stable alongside George and Two. He still picked up the kitchen like he always did after meals except for breakfast when he had to get to school. At night, he'd wander into the family room, check out what the others were watching, and then go up to his room. He seldom sat at the kitchen table to do homework with them, and he never entered the office to do homework like had done since, well, forever.

He took long rides on one of the horses out in the back pasture and woods behind the little barn. He'd play with the dogs, especially Papa, Momma and Jasper. When Two wanted to kick the soccer ball around with him, he would. Sometimes, Jeremy would find Brett, or Billy, or Two in Brian's room talking or doing homework together. The only time Brian spent with Bobby was during their morning ritual of sit-ups, push-ups, and planks. Randy and Brian did yoga and meditation together, and sometimes talked religion. Brian did everything he could to avoid Jeremy and Vicky.

He and Brian had been so close just a few short months ago. Jeremy had been patient with Brian. He had extended himself as far as he could. He tried to spend extra time with him, but Brian had rebuffed him more often than not. It seemed to Jeremy that no amount of time spent with any of the boys did much to lift Brian's spirits around their home.

It wasn't that Brian was belligerent or defiant. It wasn't that he was disrespectful or rude. He had never exhibited those traits. It was mostly that Brian was withdrawn, sad, or depressed.

Brian had been seeing a therapist once a week and had been on anti-anxiety medication as a result of what the doctor had diagnosed. PTSD. The PTSD was a direct result of what had happened in Arizona on what was supposed to have been a fun hunting trip with Brett and George. That trip was anything but, and as a result, Brian came home with scars over and under his right eye, on his right hand, his right arm, and on his right shoulder. He had to wear glasses as a result of his cornea being scratched. While nothing damaged his vision, the glasses were worn to prevent further damage. Mostly, there were scars to Brian's heart that Jeremy didn't think would heal any time soon.

CHAPTER EIGHT

After Brian's goal, O'Connor excused himself and strolled to the concession stand. On the way, he called Eiselmann who sat with Sarah and another group of parents a small distance away from where he sat with Graff, Jeremy and Vicky Evans, and Mark and Jennifer Erickson.

The soccer community was a tight group of friends, almost one large extended family. They cheered for each other's kids, even though some didn't play as much as the others, and some didn't play at all.

This community not only knew the game of soccer, they knew the opposing players and their skills and tendencies. They knew the names or faces of the player's parents. While there was a healthy rivalry, or sometimes an unhealthy rivalry as the case may be, there was a modicum of respect.

Which was how O'Connor noticed them about halfway through the first half. The two men seemed odd. Out of place. They didn't fit, not in their dress and not their behavior. Especially since they were more focused on him than on the game.

"I saw them," was all Eiselmann said. "I took pictures and sent them to Kelliher and Quantico. No answer yet. What about contacting O'Reilly or someone in Chicago?"

"No." O'Connor shook his head as if Eiselmann stood across from him. "First lunch at *TGI Friday's* and now the soccer game? Someone's passing notes."

"My thought exactly. Fishing trip in the morning?"

"So far. We'll see."

O'Connor made two more phone calls. He talked quickly and quietly and in a kind of code that would only be understood by other cops.

Jorgy, the big six-foot-six red-head told him he'd be where he was needed at the right time. Tom Albrecht told him that he and Brooke would be in place, conspicuous, but not.

That done, Pat bought himself a bottle of water, strolled back, and stood with the rest of the parents and friends waiting to congratulate the team. He hadn't decided whether to say anything to Graff. He'd wait to see how the evening went.

CHAPTER NINE

O'Connor stayed around long enough to congratulate Brian, Stephen Bailey who was Paul Eiselmann's step-son, and Mike Erickson, the only kids he knew on the team. He said goodbye to some of the parents, promised Jeremy and Vicky he'd take good care of the George, Two, Brett, and Brian on their fishing trip, and confirmed the four o'clock departure with Graff, who would swing by his apartment to pick him up.

Eiselmann texted him even though they stood a mere five yards from each other.

Everything set?

Yup

O'Connor walked to his car at a leisurely pace mixed in with a crowd of soccer parents and fans. He didn't want to risk being isolated.

He pushed the key fob to unlock the driver's side door and climbed in, folding his long legs and lanky body behind the steering wheel. He started it up and inched his way forward into a long line of cars heading out of the parking lot.

The two men were four cars behind him in a newer dark Buick with Illinois plates. The driver kept his eyes on the road, while the passenger kept his eyes on O'Connor.

O'Connor called Eiselmann. "Paul, I have a license plate for you. Can you run it and pass it along to Kelliher? I want to know who I'm dealing with."

"Give it to me."

O'Connor recited the plate to him.

On the way to his apartment, Pat took a longer and more circuitous route giving the others extra time to get in place. He drove up Schwartz Hill towards some newer apartments, took a left on Summit and a right on Main which would lead him past the Waukesha Police Department. He wanted to see how they might react.

At this point, traffic had thinned considerably. There was only one car between O'Connor and the two men in the Buick.

Pat approached his apartment from the west and instead of parking in the structure below the building, he parked on the street a half of a block away. He got out of his car, stretched in a way that allowed him the opportunity to see that the Buick carrying the two men had pulled to the curb a full block behind him. Neither of the men had gotten out.

He feigned a sore, stiff back, twisting and turning each way, and then walked casually to his building as if he didn't have a care in the world.

A couple sat on the steps of an apartment building next to O'Connor's. They had been kissing.

They stopped just long enough for the man to say, "Still in the car. No one's moving," and then he went back to kissing the beautiful woman with long black hair.

O'Connor never broke stride.

As O'Connor used the key pad to enter the code to his building, the couple stood, kissed one more time, and walked hand in hand in the direction of the Buick.

When the couple reached the spot where O'Connor had parked his car, the Buick pulled away from the curb and drove slowly down the street, but didn't stop.

Tom Albrecht leaned against a tree and pulled Brooke Beranger towards him for a kiss, but he kept his eyes on the Buick to see which way it would turn.

The Buick took a right.

When it was out of site, he pulled out his cell and speed dialed Alex Jorgenson.

"Black or navy Buick. Might be coming your way."

No response, but Albrecht knew Jorgy got the message. He didn't waste any time speed-dialing O'Connor.

"They turned right at the end of the block. Might be using the alley. Brooke is coming to you. I'm going to Jorgy."

Before he had finished with the call, Brooke jogged up the street, punched in the code to O'Connor's entrance and walked in pulling the door shut behind her.

"Here."

Brooke followed the voice and joined O'Connor in the darkened hallway, lit only by emergency lighting.

"Stay here. Stay low. I'm going to the parking garage. Let Jorgy know."

He took off down the hallway and into the stairwell that would take him one floor down. He stayed to the side, but peered out the small square window watching for any headlights.

None so far.

He waited.

Still nothing.

His cell vibrated. He took it out of his back pocket without taking his eyes away from the parking garage. He glanced at the text from Albrecht.

Nothing

Jorgenson, Albrecht, and Beranger were seasoned veterans. For them, like O'Connor, patience was more than a virtue. It saved lives, his and theirs, many times over.

There were two entrances to the garage, one from the street and one from the alley behind the apartment building. From O'Connor's vantage point, he could see both.

From the street side, O'Connor saw the flash of headlights on the cement wall.

A car drove in and parked in a numbered stall meant for residents, not in one marked with a large V for visitors. At first it sat there, its motor ticking hotly. A man emerged. Young, in his thirties, O'Connor guessed. No one else emerged, and the guy was definitely not one of the two men he saw at the soccer game. The car was not a dark Buick either.

His cell vibrated.

O'Connor stepped fully into the garage but hung against the brick wall. He slipped his cell out of his pocket.

It came from Jorgy.

Nada

The cops remained in place until 11:30 PM, a full two hours after leaving the soccer game. Jorgy called in a BOLO on the Buick with the two occupants as persons of interest. So far, there had been no action and nothing suspicious. There was the possibility that the two men could come back at some point when they believed O'Connor might be asleep, or they might come back in the morning when Graff picked him up. Their disappearance puzzled and concerned him as did their whereabouts.

CHAPTER TEN

He made a quick phone call and explained the situation. The recipient of the call gave the okay in his normal mumbled fashion. The man couldn't tell if he was drunk, fuming, or if he didn't give a damn.

The man made another call and asked for a meeting.

He waited for them in the back of a vacant lot off Saylesville Road and River Road. The area was commercial, but somehow rural at the same time. A perfect location for a private meet up. As he sat there, he smiled, wondering how many high school kids came here for a quick one before heading home.

Forty minutes after sending the text, a car slowed at the entrance. When he was certain it was them, he flashed his lights once and waited.

The car pulled forward and parked side by side. He got out and climbed into the backseat.

"What took you?"

Sasha Bakay glanced at his long-time partner, and then shifted to take a closer look at the man in the backseat.

"We thought we could take him at his apartment."

The driver, Misha Danilenko, said, "It was too risky."

The man nodded and said, "Yes, it was. The cop spotted you at the soccer game."

"How do you know?" Bakay asked.

"Because he isn't stupid," the man said.

He had already slipped his silenced Walther from his jacket pocket. It spat once, then twice. One bullet apiece to the back of Bakay's head, and then the back of Danilenko's head.

Blood spattered the front windshield, side windows, and dashboard. Both men, still strapped in by their seatbelts slumped forward. Heads bleeding.

He never took chances, so he fired his weapon two more times into the base of each man's skull.

Before he left the vehicle, he wiped down the backseat, the door, and the handle. After, he got into his own car and drove away already thinking of his next move. He smiled. He liked operating alone.

CHAPTER ELEVEN

Brian placed both of his hands on the ceramic tiles and stood under the steamy shower not wanting to leave. He didn't realize just how exhausted, stiff, and sore he was. He would alternately tilt his head up to the steaming water jetting out of the shower head and then hang it so it beat on the back of his head, neck and shoulders.

His upper thighs on both hips were ripped open from his slide tackles on the turf field. Each game they opened back up and screamed at him as water hit them. It was no different this time. Only the bruise and gash from Ruiz's cleats on the outside of his left ankle hurt worse. The skin had been torn and it had bled into his sock. When he had peeled his sock off before his shower, it bled again.

"You okay in there?"

Bobby had come in, peed, washed his hands, and then brushed his teeth. He had left, but must have come back. Brian hadn't heard him return.

"Yeah, just tired."

"I took your uniform and stuff to the laundry room. Billy's going to do laundry in the morning."

"Thanks. Everything was kind of sweaty and gross."

"No worse than our stuff after football."

He turned off the water, shook his long dark hair out and slid the shower curtain open. He took the towel off the bar and dried off, starting with his hair and face, working his way down.

He stepped out onto the mat and smiled tentatively at his adopted brother.

When Bobby and Brett were younger, they looked like Tom Brady clones without the cleft chin. As they got older, they mostly lost the Tom Brady look and looked less like twins. Bobby had a softer face. Brett's, harder with an edge. Bobby was younger by eighteen months, but taller by an inch. Bobby stood two inches taller than Brian, but Brian was built more solidly and was more compact.

Bobby had let his chestnut-colored hair grow to about the same length as Brian's. Jeremy had joked that they were two of the lesser known Beatles. Only George and Two had longer hair. Their black hair hung below their shoulders, which was typical for full-blooded Navajo.

George and Two were the shortest of the brothers, but all of them had sprouted up over the summer and early fall. The identical twins, Randy and Billy were the tallest and stood a hair over six-two. The rest fell in like dominoes. Bobby measured six-one, Brett at six-foot even, and Brian at five-eleven. George was an inch shorter than Brian, and Two, the youngest, was two inches shorter than George.

"Geez, Bri. Your legs are bleeding."

Brian looked down at his legs and then checked the towel for any stains. Sure enough, there were traces. Not much, but some.

He was used to it. He had scarring that didn't tan as the rest of his legs did. During the soccer season, those spots on his legs were raw, opening up during each game, healing a little between games, only to open with the first slide tackle he threw.

"Stay there," Bobby said as he bent down and dug around under the sink for Neosporin, gauze, tape, and scissors. "You need something on them or you're going to bleed all over your sheets."

Bobby sat down on the toilet and as gently as he could, smeared the antiseptic gel onto each thigh, covered the wounds with gauze and then taped the gauze down. Bobby gently ran his hand over each thigh as Brian stood naked inches from Bobby's face. They hadn't been in this position or this close in ages. Brian felt a familiar urge from the distant past and he was pretty sure Bobby did too.

Bobby smiled up at Brian who smiled back and said, "Thanks."

"Let's fix your ankle. How badly does it hurt?"

"Worse than my hips."

"Put your foot here," Bobby said patting the toilet seat between his legs.

Brian did, and Bobby performed the same task that he had done on Brian's hips.

"When you take the tape off, you might pull some of your hair off. I did the best I could," Bobby said.

"I'll be okay."

"I think you should ice it."

Brian made a face and said, "I'll just take a couple of Motrin."

"Up to you. It's getting late. I don't know what the weather will be like up there, so I packed both warm and cool clothes for you."

Brian smiled and said, "I saw. Thanks."

Bobby smiled back and said, "I'll catch you later."

Brian slipped on a pair of loose-fitting shorts and brushed his teeth. Before he pulled on a t-shirt, he took the time to inspect the scars he received in Arizona almost two months earlier. The scar above and below his right eye bothered him the most. The scars on his shoulder, upper arm and forearm were noticeable, but he didn't care about them as much as the scarring above and below his eye. The scarring around his right eye changed his looks. Not dramatically, but enough.

The biggest change was the tuft of blond hair that sprouted out of the scar on the right side of his head. The doctor said that though the condition is rare, under stress or even with a hormonal change, hair might do this. More common was a loss of hair, but even then, that was rare. He pursed his lips, shook his head and walked out of the bathroom and across the hall to his bedroom.

Momma had taken up her post just outside of his door facing the stairs. Brian bent down to pet her, nuzzling his face into her fur. She rewarded him with a doggie kiss.

He entered his room and shut the door only partway. In his old life, he would have shut the door completely. Now, no way. No one had told him to keep it open. Everyone else except for Brett slept with their doors shut. Brett didn't because of his previous life. Brian didn't because he felt he couldn't, and it bothered him.

Papa laid at the foot of the bed and didn't move a muscle when Brian entered. Jasper, the pup laid at the side of the bed facing the doorway. Only Jasper's tail moved. It thumped softly and rhythmically on the carpeted floor.

Brian got down on all fours and gently rammed his head into Papa's side. Papa rolled over inviting Brian to pet him. Jasper came over to get his turn too.

After showing them a bit of love, Brian stood up, grabbed a duffle bag and a backpack out of the closet. It was Bobby's way of packing. Clothes, neat and orderly, laid out in two rows. Underwear and socks, t-shirts, shorts, a swimsuit, jeans, sweat pants, a sweatshirt, and rain gear, just in case.

Brian smiled as he packed the clothes neatly into his duffle, saving his backpack for smaller items like a flashlight, cell charger, a book or two, his Buck knife, and anything else he'd find along the way.

As he was finishing up, Bobby walked in and shut the door behind him.

"I'm sleeping in here tonight."

Stunned, Brian cocked his head and said, "You sure?"

Bobby's answer was to climb into bed and pull the sheet up to his waist.

"I think we better keep the door open."

"No, shut it. I want to talk to you privately."

Brian hesitated, caught between opening the door and climbing into bed with Bobby, something they had not done since early spring. Finally, Brian got into bed, but made sure he wasn't touching him.

Bobby rolled onto his side up against him, slipped his hand under Brian's t-shirt. His hand warm, soft. Brian was certain Bobby could feel his heart trying to escape.

Feeling the need to make it less awkward, Brian said, "Your voice got lower."

"Yours too. It happens when you hit puberty."

The two boys smiled at each other.

"It screwed up our harmony, though. We have to rearrange our songs a little. Not much, but some." Bobby shrugged and said, "All of us grew. Even you, but you're still stubby," he said with a smile.

"I can still take you," Brian said with a chuckle.

Randy and Bobby were in a band that had become local favorites. Danny Limbach, who lived two hundred yards down the path between the woods that separated their properties, was the leader because he was the musical genius. He could play guitars- lead, rhythm, and bass, acoustic or electric, six-string or twelve. He played keyboards, any brass instrument, as well as drums. He found banjo and mandolin interesting, and took those up, too.

They wrote songs. At first, crappy. Then crappy turned into not so bad, and not so bad turned into pretty good. Eventually, their songs became really good. So good in fact, that Danny sent six off to Tim McGraw's manager. Three of them were optioned for an upcoming album. McGraw told Danny that the other three needed to be recorded by them. He felt he couldn't do them justice because they were so personal. In his opinion, no one else could do them justice, either.

It was their harmony that caught everyone's attention. Randy usually sang melody, unless the song was in an upper register. Then Bobby would sing lead. Chris Granger, who had been in jazz band, played the drums and sang the low parts. Troy Rivera played cello and bass in the orchestra, but liked electric bass the best. He never wanted to sing lead, but sang the hard, middle harmony. Sean Drummond sang high harmony and played keyboards. When the arrangement called for both organ and piano, Bobby switched from guitar to piano, while Sean played organ. All of them could sing well enough to be a lead vocalist in any band.

Bobby ran his hand across Brian's chest and said, "Sometimes my body aches. Mom says it's because I grew too fast. We all did."

Brian smiled and said, "I think most of us are done though. Two is still groing."

"I bet he'll be taller than George."

Brian chuckled and said, "That'll piss George off."

"Have you and Randy gotten any more of those letters?"

Randy and Bobby had received anonymous letters, both derogatory and rude. The gist was how Randy and Bobby ruined Danny's chances of musical stardom by taking the spotlight from him. Danny received similar letters encouraging him to strike out on his own and leave Randy and Bobby and the others behind.

Bobby shook his head and said, "No, just the four or five."

"Do you have any idea who's sending them?"

"Nope. Danny laughs them off. Randy mostly ignores them."

"They bother you, though."

Bobby pulled his hand out from under Brian's t-shirt and traced the scar around Brian's eye with his thumb. "Yeah. A little, I guess."

The two boys stared at each other. Bobby's physical closeness and his hand first on Brian's chest and then on his cheek had caused a spark between the two of them that Brian was all but certain had disappeared the morning he, Brett, and George left for Arizona at the end of July. The gentleness of Bobby's touch on Brian's face threatened Brian's heart to jump out of his chest.

"I want to talk to you, but before you say anything, I need you to hear me out. Please?"

Brian nodded, staring at him apprehensively.

Bobby launched into what he had come to talk about. It was abrupt, but in Bobby's mind, necessary. It was also Bobby's way. He was direct when he felt he needed to be, which was most often.

"I read the letter you sent me from Arizona every day for a month. Even now, I read it. I think I can recite it from memory."

"I didn't write it to make you feel guilty, Bobby. I just wanted you to understand."

Bobby placed two fingers on Brian's lips, then brushed his cheek with a thumb.

"I know, Bri."

Before Bobby shifted his hand back to Brian's chest, he gently brushed Brian's lips with his thumb. He said, "I want to apologize for what I said to you before you left on that trip."

Brian didn't react. He couldn't react. The hurt had never left his heart. He could picture the scene in the bathroom, and could still hear Bobby's words as if it had just happened.

"I was scared, Bri."

"Why?"

"Because I'm gay."

Brian stared at him. He began to object, "No . . ."

"Shhh, let me finish."

Brian rolled over onto his side and faced Bobby. Their faces only inches apart.

"I tried to fight it. I went out with Megan O'Donnell. We did stuff," he shrugged dismissively, and said, "nothing like you and Cat, but we did stuff. It was okay." He shrugged again. "I dated a couple of other girls, but you know that." He shook his head and said, "Nothing."

"What do you mean, 'nothing?'" though Brian knew what he meant. He needed to hear it from Bobby himself.

"I didn't have any of the feelings I had when I was with you. I got scared because I kept thinking of you and me. I liked what you and I did more than what I did with Megan or the other girls."

He rolled over onto his back and said, "The thing is, I kind of wondered if I was gay back in sixth or seventh grade. I had a crush on this guy. We," he searched for the right word and settled on, "experimented. Not as much as you and me, but we did stuff. I liked it."

He turned to Brian and said, "Then, Brett was abducted. You know the whole story about Brett, my uncle, and me."

Brian nodded. He reached over and took ahold of Bobby's hand, lacing his fingers with his.

Bobby had big hands. His fingers were long. His hands were smooth and soft. Brian had always liked to hold hands with him.

"After we moved to Waukesha, I did stuff with a couple of guys. Not much and not often." He turned to Brian and said, "I don't want to tell you who, because that's private."

Brian nodded.

"Then you started spending nights at our house. When your parents . . . *died*, you and I became friends, and then we . . . you know."

Brian didn't say a word.

"The thing is, I got scared. I know both of us wondered whether we were gay. I know you liked both Cat and me."

Brian took a deep breath and whispered, "My therapist helped me understand that I'm bisexual. I think I am, anyway. I'm attracted to both girls and guys. I haven't told that to anyone. I don't think my therapist told mom and dad. The confidentiality thing. But dad and mom might know. Maybe they just suspect. I'm not sure."

"I'm gay, Brian. I'm sure of it."

"You're sure."He said this as a statement, not a question.

Bobby nodded. He wiped tears out of his eyes and took a deep breath.

Bobby used his thumb to trace the scar around Brian's eye and across the smattering of small freckles under his green eyes. All of his brothers were good-looking. Handsome. But Brian was special.

"I know I'm gay. That morning you left for Arizona, I said that if we stopped doing stuff, maybe we'd like girls more."

"I remember. I didn't understand what you meant."

Bobby sighed and said, "I didn't want to accept it. Me being gay, I mean. It scared me. I thought that maybe if we dated girls instead of doing stuff with each other, I . . . we might be different. But deep down, I knew that no matter what I did with Megan or any girl, I was gay. I am gay. It scared me. It still does kinda."

Bobby rolled onto his back. Brian had never let go of Bobby's hand. He snaked his right arm under Bobby's neck and held him.

"I know you might be involved with Mikey. You two spend every weekend together. I see how you act with him and how he acts with you. It's not like how you and I acted around each other, but pretty close."

He smiled sadly. A tear fell and rolled down his cheek.

"Bobby, Mikey and I are friends. Yeah, we've done some stuff, but not like you and me. I like him." Brian left it at that. Not willing or able to add anything else.

"I know. Mikey's one of my closest friends. We talk all the time." He smiled and said, "He's talked about you."

Brian could feel himself blushing.

As if Bobby read his mind, he said, "He doesn't tell me what you two do or what you talk about, if that's what you're thinking. And I wouldn't ask. I promise. But he likes you. *Likes* you, likes you."

Brian breathed easier.

"The thing is, I love you, Brian. I always have and I always will. I know you and Mikey are in a relationship and I don't want to interfere with that."

"I love you too, Bobby. I never stopped loving you. I just didn't know how to act around you. I was afraid to be close to you. I didn't want you to think I was pushing you. I didn't want mom or dad to get pissed at me.

I didn't know what to say. I didn't know what to do. So, I stayed away. From you. From them. I stayed away from everyone."

Brian began to weep. He shook his head. He felt lighter letting it all out. He could breathe again. But the hurt was suffocating. These were the first words about his living situation he had spoken to anyone other than the therapist. No one had known what he was thinking or feeling. He had kept it locked deep down inside of him. He dared not bring any of his feelings to the surface for fear of how it might come out and how it might be received. The little he had shared with Randy and Brett was nothing to what he had just unloaded on Bobby.

"I didn't want to live here, but mom and dad didn't want me to move out." He shrugged and said, "I still don't think they'd let me. I don't think the guys want me to move out, either."

"No one does, Bri. None of us want you to leave."

"It's so hard living here, Bobby. Mom and dad don't trust me. I don't even think they like me all that much. They would go crazy if they knew you were in here."

Bobby smiled and said, "They know."

"What?" He sat upright and stared at the door.

"Relax, Bri. I told them I needed to fix things between us. They don't know what we're talking about. That's between you and me. I don't want anyone else to know until I'm ready."

Brian lay back down but kept glancing at the door.

Bobby took hold of Brian's face. He ran his thumb over Brian's lips, and said, "The thing is, I love you, Bri. I miss . . . us. I miss you holding me. I miss talking with you and being with you. I miss everything we did. All of it."

"Me, too."

"But I know you're in a relationship with Mikey. I'm okay with that. I hope it turns out alright. I know we might not have sex for a while, maybe never, but," he smiled and shrugged and said, "you never know."

Brian smiled at him. He desperately wanted to kiss him.

"I told mom and dad that when I turn eighteen, I'm not going to be adopted."

"Why?" Brian had thought that both Brett and Bobby couldn't wait to turn eighteen so that Jeremy could adopt them legally. They both wanted to be Evans, not McGovern, but their biological father, Thomas, wouldn't sign any document relinquishing parental control or authority.

"I want to stay McGovern."

"Why?"

"Because our band is beginning to make a name for ourselves. Everyone knows me as Bobby McGovern. If Tim McGraw puts our three songs on his album, my name will be in the credits. Randy's and Danny's too, but you know what I mean."

"Couldn't you use that name as a pen name?"

Bobby shook his head and said, "No. I want to be me."

He paused and whispered, "Mostly, if you and I ever do end up together, we don't have to worry about both of us being Evans. We aren't related. Yes, we live in the same house and we're raised like brothers. But technically, we aren't."

"But Bobby . . ."

"Shhh, it's okay. Even if we don't end up together, I like being Bobby Mac and Little Mac." He smiled. "I'm good with that."

"Are you sure?"

Bobby smiled and said, "Positive. Just so long as we can go back to the way we were, even if we don't have sex."

"I want that, too," Brian smiled, the first genuine, honest smile around his brothers, or sort of brothers, in a long time. His first genuine smile directed at Bobby. It was a relief. His heart pounded. He couldn't help it, but he kissed Bobby on the lips. It was soft and pure and gentle.

"We're good then?"

Brian leaned forward and the two boys kissed again. Gently, tenderly.

Bobby rubbed noses with Brian and said, "This conversation is between us, right?"

Brian smiled and kissed Bobby again, this time a little more passionately, and at some point, he whispered, "Just us."

There was a knock on the door causing both boys to pull away in a panic.

CHAPTER TWELVE

"Sasha Bakay and Misha Danilenko are suspects in several unsolved murders in and around Chicago. They are employed by an import-export business. Eastern Europe Exchange."

"I know that name," Eiselmann answered.

He had been asleep when his cell buzzed. Sarah woke up briefly, but went back to sleep when she was certain Paul wouldn't be pulled into a case until morning.

Kelliher continued, "You should. It's owned by Dmitry Andruko."

Pete Kelliher was officially an instructor at the FBI Academy in Quantico, Virginia. However, it was understood that from time to time he would work in the field in order to stay fresh. That had been his idea. His former partner, now a Deputy Director, Summer Storm, and her boss, Senior Deputy Director Thomas Dandridge, agreed with him.

Of course, Whitey would agree with him. They had been friends since the academy days. They'd share a pizza and a beer or two as they watched Clint Eastwood movies. Dandridge was a fit and trim figure with a full head of silver-gray hair, hence Pete's name for him. As far as anyone knew, Pete was the only one to call him that. Or at least, the only one to survive calling him that.

Kelliher could have retired. He was past the age of retirement. But Kelliher was legendary in the bureau as an investigator, and he was also a friend of Dandridge, who convinced him to stay on for a couple more years so they could retire together.

Pete had worked cases with Graff, O'Connor, and Eiselmann, including the sex ring that freed thirty or so boys from captivity. The ring that had included Brett McGovern for twenty-two months, and Stephen Bailey and Mikey Erickson for twenty-four hours.

Eiselmann and O'Connor ran the raid in Long Beach, California, at the same time Kelliher and Graff raided a warehouse in Chicago. That was where Brett, Stephen, and Mikey were held. Bailey and Erickson had been abducted off the street less than twenty-four hours previous. It was the search for them that led them to Chicago, Long Beach, and a hotel in Kansas City.

"Bakay and Danilenko sure as hell don't look like salesmen," Eiselmann said. "I'm thinking enforcers."

"The FBI would agree with you."

"And they're after O'Connor."

Kelliher hesitated and said, "Given their timing with O'Connor's testimony in Chicago, I would agree. We are looking into other individuals tied to that case."

Eiselmann got up out of bed after kissing Sarah's cheek. He walked out into the hallway. Took a peek into Stephen's room. He was sound asleep on his back, arms to the side. He took a peek into Stephen's younger sister's room. Alexandra was curled up on her side, hugging her pillow. All good, all peaceful in the Eiselmann house.

He checked his watch. In a couple of hours, O'Connor and Graff would be heading north with the boys on their trip. He sat down on the top step.

"If anything happens to O'Connor, the case against Andruko turns to shit."

"Yes. Pat's testimony is key to all of it."

"Pete, three guys followed us to a restaurant. Two different guys, Bakay and Danilenko, come to Waukesha to a soccer game. As far as I know, only three people knew Pat was going to that game tonight."

"That's why we're looking at other individuals. It could be one of the lawyers. It could be someone from their office who overheard them talking. We'll put them under a microscope and see what we find. Discreetly, of course."

"Keep me posted," Eiselmann said.

"I think it might be wise to get some protection for you and your family, too. Just to be safe. You were in Chicago, in that courtroom, and at that restaurant. You are known. They don't know to what extent, but they know you. Don't put yourself or your family in jeopardy," Kelliher said.

Eiselmann nodded even though Kelliher couldn't see it. Before his marriage, he was single and could take care of himself. The marriage brought with it not only a wife, but two step-kids. He was now accountable to a family.

"I'll get on it."

"The sooner, the better," Pete said softly. "What about O'Connor?"

"He's going up north on a fishing and hunting trip with Jamie Graff, Brett, Brian, George, and George's half-brother, Michael Two Feathers."

There was some silence on the phone and Eiselmann thought he had lost a connection.

"Is that wise? Not so much the fishing trip, but who is going with him? Those boys had a helluva time in Arizona."

Eiselmann had wondered that himself.

"After we hang up, I'll call O'Connor and talk it over with him."

"I think it's important to do so. Like I said, those boys have been through a lot."

CHAPTER THIRTEEN

"Mind if I come in?" Jeremy asked half in, half out of the doorway.

"Sure," Bobby said.

"We weren't doing anything," Brian said quickly. "We were just talking."

Jeremy sighed and said, "I know."

"That's why the door was shut," Brian said.

Jeremy stepped into the room and shut the door behind him.

Papa kept his eye on him. Jasper lifted his head and wagged his tail, and Jeremy rewarded him with a pet or two.

Jeremy was about the same height as George. He was slender with brown hair that had streaks of gray at the temple, and friendly blue eyes. A counselor at the high school and former basketball coach, he was popular with students, and respected by parents and his colleagues.

"I wanted to say a couple of things, if that's okay."

"We weren't doing anything," Brian repeated.

It was a little too panicky Jeremy thought. Perhaps he had walked in on the start of something. He was uncomfortable at the thought.

"Brian, stop." To soften it, he added, "Please."

Papa got up, padded to the side of the bed and sat facing him. That unsettled Jeremy, because Papa looked to be guarding Brian.

He sat down at the foot of the bed and said, "First of all, I wanted to tell you that I thought that was the finest game you played this season. That might have been the best game you played since I've been watching you play soccer. You took control. You directed traffic. You stopped any run they had up the middle. You made a great shot, and now you're in first place by yourselves."

"Thanks."

"I also wanted to apologize for not speaking to you before the game. I know that's important, but there was a fight in the parking lot. Bob Farner has heart trouble, and he was the only staff member on duty. I didn't want him to be by himself. So, I apologize."

Brian tried to play it off by saying, "It's okay."

"No, it's not, Bri, but I felt I needed to help Bob."

Brian shrugged.

"But I am sorry."

"It's okay."

Jeremy knew it mattered to Brian more so than he let on.

"What I was most proud of was your speech to the team after the game. You gave everyone credit for that shot and that win. That was humble of you. That was a sign of a real leader."

"What I said was true, though."

Jeremy lifted a hand in surrender.

"True or not, what you said was impressive. I'm proud of you."

Brian felt himself blushing and said, "Thank you."

"Lastly, I wanted to say, goodnight."

He got up to leave and Brian said, "You can keep the door open."

Jeremy hesitated, and then said, "No, you two probably have more to talk about. This conversation between the two of you was too long in the making. It's about time you made peace."

"We weren't doing anything," Brian said once again.

Brian had finally gotten under Jeremy's skin. He snapped, "Like I said, I came in here to say what I said. And you know, Brian? It might be nice to trust me like you did once upon a time. Maybe trust your mom and me like you want us to trust you."

"I do trust you," Brian protested.

"We haven't been the same in a long time and you know it. So, when you get done making peace with Bobby, maybe you should spend some time making peace with me. Maybe you can find the time to make peace with Vicky. She still feels responsible for what took place in Arizona, and you've done nothing to lessen that guilt. Think about that. Maybe you can find some time to make peace with George. You two haven't been the same since you came back from Arizona."

Brian wanted to object, but his mouth wouldn't work. And he got the shakes. His right hand shook. It happened from time to time, mostly without warning. He and the therapist were working on finding the triggers.

Bobby noticed and said, "Give me your hand."

Brian tried to hide it, but Bobby reached over and took it, lacing his fingers with Brian's. That done, Bobby glared at Jeremy.

Jeremy knew he struck a nerve and that he had gone too far. Any positive advances he had made with Brian vanished with his mini-tirade.

Yes, Brian needed to hear what he had said. But not in this way and not at this time. Jeremy knew it, but didn't know how to fix it, at least at that moment.

"Goodnight. See you in the morning."

It was a lame way to end it and he knew it.

He left the room and shut the door behind him, leaving both Brian and Bobby staring at the closed door.

CHAPTER FOURTEEN

"So, are you still going on that trip, with the boys, I mean?"

Eiselmann had relayed the conversation he had had with Kelliher. Pat took it in silence, which was his way. He stared out the window at the street below. All was quiet, peaceful. Houses dark. He was dressed, packed, and waiting for Graff to pick him up.

"I. I think. I think Jamie and I will talk it over. Depending upon what he says, we'll talk to Vicky and Jeremy and boys." When he thought things through, he had a way of starting and stopping that bothered some. Paul and Jamie and those who knew him best accepted it as a quirk.

"Just be careful. You and them."

"You, too, Bro. We might be safer up north than you might be here. We can hide up there. Miles of nothing and no one. Two city dudes running around up there will stick out. And, I've seen them. They don't know that, but I've seen them. I have an advantage."

"Not if you're protecting yourself and the boys."

"I think we'll be fine. If something's going to happen, I'm guessing it would have been by now."

Or when Graff picks him up. He thought it, but didn't voice it. Chances were that Eiselmann thought of that too.

He spent the night catnapping in the lazy boy off the kitchen. It was set at an angle from the door. He had taken the further precaution of placing a table in front of the door so that if someone tried to pick a lock and sneak in, it wouldn't be easy.

Just like O'Connor thought, Eiselmann said, "Maybe when Graff picks you up. Maybe on the ride up. You never know, Hoss."

"I'll talk it over with Graff and we'll see."

CHAPTER FIFTEEN

Brian slipped out of bed slowly so as not to disturb Bobby. He pulled the covers back up, because he didn't want to wake him.

He stood at the side of the bed and stared at his friend, his sort of brother, his once-upon-a-time lover. Bobby slept with his lips slightly open in a smile. Face relaxed. Skin smooth and dark, muscled and defined. Though built the same way, he slept differently from Brett, who slept with a frown, jaw tight, and brow furrowed. As intense in sleep as he was awake. He loved them both, but differently. Perhaps not that differently.

He padded softly out of the bedroom and bent down to pet Momma. He could hear someone snoring lightly, but he couldn't tell which room it came from. Could be Billy or Randy. Maybe Jeremy. He used the bathroom across the hall, flushed, and washed his hands.

He tiptoed down the hallway and down the steps, his feet silent on the carpet.

A light above the window and the kitchen sink remained on each night. The pale-yellow moon glowed through windows, giving the middle of the night an unusually bright, almost eerie, look. He peeked into the laundry room and saw that the light on the alarm showed red, indicating it was on. On ever since the psycho in the woods the past winter. Brian shivered.

His bare feet were cold on the kitchen tile. The area rug hardly made a difference.

Brian walked down the hallway past the living room and family room to the study, his favorite room in the house, though he seldom entered it any longer, especially if he suspected Jeremy or Vicky might be in there. His visits to the study ended upon his return from Arizona.

He curled up on one end of the couch facing a cold, empty fireplace that had a TV over the mantle, and covered himself with a light and colorful Navajo blanket that had been folded over the back of the couch. He shivered, but the cold from the AC was only a small reason. His right hand shook as if he had palsy or Parkinson's. He had neither.

The shakes, as his brothers referred to them, mostly affected his right hand, less often his left, and came and went on their own free will. Most of the time the shakes appeared after the nightmare Brian had once or twice a week. Sometimes when he felt stress. Oddly, never during a soccer game and never when he kicked field goals or extra points in football. The therapist thought that was interesting and began exploring that with Brian.

The therapist he saw once a week told him he suffered from PTSD. The psychiatrist prescribed Zoloft, but Brian only took it sporadically and when he did, he cut it in half, because he didn't like the zombie-like, lethargic affect it had on him. It dulled his feelings and he didn't like that. He also liked eating, and the drug affected his appetite.

Unfortunately, when he didn't take it, he sometimes became agitated and at times couldn't control his temper. Normally, Brian was easygoing, typically one of the quieter ones among the adopted brothers. He was probably more so since the trip to Arizona. But when he didn't take his meds, he found himself impatient and angry. He could feel it coming on and worked to control it.

Randy, one of the twins, taught him Yoga and meditation, and that helped. So much so, he toyed with asking his father and mother to cut back on the therapy. It was too soon, even though it had been almost three months.

The nightmare.

Brian knew he needed to analyze it and then jot his thoughts down in his journal so he could discuss it with the therapist. It appeared in several variations ever since he, Brett and George fought and almost died on the top of the mesa in Arizona on the Navajo Nation reservation.

In it, he shot two men and watched them die. Then two others fired and wounded him. He carried a scar above and below his right eye, forcing him to wear glasses as a precaution to further damage. He had other scars. Perhaps the biggest scar was etched into his heart.

The nightmare was consistent, for the most part, with what actually happened. The ending twisted on its own and in a way all nightmares did.

Men charged and shot their way up the path. Sometimes the two men would leer at him and then shoot and kill Brett, but leave him alone. Sometimes the men would shoot and kill both George and Brett. Both of his brothers were there that early morning, but neither of them had been shot. The nightmare didn't care. Sometimes the two men would shoot Michael. While Michael was there and did shoot and kill one of the men, he had not been shot. Again, the nightmare didn't care.

The nightmare turned worse when the two men shot and killed Bobby. Bobby was never there, had never been involved in the gunfight, and Brian didn't think Bobby was capable of shooting anyone. Sometimes, the nightmare twisted and the men shot and killed Mike Erickson, Brian's teammate and best friend. More than a friend.

Brian shut his eyes and practiced his deep breathing just as Randy had taught him. He was so into it, he never heard him.

"Hey," Brett whispered, reaching out and pushing the bangs off Brian's forehead. "You okay?"

Brian nodded. He embarrassed easily, and thought of the tremors in his hand and the reoccurring nightmare as weaknesses.

Brett sat down next to Brian, slipped an arm around his shoulders and pulled him close. Brian wiggled the blanket free and wrapped himself and Brett in it.

Brett said, "Give me your hand."

Brian hesitated. Even though his brothers knew his hand shook, he didn't like showing them.

When Brian didn't give Brett his hand, Brett reached out and held it.

"It's okay," Brett said lacing his fingers with Brian's.

Brian lowered his chin to his chest.

"Hey, it's okay."

Brian shrugged.

"Tell me about it."

Brian's immediate response was to shake his head.

Brett ran his lips and nose in Brian's hair and whispered, "You need to talk about it. Telling someone about your nightmare makes it less."

That was something Billy, Randy's twin, had said to one of them a long time ago. Brett couldn't remember who he said it to, but knew instinctively Billy was right.

"It's the same one, only this time, they shoot Bobby."

Brett nodded.

Brett had been jealous of Brian's and Bobby's exceptionally close relationship. Even to this day, and even though that closeness had vanished the morning he, Brian and George flew to Arizona. Brian and Bobby were never able to get that friendship back to what it once was even though Bobby had tried. Maybe that might change after the talk he and Bobby had.

"How did that make you feel?" Brett asked.

Brian shook his head and then he shrugged. Brett squeezed his shoulders.

"You felt . . ." Brett started for him.

Brian shrugged again, but said, "Helpless. I couldn't help him."

He brushed some tears off his face.

"You still love him."

Brian shrugged and said, "I always will."

"All of us know that. Even mom and dad."

Brian glanced at Brett, wondering if Brett knew what had taken place earlier that night. That worried him.

"Did you and Bobby get it worked out?"

Brian squirmed. Of course, Brett knew. Everyone knew. There were no secrets among the brothers regardless of how one tried. What Brian didn't know was how much of the conversation with Bobby was heard by Brett or anyone else. Or, how much of what Jeremy had said was heard.

"He still loves you."

Brian wanted to say something, anything, but nothing came out.

"Bobby loves you," Brett said again.

Brian shrugged. "I know, but it doesn't matter," Brian whispered.

Brett shifted and held Brian with both arms as Brian wept quietly. He used the blanket to wipe his tears off.

"You scored the winning goal last night. In the last football game, you kicked two field goals and three extra points. You didn't miss one. You were perfect. In fact, you haven't missed yet this year."

Brian shrugged. Whatever success he felt in football didn't matter to him. He only cared about soccer. That was his sport, the one that mattered.

"That fake field goal was gutsy, but you got the first down by an extra twelve yards."

Brian had no response.

"In your soccer game, you played like you were pissed at the world. Possessed. When the crowd chanted your name and gave you a standing O, you stared up at mom and dad. Why?"

That brought fresh tears to Brian's eyes. It was hard to explain.

"Dad never talked to me before the game. He always does, but he didn't last night."

It had been a ritual that had begun in basketball their freshman year. During warmups, Jeremy would stand on the sideline and speak to each of the boys one by one. Sort of a mini pep talk. He had never missed a game. It carried over to the fall. For George and Two, in cross country. For Brian in soccer and in football. Each boy, each game.

"There was a fight in the parking lot and he went to help. When he got back, the game had started."

Brian turned his head away from Brett. He couldn't explain his hurt. It was more than just the talk before the game. It was a lot more than that. He and Bobby had shared a bedroom just like George and Billy did. Ever since Jeremy and Vicky found out that he and Bobby were experimenting, they made them sleep in separate rooms. Brian felt as though he was watched all the time, that Jeremy and Vicky worried about what he might do. He felt they didn't trust him, and that they were disgusted with him.

Now that he and Mikey were together, he worried they might put an end to Mikey sleeping over and would prevent him from sleeping at Mikey's.

Both Jeremy and Vicky had assured him he was wrong, but Brian didn't believe them. He slept with his door open, though he hated doing so. He didn't risk shutting it, believing that Jeremy and Vicky would wonder and worry. He worried that Billy or Two, who sometimes slept with him when one or the other wasn't sleeping with George, might get weird about sleeping with him.

Brian no longer felt he belonged in the family, even though he had been adopted and carried the Evans name.

Randy and Billy, identical twins, had been adopted by Jeremy when he was single. Billy kept his last name, Schroeder, out of respect for his first adoptive father. Along came George during the summer of death. He was adopted, but kept his Navajo name, Tokay.

That same summer, Vicky, Brett and Bobby moved to Waukesha from a suburb of Indianapolis. Vicky was recently divorced, and Jeremy had been counseling both boys because of what they had been through. Eventually, Jeremy and Vicky married, and the two boys lived with Jeremy and the rest of the boys.

In August, George, Brett and Brian went to Arizona, and they came back with Michael, George's step-brother. Neither boy had known they were related. Michael's mom died of an overdose, and his father- George's father also- had disappeared. Michael had been living with a bar owner. Two, as he was known by everyone, would eventually be adopted by Jeremy and Vicky, but he had decided to keep his Navajo name, Two Feathers.

Brian was the only adopted brother who didn't have a true sibling, and that further separated him from the rest of the family.

"Hey," Brett whispered. "What are you thinking?"

Brian shook his head. "I'm so fucked up," he answered. "Just. Fucked. Up."

"Brian, we love you. I love you. You've got to believe that."

Brian had asked Jeremy and Vicky if he could move out, but they had told him that families work through things, that they don't give up on each other.

"I keep telling myself I have two years left and then I leave and go to college."

"That's all of us except for Bobby and Two," Brett said, though he knew what Brian meant.

Brian shook his head, his chin low on his chest.

Brett held up Brian's right hand and said, "The shakes are gone. Let's go back to bed. We have a couple of hours before we leave."

They left the study and walked back upstairs. They hugged in front of Brett's room, and then Brett whispered, "Goodnight. You worry too much. We love you. I love you. Remember that."

Brian nodded and tiptoed to his own room. He scratched Momma behind her ear, opened up his door and shut it.

Brian climbed in and Bobby threw an arm across his chest and a leg over his. That was the way they had slept when they were together a long time ago.

"You okay?" Bobby whispered.

"Yeah. Go back to sleep."

Bobby shut his eyes and nodded, but he knew Brian wasn't.

CHAPTER SIXTEEN

Brian had bought the maroon Ram 1500 Crew Cab short bed with some of the money his parents had left him upon their death. He still had a pile of it in savings, as well as in a trust, and still more safely tucked away in a couple of 403b's. Of the boys, he had the most money by far. Even more than Jeremy and Vicky, though you'd never know it if you talked to him.

George and Two had packed Brian's truck with their gear and most of Brian's and Brett's stuff. Then George hitched Brian's Bass boat with the 75 horse power Mercury loaded on the Single axle Load Right trailer onto the back of the truck. George had gotten up earlier than the rest of the family in order to run, but because it was still dark, he couldn't say his prayers to Father Sun, which was part of his Navajo ritual.

Vicky got up and made the boys a quick breakfast of eggs, bacon and toast with orange juice to wash all of it down. Randy and Billy traipsed down the stairs to say goodbye, saw the food, and decided to eat. It was a fact that Billy could eat anything at any time. Brian knew they would go back to bed when the goodbyes were over.

There hadn't been much talking. Everyone was still sleepy. Even Vicky, who was used to getting up early because of her shifts at Froedtert Hospital, read the paper and kept to herself. Mostly just "Please pass the . . ." and "Thanks."

The last of the brothers to come down was Bobby. He chose a chair next to Brian and before he sat down, he slipped an arm around Brian's shoulders and hugged him. Brian slipped an arm around Bobby's waist and hugged him back. It did not go unnoticed. It brought smiles to everyone's faces. Brian and Bobby chose not to pay any attention to them.

"You guys packed up and ready?" he asked as he piled eggs onto his plate.

"Mostly. Bri and Brett's fishing gear is out there, but George and I didn't know what to take," Two said.

"I'll look through it," Brian said as he ate the last bit of his toast.

"I'm taking the Glocks," Brett announced. "Might target shoot."

Vicky didn't like guns, especially since Arizona. She frowned, but said, "Make sure you have your permits. All of you. Just in case."

Brian cleared his throat and said, "When we get back, maybe next weekend, do you guys want to do something? I mean, all of us together?"

The boys looked up and blinked at him.

"It's been a while since we all did something together," Brian explained.

Billy smiled and said, "That sounds good. What do you have in mind?"

Brian said, "I don't know. Anything. You guys can decide."

"We'll decide together," Randy said with a smile.

Vicky got up from the table with her coffee cup in hand and headed for the coffee pot for a refill. When her back was to them, she dabbed at her eyes with a napkin, but she was smiling.

"We better get going," Brett said. "Jamie and Pat probably left already."

"Do you have directions?" Vicky asked.

"Yes. I put them in the Nav system," George said.

"Where is your father?"

Jeremy had told her that he'd be down before they left. He had hoped the boys would leave him something to eat. They did, but it was minimal.

The boys got up and took their plates to the sink. Brian hesitated. He had been the one to clean the kitchen after meals, something he had done since before he had moved in with them and before he was adopted.

"Bri, I have it," Vicky said as she came up behind him kissing his cheek. "You guys have to get going. But promise me you'll drive slowly and take your time."

"We will." Brian answered. He turned to George and said, "George, would you drive as far as Crivitz? I didn't sleep well last night."

"Oh my God!" Brett said. "If George drives, we won't get there until Noon."

The boys and Vicky laughed.

George was known for going five miles under the speed limit. With the boat and trailer on the back of Brian's truck, it might be even slower.

"Sure, no problem," he said with a smile. "We'll strap Brett on the back of the truck so we won't hear him complain."

Brian handed the key fob to George, and said, "I'll be out in a minute."

The boys left the kitchen.

Vicky said, "Brian, is everything all right?"

He faced Vicky and said, "Yes." He dipped his chin briefly into his chest, then looked up and said, "I want to apologize to you . . . for everything. Doc said no one can ever start over, but we can start where we are and move forward. I would like to do that with you, if you want to."

Vicky burst into tears and the two embraced.

"I would like that very much, Brian Evans. I would like that very much," she said as she kissed his forehead and cheek.

"And I don't want you to feel guilty about what happened in Arizona. You didn't have anything to do with it. I made the choice. I made the decisions."

"Bri . . ."

"Seriously, Mom. Please don't feel guilty anymore about that, okay?"

"I'll try."

Jeremy entered the kitchen, took in the scene and nodded. He had heard Brian from the hallway.

Brian walked out of the kitchen with both Jeremy and Vicky following.

He said his goodbye to Randy and Billy, and said, "I would like us to get back to the way we were before . . . everything. If, that's okay. Maybe we can all do something together, and then the three of us can do something."

"I'd like that, too," Randy said as he hugged Brian.

"Me, too," Billy said with a hug.

That done, Brian and Bobby faced each other.

"Thanks for last night," Bobby whispered.

"I love you, Bobby. I always have and I always will."

The two boys embraced for a long time, each kissing the other's cheek.

"I love you, too," Bobby said.

"You guys have everything you need? Driver's licenses? Hunting and fishing permits?" Jeremy asked.

A chorus of "Yes!"

"Drive slowly and take your time," Jeremy said to Brian.

"George is driving," Brett said. "Driving slowly and taking our time is a given."

Jeremy cocked his head at Brian. He knew that Brian seldom let anyone drive his truck.

"I'm tired. I'm going to take a nap in the back with Two."

Jeremy nodded and handed him a twenty-dollar bill. "This will help with gas."

Brian began to object, but Jeremy cut him off and said, "Just take it. A gift is a gift."

Jeremy said quietly, "I heard your apology to Mom. That was a nice start. But an apology is only as good as the action that takes place after it. I'm just wondering what comes next. On your part, that is."

Brian hadn't expected that. The boys and Vicky hadn't expected it either. Jeremy had always been conciliatory and compassionate. He was a bridge-builder. Yes, he rebuked and reprimanded when necessary, but because Brian had reached out to Vicky and to the brothers, none of them understood why he said what he did.

Vicky stepped in between Jeremy and Brian, actually moving Jeremy behind her. She placed both hands on Brian's shoulders, and said, "Brian, I already accepted your apology, and you and I will work on things together. You and I are good."

Brian wanted to answer, but couldn't. Jeremy's words stung. They hurt. He was trying. Perhaps, Jeremy didn't recognize that. Maybe he didn't want to.

Randy and Billy looked at each other, then at Brian, but didn't know how to rescue him.

Bobby put a hand on Brian's shoulder, but Brian turned and got into the backseat and shut the door behind him. Everyone noticed that his right hand was shaking.

Randy and Billy walked back into the house, looking over their shoulder as they did. Vicky put an arm around Bobby's shoulders and the two of them stood apart from Jeremy. They smiled and waved as the truck and boat pulled out of the driveway.

"Bobby, why don't you and the twins go back to bed," Vicky said as she hugged him. "I'm going to talk to your father."

Bobby found Randy and Billy in front of the kitchen sink staring out the window, watching a very one-sided conversation with a lot of finger pointing. Vicky started for the house leaving Jeremy staring at his shoes with his hands in his front pockets and rooted to a spot in the driveway. Before she got to the backdoor, the boys sprinted from the kitchen and climbed the stairs without saying anything, though their minds were definitely full of thoughts.

CHAPTER SEVENTEEN

"I found your BOLO."

Patrolwoman Lisa Vickers had been on her way to the station after her graveyard shift, but had decided to check the lot before doing so. Horny teenagers used it to get their rocks off or guzzle beer. Burnouts used it to make their purchases from dealers. The homeless slept on moldy bug-infested blankets or cardboard in one of the empty warehouses.

"They are armed and dangerous. Backup is on the way," Dispatch answered.

"They might be armed, but they aren't dangerous. They're dead."

Vickers, all five-foot-five of her, was a four-year veteran who acted and carried herself like a fourteen-year vet. Following normal protocol, she roped off the crime scene and placed a call to the detectives on duty. She did a cursory look for evidence, but found none. Tempted to search the victims and car, she resisted and waited until the crime scene techs arrived.

Detectives Greg Gonnering and Carlos Lorenzo were the first to arrive on the scene. She filled them in on what she saw and did, and then passed it off. By then, it was 6:17 AM.

Gonnering noted the Illinois plates, and after Lorenzo fished out their IDs, Gonnering called O'Connor, who was in Crivitz filling up with gas and getting a light breakfast with Graff.

"How?"

"Executed. Close range. You can see powder burns and stippling. Whoever did it sat in the backseat. We're checking for prints and fiber, but whoever did this is a pro. We won't find anything."

Graff squinted at O'Connor but didn't say anything. He and O'Connor were long-time friends and worked any number of cases together. The most recent was in Arizona where O'Connor and the boys nearly died.

"Get this to Eiselmann. He'll let Kelliher know."

O'Connor ended the conversation. Whatever appetite he had- which was never very much- had disappeared.

"What's up, Hoss?"

O'Connor checked their surroundings to see who was nearby. There were too many ears, and too many people in close proximity.

"Let's finish up."

Graff nodded and finished the last bite of egg sandwich on his paper plate, and chased it with the last of his second cup of coffee. O'Connor pushed his plate away with his half-eaten eggs and bacon. He took the Diet Coke and stood up. Graff followed.

It didn't take long for O'Connor to give Graff the highlights. Jamie leaned against the front bumper of his black Silverado and listened without asking questions. Once O'Connor was done, Jamie pushed around a stone with the toe of his tan work boot.

"Have you heard from Eiselmann since last night?"

"Just before you picked me up. He had spoken to Kelliher and filled me in on their conversation. The FBI had ID'd them. They worked for Andruko, and Kelliher thinks they were enforcers."

Graff pulled out his phone, speed-dialed Eiselmann, but didn't put it on speaker in case there were extra ears.

"Paul, this is Jamie."

"Figured you or Pat would call."

"You heard?"

"Yup. I already called Kelliher. He's looking into it and will get back to me. I'll make sure Greg and Carlos copy me in on the investigation. You know, if those two guys were killed, it had to have been by another pro. That means, someone else is out there, and we don't know who or where that someone is, and neither does Kelliher. Could be more than one. He said they would do some digging."

Graff stared at O'Connor, then glanced around the parking lot. It didn't look like anyone was paying attention to them. It also didn't look like anyone was trying *not* to pay attention to them, either. There were several cars with Illinois plates sprinkled in the lot among the Wisconsin cars, but there was no one obvious who didn't belong. Most of the vehicles were empty. Their occupants were lined up at gas pumps, in the store eating, or purchasing items for the road.

Crivitz was the last major stop on the way "up north." For as small as it was, it was busy and traffic was constant. There were two other stores with gas stations across the street, along with a diner. Someone could be sitting in one of the parking lots watching them, and neither Graff nor O'Connor would know it.

Northern Wisconsin was a playground for many from Illinois, second only to Wisconsin Dells. To a lesser extent, some folks from Indiana felt the same way about Northern Wisconsin and the Dells. Because it was a long weekend, there would bound to be Illinois or Indiana traffic headed north. Travelers from those two states could be using this weekend like the Wisconsinites, as a mini-vacation and a welcomed break from the work race.

Graff bit the inside of his cheek.

Eiselmann said, "What are you going to do with the boys?"

"We'll call Jeremy and Vicky, and we'll talk to the boys. The boys are about thirty minutes behind us. George is driving."

Eiselmann laughed. "If Brett was driving, they'd be thirty minutes ahead. George drives like an old man."

Graff smiled. "Safer that way."

He got serious again and said, "I'm not sure why those two men were killed. It could be that someone found out they were made and they ended up being loose ends."

Eiselmann said, "It could go one of two ways. One, that's the end of it. O'Connor is too hot a commodity right now. Their identity leads back to Andruko and with his sentencing around the corner, he can't afford to have anyone fuck up."

"Or?"

"It's not over. Those two were expendable especially since they were made. Andruko can't afford that. In comes one or two guys to finish them off and then try to take care of O'Connor. Whatever happens will happen quickly. They won't want you to dig in."

"Or you. You're just as vulnerable, especially since that restaurant in Chicago."

"Yeah, I've been thinking about that. Maybe. But something doesn't make sense."

Graff frowned and said, "Why?"

"How would Andruko or anyone know they were made?"

Graff picked it up from there. "Someone else was with them. Not with them, per se, but there. At the game. And at O'Connor's apartment. Someone saw it all go down and saw those two assholes get made."

"If that's the case, either someone is on your tail or already pulled out. I think he might have pulled out."

Graff was curious. "Why?"

"Because if he's from the city, he'll stick out. I doubt he'd be dressed for hunting or fishing up north, and if he is, the clothing will appear new, especially the boots. Look for someone who's limping because the boots haven't been broken in. The jacket and hat will be new. Hell, he might not have a hunting rifle. He'd carry a handgun with a silencer. Maybe something automatic."

Graff considered this. Eiselmann was an excellent detective. Thorough, organized. The way he ran a computer and analyzed details and data amazed Graff. He was the perfect control for O'Connor. The pair were the best in the tri-state area.

Either way, it warranted a phone call to Jeremy. Those boys, Brian in particular, had been through the wringer, and Graff knew Brian still hadn't recovered.

"Paul, Pat and I will give you a call later. Take care and watch your six."

"Will do. You do the same."

Graff ended the call and did a slow scan of the parking lots across the street as well as the one they were in. Again, no one stuck out.

Pat ran his hand through his long hair, sighed and said, "Look, Jamie. I don't want to take the trip away from the boys. Both of us know that's what Jeremy and Vicky will do. Instead, I'll go fishing today, and leave after dinner tonight or early tomorrow morning. That way, whoever is looking for me, if someone is looking for me, won't bother you or the boys."

Graff pursed his lips and squinted off in the distance at nothing in particular.

"How will you get home?"

O'Connor sensing a small victory, said, "I'll call Jorgy or someone. No problem."

Graff thought it over. He hated the thought of Pat leaving, but knew the boys would be safer if he did. He knew how much O'Connor loved fishing and being at a lake with the boys, and Graff was looking forward to spending time with his buddy.

"You sure?"

"It's the only way, Jamie. The boys, especially Brian, need this trip."

"Okay then. Maybe give Jorgy or someone a call and have him pick you up in the morning. Early, but not too early."

O'Connor turned around and walked a short distance away and called the big red-headed detective.

CHAPTER EIGHTEEN

Brian woke up on the outskirts of Crivitz. He wiped drool off his lips and cheek. That was a first for him. He straightened up and looked around.

"Sleeping Beauty awakes!" Brett said from the front seat. "And without a kiss at that!" he added with a laugh.

Brian wiped gunk from his eyes and said, "How long was I sleeping?"

"I don't think we were out of Waukesha," Two said with a smile. "You were snoring."

"No way," Brian mumbled.

"Way!" Two responded with a laugh.

"I thought someone started up a chainsaw," George said.

"Bull."

The three boys laughed and said, "Bro, you were snoring just about the whole trip up here. You were out," Brett said. "And you were drooling."

Changing the subject, Brian said, "We're supposed to hook up with Jamie and Pat at a Kwik Trip. Should be somewhere on the other end of town on the right. I'll top off the gas."

"We'll chip in," Brett said.

"No, I've got it."

Crivitz had less than one thousand residents. It featured a half-dozen bars, a grocery store, a post office, several antique shops, and a couple of gas stations. Graff had chosen the Kwik Trip because it had a deli and a grill for sandwiches and such.

"Don't blink," Brett said. "We might miss it."

"Up there," Two said leaning into the front seat.

George pulled up to the gas pump and the four boys got out and stretched.

"Anyone see Graff or O'Connor?" Brett asked as he looked around the busy parking lot.

"Not yet. Look for Detective Jamie's black truck and boat," George said.

He was uncomfortable calling adults, even adult friends, by their first names. He usually put a Mister or Missus or their title in front of their name.

"I have to pee," Brett said through a yawn and a stretch. "You guys coming in?"

"Here's the twenty Dad gave me. Use it for food and munchies."

Brett took it and said, "You want anything special?"

"We'll need nightcrawlers for fishing. Maybe some Twizzlers. I'll order something to eat when I'm done with the gas. Let me know if it costs more than that and I'll pay you back."

George and Brett walked into the store, while Two leaned against the door waiting for Brian.

"You okay, Bri?" he asked quietly.

Brian nodded, but kept his eyes on the pump, watching the gallon and dollar digits blink skyward.

"Bobby, Billy, and Randy texted and asked me to check on you."

"Tell them I'm okay. No worries. I'll text them when we get to the house."

"Randy said to check your phone. He thinks Dad and Mom tried to get a hold of you."

Brian didn't respond, not interested in turning on his cell. He would get to it when he was ready.

Two pulled his cell out of the back pocket of his jeans, his fingers flying over the keys. That done, he grabbed paper towel and the squeegee and washed off the windshield.

"Thanks for doing that."

"I figure I have to do something to get a piggyback ride into the store," he said with a laugh.

"You and your piggyback rides," Brian laughed. "Why am I the only one you ask?"

"You give the best ones," Two laughed.

"How would you know? You don't ask anyone else."

"Because you give the best ones," Two laughed again.

Two had grown just like the rest of them. While each day he looked more like George, their personalities were as different as could be. Two had a playful side. He laughed easily and talked more than George did. He would goad Billy or Brian into wrestling with him, no matter that they were bigger and stronger than he was. In that respect, he was more like Billy.

Two wore camo pants and a camo hat one might see in the Australian outback, with a camo long-sleeved t-shirt and boots. Brian, wore nylon sweatpants, a black Nike t-shirt, and a pair of older basketball shoes. George had dressed similarly to Two minus the outback hat, preferring to wear a Packer cap, and Brett dressed similarly to Brian. The only difference between Brian and Brett was the Wisconsin Badger snapback on Brett's head.

Two had taken to Brian from the time the two had met in Arizona, and especially once they got back from Arizona. No matter where they were or where they were headed, Two would jump on Brian's back and get a ride.

Brian topped off the tank, squeezing in a couple of more ounces, but stopped before gas leaked out. He screwed on the gas cap, shut the little door, and grabbed the receipt.

"Hop in. I'll move out of the way and park behind the store."

Two finished with the windshield, leaving no streaks. He hopped in the front passenger seat.

Brian, looking over both shoulders and using his mirrors moved out of the way slowly, and parked in a spot specifically for trucks and cars with trailers. He hopped out, shut the door and locked it up. He walked around the trailer and inspected the lashings making sure they were still tight. Everything looked good.

He noticed a few stares, but didn't pay attention to them.

"Hop on," he said to Two.

Two obliged with a laugh and a "Giddyap."

"I'm not a horse," Brian said with a smile.

Two laughed.

He carried him around to the front of the store on the opposite side away from the two men and a boy who had been staring at them.

They entered the store, spotted George and Brett at the checkout, and walked to the kiosk to order breakfast.

The store had more people in it than there were cars parked in the lot. Or so it seemed.

Two leaned in closely to observe Brian punching in his order. He had his hand resting on Brian's shoulder as he watched.

"What do you want?" Brian asked.

"Pancakes and sausage. Bacon too."

"You eat like a horse," Brian laughed.

"I'm growing."

"Take your growing body and get us something to drink. I'll take chocolate milk and a berry Propel. Get whatever you want and I'll meet you at checkout."

As Two moved away from the kiosk, he bumped into a man in his mid- to late-thirties. Dark complexion, dark short-cropped hair, dark eyes, with two- or three-day-old whiskers.

"Excuse me," Two said stepping out of the way.

The man didn't comment other than to glare at him. The man with him bumped into Two and kept walking. The boy that was with him side-stepped out of the way.

Brian saw what had happened, and it looked to him as if the two men walked into Two on purpose.

"Wait here," Brian said to him. "What do you want to drink? I'll get it."

Puzzled by the encounter, Two hesitated and then said, "Chocolate milk and an orange juice."

"I'll be right back and then we'll go to the checkout together."

Brian made his way to the glass-encased refrigerators and got the drinks. He took the time to glare at the two men, who didn't notice. The boy, a little younger than either Brian or Two, did. He blushed and turned around and stood behind the older, bigger of the two men.

Brian hooked up with Two, paid for the purchases and then Brian sent Two with the drinks to the table where George and Brett were already eating their breakfast. Brian picked up his and Two's breakfast at the grill counter.

"I might have to have a bite of your pancakes," Brett said.

Two pushed his plastic tray towards Brett, who took a small bite with plenty of butter and syrup.

He nodded his approval.

"Not as good as mom's or Randy's, but pretty good."

"That's because they use cinnamon with a splash of vanilla," Two said.

As the boys ate their breakfast, they talked about the trip.

"Do we need any supplies besides nightcrawlers?" Brett asked.

"I want to get some eggs, a carton of milk, and cornmeal," Brian answered.

"Bacon," George chimed in.

"If there isn't room in the cooler, we can get a small Styrofoam one with some ice," Brian added.

The two men and the boy sat down at a table adjacent to the four boys. Every so often they would glare in their direction and one or the other would mutter something causing the other to laugh. The boy with them remained quiet, intent on his food. He would glance furtively at the boys.

Brian noticed, but didn't say anything. He was sure George noticed them also. George never missed much.

The older of the two men, thicker with a beer gut said, "Can't tell if they're boys or girls."

The younger of the two men, the guy who had bumped into Two first, said, "Bob, you smell that? Something stinks."

The larger of the two men glared at the four boys and said, "Don't know if I can eat with that stink."

"Fucking Indians need to stay on the reservation."

Brett, who had his back to them, turned around to glare at them. George reached out and took hold of Brett's forearm. Brett shook it off.

"The only thing I smell is horseshit and BO. Ever think of showering or don't you have running water where you live?"

"You have a smart mouth. Maybe I ought to take you out back and teach you to mind your manners," the bigger one said.

"You can fucking try if you want to."

The two men laughed and the smaller of the two said to the other, "He talks a good game."

"I'm thinking one good punch to pretty-boy's mouth should do the trick," the bigger one said.

The boys went back to eating silently. Two pushed his half-eaten pancake away from him.

"Eat up," George said. "You'll be hungry before you know it." He slid the tray back in front of his younger brother. "At least eat your bacon."

Two picked up the remaining piece of bacon and nibbled it until it vanished. He finished the pancakes too.

"You guys finished?" he asked as he gathered up the empty plastic trays, the used plastic silverware, and the napkins.

"I'll go get the other stuff we need and meet you by the truck," Brett said.

"I parked in the back," Brian said.

Two piled everything up onto his tray and slid his chair back. He stood up and walked away from the table towards the garbage can in the corner of the little dining area.

The larger of the two men stuck out his foot and Two crashed to the floor. Bits of food and a little syrup ended up on his t-shirt. He was slow to pick himself up, but did so without looking at anyone.

"Fuckin' Indian is clumsy," the younger of the two men said with a laugh.

The bigger of the two chuckled as he sipped his soft drink.

Graff and O'Connor walked up to the four boys and Graff said, "Looks like you boys are making some new friends." He bent down to help Two pick up the mess.

With the paper cup still at his lips, the bigger man mumbled, "Not a fuckin' chance."

O'Connor smashed the drink into the man's face. Whatever he was drinking covered his face, the front of his shirt, and dripped into his lap.

"What the . . ."

"I must be clumsy too. Sorry about that," O'Connor said as he squared up in front of them.

The big man glared at him and pushed himself out of his chair.

"You don't want any part of him, Mister," Graff said as the man stood up and pushed Two in the direction of the garbage can.

George, Brian and Brett had already gotten up and moved out of the way. Several onlookers stopped eating. Others scurried out of the store. The two cashiers stood motionless behind the counter.

The big man easily had seventy-five to a hundred pounds on Graff, and a heck of a lot more than O'Connor. The big man used his forearm to try to move Graff out of the way. Jamie cranked the man's arm behind his back and slammed his head into the bacon and eggs on the table. He used his other hand to point at the younger man.

"You keep your ass in your chair."

To both of them, Graff said, "This is Sheriff Detective Pat O'Connor on special assignment with the FBI."

"I'm Detective Jamie Graff. We can have the two of you arrested for assault associated with a hate crime. You want to play tough, we can too."

The younger of the two men stared at Graff, and then at O'Connor as he appraised the new development they had gotten themselves into. He licked his lips nervously.

"Look, we don't want any trouble," he said.

"These boys weren't looking for any trouble, either, yet here we are," Graff said.

"These four boys are way tougher than you'll ever be," O'Connor said. "I'm confident they can handle themselves in just about any situation they're faced with. I suggest you finish your meal, or not, and get the hell out of here."

Graff yanked the big man's ear and sat him back into his chair, almost knocking him over backward.

"That sound okay with you?" Graff asked.

"He's no fuckin' FBI," the big man growled. "He looks like a fuckin' Indian, too."

Graff swatted the back of the man's bald head and said, "You need to watch your language."

He took a twenty out of his wallet, threw it on the table and said, "That should cover your breakfast. I suggest you take it and leave."

"It's a free country," the younger man said. "We don't have to leave."

"That's true," Graff answered. "It is a free country. For you and for these four boys. Remember that."

O'Connor remained facing the two men, arms at his sides, hands balled into fists. Anything but relaxed.

Graff turned to the boys and said, "Why don't you guys finish up and we'll meet you at the truck. We have about a forty-five minutes to go, and I know George and Two want to get hunting."

"We need to stop at a grocery store for a couple of things," Brett said. He turned to Brian and said, "We'll get the crawlers here, the milk and cornmeal somewhere else."

"No, get everything here," Graff said. "I don't want to stop until we reach the cabin."

Brett and Brian headed back into the store to get what they needed. George ushered Two into the men's restroom to clean himself off. O'Connor and Graff remained where they were just to make sure the boys would be safe.

Everything paid for, the boys left the Kwik Mart with Graff leading and O'Connor following. They moved at a faster than leisurely pace towards the trucks, which were now parked side by side.

"Listen," Graff said as Brett and Brian stuffed the perishables into the cooler with ice. "There's been a little change of plans. Pat is going to have to get back to Waukesha either tonight after dinner or early in the morning. Something came up on a case he's working on. We'll play it by ear."

"Oh, man!" Brett said. "Seriously?"

"Sorry, but it can't be helped," Pat said. "You guys and Jamie will stay for the whole weekend. We know how much you've been looking forward to this."

"You, too," Brian said. "Can't whatever you're working on wait?"

O'Connor smiled at Brian, slipped an arm around his shoulder, gave him a squeeze and said, "Wish it could."

"How will you get back?" George asked.

He sensed there was more to it than Graf's explanation. George was hyper-sensitive that way, quick to catch any subtle nuances others might miss. Brian and Brett were too, but not like George. His Navajo thing as Jeremy and Vicky called it.

"I'll have someone come get me. No big deal," O'Connor said trying to read George's dark eyes and the expression on his face. "No big deal at all," O'Connor repeated, specifically at George.

George nodded, but decided it was a big deal. He was pretty certain Brett and Brian understood that too.

CHAPTER NINETEEN

He watched the scene from the back aisle near the coffee pots, soda dispensers, and bakery. He heard every word.

He appraised O'Connor as the kind of guy who would act unpredictably. At the same time, predictably if he was defending someone he cared about. That might be how he would be able to get to him.

He was impressed with Graff. Good hand to hand skills. He thought that Graff wasn't as unpredictable, but acted more out of predetermination. He thought Graff would assess a situation, use what was at hand, and go from there. The two men together were formidable.

Whacking an FBI agent didn't bother him. He'd done it several times before. He lost count of the cops he whacked. In his mind, it was a photo of a person and a name on a piece of paper that presented him with an opportunity to make money. What he didn't like was doing it in front of those boys, but he would if it came to it. If necessary, he'd whack the boys. He didn't like loose ends. Of course, Graff would come with the package. One less cop and all. The world could do without and be no less for it.

He was taken with the kid wearing the Badger cap. Tough. Unafraid. The boy reminded him of himself at that age.

The difference between him and the kid was that by that age, he had already killed his stepfather and had gotten away with it. His mother suspected. So did the cops. But there wasn't any proof. Besides, his stepfather was a piece of shit, so his mother didn't care that much, and the cops didn't look very hard, because they knew his stepfather was a piece of shit, too.

When his mother died during his freshman year of college, he was free. Good grades in high school. Graduated from college with a communications and theater double-major. But it was the darkest of arts that spoke to him. Once he had a taste, he wanted the whole meal. And, the money was always good in that line of work.

With O'Connor, he would see what developed and he would plan. He had a variety of weapons at his disposal. His favorite was to look into his queries' eyes before death. While he liked the look of panic, what he most delighted in was the resignation in the victim's eyes that death was imminent. The recognition that no matter the amount of pleading or promises, death was coming sooner rather than later.

He hoped he'd have that same satisfaction with O'Connor. With Graff, too, if it came to that.

He wondered about the kid in the Badger cap. He bet the kid wouldn't plead, wouldn't beg, and wouldn't even shed a tear. He wagered that the kid was tough like that.

Same with the soccer player. From what his dad had said at the end of the game, the kid was troubled about something. If he had to kill the soccer player, he would first want to know why.

The two Indian kids weren't anything much. Not because they were Indian. He didn't care one way or the other whether they were Indian, Asian, or Latino. He had killed many different nationalities. They were just two normal, everyday kids, and the world wouldn't care one way or the other if either lived or died.

He would continue to follow the kid's truck and see where it, and they, would lead him. He would be patient. It would happen. To O'Connor. Probably to Graff. Perhaps the boys. He'd wait and see how it unfolded.

CHAPTER TWENTY

George and Two were camo copies of each other, though one was taller than the other. Both were outfitted in Mossy Oak camo that matched the fall season and terrain. However, to move into and through, and then back out of the woods, they needed 250 square inches of blaze orange. That was required by the Wisconsin DNR when moving throughout the woods. As hunters termed it, blaze in and blaze out.

Their outfits came with carbon liners that helped trap human sent in their clothes. Because it was a liner, they could take it in and out of the camo outfit. All it needed was to be thrown in the dryer for twenty minutes to activate it, which they had done when they arrived at the lake house.

On their feet were Gore-Tex boots. Because the weather wasn't particularly cold, they only had a moderate Thinsulate number. The boots were waterproof which made them a must-have in the woods, and the rubber soles wouldn't leave their scent on the ground like leather soles.

As essential as their Killer Instinct Ripper 415 Crossbows, which were accurate to about eighty yards, was a grunt tube. It made the sound of a buck when he's "looking for lovin,'" as Brett would say. The doe bleat makes the "bleat" sound of a young doe or lost fawn. The buck would check out the call to have his way with the young doe or lost female fawn.

George and Two would wait on the doe urine until they entered the woods. They would then squirt some on a sponge applicator and drag it alongside using a string while they walked in. Bucks would pick the scent up and follow it thinking it was a doe in heat.

The last item for their clothing were scent wafers. They clipped one on their hats and one on their jackets to cover their scent. The earth scent actually smelled like dirt. Both boys had hunted for a long time on the Navajo Nation Reservation before moving to Wisconsin. Two was new to hunting in Wisconsin, but George had hunted alongside Brian and Brett, and O'Connor and Graff. Both knew scent played a huge part in deer hunting. The deer's nose was their biggest defense mechanism. Once they smelled you, you were toast. Game over. Might as well go back to the cabin, drink a soda, and watch TV.

Even with carbon-lined gear and scent wafers, both boys knew they had to take wind direction into consideration. Traveling into and out of their tree stand position, they wanted the wind in their faces. Wind carries scent. Deer know this and use it to their advantage. They can smell any hunter, especially an inexperienced one coming from a long way out.

Both boys had a portable climber, which was a two-piece contraption they would carry into the woods and use it to climb a tree up to about fifteen feet and then sit in it. Both boys preferred fixed stands, because climbers were a pain in the ass. However, they didn't know the property, and they might have to move their location, so the climbers were convenient.

George and Two wanted their climbers between where the deer bed and where they fed. They knew that deer, like most animals including the human variety, were creatures of routine, except during the mating or rut season when bucks lose their mind. Deer did most of their moving around and feeding at night. They usually bed down during the day. Of course, there are times during the day they will move, usually to find water, but they were typically nocturnal. The boys knew there was a full moon the night before, and there would be a near full moon that night, so deer would be even less likely to move throughout the day.

The best time to hunt deer or any animal and catch them in their routine patterns would be at day break and at dusk, which are their transition times from bed to feed and vice versa. The boys would hunt twice. Once in the morning and then again at dusk.

Both boys were ready to leave the lake house. George hesitated.

"Two, wait here. Brian, can I talk to you a minute?"

Brian was readying his boat for fishing. He and Brett had driven to the public pier to set it in. Brett was to help Graff and O'Connor with Graff's Aluminum Craft, and then drive Brian's truck and trailer back to the lake house. Brian drove the boat straight across the lake. Because he did, he was still waiting for Brett.

"What's up?"

George fidgeted. On one hand, he needed to ask Brian a question, but on the other, he knew Brian was still fragile from the mess on the mesa in Arizona. He didn't want to push him over the edge.

It was George's hesitation more than anything that caught Brian's attention. He climbed out of the boat, but sat on the edge, and faced his brother who stood on the dock.

"I want to ask you a question, but I do not want to upset you."

Brian frowned.

"Has your brother, Brad, visited you lately. Yesterday or today?"

Both Brian and George had visions. Brad, who had died during the summer of death, had visited him as well as a couple of the other brothers since then. George had been visited by his grandfather. In those cases, the visits or visions were meant to be a caution as much as a guide. In other cases, the visits were meant to comfort. The latter occurred more in Brian's case than in George's case.

"No, not since Arizona." Brian thought it over and asked, "Why?"

George shook his head and said, "I just wondered. My grandfather has not visited me, but something . . ." He trailed off and didn't finish.

Brian looked down at feet. He wore his Nike slides, and he wiggled his bare toes. "Is this about what Graff said to us in Crivitz? You know, about O'Connor?"

George looked off across the lake and nodded, just slightly. "Yes, I think so. I am not sure."

"But you have a feeling." Brian said it as a statement, not as a question.

"Yes."

Brian sighed and said, "So do I. I am not sure why." He shrugged and said, "So now what?"

"We watch. We wait."

"Do we tell the others? Brett?"

"Not yet. I think we should wait."

George glanced in the direction of the cabin where Two was waiting impatiently for the hunt. The sound of a truck approached the cabin, tires crunching on the pea-gravel drive. The sound of a boat motor off in the distance, getting closer.

"I think that one of us needs to be with Brett and the other with Two. We do not leave them alone. Just in case." He paused as he watched Brian's face cloud up. "Are you okay with that?"

Brian hesitated. Part of him absolutely was. The other part of him didn't want to experience anything like what had taken place on the mesa ever again.

"Yes, I think so."

George stared at his brother, waiting for an explanation. When none was forthcoming, he said, "Let me know if you are not okay, Brian. I will understand."

Brian smiled at him and said, "I will be okay."

George nodded and began to turn away.

Brian said, "Good luck hunting. Two is excited."

George turned back, smiled, and said, "Two is always excited about something."

Brian laughed.

"Good luck with your fishing."

Brian smiled and said, "I'm hoping for at least ten this morning. It will make a good lunch."

George laughed and said, "I have no doubt you'll get your ten and then some."

He turned to leave again, but Brian stopped him.

"George, are we good? You and me, I mean?"

George turned back around, placed a hand on Brian's shoulder, and said, "Yes. I have apologized and I would like to make it up to you. I just do not know what more I can do. I do worry about you."

"No need to worry about me, but just answer me honestly."

George waited.

"Do you think who I am, or what I've done with Bobby, or what I might be doing with Mikey . . . are you disgusted or think I am wrong?"

86

George smiled sadly and said, "I told you once what my grandfather said. He said that if two hearts are meant to find one another, they will. I believe that, too. So, no, who you are or what you have done or are doing does not disgust me. It is out of love. I believe that. You are kind and generous. You love easily, but because of that, you get hurt easily. I worry more about that then what you do."

Brian sighed. He was relieved. He had missed being close to George. He was tired of being guarded around him, not trusting him.

"George, I," he shrugged, and said, "I'm sorry for treating you like I have been since Arizona."

George smiled and said, "And I am sorry to have caused you to doubt me. You are my brother, Brian. You are also my friend. You will always be both to me."

Brian stood up and embraced George and said, "I feel the same way. I love you."

"I love you, too."

CHAPTER TWENTY-ONE

Brett was never patient when it came to fishing. He had only taken it up to be with Brian, George, and Big Gav, and with O'Connor and Graff. Gavin Hemauer couldn't make this trip. He was on a trip with his mom, Ellie. While that was disappointing, it was okay. He was with the others and that was always good. He liked camping and the outdoors, but he considered fishing similar to watching grass grow. Right up there with golf. He was restless, anxious, and bored.

Brian was the opposite. He could, and sometimes did, fish for hours. He enjoyed it more than hunting, especially after the trip to Arizona.

To him, fishing was peaceful. The gentle rocking motion of the boat. The smell of water mixed with the earthy smell of the woods or forest. The smell of campfire and pine. Those smells soothed his soul and set him at ease.

He set his new Shakespeare Ugly Stick with a spinning reel down as he stripped out of his red Badger hoodie. It was warm enough for just his black dry-fit Nike t-shirt. He glanced around the lake and the shoreline, then sat down and pulled off his nylon sweatpants and ended up in red-checkered boxers. He pulled up a pair of khaki cargo shorts. He reattached his Buck knife in its leather sheath to his hip. He pushed his slides off to the side, content with his bare feet on the light-blue indoor-outdoor carpet of the boat.

He didn't use the Lowrance Hook 5 fish finder. Instead, he used his instinct and parked his boat in the shadows near the banks of the lake.

His hunch had paid off. Nine caught so far. A nice mix of bass and walleye, and all within the legal limits.

Occasionally, he fired up his Minkota trolling motor to stay in the shadows as the sun moved east to west overhead. The lake was big enough so that other fishermen wouldn't feel crowded. In fact, since he and Brett had set out, they hadn't come across Graff and O'Connor except at a fair distance.

Brian had begun with crawlers, washing off his hands and fingers in the water to get the slime and guts off. That lasted for only two catches, and then he switched to crankbaits and spinnerbaits. He had his favorites and used them to his advantage. He wore his dark-framed Costa sunglasses to protect his eyes- mainly his right eye- from the sun bouncing off the water. He didn't like anything on his head, so he didn't wear a hat. The sun felt good on his face and arms, though it wouldn't take long before he'd burn, especially with the sun bouncing off the water.

"You have another bite," Brett said.

He had been watching Brian closely. Like the rest of his brothers and his parents, he worried about Brian. Brian wasn't back to normal. Not yet, but he was getting there.

Brian was aware of Brett watching him, but didn't let on that he knew. He liked his privacy, though of any of the brothers, he shared his feelings with Brett and Billy the easiest. After he and Bobby talked the night before, he would add Bobby to the brothers who he could best talk to. Probably George, too.

Odd that he didn't feel that way about Randy. Randy was the least judgmental, and the most accepting and the most willing and open. He had known the twins the longest from his life before being adopted. Still, there was something that caused him to hesitate and fully open up to Randy. Or Two. He liked Two a lot, but he didn't know him well enough yet. Someday, for sure.

"Not yet. Curious, though," Brian said as he concentrated on the tip of his rod. Little waves floated on the surface each time the line was pulled downward.

He fished by feel. He supposed most fishermen did. It was something his father had taught him and Brad from little on. That, and patience.

He felt the tug, the pull on the line.

"This is a big boy."

Brian's rod dipped and he played the line out a little, then on the next tug, Brian snapped his hand up, and the match began.

He chuckled.

"He's a big one," Brian said again.

"How can you tell?"

"Just can," Brian said with a laugh.

Brian would alternately pull the rod up and then reel the fish in. The fish broke surface and dove back under.

"Told you it was big," he laughed. "Get the net ready."

Brett had been sprawled out on the front cushions. He got up, grabbed the net and stood at the ready.

"He wants to play," Brian laughed.

"Shit! He wants to live!" Brett laughed.

"That too," Brian laughed.

"Jesus! How big is that?"

"Guessing sixteen inches. Maybe bigger."

Brian gave a last tug up, and reeled it to the surface. Brett scooped it up in the net and brought the fish dripping and fighting into the boat.

"Damn! That could feed both of us," Brett said.

Brian laughed, as he gripped the big fish behind the gills and worked his spinner out of the fish's mouth.

"That's gotta hurt," Brett said screwing up his face.

"Probably."

Brian dropped the fish in the wire bucket with the others, and then lowered the bucket back under the water.

"Had to work for that sucker!" he said with a smile.

"Shit, you make it look easy."

Brian sat down on the cushions, grabbed a bottle of water from the little, compact cooler they had brought with them, and then stretched out.

"I could do this all day," he said as he nestled into the cushion, his face lifted to the sun.

Brett smiled. It had been a long time since he had seen Brian this at ease.

"You seem happy."

"I am," Brian answered.

"You and Bobby made up?"

"Think so. Yeah, we did." He couldn't hide his smile.

"What about Mikey?"

Brian shrugged. "We're friends."

Brian chose not to elaborate, but he felt himself blushing. He hoped Brett wouldn't notice, but knew he would.

"How did you two start out? I know you play soccer together, but how did it start?"

"I don't know. We just kind of talked and then hung out."

"I know that, but how did you *start* start? You know, doin' stuff?"

"Geez, Brett, that's private."

"Just tell me. It won't go anywhere."

Brian hesitated. He seldom if ever lied to his brothers. To anyone, for that matter.

"You won't tell anyone, right?"

"Of course, not. I don't share anything we talk about unless I think it's important to do so."

Brian shot him a cautionary look and then said, "We were watching a movie, and he had Twizzlers on his side of the bed. I asked for one, and he took one, bit it off, and a little piece stuck out of his mouth. He said if I wanted one, I had to start with that one, but I couldn't use my hands. I told him if I did that, I'd end up kissing him, and he smiled, like he had that planned."

Brian glanced at Brett and continued, "You know how you know if someone wants to do something with you?"

"Yeah." What he wanted to say was *how did you figure it out?* because Brian was super slow about catching onto that kind of thing. What he did say was, "How did you know Mikey wanted to do something with you?"

"Well, besides the little piece of Twizzler sticking out of his mouth," he shrugged and said, "when he talked, he'd touch my arm or my chest or my hand. A couple of times my leg and my stomach."

"So, what did you do?"

Brian blushed deep crimson and said, "I went after the Twizzler."

"You kissed him."

"Yeah." He turned to Brett and said, "I like kissing. Probably more than anything. Especially if it means something, and if I'm kissing someone that means something to me."

"Then what?"

"Geez, Brett."

"Just tell me."

Brian glanced at Brett. "We kissed and then we did stuff. Not much. Just a little."

"Does Bobby know about Mikey? I mean, that you're doing stuff with him?"

Brian nodded and said, "We talked about that. He's cool with it."

"Do you still have feelings for Bobby?"

He was a little shocked at the question, since he had thought everyone knew how he felt about Bobby. He said, "I love Bobby. I always have and I always will."

"And me?"

"Same, Brett. Always. You know that."

Yes, Brett knew, but not in the way he had hoped.

"Now the big question. Did you get the Twizzler?"

Brian laughed, not expecting it.

"I got it, and then Mikey got it and swallowed it because we didn't want to choke on it."

"So, you never got the Twizzler."

"I got something better," Brian said. It tumbled out of his mouth before he could stop it.

"Wow!" Brett laughed.

"I . . . shit, I mean . . ."

Brett laughed and said, "Never mind. I get it."

Brian ended up laughing with him.

They settled down. A couple of gulps of water. Eyes shut letting the sun caress their faces.

"Too bad O'Connor has to leave," Brett said.

Brian glanced at him, though Brett wouldn't have known. His eyes were shut.

"Yeah. It sucks."

"I don't want any job that interferes with my life like his does. I mean, I'm thinking about being a doctor, and I know I'll have to work different hours. Mom's a surgical nurse, and other than an emergency heart surgery, her hours are steady. But at the start, she worked different shifts and stuff. Bobby and I didn't like it. It sucked. But when I'm off, I want to be off. You know what I mean?"

"Yeah, me too. I think with teaching and coaching, the hours are pretty set. I know I'll have shit to grade at night, and there will be some games and practices if I coach soccer, but it won't be like O'Connor's job."

"Why do you want to teach and coach? You won't make great money."

Brian thought about the amount of money he had in accounts in three different banks, the money that had been placed in a trust fund, and what he had invested in the stock market in moderately aggressive funds, and the small portion that was placed in CDs. He was unconcerned.

He knew more about money than the average high school kid because his father had taught both him and Brad about it at a young age. He devoured the business section of the newspaper and kept track of his stocks using the Fidelity app on his phone and on his laptop.

His brothers knew he had amassed wealth, but not how much. He tried not to flaunt it and whenever he could, he paid not only for himself but whoever was with him. The tricky part was paying for his parents when he was out with them. That seldom, if ever, happened, because they wouldn't allow it.

"I'll be okay. Besides, I think I'd like teaching. I know I'll like coaching. But at some point, I'd like to be a counselor."

"Like Dad."

Brian was silent for a beat or two and said, "I guess."

He sat up and said, "Ever since I've been seeing the doc, I was thinking of going into psychology or social work. I looked up occupations in both fields, and clinical social work looks interesting. They can do pretty much what a psychologist does, but there are more options. Instead of a Ph.D., I can practice with a master's degree. Less school and about the same pay. A win-win."

He lay back down.

"Huh. I never pictured you as a shrink, but I can see that. You like helping people."

Brett stared at Brian who was stretched out on the boat cushion, his legs crossed at his ankles, his hands folded on his chest, fingers laced.

"Have you answered the texts and voicemail you received?"

"Yeah, but it wasn't easy. Service sucks up here."

"How did you leave it with Dad?"

Brian shrugged, slowed his breath down, and concentrated for a beat or two to keep his composure. He didn't want to lose it. "About as good as it's going to be for now. We'll see when we get home."

"Did he apologize?"

"Yes. I did too, but I'm not sure what I apologized for."

"Sometimes, apologizing for shit even though it isn't your shit is a good way to go."

Brian shrugged and said, "We'll see."

CHAPTER TWENTY-TWO

In her former life, Dasha Gogol, had been selected at the age of five to take part in the state-run gymnastics academy with the goal of representing her country and competing in the Olympics. The education, room, board, and the training were free. They had to be, since her parents had trouble putting food on the table and clothes on their children's back.

All of that came to an end eight years later after a horrendous landing on a vault that shattered her ankle and damaged her knee. Her gymnastics days were over, and so was the free ride of food and education. Her father had died that same year.

At the age of fourteen and after her older brother had given Dasha personal in-depth lessons, he placed Dasha on the street turning tricks and giving blow jobs to bring in money for food and clothes. Much of that money, however, went to her brother's heroin and cocaine addiction.

With her beautiful dark hair, dark eyes, and her lithe, athletic build, she had many suitors. Eventually, her brother died of an overdose. The authorities hadn't bothered to investigate too thoroughly, since he was nothing more than parasitic street scum. Had they done a complete investigation, they would have found Dasha's fingerprints on the syringe that was found at the scene.

One of her frequent suitors had been a high-ranking member of Berkut, the Ukrainian special police force. The Berkut had a history of illegal activities against Ukrainian citizens, especially physical violence and torture. The new government held Berkut responsible for most of the civilian deaths during a protest and crackdown, and acting Ukrainian

Interior Minister Arsen Avakov signed a decree that dissolved the agency, which was replaced with the National Guard of Ukraine.

Her suitor had survived and found himself in the upper echelons of the National Guard. He set Dasha up in her own apartment and spent more nights with her than he did with his wife and children.

It was through him that Dasha became trained in the art of surveillance and the darker art of death. So skilled had she become in the latter, that she had become the first person sought out by the Ukrainian government for political assassinations. After all, she was not a member of the government or the National Guard, so there would have been no blow back on them. More importantly, who would suspect a female assassin?

When death was not the preferred end game, they used her beauty and her body to compromise various dignitaries for favors that would suit the government's own means. Who wants death when a pawn can be created, owned, and manipulated?

Eventually, her skill came to the attention of the underworld and in particular, one Dmitry Andruko. He invited her to Chicago to take out a rival, and once there, she had never left. Before she left for Chicago, she had to end her relationship with the high ranking general, but that was no problem. She had grown tired of him and tired of the Ukrainian government using her for their purposes. He died in what had been ruled a mugging gone wrong, though there had been suspicions.

For years, Dasha had wanted to strike out on her own and become a free agent. She had the skill and talent, and most importantly, the looks. Andruko tried to use her body, but she put a stop to that quickly. Instead, he settled for using her for various business arrangements, mostly of the forced variety. More times than not, at the age of thirty-one, Dasha had become one of his go-to agents to dispose of anyone in his way, especially by means that would be untraceable or that might come back on him.

After the fuck-up and death of Sasha Bakay and Misha Danilenko in the vacant lot in Waukesha, she was contacted to dispose of the red-haired cop that helped place Andruko behind bars. The means had been left to her, and she preferred it that way.

She studied the file closely and decided that a suburban cop wouldn't be too difficult. To be sure, she would be careful. The kill would be clean and quick, and then she'd move on to the next assignment whenever that might be. She never knew until she read a post in the classified section of the Chicago Tribune.

The red-haired cop.

She had driven by his house twice spaced apart by a half an hour. The first drive by showed nothing but an upper middle-class home. A basketball hoop on a pole in the driveway and a futbal goal in the backyard. A modest house on a hip-high brick foundation, with a tan or cream-colored vinyl siding on top of that. The siding contrasted nicely with the red brick. There was an attached two-car garage, but no car in the driveway.

The second drive by showed the cop mowing the lawn while a strawberry blond boy, his son, she presumed, trimmed the edges along the sidewalk and driveway. No sign of his wife or daughter.

For a fleeting moment, she wondered if she could just shoot him from the car and speed off. Contract completed. However, a complicating factor was a jogger on the side of the street opposite the cop's house, and two females walking their pooches on the same side of the street as the cop's house, and walking towards him. He waved and the three of them carried on a brief conversation before the two continued on their way. His son doing the trimming would have been another complication, probably more so than the jogger or the dog walkers.

She wasn't opposed to shooting his son, the dog walkers, or the jogger, but those were unnecessary complications to an otherwise easy opportunity. Her clean getaway might be prevented.

No, she would choose a different time. One would surely present itself. They always did. There was no rush, other than her own timeline to get in and out quickly and cleanly.

She would stay relatively close and then take him out. In her mind, he was as good as dead. He just didn't know it.

As she drove away, she noticed the cop stop, turn the mower off, and reach for his cell phone.

CHAPTER TWENTY-THREE

"Paul, nothing jumps out at us. Yet," Pete Kelliher explained to Eiselmann. "We have the three lawyers on a soft watch as we dig through their finances. We haven't gone for a more thorough or in-depth warrant, because we don't have any basis for doing so."

"You're sure the leak comes from one of them?" Eiselmann asked as he wiped sweat off his mouth and forehead.

"We don't know who else would have that specific information on O'Connor going to a soccer game. Before the lunch at the restaurant, there had been no mention of it. The timing of it was too quick for it to come from someone else."

"Have you spoken to O'Connor lately?"

"No. I call and it goes to voicemail. I'm guessing cell service isn't strong where he and the boys are."

Eiselmann pursed his lips. He watched a navy blue, newer model Sonata with out of state plates drive away. A woman driver and no passengers.

He nodded to two of his neighbors, Amy Ivory, walking her pug, Sqwendel, and Alexis White, walking Camden, her brindle and white pit bull. Sqwendel struggled. His back legs didn't work like they once did and was at times incontinent. Camden, still on his leash, wandered over to say hello to Eiselmann. He bent down to scratch him behind the ear. Sqwendel didn't care and took the time to sit. Eiselmann waited until they passed before continuing the conversation. They were on their way back from their walk.

"I'll try to get in touch with him," he said. "Keep me posted on what you find."

"One last item," Kelliher said. "You sent us a picture of the guy Andruko was communicating with in the courtroom. His name is Oleg Klyuka. He is listed as Head of Security for Eastern Europe Exchange, which as you know, is Andruko's import-export company."

"Head of Security? Why would an import-export company need someone with that title?"

Kelliher chuckled and said, "Exactly. We have him on a heavy watch. But again, we don't have the grounds for a warrant, so we can't access his electronics. Yet."

Eiselmann thought for a moment and asked, "Have you thought about asking someone on the outside to see what that someone might find?"

Kelliher remained silent. He was still on the call because Eiselmann could hear background noise.

"Summer, Dandridge, and I thought of that. We don't think it is something the FBI can request at this point."

"Huh. I believe I understand."

"Yes, I'm sure you do."

Eiselmann smiled and nodded. He said, "If anything comes up on Klyuka or the three lawyers, give me a holler. I'll try to reach O'Connor. My guess he's out on a boat. And, I might make another call."

"Do what you feel you need to do. Let us know if we can assist."

The call ended. Eiselmann bit the inside of his cheek. He had never heard Kelliher speak so formally or precisely as he did in that brief conversation. He smiled as he put his cell back into his pocket.

"Hey, Stephen, I have to go make a phone call or two. I'll be back."

Stephen Bailey, Paul's adopted son, said, "Are we still playing tennis this afternoon?"

"Yup. I feel a butt kicking coming on."

"Yours most likely," Stephen said with a smile.

Eiselmann laughed as he disappeared into the house. He loved his kids. He loved his wife. And, he loved his life. He walked to the office and shut the door behind him. He phoned a friend.

"Morgan, this is Paul. I have a favor to ask."

CHAPTER TWENTY-FOUR

The first thing he did was rent a pickup. The second thing he did was purchase hunting gear. That way, he'd blend in with everyone else tromping around in the woods. Besides, if he just strode in without blaze orange, he might end up as the trophy on the hood of some hunter's truck. He didn't want to risk it.

Nothing fancy. Orange vest, pants and hat. Underneath, he wore green camo to blend in with the forest. His intention was to get to a point on the shore of the lake where he would have a clear line of sight to any boat coming or going.

When he was certain the two cops and the four boys had left the cabin, he hiked in on foot and checked it out first hand. He didn't see any weapons, which meant the cops had them. The two boys dressed in camo probably had their weapons. Had to if they were hunting.

The gear was stowed neatly in what looked like the boys' rooms. Two boys slept in each room. The two cops were in two rooms on the second floor. Nothing had been unpacked that he could tell.

Both vehicles were locked up. He didn't want to risk picking the locks because both trucks were newer models and that meant both had alarms.

After his quick once-around around the cabin and grounds, he had ruled out taking O'Connor out at the cabin. There were too many potential witnesses. He could handle taking out both men, but the four boys were needless collateral. He didn't see the purpose.

The other consideration was that the potential get-away could be fouled up. The driveway to the lake cabin was a one-way in and out on pea gravel. Too much potential for something to go wrong. By taking him and the other cop out while they were on the boat was convenient, especially using a suppressor. The hit could be made and he could get away before their bodies were discovered. His exit from the woods would be construed as a hunter being done for the day.

He carried a large black duffle. In it were the tools of his trade, including a Colt LE6920 in .223 with a variable power scope. It had a crisp trigger and a snap-down bipod for shooting support. He had been able to manufacture a suppressor for it so sound wouldn't alert anyone. Also in the duffle was a dark green tarp that nearly matched the forest floor. He would lay on it and sleep in it if need be, though that wasn't his preference. His goal was to take care of business and then get out in a hurry.

He had brought with him a variety of protein bars and two large canteens of water if he was forced to stay longer than an overnight. He also brought with him a nylon rope with a thin wire core. The rope was for insurance in case he ran into any of the kids. He didn't want to harm them if he could help it, though he wasn't opposed to dispatching them to the next world if it came to it.

On his belt was a KA-BAR Becker BK2 Companion in a polyester sheath. A nod to the military man he thought himself to be. In a shoulder holster under his orange vest was a 9mm CZ 75 B. It featured a steel frame, a black polycoat finish, three dot sights, with a 16+1 round capacity. He had manufactured a suppressor for it, and the suppressor sat on his waist tucked snugly in a polyester sheath, along with an extra ammo clip.

He had parked the rental on a sometimes gravel, sometimes dirt road that led him to property for sale along the lakeshore. Three two-and-a-half acre sites. If he was shopping for lakefront property, this would not be a bad choice. The lake was large, neighbors scarce, and plenty of wildlife living in the woods behind it. If it ever came to it, he could hide out indefinitely.

On his hike in, he had spotted several hunters hidden in and among the trees, a couple in portable stands and two in permanent structures. They had waved at him and he had waved back. To them, he was just another hunter walking in to get a good spot for a hunt.

He smiled. They had no clue what he was hunting for.

CHAPTER TWENTY-FIVE

"Have you spoken to Eiselmann or anyone lately?"

O'Connor cast his line out again and said, "About like us fishing. No bites and no calls."

Graff figured as much. Cell service up here sucked.

Graff was the thicker of the two. A head of wavy, almost curly black hair that topped off a better than six-foot height. A solid, trim build. Anyone looking at him might think he was some flavor of Latino, but he wasn't. Nothing but good German stock.

Anyone looking at O'Connor would tend to shy away, maybe even cross the street if he walked towards you. He had a narrow, gaunt, almost hawk-like look. Dark brown hair the length between George's and Two's hair length and Brian's. Brett had teased him that he looked like a burnout. O'Connor thanked him, reminding him that the look was exactly what he was going for.

Smallish eyes, but observant, catching most things others didn't see. In his line of work as an undercover detective, that was a good thing. He operated mostly by gut, by hunch, and so far, it hadn't let him down.

Graff had caught two medium-sized bass to O'Connor's one. Still, being on a boat on a lake with a beer or two was okay with him.

"Kelli and I are having a baby."

"Hey, man! Congratulations! Boy or girl?"

"Boy. We found out a couple of days ago. We're not saying anything to anyone yet."

O'Connor smiled and nodded. "That's really cool! Congratulations," he repeated.

"It will be nice for Garrett to have a brother. Kelli was hoping for a girl and I didn't care either way. But two boys will be good."

"Do you have a name picked out?"

Graff reeled in his line and set the rod down against the metal wall of his Aluminum Craft boat. It wasn't nearly as big as Brian's, nor was it as comfortable.

"We do. We were thinking Daniel or Brian. But I think we're going to go with Caden."

O'Connor smiled and said, "Good name. Caden Graff. Sounds solid. Like Garrett Graff."

O'Connor reeled his line in and stretched his long legs out. Both men had a seat cushion that doubled as a flotation device. Never used unless it was as a seat cushion.

"I think we should talk Brian into swapping boats."

Graff laughed. "That will never happen. I was shocked George got to drive his truck. Mighty protective about his boat." He was quiet for a beat or two and asked, "How is Brian?"

"Seeing a shrink. I think it's helping. He's a different kid up here. Like he is on the soccer field, but more relaxed. Happier. Intense like Brett and George. But up here," he shook his head, "he's as close to being a woodsman as I ever saw."

"I don't think I ever met his mom and dad. I knew of them. I never met his brother. Ever since the shooting at the field . . ." he trailed off.

O'Connor was at the field and saw the carnage. Not just Brad, but other boys and girls. Kids younger than Brad. Parents. A couple of grandparents who had come to watch their grandsons' game. Bodies torn apart. Lawn chairs toppled over. Blood everywhere.

An FBI agent, a good one, had died that day. He sacrificed himself so Kelliher could stop the automatic weapon from firing.

O'Connor had spotted the perp. A female assassin. Unusual, since the likelihood of a woman assassin wasn't all that common. He had given chase, but lost her. It was Brett who had killed her at the hospital. He and his friend, Tim, had been the actual targets all along. The massacre at the soccer field – and in his mind and in the minds of law enforcement who had to pick up the broken pieces of kids and adults, it was just that, a massacre – was only a diversion. Just as the bomb at the dance club had been a diversion. A needless waste of life.

"What are you thinking?" Graff asked as he eyed his friend and sometime partner.

"Just thinking of the mess at the soccer field." He shook his head and took a long pull from his can of beer.

"I think about that day. Chet Walker dying. All the kids and adults dying. Brad dying," Graff shivered. "I wonder how different it would be for Brian if his brother had lived. Where he would be now, what he'd be like." He shook his head again.

"Different for sure," O'Connor said quietly, almost in a whisper. He almost said something like it wasn't meant to be, but didn't.

"I've always had a fondness for Randy and Billy. I knew them the longest. If Jeremy wouldn't have adopted Randy, Kelli and I would have. Did you know that?"

"I suspected as much."

"George is special. Kelliher and the FBI have their eye on him."

O'Connor frowned. "I know. That bothers me some."

"Jeremy and me, too, though Jeremy doesn't talk much about it."

Neither man knew what that interest was or how it might turn out for George or the others. That was a concern. One day, Jamie would broach the subject with Kelliher. Graff took another gulp of beer, and then crushed the can and tossed it in the sack of empties.

"You seem to be closer to Brett and Brian. George, too."

O'Connor shrugged and said, "They're the most like me, I guess. George and Two, too," he laughed, liking the pun he made.

Graff laughed. "This trip is good for them, but I needed it. Both of us did. I'm surprised Paul didn't come with us."

"He's not much for fishing. Hunting, maybe. Fishing, not so much. He wanted to mess around his house this weekend. Spend time with Sarah and the kids."

O'Connor was envious of his partner and friend. He had someone he could go home to each night, spend time with.

Listening to O'Connor and watching him relax in the boat, Graff wondered if he and O'Connor had overreacted about the threat on O'Connor's life. He wondered how real it might be here in the middle of nowhere in the woods and in a boat on a lake. Maybe some. Maybe not. He would think about it some more.

CHAPTER TWENTY-SIX

For all of George's knowledge about the Navajo belief in the spirit world, he didn't understand exactly how visions worked. His grandfather had taught him that the Navajo, the *Diné*, had a connection to the spirit world that the *Biligaana* did not. And at that, it saddened his grandfather that many of the *Diné* lost that connection as they became more like the *Biligaana*.

He and his grandfather believed that dreams were messages from the spirit world. When he was younger, his grandfather would help George interpret them. There was no longer anyone to help him do this. He sought help from Jeremy and Randy, and they tried as best they could. While it was interesting and somehow comforting to speak to them about spirituality and mysticism, they lacked the depth of knowledge his grandfather had. He never faulted them for that. They hadn't lived that life, and they weren't emersed in it like he or his grandfather had been.

From time to time, he spoke with his grandfather, sometimes in his dreams, sometimes in person. Sort of. It was a conversation that took place in his head. He could see his grandfather. He could hear his grandfather. And George could speak to his grandfather. Yet, in a physical sense, his grandfather was not there.

He wasn't the only one who had seen or who had spoken to his grandfather. There were times when his grandfather would reveal himself to his friends and those close to George, but not to George himself. While that stung, George never questioned it. His grandfather had his reasons, he was sure. Still, it hurt.

On the way into the woods, he had asked Two if his grandfather had ever spoken to him or if Two had ever seen him.

Two scrunched up his face, thought for a bit, and then shook his head and said, "I never met him. I don't know what he looks like. Kind of like my dad. I never met him or saw him either."

George didn't talk about it further, but he could feel Two staring at him as they walked single file on a game path to possible hunting spots.

After walking into the woods using a game trail, they selected their positions. Two chose a spot up a stout northern red oak tree on the edge of a field. It was advantageous for several reasons. First, it bordered a field, and he thought deer might graze in the field as well as the forest. Second, because it was a red oak, it was possible deer might graze on the acorns that fell from the tree. Once in the tree, Two positioned himself sideways to the game trail where he could watch both the field and the forest.

George was not quite two hundred yards further into the woods from Two's location. He didn't have as good a view of the field, so he chose to concentrate on the forest.

So far, nothing. He could hear Two's deer call, but he had no sighting and no movement and no answering call. They might have better luck in the late afternoon before dusk, he thought. George figured they might have to change positions, though there was sign deer had been in or around them.

George had trouble concentrating on hunting, though he was ready. He controlled his breathing and watched. A quiet boy normally, he was comfortable and confident in solitude. He knew Two was similar in nature, though Two was more outgoing and liked to be around his brothers. Not that George didn't. It was just that Two needed to be around one or more, typically Brian.

George smiled. That Two had become closer to Brian didn't bother him. Both brothers needed each other for different reasons, he suspected, though Brian was comfortable with all of them, especially Brett and Billy, and now it seemed, Bobby. That was a good thing.

He felt good about his brief conversation with Brian before he left for the woods. Yet, he was troubled at the same time.

He could sense that Brian felt something, too. The woods spoke to George, just as the desert had. Though different in composition, they were the same. They were of nature and Mother Earth. Mother Earth spoke to him through dreams, through visions, and through feelings. Mother Earth spoke to Brian differently, but spoke just to him just the same.

Just as his grandfather appeared and spoke to George, Brian's brother, Brad, had at various times appeared and spoken to Brian. Just as his grandfather spoke to his brothers and those George cared for, Brad appeared and spoke to those who Brian cared for.

Brian didn't understand the spirit world as George did, though Brian was spiritual and religious. He didn't understand how or why or when Brad might appear to him, only that he would, seemingly of his own intention and reason. Brad had assured Brian that he was always nearby, in his heart, but Brian didn't know how that worked. Neither did George.

A breeze rustled the leaves of the trees around George. Though it was a warm, comfortable day, the air grew chilly. The leaves turned upside-down as if it might rain, though there wasn't a cloud in the sky. It only added to George's unease.

A hawk flew overhead, looking for breakfast. Or perhaps, for something more. George wasn't sure. It was a feeling.

As certain as he was about the hawk overhead, he was certain that before the weekend was over, his grandfather would speak to him. Perhaps Brad might speak to Brian. George would wait and think about that some more. He would be ready. He hoped Brian would be too, but wasn't sure how the battle in Arizona might have affected him. And if a situation did arise, he didn't know how Brian might respond.

CHAPTER TWENTY-SEVEN

"FBI my ass!"

This was the fourth time Bob Freeman made the statement. Not that Noah, Freeman's thirteen-year-old son was counting. He only knew he had said it often and usually with a string of cuss words describing the FBI agent and the FBI agent's mother. Colorful words Noah was not allowed to use.

"Do you think that piece of shit is a fuckin' Indian?" his uncle, Nick Roman, asked. "He had the same look."

As if he didn't hear him, Freeman said, "If I run into him or those fuckin' Indians, they're dead!" This pronouncement was accompanied with the turn of his head and a spit of thick brown tobacco juice that Noah had to dodge by hopping to the side.

Two had seen them coming before he had heard them. Frightened, he almost climbed down from his perch to hide in the deep brush off a game trail. Fortunately, the leafy tree was big enough to give him several hiding spots even if they did see the stand.

Noah spotted him. While making eye contact with Two, he shook his head slightly. Two took that to mean he should remain where he was and stay quiet and as much as possible, remain hidden. At least, that was what Two hoped the shake of the boy's head meant.

The Apache, cousins of a sort to the Navajo, believed that if you did not stare at the enemy, the enemy would not see you. Adhering to this belief, he averted his eyes until the three of them moved deeper into the woods. Noah glanced back once, nodded, and then marched in line with the two adults.

They were headed in George's general direction. He dug out his cell, but couldn't find a signal. He texted George to warn him, but the text didn't send. Two knew George could take care of himself, but it didn't prevent him from being anxious.

After the two men and the boy were out of sight, Two slipped out of his tree, put on an orange vest, and tucked his long black hair under an orange hunter's baseball cap. He didn't know if he was covered in enough orange like he was supposed to be, but he thought enough of him was so an errant arrow would not fly his way.

He followed them at a distance. They made so much noise working their way through the brush and mumbling about the incident in Crivitz that any deer that might have been in the area would be long gone. Two didn't have any doubt that George had heard them coming.

"Why aren't you in your tree?"

Two jumped and spun and in the same movement, hoisted his crossbow off his shoulder. He saw who it was and relaxed.

"Geez, George. You scared the shit out of me!" Two hissed.

George smiled and then looked off into the distance where the two men and the boy had vanished, and said, "Let's head back to the cabin. We'll go out again later this afternoon."

"What about them?" Two asked, his head jerking in the other direction.

"It's a big forest. We'll find some other place to hunt. Maybe near the lake."

The two boys stopped at Two's perch and picked up his equipment. Two dressed himself fully in blaze orange, and then they headed to the cabin with George taking the lead. Two glanced back every now and then to make certain they weren't being followed.

"They are long gone by now," George said without turning around.

Two wondered how George knew, but then again, nothing George did surprised him. George just knew stuff that no one else knew.

"The boy who was with him warned me to stay quiet."

George was silent for a beat and then said, "There is hope then that the boy might not turn out like those two men."

"Maybe," Two said, glancing back one more time.

CHAPTER TWENTY-EIGHT

Eiselmann was too preoccupied to give Stephen the match he deserved and as a consequence, Paul got an ass whipping. He managed to win one game in two full sets. Stephen controlled the net, the back line, the service- name it. Stephen owned him.

After, the two of them sat in the snack area. A water for Paul and an ice blue Gatorade for Stephen. Over the rim of the bottle Stephen drank from, he eyed his stepfather.

Paul glanced around the court area. Watched and studied people enter and exit the locker rooms.

"Earth to Eiselmann, earth to Eiselmann," Stephen said.

Paul didn't respond. When he saw that Stephen was staring at him, he said, "Huh? You say something?"

"What's going on? Who are you looking for?"

Paul shook his head and took a gulp from his bottle of water.

"You didn't play like you normally play. You weren't in the game at all. What's happening?"

Paul pursed his lips. He had an agreement with Sarah that he wouldn't bring his work home unless his family was in danger and needed to know. Yet, he decided to make an exception.

"There is a possibility, not a probability mind you, only a possibility, that someone might be after me."

Stephen took a sip of Gatorade, stretched his arms overhead, and stretched his back from side to side, taking the opportunity to look in all directions. The men's locker room was off to his left and the women's to the right, but he couldn't see the court area without turning completely around.

Paul smiled and said quietly, "That wasn't too obvious." Then he laughed.

"I'm not a cop," Stephen said with a smile.

Turning serious, Stephen asked, "Who might be after you?"

Paul bit the inside of his cheek and whispered, "It's only a possibility and I'm not that worried. The case O'Connor and I were working. It's complicated."

Stephen was pretty smart, perceptive in the way kids are, especially kids who had baggage like he did.

"You've not been yourself today. On the ride here, you took a couple of turns that took us out of the way. Your game sucked. Not that it normally doesn't suck, but you sucked worse today than normal."

Eiselmann laughed and said, "Thanks for that. You're a shit, you know that?"

Stephen smiled and said, "I learn from the best. But seriously, if you aren't that worried, why did you take the long way and why are you memorizing everyone who is in here?"

Eiselmann loved his son. No, he didn't help give birth to Stephen or Alex, but he was their dad. He was proud of who they had become and who they were becoming.

"I made a promise to your mom that my job wouldn't touch our family. I want to be sure it doesn't."

Stephen nodded. He had piercing blue eyes and sandy-blond hair that was more strawberry than blond. He had freckles under his eyes and under his nose and across his shoulders. Not as big or as many as Eiselmann, but he had them.

He had grown. Still looked a little like a plucked chicken. He was all arms and legs, but that didn't stop him from being an athlete, especially in the goal on the soccer pitch. Stephen was an excellent tennis player and a pretty fair basketball player and catcher in baseball, too.

More than that, Stephen was a good young man. Smart, kind, considerate. Perceptive. He had overcome much. Paul knew that Stephen's brief captivity in the sex ring, taken with his best friend Mike

Erickson, and freed that same evening by Graff and Kelliher, still weighed heavy on his heart and soul. Couple that with the death of his abusive and emotionally distant father, Stephen had seen and lived through much.

Much of the baggage Stephen carried had been overcome, but he still carried a Samsonite or two. While he was friends with Mike, he had drifted, or Mike had drifted, and the two didn't spend as much time together as they once had. Still, he had a good group of friends. He was more of a homebody than he was a socialite. Paul understood that might change as he became more comfortable in high school. But Stephen seemed content, and Paul and Sarah were happy with that.

"Who do I look for?" Stephen asked.

Paul blinked at him. This was more direct than Stephen had ever been with him about Paul's job.

"I won't tell mom or Alex, if that's what you're thinking."

Paul nodded and said, "I appreciate that. Look for anyone taking an interest in us. Or more importantly, anyone trying hard to show they aren't interested in us. Me, that is. A car that seems to show up more often than not. One you haven't seen before."

"Is that why Nate Kaupert is following us?"

Shocked, Eiselmann said, "How . . . when?"

"I saw you using your mirrors more than normal. I spotted him."

He said, "It's good to be observant."

Stephen gave him a sincere aw-shucks grin and shrugged.

Paul said, "I didn't see him at first. I think Graff or someone wants to make sure we're okay."

"You mean, *you're* okay."

Paul pursed his lips, took a gulp of water and said, "Yes, that I'm okay. But if I'm not, you guys aren't. It's good to take precautions."

"Is it still okay for me to hang with Mike and the guys tonight?"

"Who's all going to be there and where will you be?"

"Just the guys. Mikey, Bobby, Danny, and Garrett. I think we're either going to Danny's or Mikey's. Probably Danny's since he has a swimming pool."

"That should be okay. Do you know how you're getting there?"

"Not yet, but I'll let you and mom know."

Paul smiled and said, "You know I love you, right?"

Stephen smiled, his blue eyes sparkling. "Because I'm loveable."

Paul laughed and said, "Mostly because you're a smartass."

They laughed together, and Stephen said, "I'm a loveable smartass!" He paused, smiled again and said, "Love you, too."

CHAPTER TWENTY-NINE

Gogol spotted the tail on the red-haired cop and his son right away. It was easy enough, since he wasn't doing anything to hide the fact that he was a tail. She had hung back following, watching and waiting. As much as possible, she wanted to see what the red-haired cop's routine was. If he had a routine, given that it was the weekend.

She squinted and pursed her lips in thought.

If the tail wasn't hiding, then he wanted to be seen. Why? Maybe the tail was lazy and not a good cop or lousy at providing protection. Or, perhaps it was because a threat on the red-haired cop wasn't considered as a priority or it was judged to be improbable. Maybe they considered the threat nonexistent.

The latter was probably the answer. They didn't think anyone was going after him.

She hadn't seen anyone else following him, or more importantly, her, since he had left his house. She was good at spotting tails and she trusted her instincts and her abilities.

She smiled. Just in case, she would change cars and come back and watch the house. An opportunity might present itself and she would act accordingly. She wasn't opposed to breaking in at night and killing him and whomever was in the house. There were advantages to that.

However, if there was a tail on the cop, there might be one or more nearby.

Slowly and carefully, she took in the street. She couldn't see anyone sitting in any of the parked cars. Any joggers or walkers looked to be just that- joggers or walkers. Most were badly out of shape. Obese. The dog walkers had their poop bags at the ready and were more concerned with their pups pooping on someone's lawn than they were watching over the cop or anyone else for that matter.

She decided that the one tail was all there was. For now. At some point, there might be others. She would watch.

Gogol drove to a Speedway gas station, but instead of pulling up to the pump, she parked in a spot farthest from the entrance. She pulled out her cell and found an Enterprise on Bluemound Road not far from the east side where Eiselmann lived. She used Google Maps on her phone, set her phone in the cup holder, and drove to the Enterprise lot.

She parked her car across the parking lot in a line of parked cars in front of a Festival Foods grocery store. She hid the extra identities, the extra passport, and the extra credit cards made out in different names up and under the driver's seat.

She locked up and walked fifty yards to Enterprise. She provided the license she had chosen with a credit card that matched the name on the license. After signing the forms and waiving any extra insurance, she drove off in a tan Ford Fusion. She would have preferred gray or black, but tan was acceptable for what she needed to do. Besides, Ford Fusions were ubiquitous.

Gogol stopped at a neighborhood restaurant, walked into the woman's restroom, and entered a stall. Once inside, she removed the red wig, stuffed it into her purse, and placed a blond wig on her head. Both were designed to meet her specifications and crafted for her. Though it was a wig, it was made to look exactly like her own.

She washed her hands at the sink, taking a long look in the mirror to be certain the wig was correctly and neatly in place. More importantly, she wanted to be certain it didn't look like a wig. After, she walked out.

Back in Eiselmann's neighborhood, Gogol parked at the end of the block and around the corner facing the house at an angle. She watched the comings and goings, not only at the Eiselmann house, but on the street itself. Eiselmann's tail had parked down the block on the opposite side from where Eiselmann lived, but facing her direction. The cop looked to be taking a nap. Some protection he was.

Restless, she got out of her car and strolled down the sidewalk on the same side as Eiselmann's house. There was a house for sale two doors down, and making a bit of a show, she stopped at the For Sale sign and took one of the flyers in the plastic container below the sign that had been provided by the realtor. Not a bad looking house. A two-story brick and wood design, cream color with green trim. Nothing fancy. Just stable, solid, and not too old. Price fit, though she thought if she was in the market, she would come in at least five grand lower than the asking price.

The yard was neatly kept. No weeds grew in the front or side flower beds. Shrubs had been trimmed. The home itself looked and felt empty. A lockbox hung on the front door. Gogol decided that the owners had already moved out.

She slowed her pace as she pretended to read the flyer, almost coming to a stop just off the Eiselmann property, then tucked the flyer into her purse, turned, and walked back to her car. She got in, and drove three blocks behind Eiselmann's street, up two blocks past Eiselmann's street, and came up to a corner opposite from his house and on the opposite side of the block from where she had parked previously.

The tail stepped out of his car and stretched. First, he raised his arms over his head, and then he did trunk twists. That done, he walked across the street to Eiselmann's house and rang the doorbell. She couldn't tell who answered the door, but the tail walked in and the door was shut behind him.

Odd for a tail to introduce himself to the person he's covering. She would have to think about that.

CHAPTER THIRTY

George had been quiet, deep in thought, missing parts or most of the conversation taking place around him. The time from when he and Two arrived back at the cottage, to sitting in the boat with Two, Brian and Brett, his mood and demeanor had changed. It had darkened.

Something. He wasn't sure. More of a feeling than anything concrete.

In contrast, Brian was excited. His face radiant. He couldn't stop smiling. His eyes wide and bright. Brett was lost, not only in Brian's excitement, but in Brian's overall change in mood.

While they were in the boat fishing, Brian was relaxed, but happy. There was a calmness about him. Now, however, Brian was as animated as he had ever seen him. A happier version of the Brian on the soccer field.

They sat fifteen or twenty yards off shore. Brian had cut the engine and dropped the anchor.

"Can you imagine how cool that would be?" Brian asked no one in particular.

"That's a lot of money, Bri," Brett said.

"Three two-and-a-half acre lots just sitting there. Look at the shoreline! It's a sandy beach. We put the house on the middle lot. Three stories. Seven bedrooms. A large family room on the lower and middle levels. Lots of windows."

His arms swept from side to side.

"A big kitchen. Two sets of stairs outside leading up to the deck that surrounds the house. A real house, not a cottage. Something we can use in winter if we want."

"Seven bedrooms?" Two said.

"That's bigger than the house we live in now," Brett said.

"The way I figure it, seven bedrooms for seven brothers. Mom and dad for one, so two of us will have to double up. But if we marry and have kids, we'll have a place for them. It will be ours. Mom and dad can retire here if they want or they can come up whenever they want to."

"Bri, mom and dad can't afford this," Brett said.

Brian shook his head and said, "They don't have to. I have the money now. If you guys want to help out, I can pay for the land and half of the construction cost. The rest of the mortgage can be paid out of our trust funds. If we divide that up between each of us, we should break even between the cost of the mortgage payment and the interest earned on the balance in the trust funds."

"How do you know all this stuff?" Two asked as he shook his head.

"My dad, mostly. He taught Brad and me about banking and the stock market and stuff. Brad didn't care about it, but I found it interesting."

"Do you actually have the money we would need to get the land and build this house?" Two asked.

Brian beamed. He chuckled, and the guys wondered if his head might explode.

"I keep track of it. I think I could afford all of it, but I'd rather not. Besides, I don't want it to be mine. I want it to be ours. We'll call it, Seven Brothers."

The four boys let that soak in as they stared at the three For Sale signs, the sandy shore, and the woods behind.

Brett shook his head, not in disagreement, but in awe and his lack of ability to paint the picture Brian had placed before them.

Two tilted his head first to one side and then to the other. He shrugged, finding it difficult to imagine. In the first place, he had trouble believing he lived in as nice a house as he was living in. The house was far better, far bigger, and far more everything than what he had been living in.

Before moving to Wisconsin to live with Jeremy, Vicky and the boys, he alternated between living in the desert on the hard-packed red dirt under the stars with only a blanket covering him, and living above the bar-diner with Lou Feldcamp, sharing the one bed with the man. Feldcamp was now in prison on multiple charges ranging from narcotics possession, sale and distribution, along child endangerment, felony sexual abuse, child rape, and pornography among other things. He would die in prison, sooner rather than later because of lung cancer.

Only George remained silent. Lost in a myriad of thoughts, none of them good, and none of them about Brian's proposal to build a lake house.

"Yo, George! What are you thinking?" Brian asked with a laugh. When he didn't respond, Brian repeated, "George, what do you think?"

George blinked at him, then at Brett and Two.

"Sounds fine."

Brian couldn't hide his disappointment in George's lukewarm endorsement. He had hoped to win them over. If the three of them got excited about it, it would be an easier sell to their parents.

"Fine? That's all you can say is, *fine*?" Brett said.

George shrugged, turned to Brian and said, "It's a good idea."

Brian raised his eyebrows and sighed. His shoulders sagged. He felt deflated and defeated. Reluctantly and without another word, Brian lifted up the anchor and set it in the cubby in the back of the boat, started up the engine and motored away, looking back over his shoulder at the shoreline as he did. It didn't lessen his resolve. If anything, he was more determined than ever. The doubt of his brothers would not dampen his spirits.

The trip back to the cottage was silent except for the thrum of the motor and the splashing of waves as the boat carved through the lake. The boat bounced with the waves much to Two's delight. Several times he turned around towards Brian grinning. All the while hanging onto his hat and the boat railing, his long black hair trailing in the wind.

George frowned as the cottage came into view. His demeanor had only gotten darker. Brett glanced at Brian every now and then, but Brian ignored him, intent on the steering the boat to the pier. Every so often and between chuckles of delight, Two glanced from Brian to George to Brett and then back to George. He didn't understand George's mood change, and wondered if anyone else had noticed it.

CHAPTER THIRTY-ONE

He dared not move. Could not move. They stared right at him.

The soccer player seemed excited, but he couldn't hear what he was saying. For self-preservation if not curiosity, he wanted to inch closer and raise his head, anything to hear what was being said. But he couldn't because that would give away his position.

If he moved, they might wonder why he faced the lake and not the woods. They might spot his atypical hunting rifle. Too many questions, not enough answers, and his opportunity would be lost.

No, better to not move and remain hidden.

There was one thing that bothered him. It looked as though the older of the two Indian boys stared directly at him. The Indian boy spoke twice in answer to one or the others' questions. Again, the words were indistinguishable in the distance. His eyes, however, remained on him, or at the least, directly at the area where he was laying. He might have to do something about the kid, sooner rather than later. One more loose end. If he did somehow take out the Indian kid, one or two of the others might have to be taken care of. He would see how it played out.

He ignored the ants and the mosquitos. Sweat ran off his forehead and into his eyes. He did not move.

He gritted his teeth, because the boat carrying the two cops motored past the boys. It was a distance, but nothing challenging and nothing his rig couldn't handle. He had made much tougher shots at a greater distance. It was just as he had planned.

He felt the tingle in his finger and almost pulled the trigger. But that would mean six shots, at least, and not just the two he had counted on. The boys might react to the first two shots and dive overboard or speed away making the subsequent shots harder. Not impossible by any means, but harder.

The pop of the rifle, even with the suppressor, might alarm other hunters. He knew from experience that any suppressor would fail the more times the trigger was pulled. Soft at first, nothing more than a 'thtttt' but blossoming louder with each shot. Even the best suppressor failed eventually.

No, he would have to wait it out. He was patient, but he didn't like waiting, especially when his plan had been thwarted.

By the time the boys in the boat pulled away and sped off, the two cops were out of sight and around the bend. No shot possible. He still couldn't move because the soccer player kept turning around and looking back until they, too, rounded the bend.

Finally, he was able to move, but not relax. Tentatively, cautiously. He first wiped the sweat off his face, and then he brushed ants off his jacket and pants. He stood, moved over to a tree and relieved himself, taking the time to scan his surroundings.

No other hunters visible. No deer moving through the brush or on game trails. He was alone.

He had to reexamine his situation and perhaps, he'd have to hurry and take the cops sooner at a more inconvenient location. He would have to think it through and plan.

CHAPTER THIRTY-TWO

Mark Erickson drove his son, Mikey, along with Stephen and their friend, Garrett, to Danny Limbach's house for the evening.

Paul and Sarah dropped Alexandra off at the Germaine house two miles away for a sleepover. They had the evening to themselves, which was a rarity. Keeping up with Stephen's and Alexandra's soccer practices and games, dance classes and competitions, left them precious little time for each other. They were happy, though, and enjoyed the time they did spend together, not only with each other, but with the kids.

They sat down at a table at Jake's Restaurant in Brookfield. It was early evening, so the sun began its decent down the western horizon. It wasn't quite ready to retire and be replaced by the moon. That would occur soon, however.

Paul debated whether to let Sarah know they were tailed by no less than four cops in three different cars. Kaupert remained the most visible. Hidden to most anyone except another cop were Tom Albrecht and Brooke Beranger sitting at a table towards the front. Sarah thought it was a coincidence the two arrived at the same restaurant just after Paul and Sarah sat down. She and they waved across the room. Outside sitting across the street was Nate Kaupert.

Down the street in car parked facing the direction Paul and Sarah would most likely travel after their dinner was Alex Jorgenson, the six-foot-five redheaded detective. The former high school all-state tackle and college football player was hard to miss. He window-shopped here and there, but spent most of his time inside his car playing a word game on his phone.

Eiselmann's cell buzzed. He picked it up and saw who was calling.

To Sarah, he said, "I need to take this. Sorry."

She smiled, nodded, and sipped her white wine.

"He uses two phones. His personal phone and a burner."

Paul glanced around to see who was nearby and who might listen in. They were in a booth at the back of the restaurant as was Eiselmann's customary position in public. On one side, a foursome laughed and clinked glasses at something someone had said. Behind him on the other side, a couple wrangled with their kids over the drink menu. No one sat at the tables nearest them.

"How do you know he has a burner?"

Billias chuckled. *"Because the idiot answered a call on it without turning off his main phone."*

"You can listen in on calls now?"

A pause. *"You'd be surprised at how technology has changed in just a couple of years. Not everyone has it or uses it, but some do. Like me."*

"I don't think I want to know."

"A discussion for another day. Soon. You should know. Everyone should know."

"Oh."

"Anyway, something is going to take place either this evening or tomorrow. Time wasn't specific."

"He was clear about that? I mean, something happening tonight or tomorrow?"

"Not as clear as you or I would like it to be, but clear enough. Not sure who it is or where it will take place."

"Huh."

"The caller was a female. But . . ."

"But, what?"

"I got the impression that there are two bad actors, so to speak. I also got the impression that the two are working separately."

"And how did you arrive at that?"

"Like I said, just a feeling. Why would he tell the female that something was going to happen if two individuals were working together? Wouldn't she already know?"

"Shit," Paul muttered into the phone.

Paul blinked at his wife, who tilted her head. She was privy to only one side of the conversation, and it had sparked her interest.

"That . . . doesn't . . ."

"I know, right? I've read enough mysteries and seen enough movies. I worked with you guys long enough to know most of the killers out there are male. It took me by surprise, too."

Eiselmann's mouth went dry. The hairs on the back of his head stood at attention. Slowly, he looked around the room looking for anyone, a female, sitting by herself. The bar area was towards the front door. He and Sarah had walked through it to get to the dining area. He didn't look closely enough, and he wanted to kick himself for not doing so.

"When you called, you mentioned that there were two men following your partner around. They ended up dead. I'm wondering if this lady took care of them."

Paul shook his head. Then he bit the inside of his cheek. Maybe. Perhaps.

"You sure it was a female?"

"The voice was a husky, smokey alto, like she could sing the blues. Maybe tobacco enhanced. A hint of an accent. Eastern Europe, I'd bet."

Paul sighed. He glanced up at Sarah, who had a quizzical look on her face.

"I'll call O'Connor and let him know. I know he's on a short vacation, but I promised I'd keep him in the loop." He would also let Kelliher, and the two detectives on the case, Greg Gonnering and Carlos Lorenzo know. "Thanks again."

"I will keep monitoring him. If something comes up, I'll let you know. And we need to have a conversation about current technology."

There were some things Paul wanted and needed to know. There were other things he'd rather not know. He couldn't hide the reluctance in his voice when he said, "Will do. Thanks."

After ending his call and sending out a group text that included O'Connor and Graff, he stared at Sarah and said, "We're going to have a nice dinner and a quiet evening together. That's a promise."

She stared back at him and in perfect deadpan said, "Sure we are."

CHAPTER THIRTY-THREE

Brian couldn't help but feel relaxed. Yes, he was disappointed with the reception of his idea when he mentioned it to the guys, but he couldn't help feeling at peace. It was a peaceful end to a relaxing and satisfying day.

Assorted birds called to one another. He wasn't sure if they protested their presence or were just chatty. A woodpecker pecking for food. Crickets chirping. Frogs croaking. A discordant opera of nature at its finest. There was even a loon on the lake calling to its lover.

A slight breeze rustled leaves. The air crisp with the onset of perhaps an early winter. Typically, this would jeans and sweatshirt weather. But Wisconsin enjoyed a late splurge of summer warmth. It was especially warm sitting around the fire. Shorts and t-shirts, or no shirt at all in Two's and Brett's case; sandals or slides for the boys, grubby tennis shoes for Graff, boots for O'Connor, and moccasins for George.

The air thick with wood smoke. Under it, a dark dank smell of earth. Beyond it, the smell of the lake. Not fishy, though four of them had fished most of the day. Well, three of them did. Brett fished for a minute or two, and elsewise was content to sit and talk or shut his eyes and enjoy the sun and the rocking of the boat. Brian didn't mind. Brett was good company awake or asleep.

George had been quiet. He hadn't been this unnerved in a long time. He frowned. He didn't look at the fire too often because that would cause night-blindness. He wanted to be able to see into the forest. He was not sure what he was looking for, however.

130

Brian and Two poked and prodded the fire, adding logs to it to keep it going. The warmth of it felt good. Logs popped, and sparks and glowing embers danced upwards in the darkness.

Two looked up at O'Connor and Graff and asked, "What makes someone a murderer?"

Graff thought it was an odd question and random at that. They had been talking NorthStar football and soccer, and the prospects for a decent basketball season.

As for the cops, the number of dead at their hand was too many to count. Graff supposed he could figure it out if he thought long and hard about it. He knew from conversation with O'Connor that the lanky undercover detective had no interest in how many he had killed. It would drudge up too many memories. They were best buried, just like the people he had killed.

Both cops knew the four boys had shot or stabbed men either to protect themselves or to protect their family. George had shot or stabbed ten at least. No telling how many he, Brett, Brian or Two had shot and killed in Arizona.

Brett shot two in the summer of death as he helped free himself and about thirteen other boys from captivity, and in that same summer, defended himself from a female assassin sent to kill him and a friend. In Arizona on the ill-fated hunting trip, Brian shot and killed at least two, probably more. He wasn't sure and neither were his brothers. Much of the shooting had taking place in the pitch black of night, so there was no way to tell just how many men he had shot. A good number, Graff figured. And Two, one for sure. At least, that was all anyone knew. He hadn't spoken about his life prior to meeting O'Connor and before he had begun living with the family in Wisconsin.

O'Connor eyed Brian, whose expression hadn't changed. It was unreadable. Who knew what was rattling around inside his head, especially prompted by Two's question? He knew Brian was as deep a thinker as they come. His thoughts colored his heart and soul.

After a few beers one night at a campfire similar to this one, O'Connor had told the boys and men sitting around discussing this and that, *'They don't give classes in human suffering. Nobody gets to happily ever after without a few scars.'* Of course, that last statement could apply to anyone, especially the boys sitting around the fire.

It was O'Connor who answered. "Men kill each other for any number of reasons. Money. Power. Kicks. Defense. Revenge. Lust."

Graff picked it up from there, eyeing Brian. "There are some like that psycho, Nelson, who are bent around the corner. No one really knows how they got there."

"Who?" Two asked.

"There was this psycho . . . this dude who didn't believe in adoption." Brett stopped, sighed, and shook his head. "This fuckhead killed anyone who had been adopted or was somehow involved with adoption. Brian caught him in our woods."

Two's head whipped sideways at Brian, his eyes large and his mouth open. "Our woods?"

Brett nodded. "He came for George and Brian. Maybe for the rest of us. Who the hell knows?"

"What happened?"

"Brian shot him in the ass." Brett smirked, then laughed, elbowing Brian. "Twice."

"You're making this up," Two said.

"Nope," O'Connor said, watching Brian closely, especially his hands.

Two stared at Brian and said, "Why did you shoot him in the ass?"

"I knew O'Connor and Graff and the FBI agents would want to interview him. I didn't need to kill him." Then he added in a quiet voice, almost as if he thought it and didn't intend to speak it out loud, "I didn't want to kill him."

"Wow. Okay," Two said. He had a new picture of Brian. Another facet, so to speak.

Brett wanted to add that the shot was at almost fifty yards in the dark of night in a near freezing white out, but he didn't want to push it. Besides, Two had seen up close and personal how good a shot Brian was. Distance, time of day, or weather conditions didn't matter. In Brett's mind, Brian could shoot a gnat off a horse's ass at a hundred yards if he wanted to.

"It was important to not let him get to the house," Brian said, his eyes flicking up at George and then back to the fire.

George stared intently at the woods. He didn't even know that Brian had glanced at him. He was barely aware of the conversation.

Curious, Graff asked, "Why did you ask about murderers?"

Two said, "I'm reading the book, *Mindhunter*. It's written by two FBI agents. It's interesting."

"I've read it," Graff said nodding.

"Me, too," Brett said.

Two asked O'Connor, "Why did you want to be a cop?"

"The women." He tried to keep a straight face but couldn't.

"Yeah? And how's that workin' for you?" Brett asked with a laugh.

Everyone laughed except George, who appeared to not have heard the comment. Even Brian laughed.

"I don't know really. About being a cop, that is," O'Connor said after a long pull from his can of beer. "Sort of fell into it, I guess."

"What about you?" Two asked Graff.

Jamie shrugged and said, "I went to college and studied sociology. A little psychology. I wanted to understand the why behind the who." He shrugged and added, "I like the work, especially investigating crime scenes. I see an investigation as a puzzle. Each piece fits just so."

"That's what I want to do," Two said. "Crime scene stuff."

"George is good at it," O'Connor said. "Right, George?"

"What?" George responded. "I'm sorry. I wasn't listening."

Graff and O'Connor had noticed, but didn't say anything about it.

"I said, you are good at investigating crime scenes," Pat repeated.

George felt himself blush. "It is interesting. Agent Skip taught me a lot."

"But you knew quite a bit before you ever met Skip Dahlke," Jamie said.

"Who's that?" Two asked.

Graff laughed. "He is this young kid. I guess, not so young. He just looks like he's twelve or something. One of the smartest guys I know."

"Probably the whitest guy I ever met," O'Connor added. "He doesn't tan. Just burns. Mostly, he's white as snow."

Everyone laughed, including George.

"Reminds me of someone else I know," Brett said elbowing Brian.

"I tan," Brian objected.

"Uh huh. Sure, you do."

Everyone laughed, including Brian.

"Skip Dahlke was a crime scene tech working for the state of Wisconsin, but he was hired by the FBI. That's his gig now. Crime scenes. He's a specialist," Graff said.

"None better," O'Connor added.

"Don't underestimate yourself, Hoss," Graff said to him.

O'Connor shrugged it off.

"That would be so cool!" Two said.

"What? The FBI or working crime scenes?" Graff asked.

"Both! I think that's what I want to do," Two said, smiling.

Brian stood up, stretched, and said, "I'm going to walk down and check on the boats."

He playfully tugged on Two's hat down low enough to cover his younger brother's eyes, and then walked away.

"You want company?" Brett asked as he checked Brian's hands to see if either shook. Neither did, so that was a good sign.

"Nah, I got it."

The pier was around a clump of trees and down a slight hill. From the campfire, there was no way to see the pier, much less the boats.

"Is he okay?" Graff whispered.

Brett, still looking off in that direction, said, "Yeah, I think so."

"I'll give him a couple of minutes and then I'll go talk to him," George said. "I want to talk to him about his idea."

"What idea?" O'Connor asked.

Brett filled them in on Brian's plan to build a house up on the lake.

Graff nodded and said, "Honestly, that sounds cool."

"It would give us an excuse to come up here more often," O'Connor added.

"Who said you were invited?" Brett asked, barely able to keep a straight face.

"Sleep lightly, McGovern. That's all I've gotta say."

The boys and the men laughed.

Sitting at the end of the pier, his feet just above the water, Brian thought of a line from one of Bobby's poems. *'The stillness of the night brings the hope of a promise.'*

He wondered, and yes, he hoped. Hope was the one thing he had never given up on.

He lay back with his hands under his head and he looked at the stars and the not-quite-full moon.

Funny how he thought about Bobby and not Mikey. Maybe because his relationship with Mikey was still new. The two of them were still exploring limits and boundaries, neither one willing to risk going too far, too quickly.

With Bobby, Brian knew what he had, and so did Bobby. They had explored and discussed. They were comfortable with each other. There was a need and a hunger that both boys recognized and wanted, with and from each other.

He was aroused, embarrassingly hard. He reached into his shorts to rearrange himself, but there was no hiding it. He didn't particularly care. Maybe around Graff or O'Connor, but not the guys. They had seen one another at one time or another, so it wasn't a big deal.

He wondered if it would be as easy with Bobby as it was before they went on their break, as he referred to it. Probably. The getting-to-know-you stage all over again was an exciting thought. The touches. The kisses. The everything. Maybe more.

Then there was Mikey. The two of them weren't there yet. Not even close to where he was or had been with Bobby. Would they get there? Probably eventually, if both of them wanted to continue down that road. Mikey seemed willing. It was Brian who had held back. Maybe because he didn't want to get hurt again. Maybe because there wasn't the spark, the fire with Mikey that there was with Bobby. He sighed. That was more likely.

A frog jumped into the water from somewhere behind him. Brian heard the pier creek. The near silent footfalls.

George lay down on his stomach with his feet towards shore so that his head was next to Brian's.

"Are you okay?" George whispered

Brian nodded. Unwilling to break the silence, the peace. He had grown to love silence.

George reached over and smoothed Brian's hair off his forehead. Brian couldn't remember George ever doing that to him. Not to anyone else, for that matter.

"Your idea about the house on the lake is a good one," he whispered. "I will help pay for it."

"I didn't think you liked the idea," Brian whispered back. Not sure why he whispered, but that's what he did.

"No, it is a good idea. It was not that," George whispered.

He moved his lips closer to Brian's ear and continued whispering.

"Brian, do not say anything and do not move. Just listen."

Brian nodded. His thoughts of Bobby and Mikey melted away. Any noticeable bulge in his shorts melted away too.

"When Two and I got back to the cottage after hunting, it felt like someone had been in the house. Little things. Mostly a feeling. I think my duffle bag was moved. I think someone had been in it. I think someone went through Two's, Brett's, and your bag too. At least, that is what it seemed and felt like."

Brian turned his head, but George placed a finger on Brian's lips.

Speaking more formally, George continued, "I do not have proof. It is only a feeling. My grandfather has not visited me and if we were in danger, I believe he would come to us."

"Brad has not come to me either."

George thought that over. Brad coming to Brian was not as good a barometer as his grandfather coming to him. There was more frequency between his grandfather's visits than there was with Brad visiting Brian.

"When you left to check on the boats, Detective Jamie asked Two and me if we saw any female hunters."

Brian frowned and cocked his head. "Why?" he whispered.

"He did not say."

"That's an odd question. Kind of random," Brian whispered.

"Yes, I thought so too."

Brian thought it over and whispered, "Did you? I mean, see any female hunters?"

"No. But, we only went in one way and back out. We did not see too many other hunters. We did see those men and that boy we saw in Crivitz."

Brian tried to sit up, but George prevented him. Brian relaxed as much as he could, which was not much.

"Where? When?"

George smiled, smoothed Brian's bangs back and said, "Just before we left the woods. They did not see us. We saw them."

"What about tomorrow? Is Two going to be okay? Are you going to be okay?"

George loved the way Brian and Two had gotten on. They were close. Brian protecting and looking out for Two was special. Two looking up to and seeking out Brian was special, too.

"I will look out for him. Two and I will find another spot to hunt. It is a big forest."

Brian turned to face him and said, "Could it be that's what you're feeling? Those two men getting back at us? At Two?"

George had thought about that. It was possible that the incident in Crivitz would cause that. Still, George didn't think so. He whispered that to Brian.

He continued in a voice so hushed Brian had trouble hearing him clearly. "When you told us about your idea for the house and showed us that land, I thought I saw something."

Brian blinked at him. "What?" It came out a little louder than he intended, and repeated in a whisper matching George's voice, "What?"

George hesitated. He did not want to alarm Brian needlessly. But he also felt that of the three brothers, it was Brian who would know best how to deal with it. He hoped.

"I thought I saw someone lying in the grass behind bushes."

Brian thought about it and said, "It wasn't just another hunter?"

Slowly, George shook his head and said, "I do not believe so."

CHAPTER THIRTY-FOUR

He had a dilemma. Never having faced a catch twenty-two before, he didn't like it.

He was certain that the older Indian kid knew something or at the least, saw something. Him. The way he stared into the forest at the campfire was another indicator. He had the feeling that the Indian boy was on watching for him. It had unnerved him. The kid was more alert than the two cops. Odd.

He followed the Indian kid to the pier and watched while he spoke to the soccer kid. He couldn't hear a word, except twice when the soccer kid said, *"Where? When?"* and then later when he said, *"What?"*

How much did the soccer kid know? What exactly did the Indian kid know and how much did he tell the soccer kid?

His dilemma was that the Indian kid was now a liability. Potentially. Maybe. More than likely. If he was, the soccer kid would be, too.

He knew he needed to act. Angry with himself for his hesitation. He didn't know why he was reluctant to kill the kids. He had done so in the past without any compunction. Shot a toddler and his sister in front of their parents just because he could. Yet, this time, there was reluctance on his part and he didn't know why. That frustrated, if not angered, him.

Enough.

He pulled out his handgun, screwed on the suppressor, and took aim.

CHAPTER THIRTY-FIVE

She knew where the red-headed cop would end up, so she left the bar, walked across the street and got into her car. Before she started up the engine, she took the time to feign touching up her lipstick and makeup while she searched for anyone watching her. She didn't see anyone, so she drove off at a leisurely pace. Checking her side and rearview mirrors as she drove, she didn't see anyone tailing her.

Sitting at the bar, an idea had occurred to her. On the drive back, a plan formed. She knew it would. It always did. She knew an opportunity would present itself. She would seize it and be done with it. And be done with him.

CHAPTER THIRTY-SIX

He was about to shoot them both when the two other kids showed up. The young Indian boy ran down the pier, while the brown-haired boy took his time.

"We're going skinny dipping!" the younger Indian boy said.

"Seriously?" the soccer kid asked. He looked across the lake and could see in the distance two other fires and lights on in a house or cottage. Laughter and voices carried across the lake, though he couldn't understand a word that was said. "We're not that isolated."

"Unless they have binoculars, we're good. And if they have binoculars, they'll take one look at me and get jealous," the brown-haired kid said with a laugh.

The two boys shed their clothes and jumped in one after the other.

"Come on in," the young Indian boy said. "It's not too bad."

The older Indian boy stripped down and jumped in, leaving the soccer kid the last one on the pier.

The soccer kid inspected the gauze and tape on his upper thighs and on his left ankle. "Fine," the soccer kid muttered.

"Horse fights!" the little Indian kid said. "I ride Brian."

"George, get on me. We'll win," the brown-haired boy said.

"Oh bull," the soccer kid said as he cannonballed the three boys in the water.

In the dark of the forest, he couldn't understand how they were comfortable with their nakedness in front of each other, much less riding the shoulders of each other. Something he would never do, would never even think of doing. Not in this lifetime.

He watched the four boys for just a short moment, and then slowly made his way back to the cottage to see if he could get rid of the two cops. The four boys swimming would give him not only an opportunity to dispose of the cops but to make a clean getaway.

He made his way through the heavy bush on the edge of the forest up to the cottage, but stopped fifteen yards out. The campfire was only embers. There was no sign of the two cops.

He crouched down and waited. His eyes everywhere. His ears searching for any sound.

Could they be watching him? Listening for him?

He waited. There was no one. He had no idea where the cops went. Perhaps in the house?

He dared not move in the event they were waiting for him. He didn't want to risk a shootout.

He couldn't glance at his watch for fear of the glow from the digital dial would light up and they'd spot it, him. He had to wait it out.

He heard the boys before he spotted them. They trudged up the hill and around the corner, still naked, each carrying his clothes, except for the soccer boy who carried the smaller Indian boy on his back.

"Losers have to put out the fire," the brown-haired boy said.

The man thought it was the brown-haired boy by his voice, though in the dark, he couldn't tell for sure.

"Only because you grabbed my dick and wouldn't let go until I threw Two off of me," the soccer boy said.

"Well, it was hanging there, so I figured, 'What the hell? Might as well,'" he said, causing all the boys to laugh.

"I'll remember that for the next time," the soccer boy laughed.

The bigger Indian kid and the brown-haired boy went into the house.

"We can use the water in the bucket to put out the fire," the little Indian boy said.

"Do it carefully. You don't want any of the embers to burn you," the soccer boy cautioned.

The smaller Indian boy poured water onto the dying embers and what remained of the fire blinked out with a hiss and cloud of smoke and steam. After, the two boys disappeared into the house with the others.

The man couldn't hear anything once all were inside, and he still didn't know where the two cops were. It occurred to him to peep into the windows to see where everyone was, but he discarded the idea as quickly as it came. He couldn't risk it. He didn't know where the cops were. He had no choice but to wait it out.

Another opportunity that turned to shit.

He gritted his teeth and hunkered down to wait.

CHAPTER THIRTY-SEVEN

She hadn't seen a dog, but that didn't mean there wasn't one. She viewed dogs and cats as nuisances. Small dogs yipped and yapped incessantly. Large dogs, depending upon the breed, could be dangerous, especially to someone who wasn't known and who was about to trespass on the owner's property.

Picking a lock was easy. Her pick set was as necessary as her FNH FNX-45 Tactical 45 Auto Black Pistol. Her weapon of choice. She liked- no loved- the weapon. The three magazines carrying fifteen cartridges each, and the fact that it carried a threaded barrel to equip a suppressor made it the perfect weapon. Not too heavy, not too light, just right. She smiled at her little poem.

She frowned.

Fortunately, before she set to picking the lock and opening the door, she took a moment to glance through the windows on either side of the door. There it was in the hallway. Glowing red. Armed. Of course, he'd have an alarm system. What cop wouldn't?

She wouldn't have the opportunity to surprise the cop in his own home. She would have preferred that to taking him out in his backyard or on the street. Too much noise, even with the suppressor. Too many eyes peeking around curtains.

She straightened up and slowly turned to face the nearest neighbor. No lights on in the house, at least on the side facing the red-haired cop's house. She turned to the backyard. The bushes obscured the fence. Beyond in the house directly behind the cop's house, a light in what looked like the kitchen window. No movement. The houses on either side had lights on, but again, she didn't see anyone at them.

She assumed she hadn't been noticed, but she didn't want to take any chances.

She crossed the darkened yard to the side of the garage. There cloaked in darkness and hidden by bushes, she crouched down and waited.

A car drove down the street without slowing. Just a driver. No passengers. Another came from the opposite direction. A man and woman. People getting back from dinner or shopping or something. Whatever it was suburbanites did on Friday nights.

All was still, but not quiet. A dog barked. Soft music from one of the neighbors behind the cop's house. Some pop song, she decided, though she couldn't place the tune.

It wouldn't be long now.

CHAPTER THIRTY-EIGHT

The driver licked his lips. The butt of his Sig Sauer P320 visible under his right thigh and within easy access. He glanced at his passenger. She bit her lip and tried on a weak smile that failed. Neither knew what was about to happen. He grasped her hand for encouragement, his as well as hers.

The passenger read the text.

We're set. Be careful. Act natural.

Sure. Right. They weren't the ones who would be shot at. Killed.

She showed him the text. He nodded solemnly.

She pulled her Glock .23 out of her jacket pocket. A couple of used Kleenex fell out and onto the floor between the seat and the door. She glanced at them and then kept her head focused ahead. Eyes darting left and right.

Three houses away.

Alexis White walking her brindle pit gave them a wave. The passenger waved back, but the look of puzzlement on Alexis' face was present. Her hand and arm frozen in a half-wave.

No other person on the street. No walker. No jogger. All quiet. Too quiet.

The passenger hoped Alexis would be okay and out of any line of fire. If there was any. Who was she kidding? If? It was a matter of when, where, and how much.

The driver willed himself to keep the pace steady. Now, both hands on the wheel, about to make the turn into the driveway. He reached up and pressed the button to open the garage door. There was no way he would drive into the garage, but he wanted it open to keep the appearance as normal as possible. Didn't want to arouse any suspicion.

He slowed down to begin his turn. He kept the car on the left side of the driveway, and kept the car running so the lights would glow in the dark. For good measure, he turned on the brights. His gut told him that if someone was out there like they suspected, he or she would be in the back of the house, maybe on the side of the garage to rush them as they walked to the backdoor. The high beams would make it more difficult for the shooter to look into the car clearly, especially if the shooter was trying to spot them through the windshield.

The passenger sunk down into her seat. She couldn't help it.

The driver had been holding his breath. Waiting. Anticipating . . . something.

Two quick shots splattered the windshield, close enough for the driver to hear the bullets buzz by like angry bees. The shots had to have come from the side of the garage.

"Get down!" he hissed.

Two more shots on the passenger side sailed over her head.

Glass from the windshield fell into their laps and hair like snowflakes, only thicker and heavier.

"Could use some help, goddammit!" the driver shouted.

As a punctuation mark, another shot in his direction struck the headrest. Too close.

"Anyone hear me? Jesus! Fuck!" he shouted.

Paul and Alyssa Gorman, Eiselmann's neighbors on the right turned on the lights. Dogs barked.

A shotgun blast came from somewhere in the back of the garage or behind the Gorman house. The driver couldn't tell.

"Drop your weapon! This is the police! We have you surrounded!"

Greg Gonnering's voice sounded mechanical, tinny through the megaphone. He was answered by two quick shots. They were answered by another heavy, throaty shotgun blast.

A female, limping badly, left arm hanging oddly at her side, came from the side of the garage on an awkward jog. She shot once, then twice behind her into the back and side yards, which were answered by another shotgun blast. Some of the spray hit the backseat side window.

As she neared the car, she shot twice into the front seat towards the driver, but never stopped her awkward run towards the street.

A female voice from behind them, either on the front lawn or the street: "Stop right there and drop your weapon!"

A male voice: "This is the police. You have nowhere to go!"

A shot from the suppressed handgun sounding less muffled was the retort. There were four quick shots from somewhere behind the car. Had to be from the front of the house, and then all was eerily silent.

The fire fight was brief but intense. To the passenger, it seemed to last a lifetime.

Smoke and the sulfurous and metallic smell of the fire fight hung in the air, mostly in the car, like industrial-strength Taco Bell grade flatulence.

Her ears were dulled by the sound of gunfire just over her head through her now shattered passenger side window. All sound muffled, like her ears were packed with a roll of cotton.

She lifted herself upright, reached over and grasped the driver's arm. Her hand came up bloody.

"Officer down! Officer down! We need an ambulance! Now! Albrecht's down!"

■　■　■

It was Brooke Beranger who suggested that they switch cars. Albrecht nodded his approval. Eiselmann protested to no avail, knowing they had it planned from the start. Bewildered and upset, Sarah stood by and said nothing. She and Brooke exchanged jackets, as did Tom Albrecht and Eiselmann.

"We think it's nothing, but we don't want to take chances. Give us a twenty-minute lead and drive slowly," Albrecht said.

They had stood in the bar area at a table in the rear near the restrooms, away from the smallish crowd. Brooke stood with her back to them watching. Just in case. Albrecht and Eiselmann spoke in hushed tones while Sarah listened.

"Who do you have for backup?"

"Nate Kaupert will follow us just as he has been following you all day. Jorgy will run drag behind you. Gonnering and Lorenzo were in place since early morning. After your text, they were the ones who spotted a . . ." he searched for a word and settled on, "possibility."

Albrecht turned to Sarah and said, "Honestly, only a possibility. We just don't want to take any chances."

"Where have I heard that before?" Sarah said cocking her head and frowning at Eiselmann.

Eiselmann shrugged, knowing he'd have some explaining to do if anything happened.

"Ronnie Desotel is close by." Albrecht shook his head and said, "Even I haven't spotted him. He'll be following Brooke and me."

Ronnie Desotel and Tom Albrecht were best friends. They had led the raid to free the kids held captive at a hotel in Kansas City during the summer of death. Desotel had gotten shot in the leg and still had a slight limp, and it pained him especially in cold or damp weather.

"There's a cop, Lisa Vickers, who is also in place. She's staying with one of your neighbors. Amy Ivory, I think?"

Amy and Alexis White had been walking their dogs when Eiselmann and his son, Stephen, were taking care of the lawn earlier that day. Amy lived two doors down. Alexis in the next block.

"Brooke and I are going to head out. Remember, you need to give us a twenty-minute head start, and it's important that you drive slowly. We don't want you to show up until everything is over."

"You mean, if there's anything taking place," Eiselmann said, his eyes darting from Tom then to his wife and back to Tom.

"Well, yeah. Right." Albrecht smiled weakly at Sarah.

■　　■　　■

Eiselmann heard the ambulance coming and as a precaution, pulled over and waited to let it get by. It only made him more anxious. He needed to get there.

"I hope no one got hurt," Sarah said because she needed something to say. She knew someone must have because of the ambulance. She didn't know how badly.

Eiselmann, his jaw clenched, hands white-knuckled on the steering wheel, nodded once.

He drove to the front of the house and parked across the street. On their front lawn was a dark lump covered in a sheet. Blood, the color of chocolate syrup in the dark, had seeped through. Two policemen stood near it. One of them had a pad and wrote notes as they spoke to a policewoman. She was short and blond. Ronnie Desotel stood off to the side. Knowing he would have to give a preliminary statement just as Vickers was doing.

Sarah assumed the body under the sheet belonged to the person who was after Paul. Behind them sitting partly on the grass but mostly on the sidewalk sat Alexis White cradling her pit. Tears streamed down her face.

Sarah got out of the car and ran to her.

"Alexis, are you okay? Did you get hurt?"

Amy Ivory came up the sidewalk at a half-jog, half-walk, and knelt down beside Alexis and held her. She whispered quietly to her friend.

Jorgenson, the big red-headed cop, jogged up, surveyed Sarah and the two ladies, then opened the driver-side door to let Paul out.

Neighbors had begun gathering in small groups in front of houses, in driveways, or behind windows.

Not sure what to do, Sarah turned back to the car, but Paul was gone and so was Jorgy. Probably to the house or driveway, now full of cops milling around, talking in small groups. Three paramedics huddled over their car. One was inside of it. One of the three held a clipboard or something and wrote down whatever it was one of the medics said to him. A fourth pushed a gurney from the ambulance towards them. It looked like an IV was started.

Some of the cops seemed unable to look away, while others seemed not to be able to look at all. Same with the cops on the front lawn near the body under the sheet. None of them even glanced at the dead body.

Sarah saw Paul embracing Brooke. No sign of Alex Jorgenson. No sign of Tom Albrecht. She lifted a hand to her mouth. She knew who the medics were working on. That would have been Paul if they hadn't exchanged cars.

Sarah walked over to Paul and Brooke and asked, "Brooke, are you okay?"

Brooke's eyes were red and streaks of mascara were on her cheeks along with a smear of blood. Hers or Toms? Sarah couldn't tell. There was blood on her hands, on her blouse and slacks, and on the jacket Sarah had exchanged with her. There was no way Sarah would ever wear it again, regardless of how well it was cleaned.

Brooke nodded, but her face crumbled for another run.

Sarah walked Brooke down the driveway away from the car and away from Albrecht. Brooke went reluctantly, glancing over her shoulder every other step.

Amy Ivory and Alexis White stood across the street. Sarah knew they wanted to help as much as they wanted to know what had happened. She lifted a hand in a small wave and nodded. What else could she do?

A detective, Carlos Lorenzo, walked up to them. Sarah knew him from the wedding and from a couple of parties at their house.

"Sarah, Brooke, are you both okay? Are you hurt?"

Sarah shook her head.

Brooke rallied like the professional she was, and said, "I'm fine. Who is going to take my statement?"

Lorenzo hesitated and then said, "You up for it? You can wait if you want to."

"Let's get it over with."

CHAPTER THIRTY-NINE

There were no clouds in the nighttime sky, so the evening had cooled down considerably. Cool enough for he and Two to sleep in shorts and t-shirts with a sheet and a light blanket over them. Probably because of the cottage's proximity to the lake, George thought the air felt damp, which increased the chill.

Two started out on his back. He shifted to his side facing George, and then onto his stomach, his face still facing George. The entire time and with each turn, his eyes were wide open.

George said with his eyes closed, "Would you be more comfortable sleeping with Brian?"

"No. We're getting up before Bri and Brett are."

There was enough hesitation before Two answered to tell George the truth about where and with whom Two would rather sleep.

"Those guys we saw in the woods. What happens if we see them tomorrow?"

George reached out and playfully tugged Two's nose. "I won't let anything happen to you."

"But we don't hunt together. What happens if they spot me when I'm by myself? Or you?"

George smiled, trying to reassure his half-brother. There were times George felt he was looking into a mirror. The similarity between Two and him was amazing. Two also reminded George of his deceased brother, William. That memory tugged at his heart. He had never been able to make amends with his younger sibling. Perhaps he could have a do over with Two.

He said, "It is a big forest. We'll be okay."

Two stared at George, his face screwed in thought. George wasn't sure if it was fear or a question. He decided it might be both.

"In Crivitz, why did they do that to me?"

George sighed and said, "Because we're different."

Two expected more.

"I've lived in Wisconsin for a couple of years now. There are prejudiced people everywhere, just as there are good people everywhere."

He thought back to the trip to Arizona and how he, Two, Brian and Brett almost died on a mesa on the Navajo Nation Reservation.

"We had some of that on our land in *Diné Bikéyah* but there were more of us than there were of them. In Wisconsin, especially up here in the north, there are more of them. They don't like change. They don't like people who are different from them."

"But I didn't do anything to them. They don't even know me," Two whispered.

George smiled at him and said, "Men like that don't want to get to know you, and they don't care if you did anything to them or not. They see us, the *Dine'* and all Native Americans as outsiders who threaten their way of life. They see blacks and Latinos the same as they see us. All of us are outsiders. We aren't the same as they are. They see what they see and know, and they don't want to see or know anything different."

Two rolled onto his back and stared at the ceiling. He pulled the sheet up to his neck.

George thought that might be the end of it. He wasn't sure if they should hunt together or separately. He liked their placements, thinking they were ideal for hunting deer. But perhaps, they should move closer to the lake.

An added benefit to moving closer to the lake would give him an opportunity to see who was lying in the grass behind the shrubs facing the lake. He didn't want to put Two in danger, but he was curious.

Something was wrong about it. It didn't feel right. The position was wrong. He could understand if whoever it was faced the woods, and maybe he was, but was curious about the guys in Brian's boat so he turned around. But why did it look as if he were hiding from them? Why didn't he show himself or wave or say hello? It felt wrong.

He would decide in the morning.

Two turned his head towards George and said, "I hope they don't see us if they hunt tomorrow."

George didn't know what else he could say, so he said nothing. He wished for perhaps the hundredth time that he had the wisdom of Brian or Randy, or the ability to come up with a wisecrack like Billy. They would know what to say.

Instead, he reached out and rested his arm across Two's chest, hoping that would be enough.

CHAPTER FORTY

Sarah sat at the kitchen table. She held a full mug of coffee, now cold to the touch. She stared somewhere off in the distance, though to look at her, you would have thought she studied the dark of the backyard. She had not been invited into the office, and she didn't expect to be. Sarah knew it was fifty-fifty proposition that Paul would share with her what was going on in that room.

Brooke rode in the ambulance with Albrecht. The last Sarah knew was that Tom had not regained consciousness and was in bad shape. Word travels quickly in the city, Sarah knew, so she wasn't surprised when Jennifer Erickson had phoned. Jennifer offered to drive over with or without Mark to be with her, but because of the number of cops in the house, Sarah told her she'd be okay. It was a lie and both knew it. There was no way she would ever be okay after what went on in their driveway and front lawn. Jennifer even offered to pick her up. Sarah could camp out at their house for as long as she needed. Sarah almost gave in, but declined. She didn't want Paul to be by himself.

She had given Brooke back her own jacket. Brooke had apologized for the blood on Sarah's jacket and had offered to have it dry-cleaned for her, but Sarah shook her head and told her it wasn't a bother. After Brooke had left, Sarah cleaned out the pockets and stuffed it in the garbage can in the garage.

All she kept thinking was that she was relieved neither Stephen nor Alex were home when the shooting started. They didn't need that. Hell, she didn't need it, and neither did Paul. She wondered if she should call them just to let them know she and Paul were safe. Part of her wanted them to be with her. The other part didn't want to ruin their evening with their friends. She'd think about that.

Sarah always had known, at least in the deepest, darkest recesses of her being that Paul's job could lead to something like this. But to have it played out before her made it all too real. The danger. The death. Thankfully, it wasn't Paul being whisked away in the back of an ambulance with lights blazing and siren blaring. She felt guilty about that, not wishing anything bad to happen to Tom or anyone else. Not at all. She was just happy it wasn't Paul.

A tear trickled down her cheek followed by more.

Fear. Anger. Sadness. Helplessness. Each fighting for its turn. Each fighting for attention. Sarah tried to stave them off, but it was no use. She didn't know which one would be declared the winner. Short-term, fear seemed to be winning. Long-term, who knew?

Tom and Paul were close. Not as close as Paul was to Pat O'Connor, but still close. She had come to understand that as a group, they were brothers of sorts. Paul, Tom, Brooke, the others in the room. Pat and Jamie off fishing somewhere up north. She wondered if they knew.

Sarah shivered. She wrapped her arms around herself.

How could another human being shoot another? How? Why? How could someone think that was okay? What pushed another human being to think it was okay to take another's life?

Sarah got up and emptied the mug of cold coffee, rinsed it, and set it in the dishwasher. She leaned against the counter, arms folded, and stared out the window above the sink. Nothing but darkness. A moon and some stars. Nothing she hadn't seen before, but she somehow saw it all differently. She saw many things differently. Nothing would ever be the same. Nothing.

CHAPTER FORTY-ONE

"Dasha Gogol. Age thirty-one. Ukrainian. Came to the U.S. within the last three or four years, though it's unclear exactly when she arrived," Gonnering said reading from his cell. "She currently lives in Chicago."

"She has dual citizenship," Lorenzo added. "U.S. and Ukraine."

It was a small gathering in Eiselmann's home office. Detectives Greg Gonnering and Carlos Lorenzo, who ran the case, did most of the talking. Sheriff Detective Ronnie Desotel, Detective Alex Jorgenson, Patrolwoman Lisa Vickers, and Sheriff Detective Nate Kaupert stood by listening. Desotel, Kaupert, and especially Eiselmann would rather have been at the hospital with Albrecht.

Police Chief Jack O'Brien joined them by phone. "Mr. Clean," as he was referred to out of earshot, of course, was all business. He received the moniker from the animated pitchman for the household cleaner. He shared not only the same bald look, but essentially the same characteristics as the animated character. His smile, if you could call it that, scared most everyone.

Eiselmann was not technically allowed to participate because he had been the intended victim. But because he was undercover with O'Connor in Chicago, he needed to be involved. Their Chicago case led to this. However, no one spoke directly to him, and at this point, Paul only listened.

Lorenzo added, "She drove an Enterprise rental. It took some time, but we found her car in the parking lot. Once the crime scene techs finished the scene at Eiselmann's house, they drove over, took a cursory look, and arranged for towing back to the station so they can work it up proper."

"What about a cell phone or laptop?"

"For now, safely stored in evidence at the station, along with the cells and laptops of Sasha Bakay and Misha Danilenko, the two hitmen . . ." Gonnering started to say.

"*Alleged* hitmen," Vickers corrected.

"Yes, *alleged* hitmen . . . the dead guys in the lot off Saylesville Road and River Road" Gonnering answered. "We're transporting all the electronics to the FBI in Milwaukee so they can begin the forensic work on them."

Eiselmann frowned. Normally, he'd be the one doing the forensic work, but because of his involvement in the case, it was decided someone else should. They didn't want to muddy the waters.

"Is there anything, ballistics, fingerprints, that would tie her into what took place in the lot off Saylesville Road?"

Gonnering spoke. "Too early to say, Sir, but in the rental under the driver's seat was an extra passport, and credit cards made out in different names up."

"So, we were dealing with a professional. Is there enough to tie her in to what Pat and Paul were working on in Chicago?" O'Brien asked.

All eyes turned to Eiselmann, expecting him to answer.

"There might be, depending upon what the forensics guy finds out. But I want to run it by Kelliher and Storm first."

There was a bit of uncomfortable silence and then O'Brien asked, *"Is there something you're not telling me?"*

Eiselmann was employed by the county. His boss was Myron Wagner, the fat, tired Sheriff, who had broadcast that he was looking forward to retirement. That was good, because there wasn't anyone on this earth who was lazier. Technically, however, he out-ranked O'Brien. Still, he had always deferred to him and in this case, would probably do the same.

As it was, Paul didn't need to share anything with O'Brien. However, while the county was large, there was a great and productive working relationship between the Waukesha City Police and the Waukesha County Sheriff department. Eiselmann didn't want to do or say anything that might cause a rift.

"Sir, I would rather not say anything yet. That is, once I get word back from the Milwaukee office, I want to run that and something else by Kelliher and Storm first, and then the next phone call I make will be to you. You have my word on that."

Another bit of silence before O'Brien said, *"Your word has always been good with me. I trust you."*

"Thank you, Sir."

"I know you have a prior working relationship with Kelliher and Storm. Still, they're pretty high up on the food chain, so I suspect that whatever you are going to talk to the FBI about, you are shielding our investigation. You don't have to confirm or deny that. It's just a suspicion."

"Um . . ."

"I said that you don't have to confirm or deny. I trust you."

"Thank you."

"Do you know who from the Milwaukee office is going to do the forensics on the electronics?"

Again, eyes shifted to Eiselmann, but it was Gonnering who answered.

"We don't have an answer to that. If we were to keep it local, Paul would have been the logical choice. He's the best at it, but because he was the intended vic, we didn't think it was proper for him to be involved." He added, "That closely."

"Probably not. Sorry, Paul. When you speak to Kelliher and Storm, see if they can spring someone loose. That skinny, white kid. Dahlke, maybe. If, perhaps, you can look over the shoulders of the tech in Milwaukee and Dahlke, I don't think that would be too risky."

Everyone knew what O'Brien meant about the 'white kid' comment. Dahlke was pale as pale can be without being transparent. Talcum powder white. Nothing racial was intended or implied.

"Is there anything else you have? Anything else I need to know?"

Gonnering and Lorenzo stared at each other and it was Lorenzo who spoke. "Sir, we don't have preliminary ballistics back yet. We sent them off to Milwaukee and asked for a rush on it, given that a cop was shot. We need to compare those slugs to the guns in Gogol's possession."

"We should get preliminary ballistics back sometime in the morning, maybe sometime tonight," Gonnering said. "That will tell us for sure."

"I will make a call and see if I can light a fire up somebody's ass."

No one standing in that office had any doubt about O'Brien's ability to light a fire. Or set someone on fire if it came to that.

"Sir, about the cell phones," Eiselmann said. "We know from the case in Chicago that Andruko demanded that burner phones be exchanged every five days. The change out normally takes place on Friday. That's today. We don't know anything about Gogol, but we know that Bakay and Danilenko would have changed out their phones before they came to Waukesha."

"Or they could be behind because they were on the road."

"That's possible, Chief, but unlikely. Andruko would kill them himself if they didn't change out. My best hunch, and yes, it is only a hunch, is that whoever called them, and Gogol, would have their numbers in the burner phones. We need to get into them quickly, before Andruko finds out they're dead or missing."

"Let me make a phone call to Milwaukee and see if I can shake someone loose. I still want you to ask Kelliher to send the kid here to help out."

Eiselmann bit the inside of his cheek. Getting Dahlke out here was a great idea, but it would take too much time. They didn't have time.

Kaupert snuck a glance at him and then turned his head. Vickers stared at her shoes. Jorgenson turned in a tight three-sixty and then flapped his long arms before crossing them on his chest. His face matched his red hair.

"One other thing," Gonnering said. He took a deep breath before he plunged on. "Sir, looking at the wounds on Bakay and Danilenko, and looking at the weapons found in Gogol's possession including her vehicle, we don't think she was their killer. Ike confirmed it as much as he could. Off the record."

The county medical examiner, Mike Eisenhower, whom everyone called, Ike, was in his sixties and bald except for a fringe of snow-white hair that ran around the sides and back of his head like a misplaced halo. He was short and a little stooped, but his mind was clear and sharp.

Gonnering continued. "Again, it's a guess, and we don't . . . *won't* . . . know for sure until we get ballistics back."

"Fuck me," Desotel muttered. He caught himself and quickly said, "Excuse me, Chief."

"Fuck us all," O'Brien said. *"If this bitch wasn't the one who shot them, that means there's someone else out there."*

Gonnering cleared his throat and said, "We think so. We think that person might be after O'Connor."

"This is not getting any easier."

Before any of them responded, O'Brien said as if he was thinking out loud, *"Noah's Ark. They travel by two. One after Eiselmann and the other after O'Connor. How much do Pat and Jamie know?"*

After an uncomfortable silence, Lorenzo said, "We've not been able to reach them, Sir. They're in the middle of nowhere and cell service is spotty up there."

"They do know that someone was after either him or Eiselmann," Gonnering said. "Paul and I had a conversation with both of them earlier today. But they don't know what happened this evening."

"I was going to pick Pat up in the morning," Jorgy said. "He told me he didn't want to put the kids or Jamie in danger."

"The kids? Jeremy's kids? JESUS CHRIST! There is no fucking way those kids are going to be put through anymore shit! Is that understood?"

"Yessir," was repeated by everyone in the room.

"Alright, goddammit, here's what we're going to do . . ."

CHAPTER FORTY-TWO

Sarah and Paul spoke to each other in short, clipped sentences. More unsaid then said. She couldn't help being angry. If the two of them had been in their car instead of Albrecht and Beranger, Paul would be in the hospital bed fighting for his life instead of Tom, and she'd be there holding his hand instead of Brooke. Worse, if Stephen and Alexandra were home and if that shooter had gotten into their house and did something to them, she couldn't finish the thought.

"Jennifer and Mark offered to come pick me up and bring me to their house. At first, I declined. I decided to take them up on their offer. I'm spending the night there. I'll see you sometime in the morning. I'm not sure when. I'll pick up Stephen and Alex."

"I understand," Paul said meekly.

"The hell you do!" she shouted. She regained her calm and said, "You don't understand. She waited outside our house. If Stephen and Alex were home . . ." She closed her eyes and shook her head, and said, "So please, don't give me any crap that you understand. You don't!"

"I . . ." he caught himself and shut his mouth, not wanting to repeat it.

She was right. He didn't understand. He was a cop for so long and a bachelor for even longer that he didn't understand the role of husband, much less the role of being a dad. He tried. He loved her and he loved the kids. He wouldn't hesitate to give his life for them. But Sarah was right. He didn't understand.

He ignored his cell vibrating in his back pocket. He was pretty sure Sarah had heard it.

"Are you going to the hospital?" Sarah asked.

"Eventually. I'm waiting for ballistics on her gun, and the forensic work on her cell and laptop."

She frowned at him and said, "You usually do that," Sarah said.

"Usually, but I can't be directly involved this time." He didn't want to elaborate because that would be like poking the not so invisible beast that sat between them.

She nodded at him and said, "Is that what that phone call is?"

He tried to shrug it off, but couldn't hide his anxiousness. "Or an update on Tom."

"Better answer it," she said as she walked past him out of the kitchen.

CHAPTER FORTY-THREE

It was an uncomfortable goodbye when Mark and Jennifer came to pick up Sarah. As Sarah kissed him, it looked to Paul as if she had wanted to say something. He wished she had. Instead, she turned and left. He waved, she waved, and he shut the door. He stood staring at it for quite a while before he went into his office. He dialed up a three-way video conference call on Zoom that included Dahlke, somewhere in the sky headed towards Milwaukee at Kelliher's request, and Gordon Pasquale in Milwaukee.

"What program are you using on the laptop?" Dahlke asked.

Pasquale was a man with black bushy Leonid Brezhnev eyebrows that made him look older than his thirty-three years. He had thick black unruly hair that matched his eyebrows. Eiselmann wondered quietly if the guy used a plastic pocket protector.

"I'm using Ophcrack Live CD," Pasquale explained. "I cloned her computer first, so I'm just working on the clone. I don't want to mess up the original."

"What about the cell phones? You did an nslookup?" Eiselmann asked.

Pasquale sighed. Their questions slowed him down. He didn't mind them observing, especially given the circumstances.

He looked up from Dasha Gogol's laptop, stared at the split screen on the Zoom call and said, "Guys, I graduated top five from MIT. I know what the hell I'm doing."

Eiselmann cleared his throat and said, "Sorry. I'm just anxious."

"So am I. I'm nearly done, but you're slowing me down, so let me work and save the questions. When I'm done, you'll be the first to know."

When Pasquale turned his head and punched keys on a keyboard, Dahlke and Eiselmann exchanged a look.

"I saw that," Pasquale said, still typing away on the keyboard.

He hadn't looked up, so neither Eiselmann nor Dahlke knew how he could have seen anything. They watched and waited impatiently, but they kept their questions and comments to themselves.

After another twenty minutes, Pasquale stopped typing, took off his glasses and rubbed his eyes.

"Okay, here's what I found," he said through a yawn. "She's not particularly good with computers or codes. Her laptop is password protected, but like most of the uneducated world, it was her birthdate. Two-digit month, two-digit day, and four-digit year. Nothing sophisticated. Maybe she figured no one would know when she was born." This last he said with a shrug and another yawn.

"She does online banking with two different banks. Bank of America and First Midwest Bank. B of A is used like you or I would use it. Her mortgage on a townhouse in Buffalo Grove and rent on an apartment in Manhattan. There are deposits each month that come in from Ukraine. Boring stuff. More routine. Like you might find in my account or yours.

"What kind of deposits?" Eiselmann asked.

Pasquale shook his head and said, "From a bank. Oschadbank. Not sure what kind of bank that is, or who or what is behind it. You'd have to dig into that bank to find out."

"I'll let Kelliher know," Dahlke said as he jotted a note.

"Sporadically, she transfers money from her First Midwest account. Money in the Midwest account comes in from an import-export business. Eastern Europe Exchange."

"That's Andruko's company," Eiselmann said.

Pasquale shrugged and said, "That's not one of the names or numbers I found on her cell."

"No, but that's Andruko's company. I'm guessing one of the numbers in her phone belong to Oleg Klyuka."

"Yes. He's in her contact list. In fact, there was one call as recent as six-thirty-four this evening."

"James," Eiselmann said addressing Dahlke, "Billias phoned me when Sarah and I were at dinner. This is the phone call he referred to."

"Who's Billias?" Pasquale asked.

"No one," Dahlke said. "You never heard that name. Understood?"

Pasquale shrugged, the expression on his face indicated he was miffed at not being included. He plowed on.

"Her browsing history shows she canvasses the classifieds a great deal. Sixty-five percent of her browsing time is spent in the Chicago Tribune Classified section. I can't tell what she was looking at specifically. That will take time, but I'm on it, unless one of you want to take that on."

Neither Eiselmann nor Dahlke volunteered, so Pasquale shrugged and said, "Okay, I guess I'll do it."

"About the cell, can you print out numbers called or numbers from calls she received?" Eiselmann asked.

"I'll download them and send them to you both in an email. I will include the burner as well. Of course, I don't have names associated with numbers on that one. But some do match her iPhone."

"Before we sign off, is there anything else you can share right off the top of your head?" Dahlke asked.

Pasquale shook his head and said, "No, nothing I can think of."

"Thank you for your help tonight. I know it was a rush, but I want you to know we appreciate it," Eiselmann said.

"No problem. Any word on the deputy who was shot?"

Eiselmann sighed and said, "Still in surgery. I'm told that the next twenty-four hours will be crucial."

"Paul, I will land in Milwaukee in about an hour. I have reservations at the Holiday Inn Express on Bluemound. You have my number if you need anything," Dahlke said. To Pasquale, he said, "And thank you for your help. You have my number, so don't hesitate to use it."

He looked and sounded exhausted. Lines on his forehead and around his eyes pronounced. Eiselmann hadn't remembered that about him.

"Oh guys, one more thing," Pasquale said. "The ballistics came back on both shootings. She was not the shooter in the death of the two men from earlier this evening. Definitely not." He paused and clarified, "Unless she had an opportunity to dispose of the weapon that was used.

But the weapons that were on her or in her vehicle were not the ones used before the shooting of your deputy."

Eiselmann shut his eyes wanting to hear anything but that.

"I know that's not what you had hoped for."

"No, not at all. It means that we have another shooter out there. I have some calls to make."

CHAPTER FORTY-FOUR

Brian liked sleeping in his own bed. He could sleep anywhere, but he didn't like it. He never minded sleeping with someone, whether it was Two or Brett, Billy or Bobby, or most recently, Mikey. What he didn't like was sleeping alone, and no matter who he slept with, he didn't like sleeping anywhere other than his own bed.

Brett was out. His cheek rested on Brian's shoulder. One of his heavy, muscular legs lay across Brian's leg, and Brett's arm rested across Brian's chest. It was the way Brett always slept. Didn't matter where and it didn't matter with whom.

Tired, but thirsty, Brian slowly and quietly eased himself out from under Brett and left the warmth of the bed. He pulled on a sweatshirt, and after making sure Brett was covered up, he padded softly out of the room. His first stop was the bathroom where he peed, flushed, and washed his hands.

Before leaving, he stared at himself in the mirror. It didn't matter how often someone told him it gave him character, he hated the scar around his eye. He didn't like the drops he had to put into his eyes each morning and each night, and he didn't like the glasses he wore during the day.

He also didn't like the small patch of white-blond hair growing out of the side of his head where another scar lay hidden under his normally black hair. That was a recent development that occurred over the past month. His friends thought it looked interesting. Billy suggested that he could dye it. Randy told him he never notices it. Brian pursed his lips.

Randy didn't lie well. He never could, and that was something he and Brian shared. Probably why he liked Randy so much.

With a sigh, Brian left the bathroom and tiptoed into the kitchen. He found a glass and filled it from the large bottle of water on the stand in the corner near the refrigerator. He drank it down in four gulps, and then wiped his mouth on the sleeve of his sweatshirt.

He spotted the Oreos on the counter. He pulled out a plate from the cupboard. He popped one of the Oreos into his mouth and placed five others onto the plate. He opened the refrigerator, took out the milk and filled his glass. Bobby would not have been happy with him because of the refined sugar thing, but Randy would have joined him.

Brian smiled and carried the glass of milk and the plate of cookies into the living room and sat on the couch facing the empty fireplace. He set the glass and plate on the table, grabbed a blanket from the back of the couch, covered his legs with it, and began dunking and then eating the cookies.

He had managed to dunk and swallow two before he nearly pissed himself.

"Are you going to share?"

Brian jumped. A splash of milk landed on the blanket and the remaining cookies fell off the plate, one falling onto the floor.

"Jesus, Pat!" Brian hissed. "I never saw you."

"Shhh, don't wake everyone up," O'Connor whispered with a chuckle.

"What are you doing up?"

O'Connor sat in the dark corner in a stuffed chair that didn't look comfortable. Probably why he chose it, Brian thought. Pat stretched his legs out in front of him, placing them on the little ottoman that matched the chair.

Once his eyes adjusted to the dark, Brian noticed that O'Connor had never changed out of the clothes he had worn that day. He also noticed that O'Connor gripped his Beretta, but kept it on his thigh. His finger was off the trigger.

"I don't sleep much."

"You scared the shit out of me," Brian whispered.

"You were too into your milk and cookies to notice me." He chuckled, and knowing the semi-constant haranguing Bobby gave him about eating too many sweets, especially cookies, he said, "What would Bobby say?"

Brian grinned and said, "He's not here. What happens when we hunt stays where we hunt."

He popped a cookie into his mouth, chewed it, swallowed and smiled at O'Connor.

"If you're ever on a date, don't eat Oreos. Your teeth look disgusting."

"You're a shit," Brian laughed. "Seriously, what are you doing up?"

"When I'm on the job, I don't sleep much."

"You're on vacation," Brian retorted.

"I might be on vacation, but I'm still on the job."

Brian shook his head and said, "Your job sucks."

O'Connor smiled, yawned, and then said, "Someone's gotta do it."

"Sure as hell won't be me."

O'Connor chuckled and said, "Never figured you to be a cop. No way."

Somewhat offended, Brian said, "Why not?"

"Because you have too good a heart. You do the things I've done, you end up with the things I've got. It changes you. I don't wish that on anyone, especially you."

"But you help people. Those guys in California. You and Paul freed them. You helped us in Arizona. You were there the day my brother was shot and killed."

O'Connor sighed, scratched his arm with his gun still in hand and said, "But I couldn't save him, Bri. I'm sorry about that."

Brian took a gulp of milk after the last cookie disappeared, and he set the glass on the plate, the plate on the table, and tucked his feet under him.

"I don't think anyone could have. It all happened so fast. He died in Big Gav's arms. Did you know that?"

O'Connor nodded.

"If Bobby wouldn't have sprinted to the field and tackled Mario and Cem, they would have died too. I'm surprised more weren't killed." He shrugged and said, "Me."

He looked off into the darkness of the cabin and said in a soft voice, "Besides, I've done some pretty serious shit too."

"In self-defense. Bri, if you hadn't done what you did, you wouldn't be sitting here talking to me, and George, Brett, and probably Two wouldn't be around, either. You did what you had to do."

Brian shrugged and looked away, unable to make eye contact.

O'Connor noticed that neither of Brian's hands shook. That surprised him, given what they were talking about.

"Are you okay, Brian? With everything? Are you happy?"

Brian shrugged and said, "Mostly."

O'Connor waited.

"Mostly," Brian repeated.

"You and your dad are in a rough patch."

Brian shrugged, his chin ending up on his chest, and it had nothing to do with being tired.

He almost told O'Connor about the conversation he overheard Jeremy having with Two and Brett.

He was going to go into the study to use the computer to print off a paper he had written, but stopped when he heard Jeremy.

"I want to ask you a question. I know you are close to Brian."

That statement caused Brian to slow down. Brett had been ahead of him heading to the study, unaware that Brian was behind him. Brett must have heard Jeremy. Brian sped up to listen more closely.

"I love him, Dad," Brett said as he walked in.

"Me, too," Two said. *"He's a cool big brother. I never had one."*

"Yeah, but now you have six," Brett said with a laugh.

"I know you both love Brian. I don't want to make either of you uncomfortable, but have either of you done anything sexual with him? You know, experimenting like he and Bobby have done?"

Brett, whose temper could reach a flash point in seconds said, *"The answer to that is no. I love Brian, and honestly, if he wanted to do anything with me, I wouldn't hesitate. Not for a second. I've even hinted at it. But he turned me down."*

"Are you serious?" Two has asked Brett. Then he must have turned to Jeremy, and said, *"I haven't done anything with him and he's done nothing with me."*

"We're done," Brett had said. *"Come on, Two. And one more thing, Dad. Brian and Bobby love each other. They still do. Brian loves Bobby. He*

always will. What they've done and whatever they might do in the future is out of love. There isn't anything wrong with that."

They must have started out of the room when they stopped talking. Brian retreated down the hallway, but he did hear Brett say, *"You talk about wanting Brian to trust you. It's pretty obvious that you don't trust him."*

"Brett..."

"You don't. Bri already feels that you don't love him. He doesn't think you like him all that much, either. How could you, if you can't trust him?"

Brian had made it to the family room doorway and made it look like he was just coming out of that room.

Neither Brett nor Two had ever mentioned that conversation, but it was a conversation Brian would never forget.

O'Connor watched Brian struggle. He could almost hear the gears turning in his head.

"What are you thinking about?"

Brian shook his head, and said, "Dad and I will work it out." He said it, but he didn't necessarily believe it. And if he did, he understood it would take considerable time.

"I hope so. He loves you, Bri."

Brian snorted. He couldn't help it.

"Don't doubt that."

Brian shook his head, not willing to talk about it any further.

O'Connor didn't want to get into it right then and there, but he'd circle back to it at some point. He changed subjects and said, "I stand by what I said. You wouldn't make a good cop because you have too good a heart. I know Brett wants to be a doctor, and that's a good choice for him. He's so damn smart. I worry about George and Two. They're thinking of going into law enforcement. Both of them, and you and Brett, have been involved with too much. You've seen too much. Jamie, Paul and I want you to be kids, to grow up slowly, and not be involved in the crap we've. . . *I've* been involved with."

Brian shrugged and said, "Too late for that."

O'Connor leaned forward and set his Berretta on the ottoman and said, "If I could take it all back, I would. If there was a way to go back and make sure you guys didn't have to do what you had to do, I would do it in a heartbeat."

"Had to do?" Brian shook his head.

"Yes, had to do. Bri, think back to that psycho asshat in your woods last winter. If you wouldn't have stopped him, he might have gotten into your house and who knows what he would have done."

Brian shrugged.

"But I want you to remember something, and this is important." He paused, stared intently at Brian and said, "Instead of killing him, you wounded him." He repeated, "You wounded him, but you didn't kill him. You made a decision, a choice to spare him."

Brian brushed a tear off his cheek and said, "But in Arizona . . ."

O'Connor didn't let him finish. He said, "You made another choice. That choice was just as good and necessary as the decision you made in the woods. You protected Brett, George, and Two. You protected yourself. If you hadn't made that choice, the four of you wouldn't be here. I'd be talking to a ghost."

"But maybe I didn't have to kill them. Those two men." Brian stopped, shook his head, and looked away from O'Connor, then turned back and said, "I watched them die. I shot them."

"And Brian, if you wouldn't have, Brett, George, Two, and you would be dead. Graff, the FBI, and I are absolutely certain of it. Those men had murdered many others before they came after you. They had rap sheets the length of your leg. They were criminals. They came to kill you, and you stopped them before they could. And, look at you. The scars you have. The glasses you have to wear. The drops you have to put in your eyes. You know if you hadn't shot them, they would have killed you, Brett, George and Two."

To O'Connor, even in the dark, and in the shadows of the living room, the look on Brian's face was at least neutral, if not hopeful.

"Brett and George told Graff and me what happened at the Morning Star ranch. They told us that you had covered them. Again, protecting your brothers."

He paused to let that sink in.

"Up on that mesa, you purposely hid Brett behind that boulder, didn't you?"

Brian nodded.

"You deliberately sent Two with Rebecca because you didn't want him up on that mesa with you guys, didn't you?"

Brian nodded again.

"And you purposely passed up water so Brett and George could have more. You put yourself in jeopardy of dehydration to keep Brett and George safe."

Brian shrugged.

"I stand by what I said. Brian Evans, you have a good heart. You don't deserve the crap that you went through this past year or two. None of you do. But especially you. I believe that with all my heart."

"Thanks." It came out as a whisper. A bit choked, but out it came.

"Bri, I love you. I love you and George and Brett as if you were my own sons. I'm jealous of Jeremy and Vicky. You three are special to me. I'm not saying that your other brothers aren't. It's just that I spend more time with you guys, so I know you better."

Brian smiled and said, "Michael is pretty special."

"Two worships the ground you walk on, Bri. Watching the two of you together is special. Not quite like it is between you and Bobby, but the relationship you have with Two is special."

Fear flashed in Brian's eyes and he said, "Pat, Michael and I . . . we don't . . . we never-"

"Shit, Bri, I know that. Everyone knows that. You're Two's big brother. That's all I meant."

Brian relaxed, but glanced at O'Connor furtively.

"Hey, you and Bobby had a special relationship. I hope someday, you two will again. I have nothing but love and respect for both of you. Believe that."

"You don't think it's weird?"

"I don't necessarily understand it because I'm not wired that way. But I know one thing. Love is never weird, Bri. Never."

Brian didn't know what to say to that. It was different talking to the Doc about stuff. Brian didn't know him and he wasn't friends with him. O'Connor was a friend, so it was harder.

"So, I'm going to ask you again. Are you okay?"

Brian sighed, thought for a minute, and said, "I'm getting there." He smiled, lifted up both hands at O'Connor and said, "No shakes."

O'Connor smiled at him and said, "That's a start."

CHAPTER FORTY-FIVE

The morning sun was still asleep and wouldn't wake up for at least an hour, if not longer. The forest was damp from dew, and the air had a chill to it. Two could see his breath in little puffs each time he exhaled. Fog or mist covered the lake and parts of the shore. Like dead fingers, it reached into the forest. Pretty, he thought.

As George had stated, they had moved closer to the lake. As they walked in, they repeated the process using deer urine on a sponge and dragging it as they walked.

He had dressed comfortably in layers, so the chill didn't bother him. George was a hundred yards off to the north and closer to the lake. At least, that's where George said he'd be. He also said he would check on him every thirty to forty minutes. Two had told him that he might scare deer away, but George said he'd be quiet.

Before he had left, he told Two not to worry, but George knew his step-brother would anyway.

Two knew what he had meant. He wasn't talking about scaring deer away. George had meant for him to not worry about those men from Crivitz.

Two couldn't help it. He had never encountered that on the reservation. In the time he had lived in Wisconsin, he hadn't encountered that until this hunting trip. It had unnerved him. He didn't think it was right or just or fair.

Given most situations or circumstances, Two could take care of himself. In his past life of selling drugs and turning tricks for travelers visiting the Navajo Nation Reservation, there had been threats of violence by those who would try to take advantage of him. He had always found a way to turn the tables on them or at least, get even.

He had never been hurt other than slapped around. It came with the territory, and he understood that. He was tough that way. At least on the outside.

Two was happy to never have to live that life again. He had never talked about it except with Brett, and even then, it was one time and never brought up again. Not by either of them. He had wanted to talk to Brian about it because Brian was important to him. At the same time, telling Brian would be embarrassing, and he didn't want Brian to think less of him. Maybe some time. He wasn't ready yet.

As far as Two was concerned, he had a new life, a new opportunity, and he wasn't looking back.

Moving to Wisconsin was scary. He didn't know any of the brothers, even though he had spent time with Brett, Brian, and George. He didn't know what to expect. The only kind of father he had was Lou, but Lou had never acted as a father. It was a relationship of convenience. Lou gave him a roof over his head, food on the table, and a job. In exchange, Lou used him and did things with him Two knew no man should ever do to a kid. Certainly not a father. Even at that, Lou never hurt him. There was that, he supposed.

Jeremy was different from Lou, and in a good way. A much better way. He cared, and didn't expect anything in return. And Vicky was different from his real mother. Smart. Pretty. His real mom had died of a drug overdose leaving Two alone in the world to fend for himself.

The home he lived in was different from the little apartment above the diner, with the one bedroom and bed he shared with Lou. In his new home, he could sleep anywhere. Most nights, he slept with Brian. Other nights, with George or Brett. He didn't have his own room, but that was okay with him. He didn't mind sharing. Besides, he wasn't ready to sleep by himself yet. Maybe eventually, but not yet.

Wisconsin was different from Arizona. In Arizona, everything was red dirt and desert. The heat was constant. There were times when the desert cooled down. Sometimes it got cold, but that was a rarity. In Wisconsin, everything was green with so many trees, especially in the north. He had never been to a big city before moving to Wisconsin. He and his family had visited Milwaukee, Madison, and Green Bay. He found each of them interesting.

Like he could on the reservation, he could tell the different seasons in Wisconsin. He had experienced summer, and fall was just beginning. He didn't know anything about winter and the guys had told him he'd freeze. When he looked at George, all George did was smile.

His family went to Brewers, Badger, and Bucks games. He went to a Packer game. He visited parks and went swimming in pools and lakes. Life was different. Safer. Comfortable. He was happy.

He loved his new life, and it wasn't until the encounter in Crivitz that he doubted his life in Wisconsin. It wasn't that he doubted his life because of those men in Crivitz. It was just that now he saw that everywhere, anywhere, there was potential for danger. It opened his eyes, and he didn't know if he liked that.

George told him to be careful, to watch for deer and to relax. George reminded him that hunting was supposed to be fun. Two knew that, of course. Hunting was always fun, whether in Arizona or in Wisconsin.

He needed to pee.

Carefully, he checked his surroundings, searching well into the darkness and into the woods. He listened for any sound that was out of the ordinary.

Nothing, except for his own breathing, his own heartbeat.

He slung his crossbow onto his back and climbed down from the tree where he had placed his stand. He crept about twenty yards to the north, and opened up his pants, pulled down his boxers, and leaned into a tree and peed. He aimed for a low bush, hitting leaves and branches deliberately to cut down on noise.

Finished, he shook himself and was about to pull up his boxers when rough hands grabbed him by his long hair and threw him face first into a tree.

CHAPTER FORTY-SIX

Brian jerked himself awake. He was sweaty and holding his breath. He relaxed a little, enough for him to glance around the darkened room to catch his bearings.

Brett slept undisturbed wearing his normal grimace. A few lines showed on his forehead. To reassure himself as much as to let Brett know all was well, he placed a hand on Brett's arm. It was cold, so he placed it under the sheet and blanket.

Brian couldn't decide if it was a dream or a warning. Maybe both.

He settled down again on his back and glanced at his watch. George would naturally be the person he'd go to about dreams, especially one containing George's grandfather. But George wasn't around. He and Two were off hunting by now somewhere in the forest behind and to the side of the cabin.

What troubled him the most about the dream was that George's grandfather stood in front of him at the foot of the bed. He beckoned to Brian, and that was when he had woken up. Other than George's grandfather standing at the foot of the bed, there was nothing out of the ordinary about his dream, at least that he could remember. Try as he might, he couldn't recall anything about his dream other than George's grandfather beckoning him to follow.

The other thing that troubled him about the dream, and there were several things that troubled him, was that he *knew* it was George's and Michael's grandfather. *Knew* it. He had never met him. He couldn't recall ever seeing him before, whether he was asleep or awake, yet he understood it was George's and Michael's grandfather.

If it was a warning, why hadn't Brad appeared in his dream?

Unless, Brian thought, the dream wasn't about him. Maybe it had something to do with George or Michael. Maybe both.

He pursed his lips as he scratched an itch in his right armpit.

And then there was O'Connor sitting in a chair with his Berretta in his lap. What was that all about?

"What's up?" Brett whispered.

Brian didn't know how long Brett had been awake. It was still an hour or so before either of them had wanted to get up.

"Nothing. Just a dream."

Brett noticed Brian's panting and the sheen of sweat on his upper lip and chest.

"Let me see your hands."

"It wasn't that kind of dream." Brian shook his head, showed both hands to Brett, and said, "It had nothing to do with Arizona or the mesa."

"Oh. Okay then. Tell me about it."

"Not much to it." He shrugged and added, "That I remember, anyway. George's grandfather stood at the foot of the bed. Kind of spooked me. I woke up and looked for him, but he was gone."

"Our bed?" Brett asked a question, but it came out as more of a statement.

"Yeah, this one."

Brett frowned. He didn't know what, if anything, it meant either.

"Did he say anything?"

Brian shook his head. "It didn't look like he was going to, but I woke up and he was gone. Maybe if I hadn't moved, he would have."

"Like what?"

"Shit, Brett, I don't know. Maybe why he was standing at the foot of our bed."

A thought occurred to Brian and he said, "Did you see him? I mean, in your dream?"

Brett yawned, rolled over onto his back and stretched both arms over his head.

"I was having a *good* dream," he said with a wry smile.

Brian lifted the covers and glanced at Brett's shorts. The waistband had lifted way up and his shorts looked like a big top in the circus. There was a damp spot the size of a half-dollar at the peak.

"You have a boner."

"No shit," Brett chuckled.

"You always have a boner."

"Some are better than others."

Brian watched as Brett reached into his shorts, adjusted himself, pull out his hand and wipe it on the sheet.

He said, "Could it be just a dream? I mean, it doesn't have to mean anything in particular, does it?"

Brian shrugged, but just as quickly, shook his head. "It feels like there was some sort of meaning to it. I just don't know what it is. My feeling is that it has something to do with George or Michael. Or both of them."

Brett glanced at his watch and said, "They're gone already. Do you know where they might be hunting?"

"George said he was going to move closer to where those vacant lots are. Closer to the water."

Brett caught the look in Brian's eyes.

"What?"

Brian shook his head.

Brett elbowed him gently in the ribs. When that didn't work, he tugged on a tuft of dark hair in Brian's left armpit. He said, "What?"

Brian sighed, but told him George's story about the man in the tall grass and brush George thought he saw.

Brett leaned up on an elbow and said, "Why didn't either of you say anything to the rest of us?" He wasn't angry. Mostly curious.

"Because George wasn't sure. Exactly. Although he had a pretty good idea."

Brett bounced his finger on Brian's pec. "Why didn't you say anything to me? Or Graff? Or O'Connor? Not telling them stuff got us into a helluva lot of trouble in Arizona."

"I know," Brian said as he ran a hand over his face. "George didn't want me to, because he wasn't sure. He didn't want to spoil the trip."

Brett pushed down the covers and swung his legs out of bed, and stretched. His shorts were propped well out in front of him. Brian couldn't help but stare at him, trying to decide who was bigger, Brett or Bobby. Hard to tell.

"What are you doing?" he asked.

"Getting dressed. We'll go find George and Two and see what's up. Time for us to go fishing anyway."

Brian rolled out of bed on the same side, stepped out of his shorts and bent over his duffle bag in search of clean boxers and socks.

"Bri, come here," Brett said softly.

Brian stood up and faced Brett.

Brett walked over, placed both hands on Brian's shoulders, and said, "Bri, if you want to sit this one out, that's okay. We'll take the boat and drive over to those lots. I'll walk in and see if I can find them. I'll have a conversation with George, see what's what, and I'll come back and tell you."

"No, I'm coming too. I'm okay."

Brett silently stared into Brian's eyes. Brian didn't blink. He didn't flinch. He didn't look away.

"Bri . . ."

"Stop, Brett." He held up both hands and said, "I'm fine." He placed both hands on Brett's hips and said, "We go together or not at all. We'll take both Glocks, mostly because I feel we need to. We don't have much orange, but we'll wear white and bright colors. I'm not interested in getting shot in the ass by someone."

Brett smiled and said, "You know I love you, right?"

Brian smiled and said, "Of course. I love you, too."

As the two boys did often, they rested their foreheads on each other and rubbed noses. Both of them knew how important they were to each other. Nothing needed to be said further.

They dressed silently. Brian wore his red Badger hoodie and a pair of nylon sweats. In one of the closets was an orange vest and an orange hat. They looked relatively clean. Brett gave them a sniff. Shrugged and decided they didn't smell. He offered the hat to Brian who declined.

"I'll wear the red hood."

He put the hat back in the closet, and put on the vest. On his head, he wore his Badger snapback.

They were barely legal for hunting, but it was the best they could do.

"Ready?"

Brian nodded. He was, but at the same time, wasn't.

CHAPTER FORTY-SEVEN

Something wasn't right. He knew it. Though it was still dark and a mist covered the lake and flowed into the forest, the forest was more active than it should have been for that hour. More noise. Nothing big. Small, quiet sounds. Snaps of twigs. Footfalls on the earth, moving in and out of bushes. A voice or two.

It could be hunters moving into position or game moving from a feeding spot to a nesting spot. Perhaps both.

It didn't feel right, so he hunkered down and kept watch.

If anyone came upon him, he looked like any other hunter, minus his high-powered rifle. The tarp could be explained away. He could say he preferred to stay low and wait until deer came to him, rather than climb a tree. It was no one's business what he had in his duffle. He'd just say it was hunting gear and supplies for an extended period of time if anyone asked. He didn't think anyone would.

The gun would be harder to explain. Actually, there would be no plausible explanation. He didn't like loose ends, so if anyone was overly curious, he'd take care of him or her.

Curious enough to make certain his imagination wasn't driving his decisions, he decided to take a look around in a tight radius from his location. As a precaution, he placed the gun in the duffle, and hid the duffle in brush near the tarp. It wouldn't be seen unless someone was searching for it. Or maybe tripped over it.

He kept his semi-automatic pistol and suppressor with him in his shoulder holster. It was loaded with one in the chamber. He believed in being ready. His knife sat on his right hip in its sheath. He didn't wear any of his prosthetics or disguises. It was his natural look. The way he preferred to look when he killed.

Silently, he made his way to where he thought he heard the most noise.

CHAPTER FORTY-EIGHT

His stand was above what looked like a game trail. The time was right for deer to move from feeding to nesting. George could sense it. At least two deer approached, though not close enough nor clear enough for a shot. It was more than hearing them. There were subtle movements in and among the bush.

He told Two he would check on him every thirty minutes. Even though there hadn't been any sign of the men from Crivitz, he didn't want to take the chance.

George froze and stopped himself from climbing down from his stand.

Moving stealthily, slowly from the direction of the lake, was another hunter. At least, George thought he was a hunter, though he didn't have either a longbow or a crossbow. There was no rifle in his arms or over his shoulder. Instead, there was what looked to be a large caliber handgun in a holster under his arm.

He also wasn't dressed in blaze orange, only camo pants and camo baseball cap. His long-sleeved t-shirt was black.

George determined him to be in his thirties, about the same age as O'Connor or Eiselmann, older than Jorgy. Dishwater-blond hair, as he heard his mother describe someone. Even with the jacket he wore, George could tell he was trim and fit. Muscled, like a wide-receiver, but on the shorter side. Not tall. More compact.

All of this ran through George's mind, yet he wasn't sure why he scrutinized the hunter as he did. In a way, the whole scene was odd to

George. The hunter didn't fit. The look was wrong. The hunter's movements were wrong. He might be a hunter, but not someone hunting deer. He was certain of that.

George remained motionless, even holding his breath. The hunter never looked up and never saw him as he passed within ten yards of George's stand. The hunter intent on what was ahead and on either side of him.

He waited until the hunter moved about thirty yards before he descended his stand. Not sure why he did, George readied his crossbow with an arrow, but kept his finger off the trigger.

A chill traced an icy finger up George's spine as the hunter headed towards Two.

CHAPTER FORTY-NINE

O'Connor wasn't in the mood for fishing. He only dozed throughout the night, but never slept. He didn't bother sharing that with Graff, though he figured Jamie suspected as much. He couldn't help staring around the lake, even though the fog made it difficult to see much beyond fifteen or twenty yards.

He'd cast and stare at the shoreline or the lake, reel it in, cast, and stare.

Graff had noticed O'Connor's mood as early as breakfast, but passed it off on Pat not wanting to leave the lake.

"Why are you so edgy?"

O'Connor ran a hand through his long hair then over his face. He shook his head more to get the cobwebs loosened than in answer to Graff's question. "Something."

Graff frowned at him and said, "Something what?"

"Don't know. It's too." He shook his head, not willing or able to answer direction. He settled on, "It's too quiet. Quiet but not."

"What's that supposed to mean? Being at a lake at," Graff glanced at his watch and said, "five-fifteen in the morning is supposed to be quiet."

O'Connor's response was, "Something."

Graff knew O'Connor. They'd worked any number of cases together, and O'Connor had an uncanny ability to put two or three seemingly unrelated events or conversations together to make something out of nothing. Most of the time, those somethings out of nothings led to a breakthrough in the case they were working on.

"What do you want to do?"

O'Connor pursed his lips reeled in his line and set the rod down inside the aluminum boat, resting it on the metal bench. He said, "Let's find Brian and Brett," patting the handle of his revolver.

"Fair enough," Graff said, though he was disappointed. He had wanted to fish and relax, and not necessarily babysit, though he knew both he and Pat were responsible for the boys.

He reeled his line in and set his rod on the floor of the boat. He raised the anchor, fired up the engine, and respecting the no wake rule until 10:00 AM, sped off at a slow speed.

He knew Brian liked to fish shadows and shorelines, and knew he had favored the north side of the lake. So, instead of traveling counter-clockwise as protocol called for it, he went clockwise around the lake thinking that they'd find the boys faster and they'd be able to get back to fishing.

Jamie had trouble seeing anything through the fog, though as the morning grew into day, and the darkness was chased by a sun that had yet to actually appear on the horizon, the fog had gotten patchy.

Graff asked, "Where were those lots Brian wanted to build on?"

"The south side of the lake. Somewhere."

Graff muttered, "Shit," and he shrugged. He noted the direction they traveled, and said, "We should see them eventually, I guess."

CHAPTER FIFTY

Two blinked as much to clear his eyes as he did to clear his head. Blood oozed from his nose and from a gash above his left eye. Both throbbed. Those weren't his biggest problems, however.

He was face to face with the smaller of the two men from Crivitz, who leered at him. The man used his left hand to choke Two, but not so much that he couldn't breathe. His right hand held a knife up against Two's throat. Two tried to move his neck and head away from the knife, but the man squeezed Two's neck enough to force him to hold still.

"What's the matter, boy? Hmmm? Didn't expect to see me, did ya?"

Two was too frightened to answer.

The man shifted his left to Two's penis and squeezed and pulled it. His nose almost touching Two's cheek.

Two held onto the man's hand to get him to stop, but man's knife cut into his neck.

"Please don't."

"Please don't what?" the man asked. A mist of spit covered Two's face. "You have no idea what I'm gonna do."

"Please."

"See, I hate fuckin Indians. The thought of you fuckin and having little fuckin Indians runnin around makes my skin crawl."

The man shifted his left hand to Two's balls and squeezed.

"You like this? Are you one of those fuckin gay Indians?"

"That hurts! Please stop!" He groaned when the man didn't ease up.

Blood from the gash above Two's forehead seeped into his left eye. He could only see out of the right. He tried to wipe it clean, but the man swatted his hand.

"Don't you fuckin move," the man snarled.

Two didn't want to antagonize the man. Instead, he pleaded with him. "Please, let me go. I'll leave and you'll never see me again." He couldn't help it, but he began to weep.

The man from Crivitz slowly shook his head. "I have to teach fuckin Indians like you a lesson." The man's breath foul, a mixture of coffee, cigarettes and fried eggs. "We can't have any more fuckin Indians running around here, can we?"

The man squeezed Two's balls again, this time harder.

Two gasped, groaned, and he was sure he had screamed. His knees buckled and he became nauseous.

"Shut the fuck up," the man snarled, not letting up on his grip.

Two had troubled standing upright in spite of the knife at his throat. He was full out crying at this point, begging the man to stop.

"Hurts, huh?" the man asked. "I can take care of that for you." He lowered the knife to Two's sack, and Two felt the knife bite into the tender skin.

"Please, no!" Two pleaded, crying all the more. "Please don't. Please."

The man laughed, then hawked up yellow-green phlegm and spit it into Two's face.

Two didn't know where the other man had come from or who he was, but he had crept up behind the man from Crivitz. He said, "Slowly, take your knife away from this boy."

The man from Crivitz startled, and Two felt the knife bite again. He said, "You never mind and leave us be. This is no concern of yours. This is between the fuckin Indian and me."

Two barely recognized the man's suppressor on the barrel of his revolver. He saw plenty of movies and TV shows where the bad guy had used one. The man holding the gun pushed the muzzle and suppressor into the man from Crivitz's cheek, and then slid it into the man's mouth.

"I said, take your knife away from the boy. Slowly."

The man from Crivitz did.

The man with the gun said, "Back away from this kid and drop the knife."

The man from Crivitz hesitated, as a thought sped through his mind. *Could he spin quickly enough to stab the man holding the gun?*

As if the man with gun read his mind, he said, "You're not quick enough and before you move one centimeter, you'll be dead."

That clinched it. The man from Crivitz reluctantly took the knife away from Two, dropped it into the mossy grass and dirt, and stepped away from the boy. For good measure, he raised both hands slowly.

"Son, are you okay?" the man with the gun asked without taking his eyes off the other man.

"I'm bleeding," Two sobbed as he wiped the phlegm and blood from his face.

The man nodded and said, "Pull up your pants, and step away from us. You'll be fine."

Two doubted it. He stepped but stumbled and fell to his knees. He felt the sting of yet another cut or scrape. He doubled over, both hands covering his groin as blood flowed between his fingers.

"You fucker!" Two spat at the man from Crivitz. He stood as best he could and slipped his underwear and his pants up, zipped and buckled, and then stepped away. With both hands covering his groin, he moved slowly, gingerly away from them. In truth, Two knew he couldn't move quickly if he wanted to.

"Look, I don't know who you are, buddy, but I'll walk away and you'll never see me again," the man from Crivitz said.

The man with gun shoved the suppressor deeper into the man's mouth and said, "This boy offered the same to you, and you threatened him."

The man from Crivitz said nothing.

"My stepfather was a piece of shit just like you." The man with the gun glanced over at Two, then back to the man and said, "I was no older than this boy when I killed him. I never thought twice about it. The world didn't need that piece of shit and it doesn't need a piece of shit like you, either."

He pulled the trigger.

The back of his head exploded, and the man from Crivitz fell right where he stood. The man with the suppressor straddled the body and fired once more into the man's forehead.

Two noted that the gun had made a phttt noise, and the impact on the man's forehead had made a thwack sound like someone hacking into a watermelon.

The man with the gun hovered over the man from Crivitz staring at the corpse waving his gun from one side to the other, daring the man on the ground to move. Two couldn't read the man's expression. He had seen enough dead bodies to know that the man on the ground was deader than dead.

At last, the man turned and faced Two. The boy couldn't help but take a step backwards, but stumbled doing so. The man regarded Two silently. He made a decision and sighed.

"Where's your brother?"

Two had no idea how this man knew he had a brother. He dared not raise his arms, so he indicted with his head and said, "Back toward the lake."

The man glanced over his shoulder briefly, faced Two and said, "Are you able to walk out of here?"

Two didn't relax, but remained hopeful as he said, "Yes, Sir. I think so."

The man nodded and said, "I'm going to take this man's orange coat and rifle. Then I'm going to walk in that direction," pointing his revolver with the suppressor in the direction of the cabin. "You're going to stand by this tree and count to one hundred slowly, and then you will go find your brother." He paused as if he considered a different option, a more logical option, then shook his head and said, "You never saw me."

CHAPTER FIFTY-ONE

Had George not waited as long as he did before following the man with the gun, he would have seen the killing of the man from Crivitz. As it was, he crouched down in the shadow of the forest behind bushes and trees as the man stripped off the dead man's coat and rifle. He heard the man tell Two to stay put and count. And, he watched the man walk away without a glance back.

He even aimed his crossbow at the man, but decided that Two might be in danger if he shot at the man, and he didn't want that. He didn't want to risk his or Two's death, so George remained where he was until he was certain the man was out of sight and swallowed by the dark forest. It was only then when he stepped out into the open, still searching for any sign of the man with the gun in case he had circled back.

When George stepped out from the bushes and trees, Two didn't seem surprised to see him.

"Are you all right?" George asked.

Two nodded and wiped tears away. "He was going to cut my nuts off." He kicked the dead man in the ribs twice, and said, "I'm bleeding. It hurts."

George glared at the dead man and asked, "How bad is it?"

All Two said was to repeat what he had said before as if George hadn't heard him. "I'm bleeding and it hurts."

It was only the snap of a twig that momentarily panicked both boys.

George and Two crouched down and turned in the direction of the lake. Both had heard it, though whoever was walking towards them were doing so quietly.

George glanced at Two and then at the dead man. Neither he nor Two carried a gun. It might not matter to whoever walked in their direction. How would either of them be able to explain what had taken place? Whoever came upon them would think they were guilty of murder, especially if it was the other man from Crivitz and the boy who traveled with them.

CHAPTER FIFTY-TWO

Though the day promised to be warm, the air had a chill and dampness to it.

'Nida 'ałkáá'i ', you and Báhách'ii need to hurry.'

Brian blinked, but sped up, breaking the no wake rule big time. This was the second time George's grandfather used Navajo language with him, and it only confused him. He'd have to have a long conversation with George.

As Brian gunned it, Brett stared at him, gave him a *what-the-hell* look, then turned around, figuring Brian had his reasons.

Once Brian docked and anchored the boat, Brett had taken the lead. Before they crossed the sandy beach and into the forest, he had again asked Brian if he had wanted to wait for him in the boat. Brian had said nothing as he checked the magazine in the handle of his Glock, set the safety, and stood with his hand on his hips. Together, they entered the forest as mist enveloped them. Fortunately, it diminished the more into the forest they hiked.

After walking perhaps one hundred yards from the beach, Brett held up his hand, stopped, and crouched down. They were on what looked like a game trail. Brian duck-walked up next to him and crouched beside him.

"Did you hear that?" Brett whispered.

"It sounded like George and Two, but I couldn't tell for sure."

Brett sighed and said, "Tuck your Glock in the front pocket of your sweatshirt." As he said this, he slid his Glock, a twin of Brian's, behind his belt on the back of his jeans under the orange vest he wore. He said, "Ready?"

Brian nodded solemnly.

Brett picked up his pace and Brian followed dutifully behind him, searching the forest to the left and right, as well as their six. Neither boy had seen any hunters, though they did see where something had bedded down. The grass had been laid flat, pushed down. Maybe deer, Brian thought.

They came to the opening in the forest and found George crouching next a body, and Two leaning hunched over by the tree. Both boys stared at them. As Brett and Brian drew near, both recognized the dead man as one of the men from Crivitz.

"What happened?" Brett whispered as he stared at the dead man. He glanced at Two and said, "Jesus, Two! What happened to you?"

Two struggled, working to keep his tears in check and his voice low. "I was taking a piss and this piece of shit came up behind me. He slammed my head into the tree, took out his knife and threatened to cut off my balls."

"Are you okay?" Brian asked.

"I'm bleeding and my balls hurt."

Brett asked, "Did he . . .?"

"He cut me."

Brian walked over to Two, inspected the gash above Two's eye and his nose. "I have to clean you up. I don't think you have a broken nose. Maybe, maybe not. I can't tell for sure."

"What happened to this dude?" Brett asked nodding at the dead man from Crivitz.

"Some guy . . . I don't know who, came up behind him, made him stop, and then shot him twice," Two answered.

"Seriously?" Brett turned to George and asked, "How much did you see?"

George shook his head, and said, "Not much."

"I didn't hear any gunshot," Brian said.

"He used a silencer thingy," Two said.

George and Brian stared at each other.

"What?" Brett asked looking from Brian to George. To George he asked, "The guy who shot this ass wipe, is this the same guy you think you saw when we checked out the vacant lots?"

"I did not get a good look at him, but I believe he might be. I believe he is here to kill Detective Pat."

"If he's using a suppressor, he's professional," Brett said. "Which way did he go?"

"That way," George said staring off into the forest.

"We need to warn O'Connor and Graff," Brett said. He looked over at Two and said, "Can you walk?"

Two hesitated. He could, but he didn't know how far. As far as he could tell, he was still bleeding. His balls hurt, especially if he moved suddenly.

Brian said, "No offense, Michael, but if the four of us go after that guy, you're going to make too much noise. And as badly as you're hurt, I need to get you back to the cabin to see what I can do."

"Okay, you and Two use the boat and head to the cabin. See if you can find O'Connor or Graff along the way. George and I will follow this guy."

Brian licked his lips and said, "Brett, if he's a professional, he might kill you if he thinks you're following him. Hell, he might kill you anyway. I think the four of us should get back to the boat and find O'Connor and Graff before he does."

What Brian suggested made sense. It was the smart thing to do. It was the easiest thing to do. But if Brian and Two were at the cabin and the guy showed up looking for O'Connor, and if George and he were behind him, the guy would be covered from two directions. And if Brian found O'Connor and Graff, the guy would be outnumbered and out gunned six to one. He explained this to George and Brian.

"This is a mistake. You might think you're only following him, but if he spots you and if he thinks you're after him, both of you will be dead," Brian said.

"For all he knows, we're just hunting. I think it's our best plan," Brett said.

"I think it's a mistake, especially after all the crap we went through in Arizona. You know that." He turned to George and said, "What do you think?"

George searched the forest in the direction he knew the man went. He glanced at the dead man, then at Two. He said, "I do not want him to kill us or anyone else. I think we will be safe following him from a distance. If we get too close, we will back off."

Brian shook his head. "Whatever. Michael, do you want me to carry you on my back or do you want to try walking?"

"I'll try walking."

"Okay, let's get your stuff and get moving." Brian turned to Brett and George and said, "What you're doing is stupid and dangerous. You know that, especially after the shit in Arizona."

CHAPTER FIFTY-THREE

"This is a big-ass lake, but we've covered the north shore." Graff said. "We saw, what, maybe two other boats?"

"Not Brian or Brett," O'Connor said.

Because of the no wake rule, it had been painfully slow to get as far as they had. Graff kept them twenty or thirty yards off the shore. Deep in most places, shallow in a few spots.

They had finished the western portion of the lake where the two of them had fished the day before, and were slowly rounding the turn towards the east along the southern shore. The fog or mist or whatever it was had lifted considerably. They could see almost fifty yards in front of them. So far, no boats on the water except theirs and the two others, one carrying one fisherman and the other carrying two. The latter looked to Graff as a father and son.

"Bri uses his troller when he fishes, right?" Graff said.

"Only if he has to. Mostly, he likes to stay put or drift." O'Connor smiled, turned back towards Graff and said, "If he's catching fish, he'll stay put until the fish run out."

"He's patient," Graff said with a nod and smile. "Those boys are special. If I had to go to battle, I'd chose Brian as a partner. He can shoot a fly off an elephant's ass two hundred yards away," he said with a laugh. "Damn. I don't know anyone who can shoot like him."

O'Connor said, "Brett is good with handguns, but he's impetuous. Flighty. Not as careful as he should be. George is a thinker. His hand to hand and knife skills are better than anyone I know. I think I'd choose him as my partner. He sees everything. Knows everything. Deliberate. Thoughtful."

"I'm surprised you didn't choose Brian."

O'Connor shook his head. "After Arizona, I don't know that Brian will ever pick up a gun again."

"You think he's that messed up?"

O'Connor shrugged and said, "Maybe, maybe not. He's working through it, but he isn't there yet."

"What about Two?"

"Too early to tell. He is a mix of all three boys. He has George's ability to see and know. He's a pretty fair shot, maybe not as good as Brian, but he's pretty good. A little impetuous like Brett. A bit of a goof." O'Connor nodded as if he agreed with his own assessment. "Two would be my second choice, though."

"Why?"

"He's loyal. You had better not cross any of his friends or brothers, especially Brian. There would be hell to pay. He'd treat his partner the same way."

O'Connor lifted a hand, and Graff let up on the motor. They both heard it.

"Big engine," O'Connor said.

"Could be Brian and Brett," Graff answered. "Going to a different location?"

"In a hurry. A little faster than they should be moving. Brian knows better."

Graff had to agree. The two boys were far enough ahead that the wake and waves they created hadn't reached them. Maybe so far ahead they might not ever.

"Maybe the sound is louder than their actual speed," Graff said as he throttled up his motor.

"Maybe."

CHAPTER FIFTY-FOUR

He figured he had twenty minutes to a half an hour lead if the two Indian boys were to follow him. He resisted the urge to rush because that would draw attention, and he didn't want to risk it and he sure as hell didn't need it. He had a job to do and a hefty payout once that job was completed.

He wasn't sure what he might do next. The shot he had wanted to take was gone. That opportunity evaporated when he saved the younger Indian boy. He still didn't know why he had done it. He had reasoned that he hated bullies because all bullies reminded him of his stepfather. But saving the Indian kid made no sense. It fucked up his best opportunity to take out the cop.

Without knowing it, he had sped up his pace and his breathing. He stopped, leaned against a tree, shut his eyes, and breathed in through his nose and out of his mouth. In no time, his breathing, and his pulse rate, were back to normal.

He saw them before they saw him. He recognized the big tall bald man in the orange stocking hat, orange coat and orange pants. His son, younger and smaller than the younger Indian boy, walked behind him. At least he assumed it was his son.

He attempted to walk past them on the same path.

When he got within three yards of the big man, the big man blocked his path. "Why are you walking and not up in a stand?"

"Looking for a better position. Not much happening back there," the man said gesturing with his head.

The big man squinted at him and said, "That rifle over your shoulder. It looks familiar."

The man smiled and said, "It's not much different from any other rifle other hunters have who aren't using a bow."

"That's a bolt action .306. That's a Vortex Diamondback scope."

The man nodded.

"Can I see it? My brother-in-law has one exactly like it."

He could barely hide his impatience as he slid the rifle off his back and handed it to the big man.

The big man from Crivitz nodded, then spit tobacco juice to the side. A little dribbled down his chin. "You see these six notches on the underside of the stock? My brother-in-law carved them for each deer he shot. So, unless you do the very same, I wanna know where you got this rifle."

The man half-turned away and unzipped the orange jacket he was wearing in the same motion, reached inside and took out his revolver with the suppressor. He pointed it at the big man.

"Whoa! Hey! I'm just asking a question."

"I'm about to answer it," the man said.

He fired one shot into the man's forehead, dead-center above the eyes. The big man dropped like a sack of shit, falling into his son who had stood off to the side, but behind his father. The boy was knocked off his feet and landed on his ass in a bush.

The man played the gun over the boy's face watching his reaction. The kid's chin trembled, but he remained motionless and silent. The man took a deep breath, sighed and said, "Hand me your rifle, butt first."

The boy did as he was told. He glanced at his father once, but otherwise had his eyes locked on the man holding the revolver.

The man took it. The boy saw the man's grip tighten, so he clamped his eyes shut and steeled himself for the coming shot.

"Kid, get up and run," the man said softly.

The boy wasn't sure if he had heard correctly, so he remained where he was, frozen.

"If you want to live, get up and run. Now."

Still not believing what he had heard, the boy stood, and glanced at his dead father. His father's eyes were wide open. His mouth formed a perfect O, caught by the surprise of his death.

The man repeated, "I won't say it again." He pointed behind him and said, "If you want to live, you will run. You're not going to stop. You won't slow down. You won't come back. If you do, I'll shoot you just as I did your father."

The boy took off, all the while thinking that a bullet would hit him in the back or his head. He zig-zagged left and right randomly to prevent that.

He hadn't realized he was crying. He fell once, then again. He chanced a look behind him, knowing that would bring about a bullet, but as he turned to see what the man was doing, he kept running.

Noah didn't see the man any longer. He kept going, took one more look back, and ran right into George.

CHAPTER FIFTY-FIVE

Brian heard the voice. He didn't see him, but he heard him just the same. More than that, he knew who it was.

"You need to warn them."

It was all that was said, but Brian knew exactly what was meant. He turned and said to Two, "How bad does it hurt?"

Michael shrugged. Both hands were clamped on his groin.

"We need to warn Graff and O'Connor. I don't want them walking into a trap."

Michael nodded solemnly. He understood.

After the hike back to the boat, Two had been in pain and he knew that if it had once upon a time quit bleeding, it had started up again. He thought that since he had climbed into the boat, the bleeding had stopped. He had tried to show that he wasn't in pain, because he didn't want Brian or anyone else to think he was a baby.

Brian knew Michael was in a great deal of pain. After all, Michael almost had his nuts cut off. He also knew Michael was trying hard not to show how much pain he was in, which made Brian's decision all that much harder.

"Michael, hang in there. This won't take long."

Brian knew Michael was tough. Possibly only second to George or Brett. As hard as he tried, Michael couldn't hide the pain he was in. Maybe it was embarrassment or shame, Brian didn't know for sure.

He swung the boat around and headed back the way they had come. He didn't exactly know where the two cops were, but it felt right to head back the way they had come.

The mist on the lake had diminished to the point where Brian could see into the distance the length of a football field. It wasn't too long before he spotted Graff's aluminum boat in the distance.

Michael pointed and said, "There!"

He had gotten Brian's attention, and then Michael's hands landed right back in his lap, and he hunched over as he held his groin.

"Let me do the talking, Michael."

He slowed his boat and pulled up alongside. Michael hung onto the side of the aluminum boat, as O'Connor hung onto the side of Brian's boat.

To Michael, O'Connor said, "I thought you'd be hunting with George." To Brian, he asked, "Where's Brett?" He took a closer look at Two and said, "What happened to you?"

"I don't have time for details. Remember those two guys from Crivitz?" Before either of them answered, Brian said, "He's dead. The smaller one. Some guy shot him in the head. Michael saw it all."

Both men shifted their attention to Two. It was Graff who said, "Two, your face! Are you alright? What happened?"

Brian gave Michael no chance to answer. He said, "Listen. You don't have time. George and Brett are following the guy. He's headed east. They don't want him to get away. The guy is a professional. His revolver had a suppressor on it. There is no hunter anywhere who uses a suppressor."

Graff and O'Connor exchanged a look, their thoughts mirroring each other's.

"Show us where they are," Graff said.

"No. I mean, you'd be behind George and Brett, and too far behind that guy. It would be better if you got ahead of the guy so he'll run into you."

O'Connor frowned at him and said, "Why aren't you with them?"

The partial lie tripped off Brian's tongue. "Because Brett and George wanted us to find you and warn you. We think that guy is after you."

It didn't look like Graff or O'Connor were going to move, so Brian said, "We have to move. Now! I don't want anything to happen to Brett or George. I can lead you to a point where I think you need to be for you to catch him."

Brian knew the men were thinking it over, but his logic was sound. He said to Two, "Michael, shove off." To Graff, he said, "I'll spin around and lead you. I'm going to point to where Brett and I put in. Then I'm going to slow down and stop at a point I think you need to be. You have your guns, right?"

"Of course," Graff said.

"Okay, let's do this."

CHAPTER FIFTY-SIX

The guy was pissed. Two loose ends running around the woods. Any other time, he would have shot both. Should have shot both. He knew it, and he knew he had blown it.

There was something about both boys in both situations.

The Indian kid being bullied by some redneck asshole, and the other kid growing up in a redneck asshole's house. Either man could have been his stepfather. The similarities were striking.

Fuck it.

He had to come up with a way to salvage whatever he could from this fucked up situation. Take the cops at their cabin. Take them on the road somewhere between here and Crivitz. Somewhere. Somehow.

He pushed on.

In the back of his mind he heard, or thought he heard, two outboard engines. Boaters out fishing. One bigger and louder than the other. He didn't know if he should be concerned about that or not.

He stopped as if struck by a thought. He smiled.

Maybe this wasn't the monumental fuck up he thought it was. Maybe the two cops would come to him. If they did, he'd be ready.

CHAPTER FIFTY-SEVEN

George clamped a hand over the boy's mouth and bear-hugged him. Noah thrashed, swung elbows, and hit whatever he could. George held him and spoke to him in a calm, quiet voice, but the boy either didn't hear or didn't want to hear.

Brett stepped in front of the boy and said, "Shhh, kid. Stop. We're not going to hurt you, but if you don't stop making noise, that guy is going to come back and kill all three of us. Is that what you want?"

The boy burst into fresh tears and he shook his head.

George whispered into the boy's ear, "Shhh, we're not going to hurt you. I'm going to take my hand away from your mouth, but you have to remain quiet. That guy might come back. Do you understand?"

The boy nodded.

"Okay, here I go."

Brett knelt down in front of the boy. George took his hand away, but held onto the kid just in case.

"What's your name?" Brett asked.

The boy sobbed too loudly, "Noah."

"Okay, Noah. You have to be quiet. Please."

"He shot my dad and he told me to run. He said if I turned around or followed him, he'd shoot me just like he did my dad."

"Okay, Noah. You're safe now. You're with us."

"Where is your rifle?" George asked.

"That guy, he took it. He told me to run. I don't know where he is."

As if struck by the thought, Noah looked around in a panic. "We have to go. He might come back." He started to get up ready to bolt.

George said in his most soothing voice, "Noah, listen to me. We have to follow him. He is here to kill our friend. You met him in Crivitz. The tall, long-haired cop. That man who killed your father is a professional killer, and he is here to kill Detective Pat."

"But we can't follow him!" the boy panicked and threatened to bolt.

Brett reached out and put a hand on his shoulder and said, "Noah, listen to me. George and I can't leave you out here by yourself."

"My uncle should be up ahead. I can go to him. He'll know what to do."

"Noah, you can't go to your uncle. He's dead. The man who shot your dad also shot your uncle."

"My uncle is dead?" Noah whispered. "He's dead too?"

George said, "Yes, Noah. Your uncle is dead. Brett and I cannot leave you in the woods by yourself. You need to come with us. We will protect you."

Noah considered his utter aloneness. His dad, dead. His uncle, dead. Alone now, in the forest with two boys he didn't know. He began to sob.

"What about my dad and uncle? We can't leave them here."

"We will come back for them," George said. "That is a promise."

"Look. Noah. We're wasting time. We have to get moving. The longer we wait, the further ahead that fuckhead gets. We can't let him get close to our friend or our friend dies. Do you understand?"

Noah looked from Brett to George and then back to Brett. "But what if he kills us?"

Brett smiled and said, "Then I guess the three of us screwed up. But what the hell. We have to try. Together, the three of us, we have a chance to stop this shithead from killing anyone else."

Noah licked his lips, took a deep breath and said, "The last I saw him, he was headed east."

CHAPTER FIFTY-EIGHT

As they sped by, breaking the no wake rule, Brian pointed at the beach where he and Brett put in, and from where he and Michael had taken off. He slowed down as they rounded a bend. He searched the forest as he figured where the man might be. He glanced at his watch and decided that they were still not ahead of the man, so he pushed onward.

He sped on and he heard the same voice.

"Up ahead. There is a turnout. It is shallow and there will be rocks. Be careful."

As Brian did when Brad spoke to him, in his head he said, *"Thank you for guiding me."*

Brian couldn't explain it, but it felt as though a hand rested on his shoulder. Of course, he couldn't see anything, but it felt as if the old man stood next to him.

"George loves you," Brian said. *"He misses you."*

"I love Shadow. You are good for him."

Brian smiled and tears threatened to spring to his eyes. He fought them off.

"Nida'ałkáá'i', up here."

Brian didn't know what George's grandfather called him. He'd have to ask George. He knew Michael didn't speak the Navajo language as well as George.

He slowed to a stop, drifting in the wake from both boats. Graff pulled up alongside of him.

"There," Brian said. "That turnout. Be careful. It's shallow, but it's rocky. Raise your engine up and use your oars. Travel fifty yards into the forest at least, maybe seventy-five. There will be a game trail. He'll be on it." Brian had no idea how he knew this. It was as if the picture of what he described and the words appeared in his head. Maybe he imagined it, but at the same time, knew it to be accurate. "He's wearing the blaze orange jacket he took from the dead guy. He also has the dead guy's rifle. So, he has a rifle and his revolver."

"He's right-handed," Two said. "He has a holster under his left arm. I saw it. He's wearing a camo baseball hat and camo pants. He has short blond hair. In his thirties, I think. Not as tall as either of you. Slimmer, but strong. Built like George, but taller. Like a runner."

Graff frowned at the two boys. There was more to all of this, but there wasn't time. At some point, he would have a conversation with them. With all of them.

"Where are you two headed?"

"To the cabin. I want to take care of Michael's eye and nose."

O'Connor said, "Jamie, let's get moving. We need to cut him off from the cabin and make sure he doesn't double-back on George and Brett."

Graff pulled out an oar and handed it to O'Connor. Graff raised the motor out of the water, took the other oar, and used it as a pole to push off the bottom of the lake to get them to shore. O'Connor did the same.

Two gave them a push, causing O'Connor and Graff to almost lose their balance. Brian turned his boat and headed for the cabin.

"Michael, keep your crossbow loaded and ready just in case."

Silently, Michael took the crossbow off his back and loaded an arrow on it. That done, he set the crossbow on his knee, held onto it with one hand. The other hand held his groin.

"You okay?" he asked.

Michael glanced back and said, "It hurts."

CHAPTER FIFTY-NINE

Noah touched Brett's shoulder and whispered, "My dad is up here."

In turn, Brett took hold of George's elbow and whispered, "Noah's dad is up here. Be careful."

George had been leading. There was sign that the path had been used. Turned up dirt. A footprint or two. A broken twig. When he saw the dead body on the trail, he stopped and crouched down and the two boys, Brett and Noah crouched down behind him.

"You okay?" Brett whispered to Noah.

Though he brushed some tears off his cheeks, he nodded.

Brett stared at him for a beat and then focused on the body. He supposed he could understand Noah caring for his father, but in Brett's mind, the guy was a piece of shit who picked on Two for no reason. A redneck asshole.

In a flash, he thought back to his biological father, Thomas McGovern, the Butler University English professor. There were any number of students who liked the man, thought he was the best thing to English next to Shakespeare or C.S. Lewis. Especially those girls who ended up in his bed. Personally, Brett couldn't stand the man and never wanted to see him again. Not after cheating dozens of times on his mom, on Bobby or himself. He didn't care so much about himself as he did about his mom or Bobby. But it stung nonetheless. Even though the two men were as different from each other as was a greasy fried hamburger to a juicy sirloin steak, both men sucked the big one. If his biological father were lying there in the mossy grass and dirt, Brett might have spit on him.

212

The forest was silent except for birds calling to one another. They had seen two squirrels and several chipmunks. As the boys neared them, they scampered up a tree or under the brush out of harm's way. The mist had not traveled this far into the forest and the day had finally woken up, so the boys could see farther into the trees and bushes.

Brett tapped George on the shoulder and whispered, "I haven't seen anything so far, have you?"

George didn't turn around, but he shook his head once.

He turned around and faced Noah and said, "We will come back for your father and your uncle. I promise."

Noah sighed, shuttered a little, and nodded. "I want to take my father's rifle. I don't know what that guy did with mine."

As he did whenever there was a dead body nearby, George offered a small silent word to the man's *chindi* requesting permission to come close, offering to help find the man's killer and bring him to justice.

Knowing this was George's routine, Brett waited patiently, and put a hand on Noah's shoulder to prevent him from moving forward.

George was almost finished when Noah leaned in between the two boys. He didn't say anything, but pointed ahead and to their right. Both Brett and George saw the flash of orange in the distance. None of them, however, could verify if who they saw was the man they were following.

George stood up slowly and the boys did the same. They stopped only long enough for Noah to get his father's rifle still on his back. He had to roll him over onto his side to do it, and then reverently, positioned the man's hands across his chest.

George didn't approve of moving the body and potentially messing up crime scene, but it was Noah's father.

That done, they moved on, picking their way slowly through the brush, parallel to the game trail George thought the man had used.

The trouble was that they were making more noise than they had wanted to. The man they were following didn't need any signal or sign he was being followed, especially since this man was as dangerous a target as he seemed to be. Because of that, George moved back to the game trail.

Up ahead a little over a hundred yards ahead was another flash of orange. This time, George saw only an orange coat, not an orange hat or pants. As he walked, he pointed ahead at the figure who weaved in and out of sight as trees or bushes hid him when thick, exposed him when the forest was less dense.

When the figure stopped, George crouched down behind a copse of trees and bush. He and Noah were outfitted in blaze orange and Brett was partially so. No matter where they hid, the possibility existed that they would be seen. There was no way around it. Yes, they could pass as other hunters. But George knew the man was a professional. As such, he was smarter than that. It was far too chancy for them, and silently, he regretted not following Brian's suggestion.

CHAPTER SIXTY

"I will not like it if we got shot," Graff muttered.

"And I won't look good with an arrow stuck in my ass," O'Connor said.

That was the only friendly banter they shared as they made their way into the forest. It was far too dangerous for either of them because they weren't dressed for hunting. If a game warden or ranger happened by, they would be fined and sent away. That was the least of their problems, but it was considerable. Of greater concern was that they hunted a professional killer. Not only were they dodging game wardens, rangers, and other hunters, they had to locate and detain- hopefully alive- a professional killer.

Graff shook his head and sighed. This was not what he had planned for the weekend that was supposed to have been relaxing and enjoyable.

"Fuck," he muttered.

Just as Brian described, they came to a game trail. O'Connor stopped, ran a hand through his long hair and said, "How in the hell?"

"What?"

"How did Brian know this trail was here? Right where he said it would be?"

"A visit from Brad?" Graff suggested, who put stock into George's and Brian's visions.

Not answering directly, O'Connor said, "What the fuck is going on?"

"One thing at a time, Hoss. One thing at a time."

Both men knelt down and studied the terrain and their surroundings, looking for any oncoming orange, whether out in the open like a real hunter, or someone dressed in orange who flitted in and out of trees and bush, like someone pretending to be a hunter. Neither man thought the professional would try hiding. He was on a mission, and the mission was O'Connor.

They considered their placement.

"I'll take up a position south of the trail. Up there in those trees. High ground, I think."

Graff looked around and said, "I'll move back about fifteen yards. I'd prefer to keep track of you visually."

"Same."

Both men moved off and settled into a position to wait. O'Connor was much better at waiting than Graff, given the number of stakeouts he had been on. His personality fit his job. Naturally laid back, easygoing. He never ruffled. That aspect of his personality probably saved his life more than once.

O'Connor climbed a tree that not only gave him a better visual in almost three-hundred-sixty degrees, but also gave him a modicum of coverage. If he was still, his dark sweatshirt and jeans might blend in.

Graff took the low ground, though it did give him a good vantage point to watch the trail, yet remain relatively hidden, given that his sweatshirt was brown.

They settled in to wait, not knowing how long it might take. Graff hoped they would find the killer before the boys did.

CHAPTER SIXTY-ONE

Brian was worried about Michael and what he might find once Michael stripped down. He walked stiff-legged as he tried not to move too much, even though he had to walk uphill on an uneven path to get to the cabin. Each step was painful to watch. Brian was certain Michael felt each step.

At the door, Brian reached under the side of the house just to the left of the steps, found the nail with the keys on it, and slipped them off the nail. He found the right key and opened up the house. After Michael entered, Brian shut and locked the door, and set the keys on the counter in the kitchen.

Two shed his crossbow, his jacket and boots, then his orange pants and hat. He leaned the crossbow against a kitchen cabinet, and put everything else over a chair at the kitchen table.

"Michael, let's go into the bathroom and I'll see what I can do for you."

Michael led the way, stood in the middle of the bathroom and waited until Brian came in and shut and locked the door behind him. "What do you want me to do?"

"I want you to strip off everything and stand in the bathtub."

Without thinking about it, Two pulled off his shirt and camo pants, pushed down his boxers which were spotted with dried blood, and slipped off his socks. Carefully, gingerly, he stepped into the bathtub and faced Brian.

Blood had run down Two's legs. Dried blood crusted in his pubic hair, and on his penis and scrotum. He looked down at himself and began to cry.

"Shhh, Michael, let's see what we have. But before I do anything, I need to tell you I'm going to start by washing all the blood off of you. That means I'm going to touch everything."

Two nodded.

"If you're not comfortable with me doing that, we can wait until George or Brett come back. It looks like the bleeding stopped, so it wouldn't hurt to wait."

Two shook his head and said, "I don't want George or Brett washing me. I don't want anyone else touching me. I mean that. I want no one else touching me."

"Okay, let's do this," Brian said with a smile. He wanted to relieve the tension, but a smile wasn't going to cut it. "Just so you know, dad or mom will ask to take a look at it."

"Only you."

Brian shrugged and said, "You have to tell me if the water is too cold or too hot."

It took time to get the temperature bearable for Two, but at last, the warm water was up to his knees. Brian washed his hands in the sink, and grabbed his bodywash off the counter. After rinsing Two off, Brian soaped up his hands and worked from the top down.

Two winced twice, and sucked in and held his breath once as Brian worked around his scrotum. Brian apologized twice, eliciting no response from Michael.

When Brian was finished washing him, Two asked, "How bad is it?"

Brian said, "The blood everywhere made it seem worse than I think it is. I think. You have two small cuts on the left side, one towards the back and one towards the front. The one in the front is a little longer. Maybe deeper."

"Will I be able to get married and have kids?"

Brian looked up at Two, smiled and said, "I'm not a doctor, but I think everything looks normal." To lighten it up, he added, "You even have a cool birthmark on your right nut."

"A crescent moon," Two said without emotion. "Lou told me about it one time when he was down there doing stuff. He would kiss it for good luck," he added with a shrug.

"My mom used to tell Brad and me that birthmarks were angel kisses. I don't know about the good luck thing."

"I think Lou was just saying that."

"Did it bother you . . . you know, doing things with him?"

Two blushed deep crimson and said, "He gave me a job. He gave me food and a place to stay. He never hurt me."

Brian nodded.

"I kind of miss him. I know what he did was wrong. But I miss him. He was all I had." He was silent for a beat, and then said, "Sometimes I miss doing stuff, but I like girls," Two added.

Brian smiled at him and said, "I know."

That had been the first time he had ever spoken to Brian about that part of his life. In a way, he felt relief. Of anyone in his family, he felt the most comfortable talking with Brian about it.

Brian dried Two's legs, butt, and pubic hair off with a towel. He pat-dried Two's penis and scrotum with Kleenex.

"Now what?" Two asked.

"I want to put some Neosporin on the cuts, but before I do, I want to use some Rubbing Alcohol or Hydrogen Peroxide first. I want to make sure you don't get an infection. When we get home, I think you'll need a tetanus shot because we don't know how dirty his knife was."

"The Peroxide is going to hurt."

"Sting, mostly, but only at first. You're tough. Just hold onto my head and grit your teeth."

Two nodded, though he wasn't quite sure he was ready for it.

Brian rummaged around under the sink, found Peroxide and some cotton balls. He soaked a cotton ball by tipping the bottle upside-down, while holding the cotton ball over the opening.

That done, he looked up at Two and said, "Ready?"

Michael put both hands on Brian's head and said, "Do it."

Brian did, wiping both with one swipe. Two didn't make a sound, though Brian felt Two's grip.

"One more time to be sure, okay?"

"Go," Two said quietly.

Brian prepared a second cotton ball and repeated the process. He could tell it didn't sting as much because Two's grip wasn't as strong.

Next, he took the Neosporin and wiped a generous amount into both cuts. After, he took gauze and placed it onto the left side of the scrotum over both cuts, anchoring it with a strip of gauze around the top and bottom of the scrotum in a loop using Vaseline to hold it together.

"I don't know how long it will hold. We might have to change it a couple of times."

Two nodded and said, "Thanks."

He started to step out of the tub, but Brian held him back and said, "Michael, your balls are swollen and bruised. How bad do they feel?"

"They hurt. Am I going to be okay?"

Brian shrugged and repeated, "I'm not a doc, so I don't know. But you're going to put on clean boxers and you're going to sit in a chair with ice on your balls. Two minutes on, one minute off for twenty minutes. That should help with the swelling. I'll also give you Motrin."

"How will I know if they work? You know, if I can have kids?"

"You'll have to see a doctor for that."

"Will you go with me?"

"If you want me to. Dad will probably have to come too. We're minors."

"I don't want anyone touching me besides you and the doctor. I don't want anyone looking at anything besides you and the doctor."

Brian smiled and said, "That's fine with me, but I can't guarantee it. You know mom and dad."

Dismissing the last comment, Two asked, "What am I going to tell Graff and O'Connor?"

"The truth. You didn't do anything wrong, Michael."

"Why did that guy do that? Why did he hate me?"

"Because he's a redneck asshole. He doesn't know you. He didn't want to know you. He saw you were an Indian, a Navajo, and that's all he needed to know."

"But George is Navajo," Two said. "He didn't do anything to him."

"He is a bully, so he picked on the smallest guy, just like any bully would." Brian laughed and added, "Did you see how Graff handled the redneck? George would have done that."

Two had no answer to that, but he said, "That guy who shot him. Why did he kill him and not me?"

"I don't know. Maybe because you're a kid. I think he came here to kill O'Connor."

"Before he shot the guy, he told the guy from Crivitz that he had killed his stepfather when he was my age."

Brian thought that over and said, "Maybe that's why he didn't kill you. You reminded him of himself." He shrugged and added, "I don't know."

"Bri, I know it bothers you that you . . . *shot* those two men on the reservation. I know George feels guilty about all the killing he's done. I don't like killing either. But that guy . . . it was like, when he killed that asshole, there was no expression. When the guy dropped dead, the man stood over him, like he was daring him to get up."

Brian stared at him blankly. He wasn't sure how to respond to that. He finally said, "I think when you kill over and over again, you become used to it. You become numb. It doesn't faze you ever again." He shivered.

"I'm glad you and George aren't like that. I never want to get like that." He thought for a minute and said, "That's the one thing that bothers me about being a cop. I don't want to have to do that. Kill people. I know I might have to, but I don't want to."

Brian took hold of Two's shoulders, put his forehead on Two's and said, "I'm going to tell you something that someone told me. He told me that he couldn't see me ever being a cop because I have a good heart. I don't know if that's true or not, but I think that same statement applies to you and George. You have a good heart, Michael. I don't ever want to see you change. You have to stay happy. You have to stay excited. You have to be you."

Two hugged Brian for the longest time, then he pulled back. Two knew he had broached a touchy subject with Brian. He glanced at Brian's hands, but they weren't shaking.

Brian noticed, smiled, held up his hands and said, "All's good."

Two smiled, and stepped out of the tub and said, "You and mom are the only ones who call me Michael."

"Does that bother you?"

Two shook his head. "I like my name. I like Two, but I like my name. Thanks."

"For what?"

He smiled, shrugged and said, "For calling me Michael. And for helping me," Two said. "And for being a big brother and a friend."

"Hey, that's what big brothers are for," Brian said with a laugh. "Anytime."

CHAPTER SIXTY-TWO

The man knelt down and studied his surroundings. He knew he was headed east. He knew the cabin was another sixty or seventy yards. He hadn't seen any other hunters since he had killed dumb and dumber. That was strange to him. There were several times he had spotted deer, but no one shot at them. Not one arrow.

The morning broke bright and sunny, though with the tree canopy overhead, he only caught glimpses of the sun and sky.

What to do next? he thought. He could stay where he was, but that would be foolish, since he had no doubt that the two Indian boys would be tracking him by now. Probably the other kid was with them. Just how far they were behind him, he didn't know. What he did know, or at least what he believed, was that they were on his ass and getting closer.

He didn't understand his reluctance at killing either boy. It would have made his mission that much easier.

Okay, that wasn't altogether true. He knew why he hadn't killed the Indian kid. He saw himself in that boy. He saw himself at the mercy of a piece of shit and he wasn't going to have it. No, his stepfather never put a knife to him, but there were threats. There were bruises and black-eyes and fat lips. Once, his ear had swollen and he had temporarily lost hearing in it. That was when he began to plan. That was when he knew what the outcome would be.

The second boy was similar to himself, before the stepfather turned pathological. The man could see the beginning stages of the life that was to come for the boy. Again, he wasn't going to have it.

But in both cases, he risked his mission. More importantly, he had risked his life.

The man made a decision. He slipped off the orange jacket. That way, with his black shirt and camo pants, he would blend in. He didn't, however, place it on the ground. Instead, he placed it over a bush. In the distance, it might look like a hunter in position.

That decided, he had to come up with a concrete plan. He could move south and once coming upon the gravel or dirt road, follow the fringe of it to the cabin and wait. Or, he could head north towards the lake and follow the shoreline to the cabin. Maybe, by using the shoreline, if the two cops were out fishing, they would come to him and he'd get both of them and then he'd head home.

The other option was to continue traveling east straight to the cabin. It was the fastest route. Perhaps the most dangerous route, but in actuality, if he hadn't seen any hunters thus far, the closer he got to the cabin would negate the possibility of any hunters. Not with only sixty or seventy yards to go.

He thought it over and decided to head to the lake and use the shoreline. He could hide and wait until the two cops showed up. That was his best bet.

CHAPTER SIXTY-THREE

Eiselmann hadn't slept. He hadn't even catnapped. His body and clothes smelled sour. Even the cologne he had used for dinner with Sarah had worn off. His mouth tasted of stale coffee and garlic from his steak. He could only imagine what his breath smelled like.

As soon as he had gotten off the phone with Gordon Pasquale and Skip Dahlke, he contacted Kelliher and Storm. They had been expecting his call, though both were asleep. He filled them in on the entire conversation and sent them via secure email the phone numbers and contact list from Dasha Gogol's cell, asking them to share it at an appropriate time with the U.S. Marshall's office and ATF. They said they would run it up the chain to see if there was enough for a warrant. Best they could offer at the moment.

Next, he called Chief Jack O'Brien, who set up a conference call with Gonnering and Lorenzo, the detectives running the investigation. He filled them in on both the conversation with Pasquale and Dahlke, and the conversation with Kelliher and Storm. He also confirmed for them the existence of a second gunman, who was presumably after O'Connor, though he left out any mention of Morgan Billias and his listening in on conversations.

"We think we have the second gunman covered," O'Brien had said. "They should be in place by now."

Eiselmann had waited for more, wondering who the 'they' were, but nothing was coming, at least on that subject.

"For safety's sake, we have you under a two-person watch. Both of your kids are covered too."

"My wife . . ." Eiselmann began to say, but O'Brien cut him off.

"We have her and your two friends under watch also." A little more gently he added, "Your family is as safe as can be."

"Thank you, Sir. I appreciate that."

O'Brien cautioned him, "Don't do anything stupid or rash. Vary your routine. As soon as practical, it would be nice to keep your family together. You have to understand, and I think you do, that you are on the sideline."

"I understand."

"It's just the way it has to be, for the time being anyway."

Eiselmann looked at his watch and said, "Sarah said she would pick up both kids in the morning." He shook his head. The morning was in a couple of hours.

"How are you and your wife, Paul?"

Eiselmann didn't know how to respond, because he simply didn't know. He had hoped for the best, but wondered if the best was out of reach. Eiselmann tried to be noncommittal, so he said, "We're okay."

After he hung up, he splashed water on his face, brushed his teeth, changed his clothes, and chewed a stick of gum. Then, he drove to the hospital.

The scene was on the dark side of grim. Kaupert and Desotel had their dinner from a vending machine. They had drunk about fifteen cups of shitty coffee apiece. The taste was similar to gasoline, but the caffeine was good. A couple of crumpled paper cups were tossed under their chairs in the waiting area. There was no sign of Jorgy.

"Any word?"

Kaupert shook his head. Desotel stared at his shoes and didn't respond.

"Where's Brooke?"

"With Albrecht," Kaupert answered.

Neither man wanted to talk and that was understandable. He didn't either. He drifted away to the nurses' station and asked for Albrecht's room. With hesitation, if not outright reluctance, he got the room number and walked toward it.

He pushed the door open and stood frozen to the spot.

Albrecht lay in bed attached to tubes and wires. Intubated. IV. Catheterized. Heart monitor. Breathing monitor. Beeps and blips and colored digital graphs.

Albrecht seemed small, vulnerable. Maybe losing the battle. Eiselmann didn't know for sure, but it sure looked that way.

Brooke Beranger sat on the edge of a chair at the side of the bed holding onto one of Albrecht's hands. Her head was down. Her eyes were closed. Shoulders sunk. Yet, Eiselmann knew she wasn't sleeping. Hadn't slept.

He walked over to her side and cleared his throat so as not to startle her. He put a hand on her shoulder and said, "You need a break?"

She glanced up, then resumed her position without answering.

Whether or not she had intended to make him feel unwelcome, he didn't know. But he did feel like the shit garnish on a buffet table. He didn't blame her. He couldn't blame her. He was the reason Albrecht lay close to death.

The thing about cops most people don't get is that they are a family. A true brother and sisterhood. Spouses and children mattered. They mattered a great deal. But the family made up of cops was thicker than blood, almost a marriage unto its own.

There was unspoken bond of trust and loyalty, and a bond of love that existed that had nothing to do with sex. Each man and each woman knew their life was in each other's hands each time they put on the badge and stepped out the door. That brotherhood survived because each man and each woman understood and recognized it existed. It was real. It lived.

Eiselmann said, "Anything you or Tom need, anything at all, ask. Please."

Brooke didn't acknowledge that he had spoken. It was as if he was never there.

He left not only the room, but the hospital.

He got into his car and drove. Aimlessly. Mindlessly. At some point he sat outside of O'Connor's apartment. He was surprised no one had called in a complaint. If they had, the complaint found a wastebasket on the first toss. His tail would have called it in and cleared it.

He drove past Mark and Jennifer Erickson's house. He wanted to speak to Sarah, to be with her. He didn't want to be alone. He almost pulled into their driveway and rang the doorbell, but chickened out. He didn't know what kind of welcome, if a welcome, he'd receive.

He was lost and alone, in spite of the tail.

He drove home. He parked the car in the garage. He opened up the house and locked the door behind him. He didn't bother turning on any lights. He sat in the dark of the living room alone. Waiting for a phone call. Waiting for Sarah. Waiting for his kids. Their kids.

And he wept.

CHAPTER SIXTY-FOUR

The three of them huddled together behind bushes and a large oak tree for fifteen minutes. They were off the trail, but still close to it.

"He has not moved," George said.

He was the first to have spied the splash of orange in the distance. George guessed the man was at least fifty yards ahead of them. He searched beyond the man to see what or who the man was looking at or hiding from. George saw no one. He also wondered if the man knew he, Brett and Noah were trailing him.

"I am going to go ahead. Both of you stay here."

"We should all go," Brett cautioned.

George shook his head and said, "Too much of a chance we will be seen."

"You don't think your bright orange jacket and bright orange pants might be seen from a mile away?"

George thought for a minute and took off his jacket. He leaned his crossbow against the three, slipped off his boots, took off his orange pants, and put his boots back on. Now, dressed in camo green and black, he blended into the forest and had a reasonable chance of getting close without being spotted.

"Okay, so now that you're not wearing blaze orange, if a hunter sees movement, you end up with an arrow or two or three."

"I will be careful."

Brett shook his head and said, "You're a stubborn sonofabitch."

George smiled and said, "Much like you, my brother."

George moved slowly and quietly, hiding among bushes and behind trees. He not only searched ahead of him, but up in the trees looking for other hunters. He didn't see any thus far, and he hoped to spot whoever was hunting well before they spotted him.

George got within twenty-five yards of the man, when he discovered it wasn't a man. Just an orange jacket hung over a bush to make it look like it was a man. He ducked down and searched in all directions. He could be as patient as needed. His eyes strained into the distance searching for the man or anything that might indicate where the man was. He saw nothing.

Carefully, slowly, he retraced his steps back to Brett and Noah and explained to them what he saw.

Brett searched off in the distance. Noah turned around and searched behind them.

"I do not know where he is," George said.

"He could be anywhere," Brett said.

"He could be looking right at us," Noah said as he licked his lips. "What do we do now?"

George said, "Our cabin is beyond those trees. Maybe two hundred yards. Maybe more. For all he knows, we are heading back to the cabin because we are done with hunting for the morning."

Brett nodded and said, "We walk out like nothing happened. We get to the cabin and wait for O'Connor and Graff to show up. By now, Bri and Two warned them, and they are back at the cabin."

"I think that is our best bet," George said.

"What about my dad and uncle?" Noah said.

"I made a promise to you," George said. "We will come back for them."

Noah nodded, turned back toward the way they had come, as much to look for the man as to look back in the direction where his father lay dead.

George pulled off his boots, pulled up his orange pants, and put his boots back on. He put on his jacket and said, "I will lead. Then Noah. Brett, watch our back, but stay close. You have the least amount of orange on."

Brett nodded, and said, "No shit." He smiled and said, "Let's go."

CHAPTER SIXTY-FIVE

Being up in a tree helped O'Connor's cell reception. So much so, his cell had vibrated almost nonstop. At first, he thought someone was calling him because of the constancy of the vibration. Slowly because he didn't want to bring any attention to himself, he pulled his cell out of his back pocket and glanced at why his phone was blowing up. While there were three voicemail messages, the rest were text messages. At least a dozen of them.

O'Connor decided to wait to read any of the texts or listen to the calls. He didn't want the distraction when his potential killer might be coming their way.

Still, there was the feeling that those messages contained something important. He pushed that feeling aside, thinking that a bullet to his head would be more dangerous than anything a text or voicemail message had to say.

Every so often, he'd search in Graff's direction, only seeing Graff and no one else. While Graff faced the trail, O'Connor was in a position to see not only the lakeside flank, but the road side flank. Graff searched ahead of them, behind them, and the side where he knew the lake to be. Neither of them had seen anything. No movement. No other hunters.

Used to long waits while he was on the job, O'Connor settled in, found a branch that not only hid him well enough, but made it comfortable for him to sit. If anyone were to shoot at him and hope to hit or kill him, it would have to come from the trail itself, or at the least, within a few yards of Graff's side of the trail.

While he never drank on the job unless his persona called for it, he wished he had some Peanut M&M's and a beer. Hell, he'd even take a couple of Brian's Oreos.

Other than the soccer pitch, he had never seen Brian take charge like he had done with him and Graff. Brian was adamant about what the two men should do, almost ordering them around.

What he admired most was how in control he was. What puzzled him was how Brian knew where the trail would be. To O'Connor's knowledge, Brian had not ventured into the forest. But clearly, he knew what he was talking about.

What neither Brian nor Two told them was exactly what had taken place in the forest. Yes, there was a man with a gun with a suppressor attached to it. Yes, the man shot one of the guys from Crivitz and then took off. But as Graff had suggested to him, there was a lot more to the story than what was shared.

Two looked as though he had been beaten up by a playground bully. The blood over the eye. The bloody, swollen nose. The way he moved. The way he sat in the boat. Neither he nor Graff missed any of it. He and Graff would get to the bottom of it before the day was over. He was not about to have a repeat of what had taken place in Arizona. Especially anything involving Brian. Not if he could help it.

CHAPTER SIXTY-SIX

The man stopped dead in his tracks, dropped down, and rethought his decision to head to the lake. If he continued on, there was the possibility of being cornered and captured, or worse, killed.

He made the decision to head back along the lake to his original hiding spot, pick up his black duffle, dress in orange and make his way to his rental truck. He'd live to see another day, and choose a different strategy and day to carry out his plan.

He judged he was twenty or thirty yards from the trail leading to the cabin. He was still fifteen to twenty yards from the lake, which he could see in the distance between the trees. If he continued west, his course would take him directly to his hiding spot and within a short walking distance to his truck.

He had encountered no one and had not seen anyone thus far. But he also knew he was being followed by three of the boys. He didn't know which ones because he hadn't gotten that close, and he didn't allow them to get close to him. Their close proximity would unnecessarily complicate things.

It wasn't about preserving the kids. It was solely and purely self-preservation. A shootout would put him in unnecessary jeopardy and lessen his chances of a clean escape.

He picked his way through the underbrush. It wasn't a trail per se, but a game path. His head was on a swivel. It had to be, because hunters, in position because of this path, could be perched in trees above him.

He looked for any telltale movement, any shadows or shades that shouldn't have been where they were. Nothing yet, but that didn't mean there wouldn't be eventually, somewhere up ahead or on the side of him.

The three boys tailing him were still twenty to thirty yards behind and another twenty yards to his south. He made the decision to let them pass.

He crouched down to a kneeling position at first, then lay prone, his revolver with the suppressor out and aimed. His breaths short and slow. His muscles relaxed. His eyes open.

The three boys had pulled abreast of him, but still twenty yards to his south. They had made no apparent pretense of looking for him, or for that matter, hunting. It looked like they were heading back to the cabin.

The older Indian boy was in the lead. The man could see the boy's eyes darting everywhere. The man smiled. The kid was good. To any casual observer, it would appear as if he was marching forward along the trail, looking straight ahead. The man knew differently. The Indian kid was anything but relaxed.

Next came the redneck boy. He must have run into them when the man sent him off. The man noticed the rifle he carried. Must have been his father's. Of the three, he was the least relaxed and did nothing to hide it. He would be the most dangerous because of his lack of discipline. The lack of discipline would make him unpredictable.

Bringing up the rear was the kid in the Badger baseball cap. He didn't look as relaxed as the Indian kid. The man wondered about that. Maybe it was his nature. Maybe it was the lack of orange he wore. Maybe the kid was on the lookout for him.

Twice, the redneck boy looked over in the man's general direction, but his expression hadn't changed and it didn't appear that the boy had seen him. There wasn't a faltered step that would be a giveaway that he had been spotted.

The boy in the Badger cap did more searching above them in the trees than he did searching behind them. He carried a Glock, though the man couldn't tell the size or model. The way the boy carried it looked to the man as if the kid knew how to use it. That kid would bear watching as much as the Indian boy.

The man kept his revolver trained on them, particularly on the boy in the Badger cap as they marched onward without hesitating or slowing down.

He waited until they were thirty yards ahead before he even thought about getting up and moving on.

The man got up, first in a one-knee-down position, and then in a crouch, before he hunched over and moved ahead on his mission. He needed to secure the black bag, get to his truck, and get out. If he was able to do that, he'd consider it mission accomplished. At least, for the time being. He still had the contract on the cop to fulfill.

CHAPTER SIXTY-SEVEN

From his vantage point, O'Connor saw them first. Graff saw them shortly thereafter.

Three in a row, George leading, Brett trailing, and . . . *'Who is the kid in the middle?' O'Connor thought.*

It was George who spotted him. It was subtle, but there was brief eye contact and a slight nod that anyone watching would have attributed to a misstep on uneven terrain. The unknown boy never saw him, but Brett saw both O'Connor and Graff. When he did, he turned and searched behind them.

George stopped on the trail far enough away from O'Connor's tree to not bring attention to him, and at a space equidistant between O'Connor and Graff.

"We will wait here," George announced.

Neither Graff nor O'Connor spoke, but George, seemingly speaking to Brett and the other boy, said, "I do not know where he went, and I do not know how we missed him."

"Could he be further ahead?" the boy asked.

"Doubt it," Brett said with his back turned to them, still facing the trail and area from where they came. "He would have been seen."

"How? By who?" the boy asked.

Neither George nor Brett answered, but Graff stepped out of his hiding place with his gun out but pointed at the ground. He stretched his back and said quietly, "About how far in front of you was he?"

The boy startled, but George turned to him and said, "We are safe now." To Graff, he said, "We stayed within sight. At least, we thought we did. He hung his orange jacket on a bush and that was when we lost him."

"How long ago was that?"

George turned to Brett and the boy, then said, "I think twenty minutes, maybe thirty minutes ago."

"So, he could be anywhere," Graff said.

"Could he have flanked you?" Brett asked, still with his back to them. He was taking no chances.

"I doubt it," O'Connor said as he climbed down from the tree.

"I didn't see you up there," the boy said. To George he asked, "Did you know he was up there?"

George smiled and said, "Yes."

"Never saw something so ugly up in a tree before," Brett added. He turned around, deciding the man wasn't anywhere nearby.

"Where are the two men you were with?" O'Connor asked the boy. Then he remembered that one of them was shot and killed.

The boy hung his head and said, "Back there. That man shot my dad."

"He also shot Noah's uncle," Brett added.

"We knew about the uncle. Brian told us. Let's head back to the cabin. We have a lot to discuss," Graff said.

"Detective Pat, I will lead. Then Noah, then you and Detective Jamie, and then Brett."

O'Connor glanced at Graff who pursed his lips.

"It is best if I lead in case he did get around you somehow. You and Detective Pat will be protected."

George didn't wait for a response or objection, but began walking. Noah followed. Brett waited until O'Connor and Graff fell into the line, then followed at the end. The five of them looking left and right, as well as ahead. Brett took care of watching their six.

It had been a long time since O'Connor was babysat, and this was how he felt. Babysat by the kids who he and Graff were supposed to be taking care of.

He couldn't shake the feeling that they were being watched. The hair on the back of his neck and on his arms stood at attention. He felt a chill, though the day was shaping up to be a warm one.

He could and would take a bullet if it came to it, though he didn't want to. He just didn't want anything to happen to the boys. Not if he could help it.

CHAPTER SIXTY-EIGHT

It was slow going, but he made it without being seen. Perhaps he was seen, but he didn't end up with an arrow in his back or stomach. That in itself was a win.

He waited until he was absolutely certain no one saw him or was coming after him before he retrieved his back duffle. Once he did, he acted quickly. He slipped on his orange pants, jacket, and orange stocking cap that he had brought along just in case. He pulled it down to cover his hair. He wanted his revolver handy, so he kept his jacket only partially zipped up.

The duffle came with shoulder straps, making it look like he carried a large crossbow on his back. With it on his back, it would make his progress through the woods faster, but more importantly, he had both arms free.

He took off. Not too fast, but not too slow, either. He needed to get to his truck before anyone else came looking for him. He also knew that the boys would report the death of the two men, which would bring law enforcement into the forest. That would only increase the chances of him being caught. He couldn't risk that.

On the way to the truck, he considered his options. He needed to fulfill his contract, but the timing of the contract was on his terms to a degree. Any contract he had worked was always left to him on how and when to execute it. Of course, there were times when the terms were dictated, but those instances were rare.

He sighed. He had come close, but not nearly close enough. He could take him on the road, preferably between the lake and Crivitz. He could take him out in Waukesha. Perhaps wait until he stepped out of his apartment, or wait until he showed up at the next soccer game. Either would be risky, but doable.

It might have to be long distance, but he had the patience, the equipment, and most importantly, the skill. Though he liked killing up close, distance might be his best bet.

As he walked, he thought back to O'Connor's apartment. Third floor, which was the top floor. Over-looking the street. Another apartment building across the street. Perhaps from the roof. He'd have to check the access, but it was a possibility. Quick, lethal shot. Leave in a hurry. In and out, the way he liked it.

He was within a half-mile from where he had parked his truck, when he saw a hunter walking in, with a hunter on either side, but at a short distance apart. It looked as though they were hunting together, but he couldn't tell for sure.

As he approached them, he was certain the guy was a cop. That meant the other two might be too. What he didn't know was whether they had been called in and were looking for him, or if they were hunting on their day off. They were dressed as hunters, but he wasn't about to take any chances.

He said with a smile, "Good luck. I haven't seen anything in two days."

"Giving up already?"

The hunter was of a thicker build with a barrel chest. Thy guy had him by forty pounds at the least. A bullet head in a crew cut of brown hair, dark eyes, and a couple days' worth of beard. He carried a long bow with a quiver of nasty looking arrows that would rip into and probably out of anything he shot at, depending upon the distance. He also carried a firearm on his hip. The man could tell by the bulge.

"Yeah, not feeling well. Flu, I think."

"That's a bummer," he answered with no expression.

"Yeah, well, it happens. I think if you're looking for deer, a couple of hunters said they had better luck west of here," the man said, point to his right. "At least, that's what they said." This last he said with a shrug.

"We'll keep that in mind."

"How far do you have to walk?"

The man was getting antsy. Too many questions. He said, "My ride is up ahead. I'll be okay. Good morning for a walk."

He started past him, turned, found the guy staring at his back and said, "Take care. I saw some kids in here. I don't know how seasoned they are, but you might want to watch your back."

The guy nodded, stared at him, but eventually turned around and motioned to his two partners to move onward.

The man breathed easier, but he didn't relax. Too early for that. He still had to get to his truck.

CHAPTER SIXTY-NINE

Brian moved from window to window. He'd peek out, look to the left and to the right, and then move onto the next, before repeating the process at the first window. Every now and then, he'd check the lock on the doors.

When he noticed Two staring at him, he asked, "How are you feeling?"

Two shrugged and said, "My balls don't hurt as much. The cuts do, but not my balls."

Just as Brian wanted him to, Two sat in a stuffed chair in a shirt and his boxers, and had placed a package of frozen peas between his legs and under his scrotum for twenty minutes. He actually did this twice for a total of forty minutes, two minutes on, one minute off. It was uncomfortable at first, but he got used to it. When the coolness of the peas wore out, he switched to a bag of green beans, and placed the peas back in the freezer.

"Can I check the swelling?"

"Yeah. Here or in the bathroom?"

Brian thought it over for a second or two and then said, "In the bathroom. Just in case."

Two got up out of the chair in the living room, and walked to the bathroom. Brian noticed that he was walking in a near normal gait, which was considerably different from the way he had walked out of the forest to the boat, and out of the boat to the cabin. Brian nodded his approval.

JOSEPH LEWIS

Without being asked, Two pulled down his boxers, and stood with his legs apart. Brian came in and shut and locked the door as he had done before, knelt on one knee and inspected Two.

"Do you mind if I touch you?"

"I don't mind."

As gently as Brian could, he touched first the right side and then the left. As he did, he looked up at Two to see what his reaction was. He didn't see any.

"Feeling okay?"

Two nodded, then smiled and said, "It tickles, but it doesn't hurt like it did. Your hand is warm."

Brian smiled at him and said, "Do you think we need to change the bandage and put some more Neosporin on the cuts?"

"Sure, as long as we don't put any more Peroxide down there."

Brian chuckled and said, "I don't think we have to do that until we go to bed. Just to be safe."

Brian peeled off the gauze, pleased that it held up so well. He took off the gauze covering the two cuts and showed it to Two. "No blood."

Two relaxed, and Brian could tell he was relieved.

"I know I already asked you this, but do you think I'll be able to have kids?"

Brian shrugged and said, "Only a doctor will be able to tell you for sure."

As he did earlier that morning, Brian coated the two cuts with Neosporin, covered them with gauze, and then looped gauze around the top portion of Two's sack, around the gauze over the cuts, and anchored it in place with Vaseline.

"I'm not as big as you or Brett."

Brian laughed and said, "There is no one in the world as big as Brett and Bobby. And remember, you're two years younger, so you're still growing. But I want you to remember something."

"What?"

Brian said, "The wand doesn't make the magician. The magician makes the wand. If whatever you do with someone you really love is out of love, then whatever you do will be perfect."

Two nodded solemnly, and then reached out and hugged Brian. "I love you, Brian."

"I love you too, Michael. That's a promise."

CHAPTER SEVENTY

Mark and Jennifer Erickson dropped Sarah off at the house, and waited until she had unlocked the front door and entered. It was only then, when she shut the door behind her, that they drove off. Mark told her that he and Jennifer would pick up Mikey and Stephen, and drop Stephen off, before they went home. Sarah thanked them, and thanked them for letting her stay at their house. She and Jennifer, her oldest and closest friend, had talked far into the night. Rather, Sarah had talked, and Jennifer had listened.

Paul was still sitting on the couch facing the front picture window. It was the same position he had been all night. He hadn't moved.

The front door was in a hallway just to the left of the living room. Sarah paused at the door, reluctant to enter, and feeling sorry if she had woken Paul up. She wasn't sure she had.

His eyes were red and puffy. He seemed pale, and his shoulders sagged. He looked small to her somehow.

She hung her jacket over a stuffed chair and sat down across from him. The two of them stared at one another. Neither wanted to be the first to look away.

"I'm not angry at you," Sarah finally said.

Paul flinched, but otherwise, didn't respond.

"The whole thing just scared me. I kept thinking, 'What if we were in that car? What if that was you the EMTs were working on? And what if Stephen and Alex were in the house and that bitch . . .'" Her voice trailed off and she shook her head. "I already lost one husband. The kids already lost one dad."

It was Paul who looked away. He swiped at his eyes, and he nodded. He didn't dare say anything for fear of it coming out wrong. Mostly, he didn't know what he could say.

"Paul, I love you. That hasn't changed." She paused, looked up at the ceiling, perhaps above the ceiling looking for inspiration. "I always knew there was a possibility that . . ." she shook her head. "But last night, it was real. It wasn't just my imagination anymore. It was real. It really happened."

Paul couldn't look at her. He wanted to disappear.

Yet, he wanted to be with her, needed to be with her. One of the best things about their relationship was the ability to be together, present, and in silence. No words were necessary between them. This wasn't one of those times, however.

He needed Stephen's smartass comments and to hear his laugh. He needed Alex's gentleness and to see her smile. Mostly, he wanted to turn back time, before what had taken place the night before, and before working undercover in Chicago. Before any of this, all of it, had taken place. He wanted his simple life with Sarah, with Stephen, and with Alex.

"Paul, are you okay?"

He nodded, but still couldn't look her in the eye.

"Oh my God, did something happen to Tom? Is he, is he . . .?"

He shook his head, then shrugged and said in a voice barely above a whisper, "I don't know."

"Did you go to the hospital? You said you were going to at least call."

"I did. He is . . . *was*, still unconscious." He shook his head. "I haven't heard anything."

Sarah leaned forward and said, "Do you want to go to the hospital? I can have Mark and Jennifer keep Stephen with them until we get back. Alex is fine at Germaine's. I'll call them and explain."

Paul's resolve crumbled. He leaned forward with his elbows on his knees, his hands on his face and he wept. He said, "I didn't want anything like this to happen to you and the kids. Our kids. I didn't. I wanted that part of my life, the cop part, separate from our life. I didn't want it touching this, what we have." He shook his head, and through another sob, said, "I didn't."

The two of them sat on separate sides of the living room. Both wept, but couldn't bridge the distance between them.

Fortunately for them, or unfortunately, Paul's cell buzzed. He lifted it off of the couch cushion next to him and looked at the caller ID. It was Nate Kaupert at the hospital. He must have an update on Albrecht.

Paul shut his eyes and said a silent prayer. He wasn't ready to hear any news. He didn't know if he would ever be ready to hear any news. He wanted to answer, but at the same time, he didn't. Whatever had happened to Albrecht, whatever it was, good or bad, it was because of him.

CHAPTER SEVENTY-ONE

Detective Alex Jorgenson sat at the picnic table facing the woods. No matter how he sat, his six foot-five inch, and two-hundred-and-thirty-pound body wasn't comfortable. His .306 was on top of the table with his right hand near the grip. He wore mirrored Oakley sunglasses in a silver frame, so neither Brian nor Two could tell if his eyes were open or closed. Both assumed he was awake.

On his right was Brian with a can of Sprite at his left hand, and his Glock on his lap within easy reach of his right hand. Two sat slouched in a lawn chair, his legs splayed out in front of him with a bottle of water in his hand and his crossbow on his lap.

When Jorgy first showed up, Brian and Two tag-teamed what had taken place earlier that morning. Two, however, hadn't mentioned the knife to his nuts, and it wasn't Brian's place to speak for him. Brian figured it was Two's story to share or not.

They sat in silence basking in the sun and the quiet. Birds chirped. A thick, pungent smell of wood smoke from someone's campfire mixed with pine filled the air. It was at once comforting and pleasing.

"I'm going to go clean out my boat," Brian said, getting up from the table.

"Maybe you should wait until Graff and O'Connor come back, since there's two of you and only one of me," Jorgy said in a low voice, never taking his eyes off the woods. "Please," he added to soften it.

Brian didn't know Jorgy all that well, so he shrugged and settled back down. He didn't feel like arguing, because it was more out of boredom than anything. Cleaning out the boat could wait.

George appeared at the edge of the woods. He held up a hand to stop the procession until he searched his left and right. When he was satisfied all was quiet and nothing threatening, he led the procession out of the woods up to the cabin. To be safe, George stood to one side facing the woods as Graff and O'Connor and Noah walked to the cabin.

Brian looked over at Two, who met his gaze, and then the two of them faced the group. Both wondered why Noah was with them. Last to leave the woods was Brett, who stood on the other side of the path and faced the woods just as George did. Neither was about to let their guard down.

"You're here early," Graff said with a laugh. "You must have left, what, about four or so?"

Jorgy squinted at him and said, "We got up here around two this morning. Been on the perimeter of the forest most of the night and early morning."

"Seriously?" Graff asked. He shook his head not understanding why he didn't knock on the cabin door earlier.

"You said, 'We.' Who is with you?" O'Connor asked.

Jorgy's mouth hung open. Finally, he tilted his head and slowly said, "You . . . don't know what happened last night, do you?"

Neither man answered.

"I know you were called. You must have a half-dozen voicemail. I sent you at least two texts, maybe more. So did Lorenzo and Gonnering. I think you got a call from Mr. Clean, who, by the way, is more than a little pissed no one had heard from you. Which is why I got here so early."

O'Connor stuck his service revolver in his belt, and snagged his cell from his back pocket. "I didn't have service until I climbed a tree about thirty or forty minutes ago."

He thumbed through his texts. Every now and then, he'd run his hand through his long hair or over his face. A couple of times he muttered, "Jesus." Once, he said, "Jesus Christ."

"What? What happened?" Graff asked, loudly enough for both George and Brett to turn and listen.

Jorgy shook his head and said, "You better sit down. And to answer your question, I met Earl Coffey and two of his deputies up here. One of us watched your cabin, while two patrolled the fringe of the forest. We rotated on the hour so one of us could get some sleep in between rotations."

"Albrecht was shot," O'Connor said to no one in particular. To Jorgenson, he asked, "Any word on his condition?"

Jorgy held up a satellite phone and said, "I've been in contact. Last I heard, there was no change."

"Wait, wait!" Graff said, holding up his hands to stop them from the half-assed bit by bit information. "Start at the beginning and tell us what happened. All of it."

George and Brett forgot all about watching the woods and joined the others around the picnic table.

Jorgy glanced at the boys, wondering how much he should share, but then in answer his own question, he said, "Fuck it," and in his slow, but thorough style, he told them from beginning to end what had taken place the night before.

He began with the tip that there were two shooters, one after Eiselmann and one after O'Connor. He went into detail about the set up at Eiselmann's house, the shooting, the meeting in Eiselmann's home office, and the hospital. After, he waited patiently for the questions, but none came.

Two cleared his throat and told them about his encounter with the redneck without telling them about his nuts almost being cut off. He told them about the man with the gun and about the man telling the redneck that when he was Two's age, he had shot his stepfather.

Noah chimed in and told them about the man killing his father and ordering him to run and not stop or he'd be shot.

George and Two described the man, including what he was wearing when they last saw him.

"Hand me your sat phone," Graff said. He punched in a number, walked a short distance away, and in a low voice so others couldn't hear, spoke to someone on the other end in a long monologue. No one knew who he was speaking with.

Graff listened for a bit, and then asked a series of questions. Nodded or shook his head, depending upon what the answers were. He kicked a stone or two, and pushed around a couple of others with the toe of his boot.

He ended the conversation with his left hand gripping the sat phone like it was alive and threatening to jump out of his hand, while his right hand flexed into a fist, only to relax for a second or two, before he flexed it into a fist again.

"How bad is it?"

"Bad. We need to pack up and leave. Now."

CHAPTER SEVENTY-TWO

By the time Paul and Sarah got to the hospital, Albrecht was still in surgery, the second since he had been shot the night before. This latest was to close off a bleeder from somewhere inside of him. He also had not regained consciousness, which, though alarming, was a blessing since how badly he was shot up.

Desotel, who was Albrecht's closest male friend, stood facing out the window with the fingers of both hands stuffed into the front pocket of his jeans. Eiselmann recognized that Desotel hadn't changed his clothes, which meant that he hadn't left the hospital.

Kaupert slumped in a chair, his feet out in front of him, his head supported by one hand. It appeared that he had been sleeping, but Eiselmann didn't know for sure. He, too, had not left the hospital judging by his rumpled appearance.

Brooke Beranger, eyes red and puffy, paced from one end of the waiting area to the other. She looked as though she had aged ten years. However, even without makeup and even as distraught as she was, she still had a grace and beauty that many women only wished for. She squeezed a crumpled Kleenex in her right hand. Her left hand was tight in a fist.

Captain Jack O'Brien, otherwise known as Mr. Clean, stood in a corner away from the deputies talking to Sheriff Myron Wagner. It was a study in contrast. O'Brien looked as though he could bench press a thousand pounds. His arms were folded tightly on his chest. Shirt sleeves and the chest of his shirt bulging from muscle. On the other hand, Wagner was grossly overweight. His jowls gave him a triple chin and a no-neck look. The only word Eiselmann could come up with was sloppy, which also described his approach to law enforcement.

Sarah made her way to Brooke. She caught her in mid-stride, and when Brooke saw her, she stiffened. Sarah felt the chill in the air and with it, the onset of frostbite. Understandably so.

Helpless, she said, "Brooke, I'm so sorry. If there is anything I can do, please let me know."

Brooke nodded curtly, stepped around her and kept pacing, unwilling to engage with her.

Eiselmann made his way to Desotel and said, "Ron, is there any update on Tom?"

Desotel, about as short as Eiselmann, shook his head, but remained facing the window.

"If you or Brooke or Nate need anything, you'll let me know?"

Ronnie nodded once. His jaw was clenched so tightly, Paul wondered if he could chew nails.

Both Eiselmann and Sarah felt like intruders, unwelcome and unwanted. They sat together in chairs at the end of the waiting room away from everyone else, as unobtrusively as possible. Sarah reached over and took Paul's hand in both of hers. Paul glanced over, and Sarah was biting her lip, her chin quivering, tears gathering in her eyes.

Head hung low, barely able to look at her, Paul whispered, "Sarah, I'm sorry."

She shook her head and whispered, "Nothing to be sorry for. Nothing. It's not you and it's not me. It's the situation. We'll get through this." And she gripped his hand tighter.

"I love you."

She smiled and whispered, "I know. I love you too. Nothing is going to change that." For emphasis, she added, "Ever."

It wasn't long before Wagner and O'Brien made their way over to Paul and Sarah, who stood up as they approached.

"Paul, are you doing okay?" Wagner asked.

Eiselmann couldn't remember the last time he had spoken to the Sheriff, but he said, "Yes, Sir, about as well as can be."

Wagner shook his head rather dramatically and said, "Damn shame." He turned to Sarah and said, "Excuse me, ma'am."

While Paul was certain the sheriff was sad to see any of his deputies on a table in surgery, there was a whiff of insincerity to his comments. Paul wondered if Wagner knew who Albrecht was.

Sarah shrugged and tried to smile.

To O'Brien, he said, "I'm heading back to the office. Keep me posted if anything happens." To Eiselmann, he said, "Hang in there, Paul." And he turned and left.

O'Brien smiled, rolled his eyes at Wagner's back, shook his head and said, "Paul, O'Connor and Graff are on their way back. So are the boys. I have Jorgenson with them. We contacted the Marinette County Sheriff Office, and they sent Earl Coffey and two deputies. I just want you to know Pat and Jamie are protected."

"Thank you, Sir."

O'Brien waved it off and said in a low voice that could only be heard by Paul and Sarah, "I noticed the chilly reception you both received. I'm sorry about that. I know they are close to Albrecht, especially Beranger and Desotel. I know it's difficult, but please don't take it personally."

Both Paul and Sarah nodded.

"Paul, when this . . ." he searched for the right word, waved his hands around, and settled on, "blows over, I would like to talk to you about an idea I have. I know we need to square away Albrecht, and you and O'Connor and the case you're working on, but when we do . . . and we will," he added with emphasis, "I would like to speak with you, confidentially. O'Connor, too." He glanced down the hall Wagner had waddled down, and then at the others in the room. "Maybe in the next two weeks, or however long it takes."

"Yes, Sir."

O'Brien softened up, smiled- though his smile scared the shit out of anyone who saw it- and said, "I know this is difficult. God only knows what you both are feeling. I want you both to know my door is always open." To Paul, he said, "I have your cell number and you have mine. Don't be afraid to use it."

"Yes, Sir."

O'Brien clamped a meaty paw on Eiselmann's shoulder, gave it a squeeze, turned to Sarah and said, "Ma'am," with a nod. He turned and left.

CHAPTER SEVENTY-THREE

Earl Coffey called in the murder of the two men from Crivitz, Nick Roman and Bob Freeman. Before anyone arrived, Graff, O'Connor, Jorgenson and Coffey pulled the five boys aside and worked through their stories.

"It's important for you to tell them the truth. But it is also important not to speculate."

Brett cocked his head expecting and wanting more.

O'Connor said, "For instance, we don't know anything about the man who shot Noah's uncle or father. It would be speculation to mention that you *think* he might have been after me. We don't know that. Tell the truth. Tell exactly what happened."

"Everyone understand?" Graff asked.

The boys nodded or stated that they understood by saying 'yes.'

The first to arrive were three deputies from Marinette County. Shortly after, Noah's mother showed up. Both Graff and O'Connor were surprised to see how put together she was. No hysterics. No screaming. Of course, there was crying. She wrapped Noah in her arms and they wept together.

She was a smallish woman with hunched shoulders, a little overweight, medium height, and rather nondescript. Graff didn't understand where Noah got his looks. He was a handsome young man. His mother wore the years of a life that hadn't been kind to her. Her husband was a loud, obnoxious man. It would not have surprised Graff if Noah or Brandy, his mother, mentioned that there had been abuse towards one or the other of them. Bob Freeman was that kind of man, and both mother and son looked to be easy targets.

The boys were called by a deputy to give statements. Two left out the cuts to his balls, though he did mention that Nick Roman had threatened to cut them off with his knife. One by one, they gave statements of what they saw, what had happened, and most importantly as far as Graff or O'Connor were concerned, the boys didn't speculate. Their statements were straight forward.

Two State Patrol officers showed up and wanted their own statements for a parallel investigation. The boys repeated everything one more time.

When George finished his statement, one of the Patrol Deputies said, "I think I remember you from two or three years ago. Two men and a naked kid died from gunshot wounds near Pembine. An FBI agent brought you in to identify the two men. By helicopter, as I recall."

"Yes, Sir."

"Seems like when you show up, there are dead bodies. Just like today."

O'Connor and Graff strolled over and said, "Everything okay here," Graff glanced at the name plate on his shirt and said, "Deputy Peterman?"

Peterman squinted at George, never took his eyes off of him and said, "I just mentioned that I remember him from a multiple murder a couple of years ago near Pembine."

"Yes, I heard you," O'Connor said. "FBI Agent Pete Kelliher asked him to come in and identify two assholes who had been involved in a sex ring. George witnessed a similar murder in Arizona. He provided credible evidence in that case, and it was because of him we were able to save about thirty kids. However, we weren't able to save his family who was murdered in retaliation for his bravery."

"Both Pat and I were on raids that freed those kids," Graff said. "Pat's right. George was key to that investigation.

"Odd coincidence."

"I guess that's one perspective," O'Connor said, clearly annoyed.

"Are you finished with George's statement?" Graff asked. "We'd like to head home and we have quite a bit to do to make that happen."

"Why the hurry?" Peterman asked.

"Because there was an attempt on my partner's life last night in Waukesha, and a deputy, our friend, is fighting for his life as a result," O'Connor said.

"If you're done, we'd like to pack up and get out. Are you done?" Graff asked.

Looking directly at George, Peterman said, "For now."

"Who is your supervisor?" O'Connor asked. "And what is your first name?"

"Why?"

"Because when I call the FBI and speak to Deputy Director Thomas Davenport, I want to make sure I have the names correct. Yours especially."

"George, why don't you go help pack up," Graff said. "I think you're done here."

"Yes, Sir."

Peterman attempted to walk away, when O'Connor snagged his arm and said, "I would like your first name. *Sir.*"

"You just put your hand on an officer," Peterman said.

"For now, just a hand," O'Connor said, as he walked away.

Graff stood waiting for Peterman to say or do anything further. When Peterman walked away, Graff did too.

Before Noah and his mother left, Two and George made sure he had their cell numbers, and asked him to stay in touch. Noah said he would, and his mother thanked them both. It had been important to George to make sure Noah knew he didn't have any ill feelings about his father or uncle. They shook hands, and Noah and his mother followed the ambulance out of the camp.

The boys had helped close up a camp many times. Each had their tasks to complete, assigned or assumed. First came the boats. Brett drove Brian's truck to the public landing on the other side of lake. One of the deputies, Brett didn't remember his name probably because he'd never see him again, drove Graff's truck behind Brett.

Brian and the other deputy, Dale something-or-other, took off in Brian's boat. Brian dropped him off at Graff's boat, and then led the way to the public landing. Once the boats were loaded onto their trailers and washed off according to DNR standards, Brian and Brett led the way back to the cabin.

George and Two packed up clothes, and the hunting and fishing gear. They stripped sheets off the beds and put them in the big black trunks where they found them the day before. Then they remade the beds with only the bedspreads and blankets on them.

Graff, O'Connor, Jorgy, and Coffey cleaned up the kitchen, emptied the trash, and ran the vacuum around the floors.

When Brett and Brian and the two deputies returned with the boats, George and Two helped load up the trucks with their gear. Most everything was tidy and put together, when Brian took Two aside and asked how he was doing.

"Better. Hurts a little. Maybe I shouldn't have lifted anything."

"Do we need to change the bandage? It's been a while."

Two glanced around at everyone milling around, reluctant to draw any attention to himself than necessary. "I think it can wait."

"We have almost a three hour drive back home," Brian cautioned.

Two sighed and said, "Yeah, probably."

"Okay, come on."

It didn't take long. Again, there wasn't any blood on the gauze, and the swelling on Two's balls had decreased considerably, though there were still some bruises and a little tender at Brian's touch.

"Looking better, Michael. Just take it easy, okay?"

Two smiled and said, "I will. Thanks."

"We will still have to see a doc for a shot and to make sure everything works."

He frowned and said, "I know."

They left the bathroom and joined up with everyone else in the living room.

"Here's how we're going to do this," Jorgy said. "Or, this is how the Cap said we are going to do this." He glanced around at the group to see if anyone was going to object.

"Brian, you drove your truck, right?"

"Yes."

"Okay, you and the guys will ride together back home, but you'll need to follow me. I'll drive O'Connor. Earl is going to drive Graff. Dale and Harvey will drive Graff's truck back."

Again, he glanced around the room. "Any questions?"

George said, "If Brett and I drive Detective Jamie's truck back, then Deputy Dale and Deputy Harvey can drive their own truck and follow. It would give more coverage."

"Why can't I drive my own truck?" Graff asked. "This is a bit over the top."

"Just doing what the Cap wants us to do," Jorgy said. "But George, that isn't a bad idea. If Jamie is okay with you driving it."

Impatient and disgusted at having to be babysat, Jamie said, "That's fine. George, you'll need to keep up."

"Yes, Sir."

"All right, a change in plans. Earl and I will drive ahead and straight through without stopping. Brian and George, you'll need to follow the speed limit. Dale and Harvey will stay with the boys. If there is any sign of anything, we have our radios. Use them."

"And what do we use?" Brett asked.

"Your cell phones. Make sure the four of you have everyone's number and keep your phones charged and handy. If you need to stop, you need to stay together."

Jorgy looked around the room and said, "Are we good?"

Nods all around, though Jamie was not at all pleased.

"Okay, let's roll."

CHAPTER SEVENTY-FOUR

The man drove to Marinette and returned the truck he had rented. Before turning over the keys, he filled it up, washed it, vacuumed it out, including the truck bed, and made sure he had wiped down every inch of the interior because he didn't want to leave any prints.

He got back into his own vehicle, a one-year-old BMW in the 5 series, and drove to an IHOP, not to eat, but to change clothes in the restroom. Part of the change was a wig of longish black hair, and brown-tinted contact lenses without prescription.

He stowed the hunting clothes in the black duffle, and wore jeans with black Nike Cross Trainers, and a black Nike hoodie with the hood pulled up over his head. He also wore cheap sunglasses with a dark frame. When he looked himself over in the mirror, he was a totally different man. He chuckled, thinking that in some respects, he looked like the Unabomber without the beard.

He jumped back into his car and drove thirty-two miles back to Crivitz, hoping he had gotten there before the cop and the kids. He'd wait a half-hour. If he did miss them, it wouldn't take long for him to catch up. All he had to do was look for a maroon Ram Short Bed hauling a boat that the soccer kid drove. Either way, he was good.

CHAPTER SEVENTY-FIVE

Not having to drive, and being driven by Jorgy who was less then talkative anyway, gave O'Connor time to think. With Eiselmann as his partner, he would bounce ideas off of him, just as Eiselmann did with him. He wasn't around, and while he knew Jorgy, he didn't know him well enough to use him as a sounding board.

O'Connor started at the beginning of the trip when Eiselmann informed him that there might be someone after him.

In Crivitz at the Kwik Trip, he was told via phone call that the two men he had spotted at the soccer game were shot at close range by a professional. Then in the forest, two men who had a run-in with the boys were shot at close range by a professional. A professional who used a revolver with a suppressor, according to both Two and George. It was used on the smaller of the two men, Nick Roman, who had threatened to cut off Two's balls. Then Noah confirmed that this same man used a revolver with a suppressor on his father, Bob Freeman. So, the same guy gets rid of two hitmen in Waukesha, drives to the lake looking for him, and ends up killing two more men for no apparent reason.

O'Connor stared out the side window at an early fall landscape of farms. Some small family run farms, some large corporate farms, along with small, modest rural homes. Yet, in the staring, he didn't see any of it. If Jorgy would have asked him what he was looking at, O'Connor wouldn't have been able to tell him.

What troubled him was why did the hitman kill those two men in the forest? Why would a "professional" risk a "mission" on killing two nobodies? And worse, or better depending on how you looked at it, why didn't he kill both Two and Noah? They were loose ends. It didn't make sense.

The man told Roman, the man who accosted Two, that he was about Two's age when he killed his stepfather. He said Roman was a bully just like his stepfather?

Was it because of what Roman said and was about to do to Two? Or was the man in the Kwik Trip and saw what those two men did to Two? How they acted towards the smallest of the four boys?

O'Connor turned and stared at Jorgy. Jorgy caught him staring and said, "What?"

"He might have been in the Kwik Trip?"

"Who? Who was in the Kwik Trip? What are you talking about?"

O'Connor turned to look out the side window again. Then his head snapped back to Jorgy. "Earl said he and the other deputies took the tags of the plates. What did he do with them?"

"Pat, slow down," Jorgy said. He knew once O'Connor had a line of thinking, it often developed into a hunch. Others had talked about it. His hunches, like George's and Brian's visions and dreams, had become the stuff of legend. He had not seen O'Connor work through a problem up close and personal until just now. It was scary.

"Answer me, did Earl call in the license tags of the vehicles he saw at the edge of the forest?"

Jorgy shrugged and said, "I assume so, but I don't know."

"Hand me your radio." He didn't wait for Jorgy to hand it to him. O'Connor grabbed it and keyed the mic.

"Earl, this is Pat. Did you call in the plates of the vehicles you and the deputies took down? The vehicles you saw in the forest?"

"Not yet. We didn't have a chance to. Why?"

"Because the shithead who shot those two men and who might have been after me probably drove one of those vehicles."

"Fuck me! I didn't think of that."

"Jamie, are you listening?"

Earl handed the radio to Graff. "Yeah, I heard."

"Get the list from Earl and get ahold of Kelliher and Eiselmann. Have them run those plates to see what we have. Have Eiselmann run the plates, and have Kelliher run background on each of those men. Have them send up the pictures of the driver's licenses of the owners to you, me, Earl, and Jorgy. We'll show them to the boys to see if they recognize the guy."

"I'll do it now."

"And have Earl meet us at the Kwik Trip. He might have been in there. We'll need the boys to stop and ID him if we can get security footage."

Jorgy's hands patted the steering wheel and said, "Ah, the Cap said we weren't supposed to stop."

"We're following a potential lead," Graff said over the radio. "If there is any heat, it's on me."

"Jamie, I'm going to text Two and Brett and tell them to meet us at the Kwik Trip. We need to speed up. We've lost time."

To Jorgy he said, "Do you have lights and a siren on this thing?"

"Ah, no! It's my personal car."

"Fuck! Speed up anyway. If we're stopped, we'll explain."

Jorgy was no stranger to speed. As a high school senior, he totaled his brand new, but used Dodge Charger when he lost control of it as he tried to see how fast it would go. He was banged up, though not seriously, but the Charger was totaled.

"What the fuck? Here we go!" Jorgy couldn't hide the smile on his face as he slammed the pedal to the floor.

Two cars back, Brian saw Jorgy's car take off and Earl's car chasing it. He said, "What the hell?"

He drove a little faster, but didn't want anything to happen to his boat, and he didn't want to risk getting a ticket.

"Something must have happened!" Brian said to Two.

Two had his cell in his hand and he looked up from it and said, "We need to meet them at the Kwik Trip."

Brian caught his look and said, "Why?"

"O'Connor didn't say, but like you said, something must have happened."

CHAPTER SEVENTY-SIX

O'Connor, Graff, Jorgy and Earl Coffey got to the Kwik Trip in Crivitz ahead of the boys. O'Connor walked in the store and up to a clerk and said, "I need to speak to your manager. Right away." He flashed his badge, as did Graff, Jorgenson, and Coffey.

"Just a minute," said a clearly flustered teenage girl. She turned off her cash register, left her post and walked to the back of the store and down a little hallway. The four cops followed her, though they didn't follow her into the room. She knocked but didn't wait for permission to enter.

Not a full minute later, a middle-aged balding man with a beer gut, walked out and said, "What can I help you with?"

Graff took charge, showed him his badge, and said, "We need to step inside where it's private." When the manager didn't move quickly enough, he added, "Please."

The manager sent the girl back to her register, held the door open for the four men, and followed them into the little room. Once the door was shut, he said, "Okay, what's going on?"

Keeping details to a minimum, Graff said, "We are involved in an investigation of a deputy who was shot in Waukesha, Wisconsin last evening, and two men shot and killed today near here. We believe the shooter might have been in your store yesterday morning between six and eight. We are waiting on photographs from the FBI to see if they match anyone on your security camera."

"Is your system working?" O'Connor asked. Without waiting for an answer, he asked, "How long does your system store footage?"

"Yes, it's working. The system stores for thirty days, so we would still have access to video from yesterday morning."

"Where do you keep it? The system, I mean?" O'Connor asked.

"Right over here," the manager said, waving his hand at the computer and monitors in the corner of his office.

Graff said, "Jorgy, can you wait for the boys to show up? When they do, please bring George and Two in here."

Jorgenson left the office, shut the door behind him, and walked out the front door to wait for the boys to show up. He knew they were fifteen to twenty minutes behind based upon how fast he and Coffey drove, and the fact that the boys pulled boats behind them, precluding any kind of speed.

Back in the office, Graff asked the manager, Norm Pitkins, to run the video back to the previous morning, starting at six o'clock. "Run it at normal speed, and we'll tell you when to go slow motion."

The manager knew the equipment well. He explained, "We have six different cameras inside, and four on the outside, with two at the gas pumps. I can bring up anything you need on one of these five monitors."

Pitkins pushed a couple of keys on the computer keyboard, and the men watched the monitors. It didn't take any time at all to back up the footage to the previous morning.

He said, "Everything is digital and high definition. There's a lot of traffic in this store, and we've had our share of shoplifters. We had two attempted robberies in the last five years. Crivitz has a police department, but it's small. One chief and two deputies. But the Marinette County Sheriff Department has been responsive."

"Okay, here we go," O'Connor said. "There we are. The boys haven't shown up yet."

They watched O'Connor get drinks from the coolers, while Graff punched in a breakfast order at the kiosk. They met up at the cash register and paid for their items. After sitting down and eating, they watched O'Connor answer his cell. He talked, shoved his food to the side, picked up his Diet Coke and both men left the store after disposing their trash.

The cameras tracked the men outside where they spoke on cellphones, had a conversation, and waited.

"There, back behind the store," O'Connor said. "There's the two guys and Noah."

The manager looked up at them and asked, "That's who was shot? Freeman and Roman?"

"You know them?" Coffey asked.

"Yeah, not well. They're both loud and obnoxious. One is worse than the other depending upon the day."

Neither O'Connor or Graff chose to give their thoughts, since it wouldn't do any good to bash the dead. Nor did they confirm or deny those were the two men who were shot.

"Okay, there's Brian's truck," O'Connor said.

They watched Brett and George head to the store, while Brian filled the truck up with gas. Two clean the windshield. After, they parked in the back of the store near Freeman's truck. Freeman and Roman stood and watched Brian park, and then watched Brian give Two a piggyback ride to the store.

Jorgy led George and Two into the office. Both boys looked unsure of themselves or exactly what to do.

"George, Two, come over here and look at these monitors. We want you to look at the video footage and see if you spot the man you saw in the forest."

George and Two huddled over the manager. George said, "Excuse me, Sir. I am sorry."

"No problem, son."

They watched a replay of the morning. Two getting bumped once, then twice on purpose. The four boys eating. Brett turning around to confront the two men. Two cleaning up the table and the big man sticking out his foot to trip him.

"Okay, you know what happened to you," Graff said. To the manager, he said, "Can you back it up to when the boys first enter your store?" To George and Two, he said, "We need the two of you to watch the men in the store who might have been watching what had taken place. See if you recognize the man you saw in the forest."

Almost on cue, O'Connor received an email with the photos of the drivers' licenses of the men who belonged to the trucks or cars parked on the fringe of the forest. Coffey and Graff received the same email. As the boys watched the monitors, the men scanned the pictures from the email. One of the pictures was of Bob Freeman, who had driven Roman, Noah, and him to the forest to hunt.

"May I see the pictures?" George asked.

O'Connor shared his cell with George. A picture popped up and George said, "Him. That is the man who shot one of the men."

Coffey looked over at O'Connor's phone and said, "Fuck me! I saw this dude. We walked right past each other. He said he was leaving early because he wasn't feeling well. Flu or some bullshit. Dammit! We could have had him."

"Not without a shootout, Earl," O'Connor said.

"He drove a rental," Graff said. "From Marinette."

"Makes sense," O'Connor said. "He would have driven up in his own car, but to fit in, he rents a truck. Probably bought all the hunting gear in Marinette, too."

"There! I see him!" Two shouted. He pointed at the monitor at a man near the coffee and soda dispensers in the back of the store during the altercation with Freeman and Roman.

"That's the man who . . . you know, in the forest," Two said.

They watched him leave the store when the Graff, O'Connor and the boys left. They watched him get into his truck and follow, at a distance, the caravan out of the parking lot.

"Sir, can you print out any still shots? I'd like to get one or two closeups without losing any quality," Graff said. "If you have a thumb drive, can you download this footage so I can turn this over to the FBI for the investigation?"

"I'll need a copy for my office," Coffey said. As an explanation to Pitkins, "The Marinette County Sheriff Department is investigating the death of Freeman and Roman."

"Yes, Sir! You got it!"

"Thank you for your help, Sir. You don't know how important this is," Graff said as he patted the man on his shoulder.

To O'Connor, Graff said, "Get word to Kelliher and Eiselmann that we have him. Let Gonnering and Lorenzo know, too. They're point on this thing."

"Um. We should." O'Connor thought as he talked. Graff and Jorgy were used to it. "We should drive to Marinette and check out the truck he used. See if he left any prints." To Earl Coffey he said, "Earl, can a couple of sheriff deputies meet us there, lock down that truck as a crime scene, but not touch the truck until we get there?"

"We'll need a print kit," Graff said.

"What do we do with the boys?" Jorgy asked.

Without any hesitation, Graff said, "We send them home. George can drop my truck and boat off at my house. I'll catch a ride home with you and Pat."

Jorgy started to object, but Graff cut him off and said, "I will call Captain O'Brien and explain what we found and what we're doing. I'm sure he'll understand."

"We'll need to keep Kelliher in the loop. Probably Eiselmann, too," O'Connor said. "And Gonnering and Lorenzo."

To George and Two, he said, "Boys, you've been a huge help! Thank you. Earl will get you to write out a statement and sign it. We'll get a copy for our side of the investigation. But you know this is all confidential. You can't share it and you can't discuss it."

To Pitkins, he said, "Sir, I have to ask you to please keep this confidential. If it leaks, it could damage the investigation and you could possibly be charged with obstruction and interfering with an investigation."

"You don't need to worry about me," Pitkins said as he worked the computer printing off several still shots and downloading the footage from that morning both inside and outside the store onto two thumb drives.

"For the first time this morning, I feel like we're getting somewhere," Graff said.

"Yeah, well, that asshole is still out there somewhere," O'Connor cautioned.

CHAPTER SEVENTY-SEVEN

"Boys, both of you and Jorgy and Earl are going to walk out of here. I want you to get something to drink, maybe a sandwich or something, but while you're doing that, I want you to look around the store to see if you spot this man. Maybe he's here, maybe not. We don't know. If he is here, he might be wearing a disguise, and he's probably wearing different clothes," Graff said.

"But you need to do this without looking like you are looking for him," O'Connor said. "Can you do that?"

"Yes, Sir," George said.

Two shrugged and said, "Yeah, I can do that."

"Earl, Jorgy, watch the boys, but also look for this guy," Graff said.

"Got it," Earl said. To the boys, he said, "Guys, let's go."

"Can you put the cameras on real time?" Graff asked.

Pitkins pushed some keys on the computer, and then said, "There you go."

The three men stared at the monitors.

Pitkins tapped one of the monitors and said, "Here are the boys entering the store from the hallway."

"Bring up the camera that shows the beverage dispensers," Graff said. "And maybe the coolers and other aisles."

Pitkins hit a key and up came the video feed in real time. O'Connor and Graff watched the various patrons. It wasn't busy at this point, not like it would be in a couple of hours as it approached the lunch hour.

There were two men near the beverage dispensers, one with longish black hair wearing a hoodie and sunglasses. There was another man, overweight with gray hair.

"The older guy is Ray Towns. He's local. He comes in for coffee and a donut twice a day," Pitkins said. "I don't know the other guy."

The look of the younger guy was suspicious, odd in some respects, but not too out of the ordinary. A woman came into the frame with what looked like her daughter. A man joined the two, and a different woman went back to grab coffee. There were other patrons in the aisles grabbing snacks or drinks from the cooler.

The older man identified by Pitkins left the drink dispenser area, while the guy in the hoodie filled a large container of coffee, added cream, and went to the register to pay.

The guy in the hoodie stood in line directly behind Brett and Brian, who were paying for their sandwiches and drinks. Once done, the boys left the register and sat at a table to eat, which ironically was the same one they had sat at the previous morning.

Brian saw George and Two, waved at them, and proceeded to eat the meal he had purchased.

Two did a tour of the coolers, then walked back to the soda dispensers, filled up a medium-sized cup with Sprite. He filled another with what looked to Graff like fruit punch, probably for George.

George stood at the kiosk and ordered, but took his time to glance around the store. He looked up at the camera and shook his head slightly.

"Okay, they don't see him," Graff said.

"Let's go," O'Connor said.

"Sir, I want to thank you for your help. I appreciate it."

"Happy to help," Pitkins said as he shook both men's hand. "I hope you get who you're looking for without any more people getting hurt."

"We do, too," Graff said.

CHAPTER SEVENTY-EIGHT

"We're meeting Gonnering, Lorenzo, and Dahlke in Marinette," O'Connor said as the three of them walked to their vehicles.

"Kelliher must have sprung Skip free from Quantico. I wonder when he got in."

"It will be nice to have an expert all over that truck," O'Connor added. "I was thinking, maybe we can get some video from the rental place. Nice to have that corroboration."

Graff nodded, and said, "Good idea." He thought for a minute and asked, "Any word on Albrecht."

O'Connor shook his head.

They separated. O'Connor climbed into Jorgy's older model Charger. Graff waited until Earl was done with a call to the department and after he explained to the two deputies who had tailed the boys what was about to happen, then he got into Coffey's car. Earl jogged up and jumped in the driver's seat.

"We're set. Dale and Javier will follow us to the Avis Rental. Things on my end are in motion."

"Let's roll then."

■　■　■

From the front seat of his Beemer, the man watched the sudden activity with the cops. It looked as though the boys were on their own, so he had a decision to make. He could either follow the boys back to Waukesha, set up and wait for O'Connor, pull the trigger and leave. Or, he could see what the cops were up to.

It was concerning to him that they spent so much time in the back room with the manager. Only two of the boys had joined them- why?

"Shit," he muttered.

He knew he had made a mistake by not getting into a disguise before going into the Kwik Trip the day before. He was on camera, so they knew what he looked like. And, the little Indian kid saw him without a disguise. He was there to corroborate. The bigger Indian kid? Did he see him after all? Spot him somehow?

"Shit," he repeated.

What he didn't know was what else the cops knew.

Curiosity got the better of him. Staying three car lengths behind the last car in the caravan, the older model black truck, he followed them. He knew where they were going as soon as the lead vehicle turned west on County Road W.

He didn't know how they knew about the rental.

"Shit! Fuck!" he pounded the steering wheel with each expletive, and then pounded it twice more.

They knew about the rental. They would have him on camera there, too. And the rental agreement with his signature. The only good thing, if there was a good thing in this royal fuck up, was that he had paid in cash. No credit card, and thus, no receipt for it.

He couldn't help but look back on the weekend as one colossal mistake after another. There was never a time when he had screwed up so much. Not one job, not one contract in the past ten years. Not screwing up was how he had managed to stay alive and how he had managed to amass the fortune he had.

He was tempted to walk away from the contract. The problem with that was that Andruko demanded absolute loyalty. Not that he was ever loyal to any of those under him. No fucking way.

He demanded that contracts be fulfilled. He saw what had happened to other operatives, who had tried to walk away after returning the money. They hadn't lived twenty-four hours, no matter where they ran, no matter where they hid. What he found ironic was that most often, he was the one who had pulled the trigger.

It came down to a choice: fulfill the contract and risk being caught or killed, or walk away from the contract and always having to look over his shoulder for the bullet or knife.

There wasn't any choice. He knew what he had to do.

CHAPTER SEVENTY-NINE

Eiselmann spent the day lounging around the house, an odd feeling of calm and peace, mixed with restlessness. While he loved watching college football and soccer on TV with Stephen, Sarah, and Alexandra, eating popcorn and playing board games, there was a part of him that felt cheap and guilty. Albrecht had been lying in the hospital since Friday night, had underwent two surgeries, and still had not regained consciousness all because he took the bullets intended for him.

He felt he had done nothing to help the investigation on any significant level, and here he was enjoying life with his family, while those closest to him were at the hospital anxiously waiting to see whether or not Albrecht would survive. And if he did, what condition he would be in. The unspoken question on everyone's mind, if Albrecht survived, was what would that survival look like and what would be his quality of life?

While he wore a smile and teased his kids like they had done ever since Sarah and he dated and married, he knew that he risked that smile falling from his face.

Sarah was still anxious at the sound of any car passing their house, any unusual sound in or around their house. She hoped the feeling would disappear.

She watched Paul closely. She, along with O'Connor, knew him best, saw right through his facade. She admired his bravery and effort. But she acknowledged only to herself, that what Paul really wanted to do was get out there and help find the assassin hellbent on killing his best friend, his brother from a different mother, O'Connor.

Each time his cell buzzed, he jumped and Sarah bit her lip, both wondering and worrying. Most were innocuous. Their friend and neighbor, Amy Ivory, called to offer any help they might need. She offered to sit with the kids so Sarah and Paul could go out, at least for dinner. Sarah politely asked for a raincheck, that given the events from the previous evening, neither wanted to stray too far from home. Alexis White called to let him know that she was bringing over homemade brownies. She did, and the batch was half-eaten not a half-hour after she left.

Dahlke called to say he, Gonnering and Lorenzo were almost to Marinette. There was a break in the case, though he didn't elaborate and he didn't go into detail. Eiselmann had the impression that Dahlke was under orders not to share what was going on with the investigation. Paul understood because Captain O'Brien had made it pretty clear he was on the sidelines.

Each time his cell buzzed, the three of them would turn expectantly. He had wanted to turn off his cell, but he couldn't. He had to keep it on in case there was a call about Albrecht or a call about the case.

Another call came in. Before he took his cell out of his back pocket, Paul shut his eyes. Neither he nor Sarah knew which call would be about Albrecht and they feared the worst.

It was Kelliher. If the FBI was calling, Paul knew it had to be something big.

Paul met Sarah's eyes and half-smiled. Sarah sighed in relief. To his kids, as much as to Sarah, he said, "Guys, I have to take this. I'll be back. Stephen, I'll want details, especially if Ronaldo scores."

"Got it," Stephen said not taking his eyes off the TV screen. Because Stephen was a goalie, he was more interested in how the defense might stop Ronaldo from scoring.

When Paul left the family room, Alex asked Sarah, "Mom, is dad okay?"

Sarah smiled and said, "Yes. This is a difficult case he's dealing with, Sweetie. That's all."

Stephen asked, "Is Tom going to be okay?"

Sarah didn't know how Stephen knew about Albrecht, but Stephen had a way of knowing things. Maybe all kids his age knew things intuitively or otherwise. She didn't know. Stephen was her first teenager.

In many respects, even though Paul had not been there when Stephen was born, Stephen was more like Paul than his biological father. Stephen even resembled Paul with freckles, though Stephen's were smaller. His strawberry-blond hair was at least three shades lighter than Paul's. Still, they could be father and son. They certainly acted like they were.

"We don't know yet, Hon. We'll see."

In the office with the door closed, Paul said, "Hi Pete."

"First of all, any word on Tom?"

Paul shook his head even though Pete had no way of seeing that, and he said, "No, not yet. I'm hoping for a call."

"Any word from Graff or O'Connor?"

"No, nothing."

Pete took a deep breath and said, "I'm going to share some things with you even though I know you aren't directly involved in the investigation. I ask that you keep it confidential and as close to the vest as possible."

"I will."

"You gave us a list of phone numbers. We are able to match one of the numbers with one of the men who drove up to that forest. We assume that number belongs to the guy who is after O'Connor. We think we know who it is. A search warrant was obtained and we have three agents and a tech crew ready to roll. However, he has surveillance set up so if we were to move on it, he would potentially find out and he might run."

"I understand. I think Pat would too."

"I appreciate that. We did let both O'Connor and Graff know, and Pat understands why we had to stand down for the time being."

Paul ran through a couple of scenarios as he was half-doodling and half-taking notes. He said, "What you're saying, but not really saying, is that Pat has a target on his back and he's being used to draw this asshole out into the open."

"That's pretty harsh, considering it was Pat's idea."

Of course, it was Pat's idea. What else could he do? Paul said, "Harsh or not, that's what's happening, right?"

"Except for we know who he is."

"Okay, I get that. But you don't know where he is."

Ignoring the last comment, Kelliher said, "We also matched some of the numbers Dasha Gogol called to both Oleg Klyuka, Andruko's head of security, and Andruko's right hand man, Andrii Zlenko. She had called both. Multiple times. We're still working on why she spent time searching the Chicago Tribune classified section."

"Isn't that enough to pull Klyuka and Zlenko in and grill them about the asshat after O'Connor?"

"We could do that, but we have no idea if either would talk, and we don't know how that might help us catch the shooter who is after O'Connor. He could up and run, and we'd never find him."

Paul had nothing to say. Kelliher and whomever he consulted with, probably Summer Storm, his former partner, more than likely discussed that angle.

"The other thing I wanted to mention is that we think we know who the leak is. I'm not going into detail on it until the time is right. I wanted you to know since you were the one who provided us with the phone numbers."

"Well, not me exactly," Paul said.

"We're not going there," Kelliher said.

"I understand," Paul said, holding up his hand in surrender.

"So, we received the phone numbers from you. We followed up on them. I told you previously that we have several individuals, who shall remain nameless, under a soft surveillance. We also have Andrii Zlenko and Oleg Klyuka under a hard surveillance. As far as we know, they don't know how deep we are on them, but we are so far up their ass, we can see their tonsils from the inside."

"Gross. Thanks for putting that picture in my head."

"One of them has been in contact with both Zlenko and Klyuka multiple times dating back a couple of years. It seems shortly after that phone call, another call is made to either Gogol or the shithead after O'Connor."

"I assume a death followed that phone call in a short amount of time."

"It appears so."

"Huh," was all Paul managed to say.

Kelliher let him mull that over. Paul said, "What you're not saying, but saying, is that right now, as of this phone call, you don't have enough to tie Andruko to the leak. And you want a clear line to Andruko."

"Bingo," Kelliher smiled. He had always liked the way Eiselmann's mind worked. He'd be a great asset at the Bureau.

"So now what?"

Kelliher said, "We watch, we listen, and we wait. O'Connor and Graff know what's at stake. They are taking the necessary precautions."

"But not enough to scare off the asshole after Pat, which leaves an opening for the shooter to get to Pat."

"Paul, I know how close you are to O'Connor. I know your relationship is beyond that of just a partner. I know the history between the two of you, and you guys are more like brothers. I get that. But trust Pat, and trust Jamie, and trust those around him."

Paul didn't respond. Kelliher expected that. He knew Eiselmann wasn't happy about it, but because Paul was a professional, he'd deal with it, even though he didn't like it.

"As I said, I know you're on the sideline. We felt it was important to fill you in on as much as we could, because we trust you."

"I understand, and I appreciate it."

"Take care. Enjoy your family. Things will shake out the right way."

"I hope so."

"And call me as soon as you hear anything on Tom."

"Will do."

After the phone call ended, Paul sat in the office. He wanted to throw his cell across the small room. He wanted to punch a wall. He hated sitting in the stands watching all the action. He had always been in the thick of it, either in the field or working with technology. He and O'Connor were a team, partners, and Kelliher was right. They were brothers.

What was worse was that he now had all this information and couldn't share it with anyone. To do so would or could put the investigation in jeopardy, Pat's life in jeopardy, and perhaps his own career in jeopardy. If he spoke out of turn, whatever happened to Albrecht would be in vain, and Paul would wear that on his reputation, as well as on his heart. Hell, he recognized that he already wore it in his heart.

Pat's life was the most important piece of this puzzle, followed by the investigation. If the investigation failed, Pat would be dead or forever be looking over his shoulder. That was no way to live.

He didn't give a rat's ass about his career. Ever since the hospital visit, he had the idea that his career might be on the same life support as Albrecht, especially the way his *friends* treated him.

But for Pat's sake, Pat's life, and his friendship with Pat, and for the sake of the investigation and whatever happened or will happen to Albrecht, Paul knew what he had to do.

Nothing.

CHAPTER EIGHTY

The driver's side window was rolled down. He sat in the parking lot of a Walmart facing the Avis Rental, watching the cops swarm over the truck like bees on honey. Interesting that the youngest member of the group, a skinny, pale, blond kid ran the show. The blond kid ordered the other cops to perform this task or that job. The man figured him to be the crime scene tech from out of town. Had to be. He didn't look or act like someone from Podunk, USA.

He was relieved he had vacuumed the truck and ran it through a car wash. He had done it right, this one thing. Too bad for him he hadn't done better on the other mistakes he made between yesterday and earlier this morning. He had never been his sloppy before, and he knew he had fucked up, but he didn't know how badly.

The blond kid called to O'Connor and the other cops, and pointed at the latch on the tailgate. He was smiling.

'Shit! They found a print.'

He thought it over and shrugged it off since they already knew who he was, or at least, who one of his identities was. Not all of them. Not the one that was the most important. Not his true identity, and they wouldn't unless they dug deep. Way deep.

He found himself starting up his Beamer and before he realized it, he was driving out of the parking lot, heading south to Waukesha.

He knew where O'Connor lived. While O'Connor and the other cops were up here dinking around on a rental truck, he would be planning and setting up his next move.

He dialed a number from memory.

"Yeah?"

"It's not done yet, but it will be soon."

And he hung up. He had nothing else to say. There was nothing else he needed to say. O'Connor was as good as dead. It was just a matter of time.

CHAPTER EIGHTY-ONE

As they neared Port Washington, Brian used the hands-free function in his truck to call Brett. He knew if he had called George, George wouldn't answer. He'd hand his phone to Brett. By calling Brett, he cut out the extra step.

"What's up?"

Brian knew Brett had put the cell on speaker so George could hear the conversation. "Do you guys want to go to a movie tonight? All of us? Together?"

Brett glanced at George, shrugged, and said, "Sure. What's showing?"

"I don't know. Anything. I'll call Randy, Billy and Bobby and ask them. I'll have them pick something out."

"Tell them to give us enough time for a run, a nap, and a shower, though."

"Will do."

He called Randy, and Randy agreed to the plan. He said Billy would pick the movie.

They got to Waukesha and drove right to Graff's house. No one was home. The four boys didn't feel right about leaving his truck and boat parked out in front of the house.

Brett called Graff.

"Did you get in an accident or something?" Graff asked.

"Yes. Four. One after another. First your boat is banged up. Probably won't float. Your pickup is beat to hell. Totaled. Blame George. He drove too slow."

Graff shook his head and said, "When did you get to be such a smart ass?"

"Always been one. I just refined my smart-assness as I got older."

"Okay, McGovern, what do you want?"

"Geez, here I am trying to be polite and all, trying to do a nice thing for you, and you take offense."

"Brett!"

"Okay, okay. We're going to take your boat to your storage place, but we need the code to the gate. No one is home, and we don't want to leave the boat out in front of your house. We'll take the oars and crap out of the boat, and I'll put the engine key along with your truck keys above the visor on the driver's side, and we'll park the truck in the driveway."

"Okay, that's nice of you. It had to have been George's or Brian's idea," Graff said with a smirk.

"Who's the smartass now? So, what's the code?"

Graff gave him the six-digit code and told him where to park it once inside. Brett ended the call, and the boys set out taking anything loose from the boat to the garage.

Brian located the house key Graff and Kelli hid outside the backdoor. He knew where it was from babysitting Garrett. He took in a few of the fish fillets and placed them in the freezer in the mud room after wrapping them in butcher paper and Glad ClingWrap he found on a shelf in the pantry. He left a note and taped it to the front of the refrigerator for Kelli and Graff to let them know what he had done.

He and Two waited outside Graff's house until George and Brett drove back with Graff's truck. Brett put the keys where he said he would, and the boys drove home.

They unpacked the truck, unpacked the boat, and Brian parked it next to the garage where he stored it. The four of them put the boat cover on it after making sure the boat was dry. Brian didn't want mold or mildew on his boat if he could help it.

Brett and George walked ahead, and Two took hold of Brian's arm to hold him back.

"Bri, what am I going to tell mom and dad about, you know . . .?"

"I'll tell them. Mom probably, because she's a mom. She would want to know these things."

"What if she wants to see?"

Brian sighed and said, "I'll handle it."

"Okay," Two said with obvious relief.

They walked up to the house, the first time in a long time Two wasn't on Brian's back. Vicky noticed.

Looking from one to the other, she said, "Are you guys okay?"

Brian smiled. He didn't know how she knew half the stuff she did, but she always knew stuff before she was told.

Brian told her a shortened, sanitized version of what took place up North. Brett and George listened, as did Randy, Billy, and Bobby.

After he had finished, just as Two feared, Vicky said, "Perhaps your father or I should take a look."

Two shook his head.

Brian jumped in and said, "I used Peroxide on the cuts."

Billy sucked in his breath and said, "That hurts just thinking about it."

"It did," Two said.

"Then I used Neosporin and covered everything with gauze. I changed the gauze a couple of times, and the last two times, there was no bleeding."

"It doesn't hurt. Brian made me sit with an icepack between my legs," Two added.

"But I think Two needs a tetanus shot and maybe a doctor should check him out."

Vicky pursed her lips, thinking it over. She stared at Two, then at Brian and said, "When was the last time you changed the gauze?"

"Before we left. I should probably change it now, and he should ice things down again."

"When was the last time he took Motrin?"

Brian looked at his watch and said, "Four hours ago. In another two, I think," already anticipating what Vicky was thinking.

"Okay. Go take care of him, and Michael, I want you taking it easy. No ruff-housing."

Two kissed her cheek, smiling in relief, and said, "Brian, let's go."

The boys left the kitchen, and the last to leave was Bobby. He caught his mom's eye and smiled.

"What?"

"Nothing. You're pretty cool."

She couldn't suppress her smile, and she said, "So are you."

"I love you, Mom."

"I know. And please believe me when I say that I love you. I always will. Always. You're my son."

Bobby smiled, nodded and went upstairs after Brian and Two.

Vicky knew the powerful feelings and urges racing through Bobby. It was only after Bobby's conversation with her that she understood what he and Brian were wrestling with.

When the four boys left for their hunting and fishing trip, at Bobby's request, she and Bobby had taken a long walk to the stable on the Limbach property, and then beyond into the field using the path the boys rode the four wheelers and horses on.

Bobby told her everything. He left nothing out. He felt it was important to tell her first. At some point, he'd tell Jeremy, but telling his mother had to come first.

Both of them had wept. It wasn't hysterical. It wasn't anger. It was relief on Bobby's part, and acceptance, if not resignation, on Vicky's part.

After Bobby finished with what he had to say, and after the questions Vicky had asked and the answers Bobby had given her, they embraced. Bobby was a full head and a half taller, but she was happy to kiss his neck and he bent down so she could kiss his cheek, and he, hers.

And then she surprised him by saying, "I think I suspected, Bobby. Back in Indiana when you were grade school. I wondered. I thought you might grow out of it. I thought it was a phase." She had shrugged and said, "Sometimes moms know these things."

"It wasn't Brian, Mom. I approached Brian."

She had nodded and said, "I know. I think because you are my son, I blamed him. And, because your dad loves me, he saw how I reacted to Brian, so he blamed Brian too."

She sighed, dried the tears off her cheeks and said, "We've been unfair to him, and because of that, we've been unfair to you."

They began their walk back to the house and were on the path in the woods almost to their yard when she said, "I owe Brian an apology, and I want you to know, both of you to know, that I love you both. You are my sons. I know Bri isn't blood related to us, but both of you will always be my sons. I will support both of you. That's a promise." After a beat, she added, "Please do me a favor and let me have a talk with Brian when the time is right. Let me be the one to talk to him."

He put his arm around her and said, "Promise."

CHAPTER EIGHTY-TWO

Eiselmann's cell buzzed again, but this time, he greeted the caller ID with a smile. Sarah saw it and she smiled.

He said, "How are you doing, Partner?"

That caught the attention of Stephen, and when Alex saw Stephen turn around to stare at his dad, she did too.

"I'm doing okay, Hoss. Where are you?"

"Almost home. Pewaukee, home of the Watt Brothers," O'Connor answered with a laugh. "Seriously though, Paul, how are you and Sarah and the kids?"

Paul got up, flashed a thumbs up to his family, and walked into the office and shut the door before he answered.

"About as well as can be expected, I guess. Sarah and the kids are on edge. The kids are mostly because Sarah is."

"You get any sleep?"

"None. I think I dozed off on the couch watching the Badgers play this afternoon."

"Good news about Albrecht, huh?"

Puzzled, Paul stared out the window and asked, "What do you mean? What did you hear?"

O'Connor paused and then said, "He came out of his coma. The surgery went fine. He's going to be laid up for a while, but he's going to be okay." He paused and said, "No one called you?"

Paul said quietly, "No. They must have been too busy or something."

"That's not right, Paul. You should have been one of the first to know."

Dismissing that topic because it stung, Eiselmann said, "When did you hear and who called you?"

"Ronnie, early this afternoon. Maybe an hour or two ago? Maybe?" It was closer to two and a half hours ago, but he didn't want to push Paul's face in it.

"I guess they got to celebrating. Everyone was beat up over it. Tired out. They got about as much sleep as I did, maybe less." He changed topics and said, "Where are we on the shooter?"

Graff cut in and said, "We think we know who he is, but the name we have is probably an alias. One of a couple probably. He is a professional. FBI are on it. We have a plan for the rest of today, tonight and tomorrow. As long as it takes."

"Good. We've had company since last night. Not used to being baby-sat."

"I understand, but we have to take precautions, especially after last night. Do us a favor since we're spread a little thin. Try not to go out much, okay? Try to stay close to home."

"I know. We are. O'Brien gave me the same message this morning."

"Good. Take care, Paul. Here's Pat."

"Paul, I'm going to call Brooke and Ronnie to see how they're doing. I'll have one or the other give you a call to update you on Tom."

"Hoss, it's okay. Don't bother. I don't want them to feel any worse about anything than they already do. But you're okay, right? You'll be safe?"

"Yeah. I have a less than average baby-sitter, though. They imported Coffey from up North."

"Hey!" Paul heard Coffey in the background protesting in jest.

Pat continued, "It seems Mr. Clean is working this. Haven't heard a word from good ol' Myron."

Paul chuckled and said, "You probably won't. Probably can't find his phone."

"Maybe he doesn't know how to use it. Just as well. Listen, take care."

"You do the same. I mean that."

They signed off, and Paul sat in his office. He had sunk into his chair. He rested his head in both hands, and he didn't know how long he had been sitting there, when Sarah placed a hand on his shoulder and asked, "Good news?"

"Pat's doing fine. Earl Coffey will be one of his baby-sitters. O'Brien called him in to help."

"That's good. I hope Pat will be safe." She thought it over and said, "Still no word on Tom?"

"It looks like Albrecht is going to pull through. He's out of his coma. The surgery went well, but he'll be in the hospital for quite a while."

"Who called you?"

Paul shrugged and said, "Desotel called Pat. He told me."

She hugged him and said, "I'm sorry, Paul."

"It is what it is."

CHAPTER EIGHTY-THREE

Billy chose an action-comedy, *Bad Boys for Life*, and the boys unanimously agreed. It was a good escape, as Randy said it would be. Brian sat between Two and Bobby, sharing a bucket of popcorn with Bobby. He bought Two's bucket of popcorn and his drink, along with his own and Bobby's.

It was casually deliberate. Brian's and Bobby's fingers and hands touched. At times the moment lingered, while at other times, it was brief. Neither apologized and neither offered an excuse. The popcorn lasted for the first half of the movie. After the popcorn vanished, the two boys linked pinky fingers. Brian made the move without making eye contact, but out of the corner of his eye, he saw Bobby smile.

It was comfortable between the two of them. Familiar. It always had been. Neither of them flaunted it nor did they throw it up on a billboard for the brothers or anyone else to notice. Yet, both boys were fairly certain Two and George noticed, because they seldom missed anything. The same was probably true for Brett who sat next to Bobby. By the end of the evening, Randy and Billy, who sat on the other side of George would know too.

During the action scene, Brian heard the voice. It was clear and direct.

"Nida'ałkáá'i' and Shadow, your long-haired friend needs to be warned. I believe he will receive a visit tonight."

Brian looked over Two's head, and met George's eyes. It was apparent George heard the same message.

George said, *"Grandfather, is there something we should do?"*

"You and Nida'ałkáá'i' need to stay away and be careful. This man is unpredictable like many Biligaana."

Perhaps on purpose, perhaps not, George slipped an arm around Two's shoulders. Two looked at him with a question on his face, then smiled, and continued eating his popcorn, drinking his soda, and watching the movie.

Neither George nor Brian knew what they were to do, if anything. They could not rush to aid O'Connor. Both were warned to stay away. Yet, O'Connor was their friend.

It was weird. It was as if George and Brian shared the same thoughts at the same time. That was a first! Brian saw George pull out his cell phone. His fingers flew over the keys.

George knew better than to question his grandfather. Brian had learned through experience to trust that voice, that man. He would do as he was told, as would George.

Brian heard another voice, a familiar voice that he had longed to hear more often.

"Order a pizza. Maybe two or three. You know how much Billy eats." This last was accompanied with a laugh, causing both Brian and George to smile.

Brian looked over at George and said in his head, *"We can do that."*

"You might need to," the boy's voice said, again with a laugh. *"You need to stay away from O'Connor, though. Seriously."*

"Are you okay?" Bobby whispered.

Brian nodded, glanced at George who wore a neutral expression as he turned back towards the screen. Brian turned to Bobby, smiled and whispered, "All's good. *Everything* is good."

Bobby caught the double meaning, and he smiled back at him.

CHAPTER EIGHTY-FOUR

Posing as a jogger, he toured the neighborhood on the lookout for cops watching for him. He had on one of his disguises. Long red hair in a man-bun, shorts, a bulky sweatshirt to hide his revolver in a holster across his chest, and of course, expensive running shoes.

He spotted four. Two were across the street from the apartment building. One in the shadows and one sitting on a stoop. There was one on the roof of the building across from O'Connor's apartment, and one sitting on the steps of O'Connor's apartment building. No doubt, there would be others here and there.

His car was parked a block away where there were other cars parked on the street. Earlier that day, he had swiped Wisconsin plates, and hid his Illinois plates in the trunk under the spare tire.

He considered whacking the cop on the top of the building across from O'Connor's apartment. He knew there had to be rooftop access, since that was where the mechanical functions of older buildings were. There was another exit over the wall of the roof and down the metal stairs. An old-fashioned fire escape that had access points on each floor. The drawback was that he would be exposed to whoever came looking for him. Yet, potentially, it was quicker. He didn't like the idea of being cornered up there.

He had watched another cop enter the building with O'Connor. He thought he recognized him from earlier that morning as he left the forest. Because of the dark and the distance, he wasn't sure. The cop had never come back out, so the man figured he was in the apartment with

O'Connor. He wondered if there was a cop or two in the parking garage below the apartment building. If it were up to him, at least one would be there.

As much as he could on his run, he watched O'Connor's balcony slider for a potential shot. The man didn't expect it to be a clean, clear shot. O'Connor wasn't as stupid as to hang out the slider of his balcony with a beer in his hand. As it was, the curtain was drawn to a slit.

There was also a window in what the man thought was O'Connor's bedroom. Of course, never having been in the apartment, he didn't know for sure. But it felt right to him.

Perhaps a pizza delivery to one of the apartment neighbors. That would get him in the door and past the cops. The pizza might be looked over. He might be searched. Whomever did the searching might end up dead along with O'Connor and the other cop. He'd see.

If there wasn't a shot this evening, there might be a gas leak in the early morning. There would be collateral damage. At this point, as frustrated as he was for the fuck ups the last two days, he didn't care who went to hell with O'Connor.

Wrong time, wrong place. Too bad, so sad.

CHAPTER EIGHTY-FIVE

There were several great pizza places in or around Waukesha, but the favorite of the boys, and at least half of North High School, was Michael's Italian Restaurant. Seven hungry boys, despite eating pounds of popcorn and drinking gallons of soda, ordered three large pizzas. One was extra cheese, one was pepperoni and sausage, and one was Canadian bacon and pineapple. Of course, what was pizza without garlic bread?

Out of all that food, there were only two pieces of garlic bread left, along with three lonely pieces of pizza. Billy was in rare form. There were stories and laughter. So much laughter, bellies ached and faces hurt. Other customers listened, watched and couldn't help laughing along. Most, though, had come, ate, and left. Not the seven boys who made up the Evans family. They hung in there almost to closing.

After the football stories, the basketball stories, and the childhood growing up stories, Billy asked in a quiet voice after checking to see who might overhear, "Bri, can I ask you a question? You don't have to answer me if you don't want to."

"What?"

"When you see that doctor, what do you guys talk about?"

Brian had only shared bits and pieces with his brothers. Randy heard the most and it was obvious he had not shared it, neither had Brett, who had heard lesser parts. He didn't mind sharing, but he'd be selective about what he told them.

Randy jumped in and said, "Billy, that's personal."

"No, it's okay," Brian said. He felt himself blushing. "I talk about stuff." He shrugged.

"Well, duh," Billy said causing everyone, including Brian, to laugh.

"We talk about my mom and dad and what happened, and how I feel about that." He shrugged again. "We talk about my brother, Brad. We talk about you guys. We talk about the stuff that happened in Arizona. Lately, we talk about what gives me the shakes. We're trying to find the triggers."

Brett felt he needed to rescue him and he said, "When you talk about our family, you probably mentioned that I was the smartest and best looking, right?"

"Of course," Brian said with a laugh. "Goes without saying."

All the boys laughed.

"How long do you think you'll be seeing him?" Billy asked.

Brian scrunched up his face, and said, "I've been thinking about that. I hardly ever take my medication. I haven't taken it since Wednesday, and it was only a half-dose. But other than Thursday night after a dream, and then Friday when we left for up north, I've not had the shakes. I don't think I've lost my temper with anyone in a long time," this last he said as he looked from one to the other, who shook their heads.

He thought about it a little bit, and the boys didn't rush him. He said, "I'm thinking on either ending it or cutting it way down. We end up talking about the same stuff over and over, and I don't see it getting me anywhere. Honestly, I get more out of talking to Randy or Father Donahue than I do the doc. It's a waste of money."

"Have you talked to mom and dad about the stuff you talk to the doctor about?" Two asked.

"No." Brian didn't elaborate and he wasn't about to.

"Will mom and dad allow you to stop going?" Randy asked.

"It was my choice to see him in the first place. I was the one who said I felt I needed to talk to someone. I don't see why they won't let me stop if I don't want to go anymore. If I don't see the purpose . . ." he let the sentence hang there.

Randy smiled at him and said, "I think it was pretty brave of you seeking help."

"I needed to, especially after Arizona," Brian said as he waved his right hand at nothing in particular. "So much had happened. George and I kind of had a fight. That's over now." He glanced at George who smiled and nodded. "Brett and I . . . I don't know . . . went through some stuff." He looked over at Brett, held eye contact with him and said, "I think that's over, for the most part, anyway."

Brett's eyes darted from Brian to Bobby, and then back to Brian, before he nodded. He reached for his water and took his time drinking it.

"I guess, I'm done. If something comes up, I might go back. If not, I have you guys."

"Always," Randy said with a smile.

"We have your back," Billy added.

Bobby reached for the last piece of sausage and pepperoni with one hand, while the other found Brian's thigh. He gave it a squeeze without looking at him, and Brian smiled.

CHAPTER EIGHTY-SIX

Eiselmann was restless. He had no idea what was going on with O'Connor. He texted him three times already, and didn't want to bother him again. Not when Pat needed to concentrate. He didn't know who was watching him besides Coffey. He hoped Earl had help, and that O'Connor had his antenna up and active.

A couple of hours after he and Sarah went to and then came back from the hospital, three more cops showed up. Two positioned themselves in the front of the house, while the other two were in the back of the house. "Just a precaution," Gibbie said over the phone when they showed up.

Chris Gibson was a veteran of the Waukesha Sheriff department. A good man. A soft-spoken, middle-aged, slender man who kept his hair short and his comments shorter. Eiselmann figured Gibbie to be the unit chief. Sarah took coffee and some sandwiches to the guys.

At the hospital, Eiselmann and Sarah felt the same arctic chill as they had earlier that day. Paul waited until Tom had woken up. The doctor told him Albrecht had asked for him, so Paul entered the room, and Brooke and Ronnie brushed past him without speaking.

Albrecht still had tubes hanging out of him. Paul didn't know what the digital numbers meant on the machine at the side of his bed. When one alarm or another went off, a nurse entered, took a look, pushed a button and the alarm was turned off. It had happened twice.

Choked up, Paul was barely able to say, "Tom, I don't know what to say."

Tom waved him off. His words were soft and garbled, but the gist was, "You would have done it for me."

Paul knew he was right, but that didn't lessen the guilt he felt. He didn't know if it was something he would ever get over.

When he left the room, he found Sarah sitting by herself in one of the chairs at the far end of the waiting room. Brooke, Ronnie and Nate stood in a tight circle on the other end.

Paul didn't know whether or not he should speak to the trio or leave them alone. It was apparent that none of them were going to extend anything towards him. Still, he wanted to be the bigger man.

He walked up to them and said, "Brooke, if you or Tom need anything, please let me know. And, if anything changes, please call me."

Brooke barely acknowledged him. Nate Kaupert studied his shoes. Ronnie Desotel folded his arms across his chest and stared at him with something slightly less than contempt.

Paul collected Sarah, and the two of them left with their baby-sitter walking just ahead of them. At some point along the way, Paul noticed another baby-sitter walking behind them.

Back at their house, Stephen had called it a night and went to bed. He and the other boys had stayed up late the night before. Alexandra went to bed shortly after Stephen did, leaving Paul and Sarah sitting on the couch. The TV was on, but neither knew what program it was, and neither cared.

Sarah rested her head on Paul, who had his arm around her. Every so often, he gave her a squeeze, one of the ways he had shown his love towards her.

He said, "When we were at the hospital, did Brooke or anyone speak to you?"

Sarah shook her head and said, "No, but I didn't expect her to, either. If you were laying in that hospital bed, I'd probably react the same way."

That didn't make him feel any better. He knew Sarah better than that. She would be gracious, even if she didn't feel like it.

"Have you given any thought to what Chief O'Brien wants to talk to you about?"

Paul kissed the top of her head and said, "Honestly, whatever he has to offer, I think I'm going to accept."

She raised her head and said, "Why? You love your job."

"I love you and I love our kids. I love working with Pat. A job is a job."

"What if what he has to offer is something you aren't interested in?"

Paul sighed and said, "I guess we'll cross that bridge when we come to it."

CHAPTER EIGHTY-SEVEN

O'Connor and Coffey were prepared. They had talked through various scenarios, each playing devil's advocate with the other. They had been, and would be, in communication with the street team, who didn't know, and wouldn't know, what O'Connor's and Coffey's plans were. That is, other than to be safe and take care of business.

The street team ran a radio check at alternating intervals, never longer than fifteen minutes apart, and no shorter than five minutes after the previous check. Unless, of course, there was an emergency. The interval schedule was designed by O'Connor. It wasn't written down, only memorized. Even the watcher initiating the radio check varied on a schedule only the participants knew. No outsider could mimic it and any variance would indicate a breach.

Pat held his trusty 9mm Beretta. Not taking any chances, the safety was off, but his finger was on first positive, which was along the barrel and not on the trigger. He also had a shotgun within reach, but preferred the Beretta.

Earl also carried a 9mm, and it was loaded with Speer's 124-grain Gold Dot hollow point +P. It was the same weapon and load the NYPD used. It was what he carried while on duty. He also had his Kimber Hunter .30-06 Springfield, which was the rifle he used for hunting. He didn't have a preference for one weapon over the other. They had both come in handy at various points in his career.

Earl preferred to sit on the floor sitting cross-legged. Now and then, he'd stretch his legs out, do a trunk twist or two, then settle back into his cross-legged position. He had his eyes shut, but O'Connor was certain that at the first unusual noise, or even a lack of noise, he'd snap to attention.

From his years undercover, O'Connor had learned to catnap, though so lightly, he never missed anything. He wouldn't this night either.

He checked his watch. Right on schedule, watcher three called a radio check. It was responded to by each watcher.

He settled back into the chair, which was offset from the door. That way, no one shooting through the door would hit him. Both he and Coffey were away from the slider and at such a severe angle that anyone gambling on firing into the room wouldn't come close to hitting either of them. To make it harder, the curtain was drawn.

Neither had eaten much. Some venison jerky. Some sausage and crackers. Plenty of water, coffee and Diet Coke. Neither man made unnecessary noise. They didn't want to give away their positions or somehow let an interested party know they were awake.

They waited.

CHAPTER EIGHTY-EIGHT

After getting home and sitting in the hot tub, the boys got ready for bed, but everyone ended up in Brian's room. All seven managed to fit on the bed. Three of the four dogs lay on the floor. The fourth, Momma, was in her night position just outside of Brian's room facing the stairs. Anyone trying to sneak up the stairs was in for rude, if not painful, surprise.

The boys were much more subdued than they were at Michaels Pizza or even in the hot tub. The talk was quieter and lighter.

Brett said with a light smack to Brian's thigh, "Tell them about your idea for the lake up north."

"Yes, it's a great idea," Two said with an elbow to Brian's ribs.

"Well, there are three lakeside lots for sale." He pulled out his cell and showed them the pictures he had taken. "All three have sandy beach access."

When the boys finished looking at the pictures and nodding approval, he said, "George, and Brett, and Michael, and I go up north during the summer, fall and spring hunting or fishing. Usually, Graff or O'Connor rent a house or cabin. I thought, we could build our own cabin on the lake. That way, it would be ours."

"Randy and Billy looked at each other, then at the others, and Billy said, "I don't think any of us are that handy with tools. Maybe George and Two, but the rest of us," he made a face and grimaced.

Brian chuckled. "No, not us. We'd hire a builder, but you're taking architectural drafting with Mr. Jett, so you would know how to design it, right?"

"Well, yeah, I guess."

He went on to explain the basic design, and launched into the financing. After he laid it all out, Bobby said, "You have that much money that you could pay for the lots and secure the loan from a bank?"

"Yes, but I don't want to pay for it all. I think I could swing it, but I would be short for college and after. But I can comfortably pay for the three lots and down payment."

He reached for his laptop, fired it up, hit a few keys and up popped a simulation that showed what monthly payments might look like.

"If each of us drew money from our trust funds, the money we take out would be replaced by the interest earned on the trust fund. In essence, we wouldn't lose any money. But we would grow a little slower than we do now. This is a simulation I came up with that monitors my investments." He looked around the room and said, "You guys know I mess around in the stock market, right?"

"Yeah," the boys said.

"I have three simulations. One for a bull market when everything is going sky high. One for a bear market when stocks sink. And one for the middle of the road, taking into account inflation and normal stock market adjustment. You can see that in two out of three, I'm still making money, which means, that each of your trust funds are making money."

"And if the stock market crashes?" Brett said.

"Then none of us make money, but we will be better off than many others."

"Bri, how much would all this set you back?" Randy asked. "I mean, three lots and the down payment?"

"Conservatively, between $200,000 and $275,000 give or take. But remember, we sold my mom and dad's house for over $300,000, so I would still have $100-plus-thousand left from that, plus my dad's life insurance, plus what was in their savings account, checking account, and in my parent's 401Ks. Guys, I won't be hurting. But I don't want this to be *my* house. I want it to be *our* house. I want everyone to have a say in how it looks and what goes into it. That's important. Everyone counts or no one counts."

The boys mulled that over. Faces clouded over. The twins stared at one another as if communicating by telepathy. Brett pursed his lips. George was expressionless. Only Michael looked sad.

Brian elbowed him and said, "Michael, what's wrong?"

Two said as he looked around at the boys, "I don't have the money everyone else has."

Randy smiled and said, "You do. You just don't know it, yet. Danny's dad, Jeff, set up a trust fund for you just like he did for each of us. We all have the same amount of money in it, except for Billy, who has extra because he inherited his dad's insurance, house, and everything else. Like Brian, only less."

"Way less than Bri," Billy said with a laugh.

"But financially, you're in good shape," Randy said.

"You, too?" he asked George. Two knew the humble beginnings both of them had.

"Yes. You and me, too," George said with a nod.

"I didn't know," Two said in wonder.

"I think you'll find out eventually," Billy said. "It's supposed to be a surprise, so you have to act surprised when you find out."

"I can do that," Two said with the broadest of smiles. "If that's the case, I'm in."

"Me, too," Randy said.

"Same for me," Billy said.

All of them ended up agreeing.

"One last thing, though. No one tells mom or dad until Billy gets done with the drawing. Not a word. Not a hint," Brian cautioned. "After he's done with the drawing and we all agree with it, I'll put together the financial picture. I might run it by Jeff. Kind of practice with him. But I think if we get Jeff's support, it will be easier to sell it to mom and dad."

"Agreed," Billy said. "All of us," he said, looking at each of the guys.

All of them agreed. Brian could feel the excitement in the room.

"I'm going to bed," Randy said with a yawn. "Church tomorrow."

"Yup," Billy said. "I need my beauty sleep."

"You need a helluva lot more sleep," Brett said.

"Two, you can sleep with me," Randy said.

Two couldn't help looking disappointed. He had planned on sleeping with Brian. "Okay."

To Bobby, Brett said, "You sleeping in here with Bri?"

"Yeah, I think so," he answered as he blushed.

"Goodnight, Everyone!"

And suddenly, the room was empty except for Brian and Bobby.

CHAPTER EIGHTY-NINE

He watched and he listened. He knew there was some schedule they were following, but he couldn't make out what it was.

There were three obvious targets he needed to avoid. That hadn't changed from his earlier recon. Three across the street from the apartment. Two below and one above. The only way to take care of the guy on the roof would be to enter the building, get to the roof, shoot him, and get back down- all without getting caught. Needlessly risky. The guy in the bushes would be easier. It would only take seconds to dispatch him.

Then there was the guy on the front stoop of O'Connor's apartment building. That sucker was out in the open probably because the guy on the roof was watching out for him. He couldn't shoot or kill him, since it would only alarm the guy on the roof.

What he didn't know was how many were in the underground parking structure, and if there were, how he could get by them without rousing suspicion and getting caught. He decided to risk it anyway to see who or what was in the parking structure.

Dressed completely in black and without any disguise, carrying both his silenced revolver in a holster under his black jacket and his knife in a sheath on his hip, he slipped into the darkness between two buildings across the street from O'Connor's apartment, but on the opposite side away from one of the watchers.

He quick-walked, but casually so, like someone taking a walk on a moderately cool evening. He traveled one block, and came at O'Connor's apartment from down the block and across the street. He stood at the corner in the shadows considering his best approach.

It wasn't two minutes later when a car pulled up to the curb. Two men and a woman climbed out of an older model Impala with a dent on the driver's side back end. They stood on the sidewalk talking and laughing. By their look, age and actions, he decided they were college students.

Taking a chance they were headed into O'Connor's apartment building, he jaywalked across the street and joined up with the trio at the back. He could smell the alcohol on them.

One of the youngish men, the one with long, curly dark hair, saw him, greeting him, stuck out his hand, and asked, "Do I know you? You look familiar?"

The man was all smiles, and said, "I moved in a couple of days ago. This is really stupid, but I can't remember the code for the keypad. I was out with a friend. He left so I took a walk, hoping someone like you would come by."

The plain-looking girl with a blond ponytail laughed and said, "I'm Olivia, and I'm on the second floor in 212. It took me a week before I had it down."

The first guy with the long, curly dark hair, said, "No, she didn't forget. She was just too drunk to remember." That earned him a soft punch to his arm, but all of them ended up laughing. He stuck out his hand and said, "I'm Rob. I live on the second floor in 215."

She said, "He's my rowdy neighbor."

The last of the trio, a dark-skinned man wearing a neatly trimmed mustache and one gold stud in his left earlobe said, "I'm Denard. I live on the first floor, in 115, so I hear everything going on in Rob's apartment."

The man said, "I'm Ray Pulisic. I just moved here from the Twin Cities."

"Pulisic? Like the soccer player?" the dark-skinned man said.

"Well, yes, but if I played soccer, I'd not only hurt myself and at least two others."

All of them laughed.

They reached the front steps where one of the watchers sat. The four of them said hello, and he nodded back.

The man kept his head down because of the camera over the doorway. He didn't want to be caught on tape.

Rob typed in the code, and the girl turned around and said, "We're going to my apartment for a beer. Want to join us?"

The man smiled and said, "I'd love that."

Just like that, he was in the apartment. He smiled broadly and thought, '*The proverbial fox in the chicken coop. Easy Peasy.*'

CHAPTER NINETY

Brian and Bobby didn't sleep right away. They talked, they kissed, and they made love in their own way, and in that order. They hadn't bothered to talk during the second time around. There wasn't any thought involved. Just pent-up emotion and adrenalin. Both had a need.

Finally finished, or so Brian thought. A light sheen of sweat covered both of them, the air in the room a musky male smell. Bobby lay in Brian's arms, his head on Brian's chest and a hand between Brian's legs. Every so often, Bobby would kiss Brian's nipple.

"Bobby?"

"Mm?"

"I love you."

Bobby lifted his head, smiled at Brian and said, "I think you made that abundantly clear. Twice."

Brian chuckled, kissed him and said, "You're a smart ass."

Bobby put his head back down on Brian's chest. His hand had never moved.

"Do you think mom and dad know you're in here?"

"Don't know and don't care."

Brian smiled and shut his eyes. It was only moments later when Brian noticed Bobby breathing rhythmically and deeply. Bobby was like that. Awake one moment and in the next, sound asleep.

Brian knew he needed to have a conversation with Mikey. He liked Mikey a great deal. He thought it could grow into love. He would be honest with him about what he and Bobby had done, because honesty was important. He knew he wasn't exclusive with Mikey. Yet, Mikey let him know that he didn't have the feelings for anyone like he did with Brian.

Brian had strong feelings for Mikey and wanted their friendship to continue, even if their relationship did not. He also knew he needed to have a conversation with Bobby.

Mikey was easy to talk to. He never judged. He never ridiculed. He teased and poked fun, but he also brought it to himself as much as he did to anyone else.

Brian loved being with Mikey and his family. What he had with Mikey was growing. He was curious to see how far it might grow. But messing around with Bobby, or Mikey messing around with someone else, wasn't fair to either of them.

He nestled his face in Bobby's hair, their bodies pressed together. He ran his hand along Bobby's side and his hips, where it settled holding Bobby's bare butt.

"I love you, Bobby," he whispered. He didn't get a response, and he didn't expect one. "Now and forever. Always." He rested his cheek against Bobby's forehead and at some point, he fell asleep.

■　　■　　■

He didn't know how long he had slept, but he found himself awake, taking quick, shallow breaths. His eyes were wide open. Bobby, however, hadn't moved.

Brian had heard the voice as clearly as if the speaker stood at the side of the bed. *"Nida'ałkáá'i', you and Shadow need to warn your long-haired friend. He is close by. He is coming."*

That was all George's grandfather said, but it was enough, and Brian knew it wasn't a dream.

Quietly and carefully so as not to disturb Bobby, Brian swung his legs over the side of the bed, the sheet and blanket no longer covering him. Both Papa and Jasper stood and faced the door. He reached for his cell as his bedroom door opened.

George entered quickly and quietly, wearing only a pair of shorts. He stood in the doorway and motioned for Brian to come with him.

Slightly embarrassed at being caught naked with Bobby, he reached down and retrieved a pair of shorts and pulled them on. He tiptoed out of the room, waited for Papa and Jasper, and then shut the door.

George pulled him by the arm down the steps to the kitchen. Once there, he whispered, "Did you hear my grandfather?"

"Yes. He said we needed to warn O'Connor."

"I texted him, but did not get a response."

Brian thought for a second and said, "I'll text Coffey. I know he's with him."

His fingers flew over the keys. Seconds later, both boys were rewarded when their cells vibrated indicating they had received a message.

K.

CHAPTER NINETY- ONE

The apartment was suffocatingly small. A tiny kitchen, white with cheap dark brown cabinets, a stove, a refrigerator, a microwave, with a toaster and a Keurig on a cheap yellow Formica counter. An island with two barstools separated the living area. A cheap round table with four wooden chairs under a dusty lighting fixture that was meant to resemble a chandelier sat in the corner. The dining area, the man decided with a wry smile.

The living room, if you could call it that, consisted of a moderately-sized flatscreen TV on a cheap stand one might get from Walmart. There was a couch and a stuffed chair. The carpet was tan and worn in places.

From his vantage point, he could see down the hallway. There were three closed doors. One had to be a bathroom. The other two rooms were bedrooms. One small, the guest room or office if she was a student, and the other her room. Maybe a bathroom was attached to it.

O'Connor's apartment had to be similar in design and layout. The man smiled and nodded.

He didn't really have time for niceties, but they did get him into the building, so he accepted a Bud Light from Olivia and settled on the couch with Rob.

Denard said to Olivia, "May I use your bathroom?"

Polite guy, the man thought.

Olivia smiled and said, "Sure."

"Are you single, married, what?" Rob asked.

The man smiled and said, "Single. Still looking." But not hard, he thought.

Rob nodded, and shifted so that he was facing the man a little more. Olivia came back into the room and sat on the floor, leaning on a couple of fluffy pillows, the kind trendy middle-America suburbs had in the houses for the kids to sit or sleep on.

"Are you in school?" she asked.

"No. Graduated ten years ago. Communications and theater from Illinois State."

Rob asked, "What do you do now?"

The man played coy, smiled, bobbed his head from side to side, and said, "This and that."

He chugged his beer, and crushed the can neatly, if not noisily. Unzipped his jacket slightly, reached in, and took out his silenced revolver and said, "Mostly this."

He plugged Olivia in the forehead and the wall behind her ended up looking like a Jackson Pollock abstract in red and gray. He didn't want Olivia screaming if he had shot Rob first.

"My God! What...?"

Rob's question was cut off by a similar shot to his forehead with results equal to that of Olivia's. Rob slumped backward, his beer spilling on the couch, on him, and on the floor. Nice guy. Might have been gay. The man couldn't decide, but he also didn't care. There was no way he was going to leave loose ends. Never again.

The man stood up and walked down the hall and peered into each room, minus the hallway bathroom. He wanted to see the bedroom set up so he could visualize what O'Connor's might look like.

That done, he leaned against the wall and waited outside the door for Denard.

He heard the toilet flush and the water in the sink running.

When the door opened, Denard never got to take a step. A shot to Denard's forehead sent him back into the bathroom where he collapsed into the toilet and then onto the floor.

Three down, one to go. More, if need be.

CHAPTER NINETY-TWO

George and Brian sat at the kitchen table. Papa by Brian's side, laying on the floor facing the back door. Jasper lay on the floor between the kitchen and hallway, but facing both boys. Both Brian and George had a glass of water in front of them, as they held onto their phones for any word from O'Connor or Coffey.

"George, your grandfather called me, '*Nida'ałkáá'i*'. What does that mean?"

George pursed his lips, tilted his head and said, "There is no word-for-word translation between Navajo and English. *Nida'ałkáá'i'* can mean several things. The most common meaning would be *scientist*."

Brian squinted at George, who smiled and said, "But in this case, I believe my grandfather means, *thinker*, or *one who thinks*."

Brian lifted his chin and smiled. "I like that." He took a drink of water and said, "Your grandfather called Brett, '*Báháchi'ii*'. What does that mean?"

George smiled and said, "You almost pronounced that correctly. That is a tough word. *Báháchi'ii* means angry one, but again, there is no word-for-word translation. Because my grandfather doesn't know Brett, I think it means more like *intense one*."

"That fits." Brian shook his head and said, "Funny how your grandfather spoke to both of us."

"My grandfather cares about you."

"But I never met him."

George smiled and said, "He cares about you." As he said this, Brian noticed that his face clouded over.

"What?" Brian asked.

George had wrestled with how he had wanted to bring it up to his family. He knew Brian might be the most difficult one to have the conversation with.

He sighed and said, "Navajo believe that dreams and visions are the spirit world sending us messages. My grandfather taught me that. However, most Navajo believe it is evil to speak to the dead. They feel that after four days, a good Navajo should quit grieving and move on."

Brian stared at him blankly and his jaw dropped. He said, "I don't believe that. There is no time table for grief. We don't get over it. We learn to live with it. And, when Brad speaks to me, he encourages me. It makes me feel good. There is nothing evil about that. When your grandfather spoke to me, it was because he felt I needed to warn Graff and O'Connor, just like he did tonight. That isn't evil. That's good."

George smiled and said, "I did not say I believed it. I said most Navajo believe it."

As if Brian hadn't heard him, he added, "It's the same thing as praying. I believe in angels and saints. I talk to God each night and most mornings. That is who I am. It's what I believe."

George reached out and placed his hand on Brian's forearm. "I know that, Brian. I know *you*. I pray, too. I speak to Father Sun each morning. And, I speak to my grandfather, though most of the time, he chooses not to speak to me."

"But I think that because you speak to him, just like I speak to Brad, it helps us remember all the good times and the good memories." He sighed and said, "I miss Brad. I wish he would talk to me more."

George smiled, nodded, and took a drink of his water. To change the subject, he said, "I am happy you and Bobby are back together," George said with a smile.

"I love him, George. So much. I think I feel about Bobby the way you feel about Rebecca." His heart thumped wildly, loudly. He took George's hand and pressed it against his chest. "Feel that?"

George smiled. What he wanted to say was that their hearts were meant to be together. With Brian seeing Mikey, he didn't know if that was appropriate. In time, Brian would know the direction of his heart.

Brian couldn't stop grinning. He said, "Watching you and Rebecca..."

George finished the statement, "Is like watching you and Bobby."

Brian beamed and said, "Yes. We're lucky."

George nodded and said, "Yes. We are."

"At the same time, I'm seeing Mikey. I like him a lot. Not like Bobby, though."

George tilted his head and asked, "How does Bobby feel about that?"

Brian hesitated. On one hand, Bobby said he understood and that he didn't want to interfere. On the other, Brian knew Bobby felt hurt.

"I think he understands," Brian finally answered with a shrug. "I guess we'll see."

That conversation ended when George's grandfather said, *"Quickly now. He is coming."*

Their fingers flew over their cell phones. George to O'Connor, and Brian to Coffey.

CHAPTER NINETY-THREE

The man tiptoed up the stairs on the west side of the building rather than taking the elevator. He had never liked enclosed places to begin with, but on this night and with this job, he needed to see what was coming at him, as well as what might be behind him.

Keeping his back to the wall, he took the steps one at a time. He spent as much time facing forward as he did facing the way he had come to make sure there was no one sneaking up behind him.

He was two steps away from the third floor landing. The door was closed, and he didn't know what might be on the other side. There was a little, fifteen-inch by fifteen-inch window set in the door.

He had a choice to make. He could open the door and slip in low and fast. That way, if someone was on the other side waiting for him, they would aim high at center-mass. Going in low would give him a moment or two so he could aim and fire.

Or, he could peek through the window to see if anyone was on the other side. That would be risky. Too risky, he decided.

He put his hand on the doorknob, turned it slowly and quietly, then thrust the door open and dove in low and fast. He made no noise other than a muffled thump. His gun was up and ready. His finger on the trigger.

No need. The hallway was empty.

He hadn't realized he was holding his breath. He squatted against the wall just inside the doorway. He shut his eyes for the briefest of moments and gathered his thoughts. He slowed his breathing, and stared down the darkened hallway.

Lit only by soft emergency lighting, he studied the shadows, not that there were any. He was as out in the open as anyone else would be. Fortunately for him, he saw no one. Again, he had been holding his breath. He frowned and willed himself to breathe slowly.

He knew O'Connor's apartment was three doors down on the right.

Keeping his back to the wall, gun ready, he took one slow step after slow step. It wasn't long before he reached O'Connor's apartment.

CHAPTER NINETY-FOUR

Coffey wanted to know how Brian and George knew. There was no earthly explanation, and that spooked the shit out of him.

O'Connor held up his hand, and then waved it.

Coffey got the message. He moved to the side of the door, revolver up.

O'Connor peeked through the door hole that allowed those on the inside to see who was on the outside.

There he was. The first thing O'Connor saw was the nasty looking suppressor attached to the revolver. He forced himself to look away from the gun and study the man.

Two had described him well. A runner's build. Short blond hair. About six- or six-one. Solid. Moved like an athlete. Right-handed, just like Two said he'd be.

O'Connor watched the man shift the revolver to his left hand as he fished out the lock pick set. He took out what he needed, set the revolver down on the carpet, and worked first the door lock, and then the dead bolt.

O'Connor nodded at Coffey. Coffey pulled out his cell and typed quickly.

O'Connor wasn't prepared for how fast the man could unlock both locks. He was fast. Too fast.

Gonnering and Lorenzo, who had been waiting in the manager's office monitoring the security cameras saw the man leave one apartment, walk down the hallway, and climb the stairs. They were just as quick. One used the west stairwell, and the other used the east stairwell.

They had talked out their plan ahead of time, since potentially, one would be shooting in the direction of the other. It wasn't textbook by any means. In this case, one would shout the order and the other would cover and shoot the intruder if need be. Shoot to disarm if possible, though neither would take any chances.

That afternoon, before O'Connor and Graff left for home, Captain O'Brien had made arrangements for the fifty-two-year-old widow, grandmother of four, to spend the evening at a hotel a safe distance from her apartment. She lived across from O'Connor, and at times when he was away, she'd collect his newspapers and his mail. In general, she would keep an eye on his apartment. He'd do the same for her when she visited her daughter and son-in-law and their children.

For fear of word leaking out, O'Brien decided not to tell any of O'Connor's other neighbors what might take place. It was risky and if something should happen, he'd take the fall.

O'Connor and Coffey were safely across the hallway in the older lady's apartment. They had moved there after spending most of the day in O'Connor's apartment. Only Gonnering, Lorenzo, and O'Brien knew where they were.

The man's back was to them, and their door was unlocked so they could move at a moment's notice.

That moment was now.

CHAPTER NINETY-FIVE

Something wasn't right. It was too quiet. Even this late at night.

He hesitated. His back tight against the wall, he glanced left. He glanced right. He licked his lips. He could feel sweat popping out on his forehead and upper lip, though that didn't have anything to do with the night air.

The door was unlocked. All he had to do was enter the apartment, fulfill the contract, and get out. He'd take out anyone in his way.

He stood to the side of the door, and with his left hand, he turned the doorknob slowly. Intent on his mission, he never noticed the movement on either end of the hallway. He never made it inside the apartment.

"Stop! Police!" Gonnering yelled, as he jumped to the floor onto his stomach.

The man spun around, but Lorenzo sprinting from the other stairwell fired twice to the man's right shoulder, disabling his shooting hand.

First Coffey, then O'Connor charged out as planned. They stayed to the side, and O'Connor repeated Gonnering's command.

Stunned, the man turned in O'Connor's direction and raised his revolver, though too slowly.

Coffey slammed his shoulder into the man and he felt at least one rib give way, and all the air rush out of him. The man crashed into the wall and his revolver went flying out of reach. He had his knife, but that was on his right hip, and his right hand was all but useless.

Coffey threw a forearm into the man's nose, and followed that up with a left hook that caught the man on the jaw. The man's eyes turned upwards and he crumpled to the floor.

O'Connor kicked the man's weapon towards Gonnering. Coffey frisked him, found the knife and held it gingerly so as not to smudge any fingerprints. The man was out cold and unable to fight for it.

Apartment doors opened. Cracks at first. Then heads peeked out to see what the commotion was all about.

Lorenzo said, "Back inside. Shut and lock your door. We're the police." He had to bark it several times as did Gonnering. Both showed their badges, though they had no doubt that 9-1-1 would be inundated with calls by now.

Without caring about the man's shoulder wounds, Coffey spun the groggy man onto his stomach and cuffed him.

The man began to waken, tried to stand, but Coffey planted a knee on his back and said, "You will stay down and not move, you piece of shit. I don't mind slamming your head into the floor if you move again. You understand?" He turned to Gonnering and asked, "Let's get him to the station. We need to get him in custody without any extra handling."

The man said nothing, but he did turn a frightened eye in his direction.

Gonnering nodded. He understood what Coffey was saying. It was important in the current climate.

As he finished reading him his rights, three other deputies, ran up and onto the floor, weapons out and safeties off. Their fingers, however, were only on first positive, not on the trigger.

"It's under control," Lorenzo advised. "It's over."

O'Connor squatted down, his back to the wall, and studied the man who had come to kill him.

He smiled. Coffey was right. That guy was a piece of shit. Any professional killer who kills others for a *job* is nothing but a piece of shit.

He pulled out his cell and texted a message to Brian and George. *Done. Thanks! Talk soon!*

CHAPTER NINETY-SIX

Eiselmann nursed an iced coffee, while O'Connor had a can of Diet Coke sitting in front of him that he had only sipped once. They were in Starbucks that was attached to the Marriott Midway Hotel. They had come down to Chicago the night before, and were supposed to hook up with FBI Agent Pete Kelliher and FBI Agent Summer Storm. Graff declined the invitation to join them. He had wanted to spend time with Kelli and Garrett.

Storm had just moved up in the agency as the Director of the Criminal Investigative Division. It was a plum position, and she was now one of the highest ranking females within the agency. Agent Skip Dahlke was coming along because he had performed some, if not most, of the forensics on the technology.

Dahlke had linked the numbers from the phones in Dasha Gogol's possession, the phones in Cameron Reis-Smith's possession, and the phones that had been in Sasha Bakay's and Misha Danilenko's possession. Ballistics showed that Reis-Smith killed the original hitmen who were after O'Connor in the vacant parking lot the night of the soccer game. It was assumed that he tailed O'Connor to Northern Wisconsin the following morning.

Gogol had failed in killing Paul Eiselmann. Reis-Smith had failed in killing Pat O'Connor. Of course, Dahlke had to uncover their true identities from their multiple alias's. Fortunately, fingerprints helped. Interpole had been helpful in both cases.

It was Graff and Kelliher who had interrogated Reis-Smith, first from a hospital bed, and then at FBI field offices in Milwaukee. Observing them were representatives from ATF, DEA, and Homeland Security. He was that big a deal. Or rather, Dmitry Andruko, was that big a deal. Because of the attempts on Eiselmann's and O'Connor's lives, they couldn't be involved in any interview. They were, however, allowed to observe the interrogation.

Anything Reis-Smith said could potentially add years to Andruko's sentence. Any evidence of Andruko ordering a hit would involve conspiracy to commit murder, accessory to attempted murder and anything else the prosecuting team could throw at him, which might necessitate another trial. He was already in prison awaiting sentencing, and while the additional charges would be nice, they weren't necessary.

They had Reis-Smith on seven counts of murder in the first degree: the deaths of the first two hitmen, the deaths of Roman and Freeman in Northern Wisconsin, and the deaths of three college students in O'Connor's apartment building. He was also charged with one count of attempted murder. He was toast.

He and his lawyer tried to leverage a deal in exchange for anything he could give on Andruko, along with his head of security, Oleg Klyuka. Afterall, Klyuka's number appeared multiple times in both Reis-Smith's and Gogol's call list. The FBI wanted the information, but didn't indicate they needed it.

In the never-ending pursuit of the bigger fish, Graff and Kelliher also wanted to flip Oleg Klyuka, Andruko's head of security. That might not be hard to do, given what the FBI uncovered from the various phones. Perhaps he would be willing to roll on Andruko.

Storm suggested making another run at both Anton Bondar and Andrii Zlenko, whose trials were forthcoming. Turning one or both would be the flowers on the grave of Andruko. But again, turning them wasn't absolutely necessary for the case against Andruko.

Both O'Connor and Eiselmann wondered privately and together who the leak was that brought the three hitmen to *TGI Friday's* the day Andruko's verdict was read in court. Neither had a clue. The information obtained by the FBI was kept from them by Kelliher and Storm specifically because they were the intended targets. The concession was that both would be present when that person was confronted.

"You okay with making the move from the sheriff department to the police department?" O'Connor asked.

"Computer crime interests me. I don't know if I will ever be as good as Chet Walker was before he died at the soccer field. I will still get to do some work in the field. Cop stuff. I won't be tied to the desk necessarily, but it will be my main job. And it will be nice to work under Graff and O'Brien." He took a sip from his iced coffee and said, "I'll miss some of the deputies I worked with. How about you?"

O'Connor wagged his head nonchalantly, and said, "You and I will get to work together some. I like Graff and O'Brien. I know most of the group on the force, but it will take some getting used to, I think." He privately worried about the latitude in working solo as much as he had done in the sheriff department.

Both men had dressed for the occasion. Slacks, dress shoes, and polo shirts with sport coats. O'Connor was not going to wear a tie. The last one he wore was for Eiselmann's wedding, and that was only because he was best man.

O'Connor said, "Tom Albrecht called me. He wanted me to discourage you from joining the police. He feels shitty about what happened to you and Sarah after . . . well, the whole hospital thing."

Paul looked off in space, shrugged dismissively, which was his only comment. He wasn't going to go there. Thankfully, he was able to tip his head towards the door.

First to enter was Summer Storm. Blond and beautiful, wearing navy blue slacks and matching jacket with a white blouse.

Eiselmann said under his breath, "God, she's beautiful. Could be a model."

O'Connor chuckled and said, "A lethal one. Wouldn't want to get on her bad side."

Eiselmann laughed and said, "No way in hell!"

Pete Kelliher followed her in. As put together as Storm was, Pete was the opposite. Older with a gray flattop, a bit of a belly, and in general, rumpled. The last to enter was Skip Dahlke, probably the youngest agent in the FBI, and without a doubt, one of the most intelligent and unassuming agents. Known for his forensic background, he had broadened out to computers and electronics. He was Pete's go-to on anything. Eiselmann would be training under and alongside of him for six weeks at the FBI in Quantico, Virginia.

Eiselmann said, "There's the war horse," referring to Kelliher.

O'Connor turned around and stood up, stuck out his hand to the three. Summer bypassed the hand and hugged both men.

"How are you two holding up?" she asked.

Pat smiled and said for both him and Paul, "Part one almost wrapped up. Just have to sit through the next two trials. Maybe a couple more depending..."

"I hear congratulations are in order for both of you," Summer said with a smile. Both Pat and Paul wondered how she found out and if she had been involved in some way.

"Hey, Pat, Paul," Kelliher greeted the two cops. "I need coffee." To Summer and Skip, he said, "Want anything?"

"Just coffee with a splash of cream," Storm responded.

Dahlke held up his can of Diet Coke and shook his head.

Eiselmann pulled out a chair for her. Pat got a man-hug from Dahlke. She wasn't even seated when she said, "Here's how we're going to play this." All business with the smile of a shark.

CHAPTER NINETY-SEVEN

They sat in a comfortable conference room with dated, but comfortable chairs, and a long wooden table that had seen its better days. Two windows overlooked the parking lot and parking structure on the other side of California Avenue. They were on the top floor of the Cook County Criminal Court Building. That was the home of the states prosecuting attorneys.

During pleasantries and small talk, Dahlke set up his laptop and linked it wirelessly to the conference room's projector. When he was ready, he nodded at Summer and Kelliher, and folded his hands as if in prayer, elbows on the table, waiting for Summer's opening.

"Gentlemen, shall we begin?" she said, smiling, teeth showing. Even her voice seemed a bit cold.

Eiselmann blinked, but didn't turn to O'Connor and tried hard not to look at anyone. Instead, he stared at a spot on the wall. O'Connor smiled as he took a sip of water, thinking that it would definitely not be good to be on her shit list.

"We collected the phones from four individuals who had been contracted to kill Pat O'Connor and Paul Eiselmann," she gestured towards both men. "One deputy almost died and is still in the hospital. His recovery will be slow and we don't know if he will ever be one hundred percent."

Overstatement, thought Eiselmann. She didn't know Albrecht. Not like he or O'Connor does. Probably for effect.

"Skip, show the slide of the major players so we know who we're talking about without having to search our notes," Summer said.

Skip pulled up a slide. On it were the names and roles of Andruko's organization, along with the two killers.

Dmitry Andruko = Head of Crime Family
Anton Bondar = Crime Family Underling
Andrii Zlenko = Andruko's Right-Hand Man
Oleg Klyuka = Andruko's Head of Security
Sasha Bakay = Contract Killer Murdered in Vacant Lot (O'Connor)
Misha Danilenko = Contract Killer Murdered in Vacant Lot (O'Connor)
Dasha Gogol = Contract Killer (Eiselmann)
Cameron Reis-Smith = Contract Killer (O'Connor)

"Just looking at this list, you can see how organized and connected this crime family is," Summer said.

The three lawyers nodded agreement.

"Okay, now Skip, will walk you through what we found. But I want you to know, each of you, the chain of custody was respected. All evidence protocols were followed. There is no hole that a criminal can crawl through. We had our legal team look everything over and it is their assessment that the case, or cases, if you will, are rock solid."

"Excuse me," Michael O'Reilly said. "Your background is . . .?"

"Law. University of Louisville."

"She will never admit this willingly, but she graduated the top of her class, which is why the FBI recruited her," Kelliher said. "We didn't need the legal division to look this over because of Summer's background, but we felt it was prudent to do so."

O'Reilly smiled and nodded. "Impressive."

"May I ask a question?" Heather Sullivan said. Without waiting for permission, she asked, "The precaution you took with this evidence, is this standard procedure?"

Storm smiled, and the room temperature fell below zero. "No, but given who ATF, DEA, Homeland Security, Interpole, and the FBI are dealing with . . . Andruko and others, we wanted to be certain all criminals will be brought to justice."

"I see," Sullivan said nodding her head.

The only member of the prosecuting team not to speak or ask a question was Daniel Keene. But that wasn't surprising, since he was the quietest of the three. He was taking notes on a yellow pad, just as he had done before and during the trial.

O'Reilly was the team lead and Sullivan was the velvet hammer. It was Keene who did the paper and detail work.

Summer waited to see if there were any other questions, and hearing none, she said, "Skip, can you take us through your presentation, please?"

Dahlke walked them through a PowerPoint that showed them what phones belonged to who, along with lists of numbers that had been collected from each contact and call list- both incoming and outgoing.

"And you have identified who these numbers belong to?" O'Reilly asked.

"Yes, for the most part," Dahlke said. "There are some burner phones that were used. For instance, you already know that Andruko required all burners be destroyed at the end of the week and new ones purchased."

"Yes, that's right," Sullivan said. She looked over at O'Connor and said, "That was part of your testimony."

O'Connor nodded.

"We know that two men, Sasha Bakay and Misha Danilenko, had gone to Waukesha and were actively stalking O'Connor at a soccer game that Thursday evening. Their intention was to murder Detective O'Connor. The theory we went with was that they were killed that same night because they had been spotted by O'Connor," Kelliher said.

"Pat and I spotted them at the soccer game," Eiselmann chipped in. "They followed Pat home, but didn't strike. Later that evening, they were shot at close range in their vehicle in a vacant lot. Execution style. Ballistics matched the weapon in the possession of Reis-Smith."

"All of that was confirmed by the phones and their call lists," Dahlke said.

"What about privacy issues?" Sullivan asked.

Summer leaned forward and said, "When the attempts on Deputy O'Connor and Deputy Eiselmann were made, we knew there was a leak. They hadn't shared they were headed to a soccer game. They hadn't shared that Pat was leaving for the weekend to go fishing."

"Except with us," O'Reilly said. He sat back in his chair, eyes darting to his right at Keene and Sullivan.

"Or someone one of you might have mentioned it to," Kelliher said.

The three of them glanced at each other, and O'Reilly's eyes narrowed as he glanced first at O'Connor, then at Eiselmann, finally at Summer.

"After we were told that two men showed up at the soccer game and followed O'Connor to his apartment," Kelliher said, "warrants were issued to have phones tapped."

"All authorized, all legal, no holes," Summer added. "Skip, before we get into that, can you walk us through the Chicago Tribune Classifieds, please?"

Dahlke showed the next slide.

Eiselmann smiled. It was all choreographed. Storm had a part. Kelliher had a supporting role. Dahlke had a role, but also was the stage manager. Professionals. Slick. He tucked this away in his memory bank for the future.

"This was puzzling," Dahlke said. "Dasha Gogol spent an inordinate amount of time perusing the classified section of the Trib. She had more than enough money so she wasn't looking for a part-time job. She wasn't looking for a house, a car or a puppy. At least that we know of. But each day between 9:00 AM and 11:00 AM, she would go to the classified section. Most of the time, she spent ten to fifteen minutes. We have the exact times charted, and for the most part, there was no discernable following activity. However, on fourteen occasions, we found advertising from Eastern Europe Exchange . . ."

"Andruko's company," Sullivan said thoughtfully, leaning forward and scribbling a note on a yellow pad in front of her. After, she sipped her Diet Dew and squinted at the screen.

"Yes, Andruko's company. After each of these advertisements, Gogol would contact a cell phone belonging to Oleg Klyuka, Andruko's head of security. Within one day, Gogol took a trip." Dahlke looked up from his laptop at the three lawyers and said, "We did forensic work on her laptop besides her phone."

"*We* didn't do forensic work. Skip did the forensic work," Kelliher said with a smile like a proud father listening to his son.

Dahlke reddened, and continued, "I had help," he mumbled. "Within a day, no more than three, in whatever city she traveled to, there was a death."

Dahlke flashed through the fourteen crime scenes. Some were of children, some of couples or families, but most pictures displayed a dead man. Ages varied. Manner of death was similar in all. She used handguns, knives, and in one case, a high caliber rifle. All of them grotesque and bloody.

"We have a timeline, phone records, all of it," Summer said.

"But I thought you said there were burner phones involved," Keene said.

Summer leaned forward and with an icy smile, she said, "Apparently, burners were used only within Andruko's company, but not with either Reis-Smith or Gogol."

"That was sloppy," Keene said. He glanced at his partners and said, "It seems Andruko wasn't as tidy as we thought."

"He was in most areas," Kelliher said. "Just not with those he contracted with."

"Klyuka and Zlenko weren't as careful," Dahlke said.

"Or to use your term, tidy," Summer said with a smile that could have caused frostbite.

"There were also corresponding deposits into Gogol's account on the day of the phone call, and then again the day of the hit. Two transactions, equal amounts."

"She was contracted to do a hit," Sullivan said.

"Will we be able to tie all of this back to Andruko himself, or just to Klyuka?" O'Reilly asked.

"Right now, circumstantial," Summer said, "but the noose is tightening."

"You're hoping to turn Klyuka or others against Andruko," Sullivan said.

"Correct," Kelliher said. "We are still gathering similar data and information on Reis-Smith, but we're confident we'll find similar contacts, communication, and deposits."

Dahlke popped up a slide with phone numbers, sat back, and folded his hands on his chest.

"Do any of you recognize any of these numbers?" Kelliher asked.

The three lawyers, and O'Connor and Eiselmann leaned forward to study the numbers. There were twenty-seven in all. Most were from the 773 area code. Others were 630 from the western suburbs and 224 from the northern suburbs. There were several from the 262 area code, which was the Waukesha, Wisconsin and surrounding area.

"Two numbers belong to Pat and me," Eiselmann said.

"I see each of our numbers on that list," Sullivan said.

Storm nodded and said, "Once we knew of the apparent leak, we had your phones tapped."

O'Reilly cocked his head, sat back in his chair, and covered his mouth with a hand. Sullivan glared at her and at Kelliher, and took two long pulls from her Diet Dew. Keene leaned to the side, a hand covering his mouth, his face red, eyes downcast.

After a stretch of silence that seemed longer than it actually was, O'Reilly said slowly and quietly, and with controlled anger, "I suppose given the circumstances, I would have sought the same."

"But surely, you didn't find anything," Sullivan said.

When no one responded to her, she said, "You did?"

Kelliher, Storm and Dahlke stared at Keene, but didn't say anything. Their expressions were neutral, but it looked to Pat as if Storm and Kelliher were fighting to control their anger.

Both Sullivan and O'Reilly picked up on it. O'Reilly, almost always unflappable, leaned forward, eyes wide and mouth open. He turned beet red.

Sullivan moved her chair away from him, but said nothing. Couldn't even look at him.

Keene thought about getting up and running, but knew he wouldn't get far. He considered denying everything, but just as that popped into his head, Dahlke flashed another slide breaking down Keene's phone contacts, along with deposits into a bank account he thought he had hidden deep enough that no one would find. Evidently, it wasn't deep enough.

"We noticed that on the day preceding an ad in the Trib, a phone call was made by Mr. Keene to either Klyuka or Zlenko. He used both contacts," Kelliher said. "Then the ad was placed in the classifieds, and, well, you know the rest."

"We noticed that thirty-three minutes after the verdict was read, Mr. Keene made a call to Oleg Klyuka," Dahlke said.

Summer said, "And it was shortly thereafter, Klyuka contacted Denys Ivasiv." She looked up from her notes and said to Eiselmann and O'Connor, "He was one of the men who showed up at TGI Friday's when all of you were at lunch. He brought along two associates."

"What we aren't sure is whether there was going to be an attempted hit or if it was just for intimidation," Kelliher said.

"Perhaps Mr. Keene would like to enlighten us?" Summer asked, this time without the smile.

He stared at the table, and said nothing.

Sullivan had had enough. Sitting in the chair next to him, she backhanded him hard across the face. Evidently, she felt that wasn't enough, so she hauled off and threw a roundhouse to his mouth, knocking him out of his chair and onto the floor.

Kelliher, Eiselmann, and O'Connor raced around the table, but Sullivan raised both hands in surrender and said, "I'm done, but damn, that felt good."

. . .

It took another forty minutes. At first, Keene, holding an icepack to his lips, was reluctant. But facing the mountain of evidence, he agreed to cooperate in exchange for a plea deal. A team of federal prosecutors, along with a team from the same office came in to depose him. Thankfully, Eiselmann and O'Connor were allowed to leave, knowing that because of Keene and his involvement with both Reis-Smith and Gogol, they'd be back to testify.

O'Reilly and Sullivan met with them and Storm in a different part of the office away from the conference room where Keene and the team of prosecutors were meeting. Kelliher and Dahlke remained behind to listen in and take notes.

"You need ice for that hand?" O'Connor asked Sullivan.

She flexed it several times. It was red and bruised and swollen.

"Probably. Hurts like a sonofabitch, but damn, that felt good. I mean, Michael and I were there with you two. Anything could have happened. Anything."

"Thankfully, nothing did," Summer said.

"Did you ever take my advice and get a small weapon. Just in case?" O'Connor said.

"Thought about it," she said, frowning, moving her head from side to side. "It will just add to the number of guns out there on the street. I'll think about it some more."

"Question," Paul said. "How does . . . *this* affect your case against . . ." he waved his hand around the room, but didn't add anything further.

All eyes turned to O'Reilly. He folded his arms and said, "Time, mostly. We'll have to doublecheck the paperwork, the trail, anything Daniel touched or worked on. Fortunately, Heather and I handled the bulk of it. Daniel did the detail work."

"But that's where it could get tricky," Sullivan said. "The question I have and won't know until we get in and do some research, is what did he leave in, but more importantly, what did he leave out?"

"Will he cooperate? Fully?" Eiselmann asked.

"We'll see, won't we?" Summer said to the four of them. "He's toast either way. Just like the others."

"Do you know why he did it? All of it?" Sullivan asked.

O'Reilly smirked and said, "Greed. Andruko evidently paid well."

"But how did he latch onto him?" Sullivan asked. "I mean, Daniel was a decent guy. Efficient. Personable. A pretty fair lawyer."

"Hopefully, he will let us know," Storm said. "There might be something he did that Andruko could have used as blackmail. Or, as Michael said, it could have been as simple as greed."

EPILOGUE

Two Weeks Later

Brian, Bobby, and Billy were in the study. Jeff sat on the leather recliner visiting with Jeremy and Vicky, who sat on the couch. Jeff and Jeremy were drinking beer, while Vicky sipped white wine.

Brian had rehearsed the presentation twice with Jeff. He had it down, including charts and graphs, and pros and cons. None of the boys said or added anything until the presentation was finished. After the few questions from Jeremy or Vicky, Jeremy pronounced the lake house a go. After inspecting the drawings closer and deciding whose bedroom was whose, Randy, Danny, Brett and George left for other parts of the house.

Brian sat on the floor leaning against the couch with his laptop. Bobby sat next him reading, leaning more against Brian than the couch. He finger-combed the back of Brian's hair. Vicky noticed, and she was sure Jeremy did, too. Billy lay on his stomach working on his math.

Two wandered in, sat down next to Brian, put a hand on Brian's shoulder, leaned in to look at the computer screen and said, "What are you doing?"

"A paper for social studies. Almost done."

Two watched him, but was antsy. Brian asked, "Did you finish your homework?"

"Yup."

"Did you have someone look over your math?"

Two sighed. "Brett did. I only made one stupid mistake. It was dumb, and he said I was rushing. He gave me five extra problems to do and I got those right."

"Good. But remember, no mistake is stupid. It's practice. A mistake means you're trying and as long as you learn from them, all is good."

"I know. That's what Randy and Dad say."

Brian smiled and said, "It's the truth, right?"

"Yeah."

"How about your paper for English? Anyone look at that?"

Two rested his cheek on Brian's shoulder and said, "Randy did." Two laughed and said, "He said I think faster than I type." To explain, he added, "I had some words missing."

"What do I tell you to do?" Brian asked, pausing from his own paper.

Two looked up at him with a smile and said, "Read it out loud."

"Because?" Brian asked.

"Because I can catch most mistakes that way. I know, I know."

Brian put an arm around Two, hugged him, and kissed the side of his forehead.

Vicky and Jeff watched them, smiling. She noticed Bobby working hard not to laugh out loud.

"But you didn't come in here to tell me about your homework, did you?" Brian asked with a smile.

Two said, "Tyler and I want to ask Kylie and Brooke to go to a movie Saturday night. Can you drive us?"

"Sure, but did you get permission from mom or dad?"

Vicky said before Two turned around, "Yes, you can go to the movie."

Brian said over his shoulder, "We might have to take your car so Michael can sit next to Kylie, and Tyler can sit next to Brooke. I'll pay for the gas."

"You don't have to pay for gas, Brian, but yes, you can use my car."

"Thanks." Brian turned to Bobby and said, "You want to come along? Maybe there's a movie we can go to."

"Sure," Bobby said with a smile.

"The thing is, I don't know what to wear," Two said.

"Clothes. Definitely clothes," Billy said.

"You're a dork," Two said.

"Now, on the second or third date, clothes are optional," Billy said with a smile.

"You realize your father, Jeff and I are in the same room, right?" Vicky said.

The boys laughed.

"What are you laughing at?" Brett asked as he came into the study and jumped on Billy's back.

"Billy is encouraging Two to go naked with Kylie on his second date," Bobby said.

"Why wait until the second date?" Brett asked. "Billy didn't with Rebecca."

"Ooooo," Brian and Bobby said together.

"That was different," Billy protested.

"What was different?" George asked as he followed Brett into the study.

"I was just reminding Billy about when to and when not to get naked with a girl," Brett said. "Right, Billy?"

George jumped on both Brett and Billy and said, "I still haven't forgiven you, Billy."

"You did too!"

Jeremy and Jeff were laughing. Vicky was laughing but beet red and embarrassed. Jeremy said, "Guys, we're in the room."

Brett said, "We hadn't noticed."

The doorbell rang and Randy went to answer it. They recognized Graff's and O'Connor's voices.

Graff, O'Connor and Eiselmann stepped into the study, followed by Randy and Danny.

"Hey guys, what brings you out here?" Jeremy asked.

"Wait, is this the lake house?" Jamie said looking up at the TV. "Where's our room?"

"We've been through this," Brett said. "Who said you were invited?"

O'Connor put him in a headlock and said, "Let's go out to the barn so I can introduce you to police brutality."

Everyone laughed.

"We wanted to bring you up to date on the anonymous letters Randy, Bobby and Danny have been receiving," Eiselmann said laughing at O'Connor and Brett.

The boys sat down on the floor, the lake house, and teasing Two and Billy a fading memory. Brian saved his paper and shut down his computer. Two shifted positions and sat down between Brian's legs, his head on Brian's chest. Brian slipped one arm around Two's waist and the other around Bobby's shoulders. Bobby scooted closer to him. Billy sat on one side of Randy with Danny on the other. George sat next to Danny.

The letters had started out as obnoxious fan mail praising Danny, but discouraging him from including Randy and Bobby and the others in the band. The anonymous author didn't think the band members were good enough, and that the two boys would hold Danny back.

The letters progressed in frequency. When they were ignored and unanswered, the letters became hate mail directed at Randy and Bobby. Recently, Danny was targeted, along with Randy and Bobby. Fortunately, the boys handed the letters to Jeremy or Jeff unopened, who turned them over to Jamie. There were seven letters apiece.

At first, Jamie had Eiselmann and O'Connor investigating them, but all three decided they were ill-equipped to deal with them, so they turned them over to Kelliher and Dahlke. As a consequence, none of the boys or parents knew how threatening the letters had become.

Jamie said, "We think it's interesting that Sean, Troy and Chris have never received any letter, and aren't mentioned in the letters Danny, Randy or Bobby received. They are included in what the author calls, 'the band,' but not mentioned by name."

"So far, we didn't have any luck in tracing them," Eiselmann said. "Neither did the FBI."

"Pete Kelliher and Skip Dahlke are running the case now, because the letters were mailed, which is a federal offense," Jamie said. "Do you guys remember Cleve Batiste?"

"Yeah. He watched over us when we lived in Indiana," Brett said.

"He's with ViCAP now, and he's involved in the case," Jamie said.

"What's ViCAP?" Vicky asked.

"Violent Criminal Apprehension Program," Graff said.

Jeff reached for Vicky's hand and held it. Jeff and Danny stared at each other.

"They have been mailed from different post office boxes in or around Waukesha, Milwaukee, even Greenfield, Greendale, and Whitefish Bay," Eiselmann said. "The FBI is certain it is the same person or persons."

Jeremy, Jeff, and Vicky stared at each other. It was Vicky who asked, "But you don't know who it is?"

Graff shook his head and said, "No."

Through it all, Pat O'Connor kept his eyes on Danny, Bobby and Randy. He saw Brian squeeze Bobby's shoulder. He watched George slip an arm around Danny's shoulders.

Just as he thought, the boys would rally around each other and watch each other's back. That was a good thing, considering how threatening the letters had become. The more eyes, the better.

ABOUT THE AUTHOR

After having been in education for forty-four years as a teacher, coach, counselor and administrator, Joseph Lewis has retired and now works part-time as an online learning facilitator.

He uses his psychology and counseling background in crafting psychological thriller/mysteries. He has taken creative writing and screen writing courses at UCLA and USC.

Born and raised in Wisconsin, Lewis has been happily married to his wife, Kim. Together they have three wonderful children: Wil (deceased July 2014), Hannah, and Emily. He and his wife now reside in Virginia.

NOTE FROM THE AUTHOR

Word-of-mouth is crucial for any author to succeed. If you enjoyed *Blaze In, Blaze Out*, please leave a review online—anywhere you are able. Even if it's just a sentence or two. It would make all the difference and would be very much appreciated.

Thanks!
Joseph Lewis

We hope you enjoyed reading this title from:

BLACK ROSE
writing™

www.blackrosewriting.com

Subscribe to our mailing list – *The Rosevine* – and receive **FREE** books, daily deals, and stay current with news about upcoming releases and our hottest authors.
Scan the QR code below to sign up.

Already a subscriber? Please accept a sincere thank you for being a fan of Black Rose Writing authors.

View other Black Rose Writing titles at
www.blackrosewriting.com/books and use promo code
PRINT to receive a **20% discount** when purchasing.

CPSIA information can be obtained
at www.ICGtesting.com
Printed in the USA
BVHW070218300821
615261BV00001B/3

9 781684 338535